ALL THE
YELLOW
SUNS

ALL THE YELLOW SUNS

Malavika Kannan

LITTLE, BROWN AND COMPANY
New York   Boston

Little, Brown and Company
Hachette Book Group
1290 Avenue of the Americas, New York, NY 10104
Visit us at LBYR.com

First Edition: July 2023

Little, Brown and Company is a division of Hachette Book Group, Inc. The Little, Brown name and logo are trademarks of Hachette Book Group, Inc.

The publisher is not responsible for websites (or their content) that are not owned by the publisher.

Little, Brown and Company books may be purchased in bulk for business, educational, or promotional use. For information, please contact your local bookseller or the Hachette Book Group Special Markets Department at special.markets@hbgusa.com.

Library of Congress Cataloging-in-Publication Data
Names: Kannan, Malavika, 2001– author.
Title: All the yellow suns / Malavika Kannan.
Description: First edition. | New York : Little, Brown and Company, 2023. | Audience: Ages 14 & up. | Summary: Sixteen-year-old queer Indian American, Maya, who falls for her white, wealthy, and complicated female classmate, Juneau, is asked to join a secret society of artists, vandals, and mischief-makers who fight for justice at their school.
Identifiers: LCCN 2022031421 | ISBN 9780316447324 (hardcover) | ISBN 9780316447522 (ebook)
Subjects: CYAC: Lesbians—Fiction. | Artists—Fiction. | Secret societies—Fiction. | Student movements—Fiction. | East Indian Americans—Fiction.
Classification: LCC PZ7.1.K278 Al 2023 | DDC [Fic]—dc23
LC record available at https://lccn.loc.gov/2022031421

ISBNs: 978-0-316-44732-4 (hardcover), 978-0-316-44752-2 (ebook)

Printed in the United States of America

LSC-C

Printing 1, 2023

To queer daughters of immigrants (who is doing it like we are?) and to my darling sister, Deepika.

chapter 1

The real kicker is that I wasn't even supposed to live in Citrus Grove. I was supposed to live in Houston with both my parents in a house with a swimming pool. But things didn't work out between them, so Amma and I moved to Citrus Grove—a sprawling suburb of Orlando with too many houses to count that has never actually felt like home.

It has two sides, like a coin. My side is filled with people of all backgrounds. There's my mother, Sujatha Krishnan, and me. There's Anya Patel, also Indian, next door to Ife Asefa, whose parents own Orlando's best Ethiopian restaurant. Ife beat me on science tests six years in a row until we finally became friends. My best friend, Silva Rivera, moved from Puerto Rico the year I did from India. There are also Cubans and Koreans and lots of people who have thick accents and even thicker blood. Amma once joked that Citrus Grove was like the United Nations—that is, if the Security Council met in the Publix deli and instead of nukes, people hurled insults in multiple languages.

Juneau Zale was from the other side. She lived a mile away, but sometimes it felt more like a light-year. Her neighborhood had bake sales, church fundraisers, and Girl Scout cookies. Her parents even fostered dogs. At first glance, Juneau's side was perfect. But then you saw the church ladies calling the cops on homeless people in the park. The realtor dads railing in their booming voices about the Immigrants and Newcomers Raising Their Taxes. Kids like Juneau roaming wild at night, smoking weed and raising hell. The white picket fences protecting their families from all forms of danger leaking from our side into theirs.

We all lived in Citrus Grove, but "we" looked very different depending on whom you asked.

I was always vaguely aware of Juneau Zale's life because I ended up in it—briefly, mistakenly—when I was eight. I was running away from home. Those days Amma often fought with my father on the phone, their voices rattling the house like a snow globe, and I'd had enough. Before Amma could notice, I walked out the door. I didn't really want to leave my mother, I just wanted to see how far I could go, if I could.

Unfortunately, I only made it a mile before the identical lawns started blending together like pages of an endless magazine. Deep in my belly, I knew I was lost. Amma had warned me that this could happen—it was all over the newspapers, TV, old bedtime stories dredged up from her childhood in India: Bad girls misbehaved and then they went missing, never to be seen again.

That was when I first saw Juneau. She was playing on the lawn of a massive house with pillars. The reason I'd stopped to stare at her house was because I thought it looked like the castles illustrated in fairy tales. Then I saw that Juneau was doing the kind of stupid shit Amma told me only white kids did. She had a pair of binoculars, and she was trying to stare directly at the sun.

I remember running up to her and saying, "Don't you know you're not supposed to stare at the sun?" or something panicked like that. Juneau Zale laughed at me, I think. She told me she was trying to figure out what color the sun was. "It's the biggest mystery of our times," she said. I had just read a book about the solar system, so I informed her it was actually just a colorless ball of gas. I asked her if she could see how many fingers I was holding up. At some point we both busted out laughing, and that's when her parents came out.

Normally, being a kid, I automatically zoned out my friends' parents, but I remembered Juneau's vividly. One reason was that they were the first white adults, besides my teachers, to ever speak to me: officious and stern, like the porcelain couple atop a wedding cake. The other is that they called Amma and snitched on me, and she drove so fast she ran into their mailbox.

"Maya," she snarled, gripping my arms hard enough to hurt. "What's wrong with you?"

Mr. and Mrs. Zale were disturbed by the great Indian spectacle we were making. Maybe they'd heard that in immigrant cultures, runaway kids got their asses beat. Maybe they wanted to look out for me. "Are you new to town?" they asked Amma. "Are you okay?" they asked me, perhaps worried about my punishment.

"No," said Amma shortly, answering two questions in one. She glared at the Zales and their lovely house, casting a curse with her gaze. "You're lucky these people didn't kill you!" she whispered, whisking me back home for a stern lecture about American stranger-danger.

I'm not sure who turned away first, me or Juneau. Because all I remember is looking back for one last glimpse of the girl with pickle-green eyes, but she was already gone. And I figured maybe I'd imagined her.

I forgot all about Juneau until she crash-landed back into my life in high school. In the eight years until then, we were occupied with other things. I was becoming a good daughter to Amma. Meanwhile Juneau was becoming a local legend: a rock star, minus the guitar smashing. Rumors followed her wherever she went—how Juneau painted portraits of each of her lovers, burned them in the dead of night. How she once hooked up with the whole football team. How she ran away the summer before junior year, possibly to hide a secret pregnancy. Lore swirled around her, and she never denied it, whether or not it hurt.

Regardless, I fell in love with her. I did it the way I learned to swim—quickly, recklessly, no lifeguards or life vests: just straight into the deep end, my lungs straining from the depth. Amma thought it was the quickest way for me to learn. I've been taking blind leaps ever since.

———

I was with Silva the night before I met Juneau all over again. It was the last night of summer before sophomore year. Anya and Ife traveled all summer, returning to their motherlands, so it was quiet at home, just the two of us. That night started like most nights—rented movies at his house, wine stolen from his brothers—and ended with our lying side by side in the yard, talking about our plans in the abstract way you do when you're half sober beneath the stars. Mine, as always, was to move to New York and open an art studio for women of color. Silva's was more practical: make a shitload of money, enough to take care of his parents for years.

We were sprawled across his lawn, sharing his headphones. Violin burst into fireworks of sound, and I resisted the urge to seize my sketchbook. We often spent hours like this, connected by the ear, but this time was different, because this music was written by Silva.

"I can't believe it," I said when the music ended. "I can't believe you composed music all summer and didn't tell me. It's just so—" I searched for a word vast enough to hold Silva's music, but I came up short. Everything was floating past the finish line of this summer. We had yet to find out where our lockers would be, whom we'd watch football games with, or whether we wanted to fall in love. But there was time to decide before tomorrow. With Silva, there was always time.

"After spending the whole summer together, I think we've transcended verbal communication," Silva said, smiling. "We're functionally telepathic."

"That's true. You always bring the exact snacks I'm craving, even before I realize I'm hungry."

Silva smirked. "That's because I know when you get your period." I laughed, and he sobered. "But the violin stays between us. I don't want everyone to know I'm working on all this."

"What? Why not?"

I still remembered finding the violin at a garage sale in the sixth grade. Silva picked it up, and something inside him seemed to soften.

"I just don't want it to become a big deal," said Silva.

"Is this about your parents not supporting your music? There's that conservatory I researched, they have scholarships for low-income students—"

"You know what my parents are like," said Silva. "*Music doesn't pay the bills*, that's what they said. I have to think about them, too."

"Maybe if your parents *heard* your music, they'd think differently," I pressed.

Silva was already putting his headphones away.

"Maya, can you not fight me on this?"

"Silva, I don't understand," I said. "You have a chance to get out of Citrus Grove and have the world. Why are you giving up?"

"Because not all of us want the world," he said, closing the box. "I think you should go home. There's school tomorrow."

I knew better than to argue with him, not even telepathically. So I walked home alone. When I got inside, Amma was gone—she worked as a nurse, and her hospital shift started at night. I barely saw her outside of weekends, and even then, she was often too tired to hang out. There was an opened Chinese takeout box with lipstick on the fork, abandoned mid-bite. Amma rarely stayed in one place after my father left—or, more accurately, never arrived. Instead, she circled between home, work, and men: a never-ending midlife merry-go-round. You'd think if she didn't stop moving she'd vanish.

Amma's mistake was falling in love with an artist. My

father, Rajendra Krishnan, is a famous painter, and when he joined us from India, we were going to move to Texas. But then my father's visa got denied. His career took off in India. He and Amma fought for years on the phone, until one day the phone stopped ringing. There were no birthday cards, no video calls, just silence, until even my memories of him faded. I forgot the sound of his voice. He forgot he had a child.

We never moved away, but we eventually had to move on. Amma did her best to raise me in this strange country alone, but I knew she really missed my dad. Once, when I was thirteen, I tried asking about him.

"I have a question," I said. We were eating dinner: home-made tacos, because Amma was feeling culinarily adventurous. *We're all brown-skinned people,* she'd said. *How different can Mexican food be from our own?* She ended up burning the tacos, but I ate them without complaint, because I wanted her to lower her guard.

It worked. "What is it, kanna?"

"Why doesn't my father call anymore?"

Amma didn't say anything, but the taco shell cracked in her hands, spilling onto her plate—undercooked beans, soft lettuce. "Am I not doing enough for you?" she asked.

I stared. "Of course you are," I said.

Amma's eyes flickered, and it felt intrusive to see her pain. Sharply personal, like reading her diary.

"He loves you, Maya," said Amma. "But he knows he can't be a stable, present parent for you. That's why he's stayed away."

Something tipped over inside me. "He *can't?*" I said. "Or *won't?*"

Amma set down her taco. "Rajendra is a brilliant man,"

7

she said. "But his true love is his art. He made his choice when he stayed in India." She smiled sadly. "Genius takes sacrifice, Mayavati. I'm just so glad he passed his talents to you."

"Why aren't you angry at him?" I demanded, surprising her. I was younger then—I rarely challenged Amma.

"Are you, Maya?" said Amma. "Angry, that is." She was using the calm, even-tempered voice she used on her patients. Rather than soothe me, her voice irritated me. I often felt this way—ignited for no reason, when nobody else was. I didn't know where my rage came from, but I knew better than to let it show. I just stayed inflamed, like a bruise that wouldn't heal.

"Of course I am," I said, and Amma frowned.

"I'm only going to say this once," she said. "When you love someone, there's no place for anger. You accept them as they are, even if it hurts. Do you understand?"

She didn't wait for my response. "But we cannot accept these burned tacos," she said. "They taste horrible." Amma dumped our plates in the trash, offered me her hand. "Come, Maya," she said. "Let's get pizza."

Amma believed that love had no place for anger, but I had plenty of room for both. I could resent Amma for excusing Rajendra and still love her more than anybody on earth. I could hate Rajendra for leaving us and still grow obsessed with his art. For years I watched him from afar, like a patron in a gallery. I started googling him, following his famous portraits of brown women, imagining the world through his eyes.

After my outburst, Amma began dating other men, but more often she rearranged the furniture. I'd come home some days and find the couch upside down on the porch. Amma said this was to prevent spiders.

But I knew better. I knew about immigrant mothers and the ways they exerted control in a changing world. Besides, I really liked spiders. Once, I watched a spider build its nest under my windowsill. I let it live, despite Amma's orders. Who was I to deny anyone the chance to choose their home?

I must've fallen asleep at the table, because the next thing I registered was Amma's prodding me awake.

"Maya?" she said. "Why aren't you in bed?"

Amma had her work face on—hair twisted back, lipstick fresh. On her name tag, the As in *Sujatha* had smiley faces drawn in. I checked the kitchen clock: 3:00 a.m.

"You worry me, kanna," she said. "I've got a date visiting tomorrow and this house needs cleaning. God, I'm hungry." She reached for her takeout, but I'd already finished it. "Did you save me the fortune cookie at least?"

I slid her the cookie. "Who's the date?"

Amma cracked the cookie to find the message. "*What we spend our lives outrunning is what brings us true peace,*" she read aloud. "Isn't that lovely?"

"*Amma,*" I interrupted.

She flushed. "His name is Ramesh and he owns a car dealership in Kissimmee. You remember him, from the Patels' Diwali dinner? He's very respected in the community." She crunched the cookie. "They should just sell these in plastic boxes at the grocery store. People would line up for all this luck."

Amma's voice swelled with an emotion I couldn't pinpoint. It took me a second to recognize it: *hope.* The same hope from back when she worked day shifts and could take me to restaurants at night, would ask me to dance after her third or fourth drink. We fought less back then, and our movements felt easier. She'd shimmy slowly, her arms linked with mine so hard our elbows poked. In those moments, I wasn't her child, I was the life she could've lived.

"I hope it goes well," I said.

Amma smiled. She was beautiful, all curves, soft laughter, easy smile, so unlike myself—I scowled too much, slouched, bounced on my feet like I wanted to make a run for it. Amma liked to joke that I got my ornery traits, including my thick wild hair, from my father. My friends loved Sujatha Aunty for her endless warmth. Sometimes I wished she wasn't mine so I could love her so easily, too.

"Go to bed," said Amma. "You have school tomorrow."

I slipped out from under her outstretched arm, headed for my room. Then I remembered. "Amma?" I said. "Can you drive me to school?"

She looked up from the kitchen table. "Isn't Silva driving you to school?"

"Not anymore," I said.

"Is everything all right between you two?"

"We had a disagreement," I said. "But hopefully we'll fix things soon."

"Of course you will," Amma said. She patted me on the shoulder but didn't say anything else. She didn't tell me what to do or pick me up while everything sank—she never did. I couldn't remember the last time we'd had a full conversation. Instead she floated off to the living room, which started to creak and groan. She was moving the couches around again.

Unable to sleep, I checked my phone in bed. There was a

text from Anya, finally back home from India—I responded with a proportionate number of exclamation points. Another from Ife wondering whether I'd completed the summer homework, which made me laugh. Ife knew full well that I'd finished in the first week of summer, because she'd done the same.

I checked Instagram next. I was a pretty private person online. There was only one person I logged into Instagram to see anyway. And that was my father.

A photo of him loaded onscreen. His dark hair, unruly like mine. His wide nose, which I'd hated on my face until I saw it on him, crinkled from smiling. I glanced at his caption: **TOUR**.

According to the post, Rajendra had won a prestigious fellowship for the arts—I didn't need to google it to know it was big because of the thousands of adoring comments. His work would be shown in galleries across the United States. He'd give lectures at museums and universities. This autumn, he'd be the artist-in-residence at the Orlando Museum of Art.

I had to reread for a few minutes before it sunk in. After all these years, he was back.

"Amma?" I almost called, but then I remembered what Amma had advised, years earlier: *You accept people as they are, even if it hurts.*

The problem is, that's not what artists do. We imagine people as the portrait versions of themselves—smooth, ideal, never disappointing. I was tired of waiting for Rajendra. It was terrible to do alone.

So I went to bed, and as the furniture scraped the floor, I wondered how life would be if I, too, like Amma, believed in fortune cookies.

chapter 2

The next morning, my mother drove me to hell. Citrus Grove High School, that publicly funded purgatory, was equally known for our town's lone football team and its propensity for brawls and mayhem. It reminded me of a medieval fortress, because the buildings were surrounded by a massive tar-black moat that was the suburban parking lot. Four thousand of us arrived from all corners of town to do daily, tireless battle. It wasn't clear if there were ever winners.

Inside the cafeteria, I opened my sketchbook to illustrate my first impressions of sophomore year.

I already knew that Citrus Grove could not be painted into submission. In seventh grade, Amma sent me to art lessons in Orlando. My teacher had studied yoga in India, but she actually had a license plate from Vermont. "Find your home," she advised, so I tried. I tried sketching the textures of our food, the footprints of mothers who worked night shifts. But the paints sneered at me. *Little brown girl plays artist*, they whispered. *Your home is not here.*

Still, the art teacher took a liking to me. She offered to drive me home in her car with the Vermont plates. But when we pulled into my neighborhood, she rolled up the windows and locked the doors. "What a dump," she said. "They ought to fix this area up."

I followed her gaze and saw squat, ugly houses. I saw Amma waving at me, but I pretended not to notice her.

My teacher smiled at me. "How much farther do you live, Maya?" she said.

"Take a right." I smiled back. She took a right, then another, dropping me off outside the house I pointed to, which was red-tiled, shiny, and also a mile away from my actual house. I walked the mile back, feeling like I'd finally found my home, but not the way my teacher wanted.

But now I was older and smarter. I knew who I was. I tried to capture the energy in the cafeteria: girls in ripped jeans, jostling, gossiping, trying to make their summers sound more exciting than they actually were. I always drew girls, because they were the most interesting.

"Miss me, bitch?"

I turned to see my friend Anya Patel racing toward me, a blur of dark hair and floral skirts. There was no chance to brace myself before she threw her arms around me.

"Seriously. Did you miss me?" Anya asked, coming up for air between hugs.

"Not a chance," I said, and she smothered me again. "Of course I missed you. I could barely function without you. How was India?"

Anya grinned. "My mom didn't try to find me a husband, but she did unfortunately consult astrologers about my SATs." She rolled her eyes. "How was your summer?"

Sometimes I envied Anya, with her unbroken family and frequent trips to India. She didn't know how it felt to be alone, abandoned, or stuck in place—all experiences with which I felt achingly familiar. "I just got drunk with Silva," I said. "Tried not to murder any of my mom's boyfriends."

"Citrus Grove is the armpit of Florida," Anya agreed. "It was good to get out of here and stop thinking about Sam. I deserve better than cheating white boys."

"Good riddance," I said.

"Anyway." Anya laughed. "I was thinking we should seduce a senior this semester so we get invited to parties. Actual parties with drugs, not just wine and Capri Suns from your mom's pantry. No offense to Sujatha Aunty's pantry."

I smirked. "It would be nice to put our juice box days behind us."

"Well, who are you interested in, then?" Anya asked. "And I can help you with makeup, if you want. I notice you're a little heavy-handed."

"I think you're better qualified for the seduction," I said, sourer than I intended. Over the past few years, guys had started noticing Anya, following her around like hired bodyguards. She knew things I didn't, like how to kiss boys without ever being taught. Standing beside her, I doubted I'd ever be seen at all.

"It's sophomore year, Maya," Anya said. "This is the dawn of our womanhood. We're not freshmen anymore, but we're not old and jaded, either. You could loosen up a bit."

Just then, Ife Asefa grabbed me from behind, squeezing me so tightly I was sure I'd grown a much-needed inch by the time she released me.

"I can't believe this," she said. "My two favorite brown girls. I lose track of you for one summer, and you both come back indiscriminately hot?"

"Oh, shut up, Ife," said Anya. "We all know you're the most beautiful girl in all of Florida."

Ife blushed, but Anya was right: Ife had unlocked herself two years ago in a dramatic rebirth as a pouty-lipped model, turning heads wherever she went. What exactly happened to some girls over the summer and not others? While Ife's and Anya's bodies molded into maturity with the ease of clay sculptures, mine did so awkwardly. As an artist, I lived only in reflected beauty, never my own.

"By the way, Maya," Ife said, turning to me. "Is everything all right with you and Silva? I saw him a few minutes ago and he seems even quieter than usual."

I told them about our fight the previous night. Anya clicked her tongue. "Lecturing Silva about his ambition like that?" she said. "You kind of sound like my mother."

"That's not true," said Ife. "Maya was just trying to help him get his shit together. I'm sure he'll come around."

I tried to return her smile. "I hope so," I said. "I would do anything for any of you. Like, I would beat up grown men of any size. You know that, right?"

"Of course we do," said Anya firmly. "And so does Silva. It'll all be fine once—"

We turned around at the sound of boys yelling. A fight was breaking out.

"Holy shit, is that *Squash?*" said Ife.

The louder of the boys was, indeed, Anya's ex-boyfriend, Sam "Squash" Harvey, so nicknamed for the football accident that left his nose permanently askew. Squash pushed someone to the ground, his blond hair shining. Both guys were massive and well matched, like Titans. The nearest onlookers formed a human ring around them, hooting and cheering.

"It's not even Fight Week," groaned Ife, referring to CGHS's long-standing tradition of student duels the week before homecoming.

"Seven minutes back from summer break, and there's already a fistfight," I said. "When is the male species going to evolve?"

To be fair, Squash Harvey had never been the poster child for human evolution, despite being the principal's grandson and football captain, all while owning the largest house in Citrus Grove. He and Anya had dated in secret from their families for months. He'd been an exceptionally bad boyfriend, cheating on her last year. It was among my dearest desires to punch his twisted nose.

"What did you ever see in him, Anya?" I said. "Besides the football body, I guess. And the fact that he drives a Porsche."

Anya bit her lip. "Sam wasn't all bad," she said. "He snuck me into his family's condo in Sarasota. He even bought jewelry for my sisters. He took care of me."

"Remember the time he called me the student council's diversity pick?" said Ife indignantly. "He's a racist dick. I hope the other guy beats him up."

Anya was covering her face—she couldn't bear violence, not even on TV, so I stepped in front of her. This gave me a close-up view of the combatants. I recognized the tackled figure to be Mateo Chavez, CGHS's quarterback. His lip bled freely as he delivered a kick.

"Let's go," I told Ife. "Before the cops get here and make a scene." We seized Anya's arms, but we'd barely waded out of the crowd when an elbow hit my jaw. It was so painful that I did an involuntary karate kick and yelled, "*Fuck!*"

Eyes watering, I caught sight of the offending elbow, which was connected to a pale arm, which was connected to the body of my erstwhile savior Juneau Zale, who'd appeared out of nowhere.

"Maya," she said, unsurprised, like she'd run into me at the grocery store. "You should watch where you're going."

Ife hissed in my ear, "*Juneau Zale* knows your name?"

Juneau strode purposefully toward the epicenter of the fight. The whispers spread like wildfire—*Juneau Zale was here.*

That was just the way she made her appearances: descending like a UFO, spreading shock waves in her wake.

Juneau shoved onlookers aside until she was standing on top of the boys, somehow immune to their violence. "Mateo, stop it," she snarled, dragging him to his feet.

Swearing, Squash stood up. I felt a sudden spike of fear for Juneau. Her back was turned as Squash towered over her. My legs thrummed with momentum. For a second, it seemed to me that Squash would hit her, and it was up to me to stop him. But then Juneau whirled back around.

"Sam Harvey, right?" she said. Squash opened his mouth, and Juneau said, "That was a rhetorical question. We all know each other's names. What I want to know is why you were astride your illustrious teammate Mateo Chavez. You looked like a pair of fumbling virgins."

The crowd laughed, and both guys reddened.

"Stay out of this, Juneau," Mateo said. "This is between Squash and me."

"It's our first day of senior year," said Juneau. "Isn't this the time we promise to be friends forever, or sappy shit like that?"

"I sold Chavez some *items*," Squash said meaningfully. "He owes me several hundred dollars. The debt has lasted too long. I'm here to collect."

Juneau laughed. Haughty and dispassionate, she had the kind of laugh that could never sound respectful. She seemed unfazed by all the attention—or she was enjoying it.

"Come on, Squash," she said. "You're way too rich to be selling weed. I've seen your mansion. Are you sure your family can't just plow down some more endangered mangroves to make it up?"

Squash opened his mouth angrily, but she cut him off. "That was another rhetorical question, asshole. Mateo, let's go."

Then Squash stood up. "At least I'm not opening my legs for any guy with a pulse," he spat. "Mind your business and have some respect for yourself. You *slut*."

Around me, people gasped. Juneau looked like she'd been slapped. Her mouth opened, but no response came out.

Mateo twisted out of her grip, snarling. He jumped on top of Squash, punching him until I couldn't tell what was his arm and what was Squash's face. The crowd started to shout—someone shouted that a teacher had called the police, but Mateo didn't hear them.

"Call her that again!" Mateo shouted. "I dare you."

"Why?" said Squash. Despite his bloody face, he was grinning. I knew right then that some men get their rush from inflicting pain. "Are you fucking her, too?"

Mateo lunged again, but our principal, Dr. Harvey, appeared, flanked by the football coach and the school police officers. They wrestled Mateo to the ground and tried to handcuff him. Juneau gasped. "You're hurting him!" she screamed.

Ife tugged my arm, but I was rooted to the ground. My heart was pounding.

Juneau knelt by Mateo, cradling his head in her arms as the police tried to drag him away. She was arguing loudly with Dr. Harvey; I couldn't believe her nerve. "Are you seriously arresting *Mateo*?" she said. "He was provoked. You can see his bruises! Your *grandson* started this—"

"This is a high school campus, not a fight club," Dr. Harvey said. He looked strained, like he was trying not to make a scene. "Juneau, please go to class. I'll handle them both in my office."

"Then why is Mateo the only one in handcuffs?" I called before I could stop myself.

Everyone, including Juneau and Dr. Harvey, turned to stare at me. I couldn't blame them: Even I half expected to turn around and see a different, braver girl talking behind me. The sort of girl who could raise her voice to the principal, startling even Juneau Zale.

"There is a cafeteria full of students who can tell you Squash attacked Mateo, and not the other way around," I said. I was surprised by how steady my voice sounded, because inside my sneakers, my feet were shaking. "The entire school just watched you treat Mateo like a criminal. If you arrest him, I know they won't accept it."

Juneau stared at me, her eyes sharp.

"Let Mateo go," she told Dr. Harvey. "I'll come with you. I'll write statements. Whatever you need."

Dr. Harvey looked around at the students, and it was like he suddenly remembered where he was. He nodded at the police officer, who released Mateo. Then he turned to Juneau. "All right, then. Juneau, come with me. You, too; you've officially volunteered as a witness," he told me. He raised his voice to address the cafeteria. "The rest of you, get to class!"

I gaped at Anya and Ife, but they shrugged. "We'll wait for you," Anya whispered, so I followed Dr. Harvey away.

The five of us made an unlikely procession through the hallways—Dr. Harvey walking briskly, followed by Juneau and Mateo, then me, with Squash lagging angrily behind. Though she held the doors open for me, Juneau barely looked at me as I passed.

The principal's office, like the rest of CGHS, was drab and unwelcoming. The glass trophy case was sparse, except for a football championship from the eighties and a smattering of academic trophies, mostly won by Ife and me.

"All right. What on earth is happening here?" said Dr. Harvey.

"Squash," Juneau said, "attacked Mateo unprovoked. Mateo was just defending himself."

Squash wiped his nose. The tissue was red with blood. "You weren't even there, Juneau."

"This is really messed up," said Mateo. "I get attacked, I protect myself, and the police come for me? Since when did the cops start cuffing students?" He was using a measured *talking-to-adults* voice that felt startlingly familiar—I had one of my own. Still, I sensed his anger, like a rubber band about to snap.

"I'll be having a word with the officers, Mr. Chavez," said Dr. Harvey. "Clearly they didn't see how it started. All they saw was you attacking Sam."

"I saw," I said. My voice had sounded deafening in the cafeteria, but now I felt small. I tried again. "I mean, I saw from the beginning. Squash attacked Mateo, so he fought back. And then the police just jumped on Mateo, without giving him a chance—"

"Who are you?" said Squash, not bothering to hide his contempt. From the look on everyone's faces, he wasn't the only one wondering. My face burned.

"Maya Krishnan," I said. "We've met. I'm Anya Patel's friend." I mentioned his ex-girlfriend to make him flinch, but it barely registered.

"Right, okay," said Squash. "So you also saw Mateo taking free throws at my face?"

"This is stupid," Juneau interrupted. "Dr. Harvey, nobody got seriously hurt. Can't you just give them both detentions and call it a day?" She had a directness that shocked me, that I'd never dare imitate. Things that should get her punished somehow seemed okay because her voice was nice and her eyes were pickle green.

"Listen." Dr. Harvey sighed. "At CGHS, there are rules. Students can't just pummel one another in our hallways. Sam and Mateo, as varsity teammates, I'm disappointed with you both."

Mateo set his jaw, but Squash stared away, scowling. If

I didn't hate him on principle, I might actually feel sorry for him—it sucked for your grandfather to run your school.

"Citrus Grove needs law and order," Dr. Harvey continued. "We're trying to protect our students."

A familiar feeling pulsed through me. Sharp, like a muscle flexing. It only took me a moment to identify it as *anger.*

"I have a question," I said. "If you're trying to protect students, why are you letting the police go after them? And why do they only come for students of color?"

Juneau raised an eyebrow. Mateo nodded his agreement. Dr. Harvey leaned forward. I watched him choose his words.

"Our officers keep students safe," he said. "Sometimes students are a threat to other students, and we need to maintain peace."

Mateo scoffed. "You seriously think I'm a *threat?*"

Juneau chimed in. "What I saw was that the cops were roughing Mateo up. That couldn't have possibly made him safer."

"I think the cops are dangerous," I said. "They're going to target students of color if you don't stop them. I think—"

"*Enough,*" said Dr. Harvey, startling me. "I appreciate your input," he continued. "But this is a disciplinary matter, not a forum on police. I think you've said your piece, Maya. You should head to class."

"What?" I hated how my voice shook, undermining any credibility.

"Close the door behind you," he said.

Mateo nodded to me as I left. Right before I closed the door, Juneau gave me one swift look up and down, finally nodding brusquely.

My heart raced on the walk back to the cafeteria. It had

taken all of my willpower to sound so confident, and now I started to shake, unable to believe what I'd just done.

In the cafeteria, Ife and Anya were waiting for me to fill them in.

"I can't believe Juneau Zale just handed Squash *and* Dr. Harvey their asses like that," Ife said. "She deserves a public service award. And *you!*" she added. "You talked back to Dr. Harvey, the most casually racist principal in CGHS history. *You*, the most law-abiding nerd I've ever met in my life." Ife looked torn between disapproval and pride.

"That's not what I am," I protested.

"Oh, Maya!" said Anya suddenly. "Look at your face!"

In her hand mirror, I saw a bruise on my jaw the precise shape of Juneau's elbow. I groaned. It was the last thing I wanted: a reason for people to stare at me. A strange, skin-deep connection to Juneau Zale.

"I can't believe Juneau knew your name," Ife said. "She's a living legend in the senior class."

"More like a living sex symbol," said Anya. "I heard Juneau's fucked every varsity athlete at least once. And honestly, I respect the hustle."

"Of course that's not true," I said, momentarily forgetting my bruise. "And Juneau and I go way back, but I don't know how she remembers me."

The bell rang, and students surged through the halls. It reminded me of Goya's wartime paintings, the wonderfully disorganized tangle of limbs. I imagined that I, too, was wild and brave like Juneau Zale. Then I walked to class.

chapter 3

My first class, AP Calculus, was as lively as a graveyard. When I entered, most of the desks were already occupied by skinny senior boys. Nobody acknowledged me, which I was grateful for. After a lifetime in advanced math classes, I'd grown accustomed to the staring, but it was nice to not be an instant Indian stereotype.

I found an empty seat near the back. Mr. Taylor began taking roll. The seniors tittered as he stumbled through the ethnic names, his face reddening with each successive syllable. By the time he reached my name, Mr. Taylor was a vivid maroon.

"Mayav—May—"

"You can call me Maya," I said.

Mr. Taylor's face broke into relief. "Much better," he said. "But I don't think you're supposed to be in this class. My roster lists you as a sophomore."

The boys stared at me, and I felt my face flush to match Mr. Taylor's. Before I could speak, the intercom crackled. Dr. Harvey's voice blared through the classroom.

"Good morning, CGHS!" The sound of his voice made my stomach tighten. "For announcements: Football tryouts will be held tomorrow afternoon..."

I zoned out when Dr. Harvey droned on about parking violations, but his next announcement made everybody sit straighter.

"And lastly, a warning," said Dr. Harvey. "As some of you may already know, CGHS has been dealing with gang activities. This morning, police investigated a broken lock on the library and spray paint graffiti."

He cleared his throat impressively. "Should I discover that Citrus Grove students are responsible for these acts," he said, "these students will be prosecuted to the fullest extent of the law. You have been warned."

The intercom clattered into silence. Mr. Taylor pointed at me. "Perhaps we should reevaluate your placement in this class," he said. "The math is quite advanced. You may find Precalculus more suitable."

"I already passed Precalculus," I said just as the door banged open and a girl burst in carrying a skateboard.

"Can I help you?" Mr. Taylor said.

"Sorry I'm late," the girl said. "My car stalled and I had to skate here as fast as I could. Can I leave the board by the door?"

For a moment, Mr. Taylor simply gaped at her. The girl looked straight out of a magazine: She had silver spikes on her nose and ears, matched by long silver box braids. I liked her tattoos, sharp against her dark skin.

"Do you need help finding your class?" said Mr. Taylor.

Maybe I just imagined it, but the skater girl tensed. "I'm in this class," she said slowly. "This is AP Calculus, right?"

"AP Calculus?" repeated Mr. Taylor. "Is that what's printed on your schedule? Can I take a look?"

The girl's eyes flashed. "Yes, it is," she said. "Maybe you don't think I look like I belong here. It's the tattoos, right?"

The entire class stared at her. The girl crossed her arms.

"I hope it's the tattoos," she said coolly. "And nothing else about me. Now is this AP Calculus or not?"

The classroom fell silent. "You're in the right place," I said, ignoring people's stares. I met the girl's eyes, and she held my gaze.

"Mark me present on the roster," she said. "My name's Patricia Lloyd." Then she added, loudly enough for everyone to hear: "And for those who were wondering, I have the quadratic equation tattooed on my ass."

Patricia rolled her skateboard across the classroom, unbothered by the stares. She sank into the seat next to mine. "Thanks," she murmured. "I'm Pat."

"Maya," I whispered, and she brightened.

"I heard what you did this morning," she said. "Standing up to Dr. Harvey."

"You did?" I said. "Are people...aware of it?" I trailed off lamely.

"You're infamous, babe," said Pat. "At least for today." She opened her notebook, and I saw it was filled with drawings, sharp and layered—a rose, a face, an eye. She saw me looking and grinned. "I drew these," Pat whispered. "If ever you need a tattoo design, hit me up."

I tried to pay attention as Mr. Taylor lectured about functions and limits, but my mind drifted to Juneau—how she'd descended into the fight, emerging from her mystery to meddle in mortal affairs. How she'd frozen when Squash Harvey called her a *slut*. I mean, we'd all heard plenty about Juneau's reputation with guys, so her reaction surprised me.

It occurred to me that I hadn't spotted Juneau in months before today—not even at the movies or mall, and Citrus Grove was a small town. To be fair, I'd never spoken to her, barely existed in her social proximity. I'd always considered myself invisible, but Juneau was a master of the art. She knew how to make an entrance, how to disappear.

When Calculus ended, I went to Spanish after which I nearly collided with Silva, waiting outside. I was surprised to see he'd brought his violin.

"I'm trying out for the school orchestra this afternoon," Silva said. "I think you inspired me." He smiled, and I recognized the peace offering. To know someone from childhood, to know their mind like your own, this was something I hadn't yet realized I'd taken for granted.

I knew we were okay again. "You're going to crush it," I said, and I meant it.

We crossed the hall. "Did you hear Harvey's announcement this morning?" said Silva. "I saw the library vandalism myself."

"Yeah, what even happened?"

"The school usually keeps the library locked up over the summer," explained Silva. "But someone broke it open and painted *Free our minds* over the door. People from town started using the library until Harvey shut it down."

"Why would anyone do that?" I said.

"I guess they thought that the books should be free," Silva said. "Kids whose school libraries close for the summer, or people without Internet at home, or homeless people without library cards, could finally use it."

"That's actually kind of brilliant."

"Brilliant, but risky," Silva said. "Whoever did it, they have guts. Where are you headed next?"

"Art Studio." I grinned.

"Is that the class you applied for?"

I nodded. Ever since I heard of it, I'd yearned to join CGHS's independent art class. The studio was designed for graduating seniors, though I'd managed to get in as a sophomore. Silva had helped me select my portfolio submissions over the summer.

"I'm so proud of you," Silva said. "Go show them for us, okay?"

I didn't have to ask him what he meant. Silva, more than anyone, knew what this studio meant to me. He'd been there for it all—the years of doodling on my bedroom floor, the 24-pack of Crayola paints Amma bought when she noticed my talent, the stacks of self-taught sketchbooks, the unquenched longing to fully be *seen*. I promised him I'd do my best.

The art studio was windowed and spacious, unlike most of CGHS. I searched for an empty easel. Everyone looked intimidatingly artistic. Even Ms. Meyer, the teacher, wore a hand-patched beanie.

To my pleasant surprise, Patricia Lloyd waved at me. I should've guessed she'd be in this class, too.

"Can I join you?" I felt like the new girl, the immigrant all over again. But Pat pushed her stuff aside, making space for me.

"Sit down," she said. "But save one spot. Put your bag down so nobody takes her seat."

"Whose seat?" I said, just as Juneau Zale walked up and hugged Pat.

My first thought was this: *I would give anything to sketch her.*

Because up close, Juneau's portrait features were even more pronounced: the architecture of her throat, her unconscious smirk, the quiet challenge of it all. My hands moved to my sketchbook, catching Juneau's attention.

"Hello again," she told me, taking the seat I'd saved.

I slowly registered the fact that Pat and Juneau were friends. Was that how Pat knew about this morning—had Juneau told her? Meanwhile, Juneau was whispering to Pat.

"Mateo's okay for now," she said. "Harvey didn't ask too many questions. Crisis averted."

I tried not to eavesdrop as I unpacked my art supplies, plus my favorite novel, for spiritual guidance. But I couldn't help it. I'd been there, so I felt invested. "What was the fight about, anyway?" I asked. "And how do you know Mateo? Isn't he a football player?"

Juneau raised an eyebrow. Right away, I regretted my childish question. This was Juneau Zale, after all, who had seen and done it all. Juneau, who'd ditched town the summer before her junior year: a mysterious sabbatical whose intent remained unknown to CGHS gossips. Juneau, who knew everybody's darkest secrets—though nobody, it seemed, knew hers.

"Mateo's an old friend," she said vaguely. She smiled, all teeth. "What are you reading?"

"*Midnight's Children*, by Salman Rushdie," I said. "It's my favorite book. I know it sounds superstitious, but I bring it for inspiration."

"*I have been a swallower of lives. To understand me, you'll have to swallow a world*," quoted Juneau.

My jaw dropped. "You've read it?"

"Nah," said Juneau. "I'm just a fan of pretentious quotes."

"Then I think you'd love it. It's full of them. You can borrow it if you want," I added.

"Sadly, I never learned to read," Juneau said. "I survive solely on my sex appeal." She rolled her eyes. "I'm sure you've already heard that about me."

"I haven't heard anybody say that," I lied immediately. I remembered the rumors Anya and Ife had repeated this morning, what Squash had called her during the fight.

Juneau actually laughed aloud at that. "Hold on to your kindness while you can."

It took me a moment to realize she'd derailed the conversation about Mateo, turning the heat onto herself instead. She was a master class in changing the subject. But now Ms. Meyer was giving us all instructions.

"Each of you was chosen because of the talent in your applications," Ms. Meyer said. "During this class, you'll be working on a portfolio exploring a theme that matters to you."

I glanced at my two new seatmates. Patricia was blowing gum in perfect, ever-growing bubbles, miraculously unhindered by her lip piercings. Juneau was thumbing through *Midnight's Children*.

"I was kidding before," she whispered. "I actually love to read."

"Please borrow it," I offered, but Ms. Meyer called, "Stop chatting, ladies!"

I jumped, but Juneau rolled her eyes.

"Over the summer," Ms. Meyer continued, "you all planned your portfolio theme. Please share those plans with the artists seated nearest to you."

"I can go first," Pat said. She emptied a Ziploc bag filled with magazine clippings: shuttered windows, sidewalk outlines of human bodies, the inside of an eye. "My project is about race, death, and police brutality," she said. "I'm calling it *Dying of the Light*. After the poem by—"

"Dylan Thomas," Juneau and I said together. I glanced at her, and she busied herself with her sketchbook.

"Mine's less exciting," Juneau said. "It's called *Facades*. It's about the exteriors that this world requires us to present, and all the shit that lies underneath."

Juneau's sketchbook was filled with evocative sketches of buildings, herself, and glass, always broken. Girls screenshotted from Instagram, posing in various levels of dress. A map of Alaska.

"Have you been?" I asked, pointing.

Juneau shook her head. "I was conceived in Alaska," she explained. "My parents were really young, so they weren't prepared with baby names. They ended up naming me after the city I was made in, *Juneau*." She rolled her eyes. "It could've been worse. They could've done the nasty in, like, Tacoma. What about your name? It's pretty."

"My dad named me," I said. "I don't know why he chose

31

Maya. It means illusion, deception. Kind of like your portfolio theme."

"Why haven't you asked him about it?" said Juneau.

My face reddened. "My dad left us when I was a kid. So he's not really part of my life."

"Mine neither," said Juneau, surprising me. "Not for years."

"Oh," I said. "I didn't know."

I remembered her parents: a churchgoing, respectable suburban couple. I'd assumed that Juneau's home life was accordingly picturesque.

"You couldn't have," said Juneau. It was true. Her life was so removed from mine, we occupied different solar systems entirely. If I were a minor planet, Juneau was a comet streaking by—a once-in-a-lifetime sighting was the most I could hope for.

"What happened?" I asked. "If you don't mind sharing."

"Divorce, when I was in middle school," said Juneau. "Despite their impeccable religiosity, my dad cheated. Not even Jesus could save that marriage."

"I'm sorry," I said.

"Don't apologize," said Juneau. "What's your theme?"

"I'm calling it *Femininity in Color*." I opened my sketchbook, heavy with paint: sharp brown eyes, pink petals, sunbeams. The entire conversation I'd felt like I was in over my head, but now my voice gained steam. "Affording flowers and sunlight to the women who usually get forgotten. I haven't figured it out entirely, I just want this art to disrupt narratives."

Patricia whistled softly as she and Juneau flipped through my sketchbook, filled with drawings of strangers, the reimagined anatomy of women who'd caught my eye. Fists in the air. Burning buildings. Resistance. As the sketches intensified, I watched them exchange careful glances. A silent conversation so fast and private I nearly missed it.

"This is brilliant," Juneau said at last. Her voice was filled with begrudging awe. She didn't like being out-shown.

"And incredibly important," said Pat. I felt a little thrill of victory.

Ms. Meyer clapped her hands. "Supplies are in the cabinets," she announced. "When you're ready, you can start working."

I had to restrain myself from leaping out of my seat. To work in an actual studio was everything I'd wanted for years. By the time I'd chosen my supplies, Juneau was already working, assembling what looked like a plexiglass frame for her charcoal self-portrait. At first we worked in silence, but I couldn't stop sneaking glances. Finally, Juneau turned to me.

"Do you have anything dangerous in your backpack?"

"Dangerous?" I said.

"A hammer, maybe?"

"I have a hairbrush."

"That'll do." Juneau held her hand out. Feeling foolish, I rummaged through my bag and handed her my hairbrush, hoping it wasn't snarled up with hair. Juneau fitted the plexiglass over her portrait, pounding it with the hairbrush handle until the glass cracked inside, lines spiderwebbing from her face like a bullet hole.

"You like it?" she asked. She asked questions in the same tone as pronouncements—soft and Southern, like sweetened tea, so it took me a moment to realize she wanted a response.

I considered. The portrait was still a sketch, but I could already tell it would become magnificent: Juneau's face was warped by the shattered glass, like she'd escaped from a fun-house mirror. *Facades*, I realized. I felt jealous, for an instant, of her creativity. In comparison, my art felt so predictable.

"I don't think *like* is the right word," I said. "It's haunting. It's so—*you*."

Juneau's eyes met mine. I knew I shouldn't keep staring at her, but if I looked away, it felt like admitting wrongdoing. So I held her gaze. But before I could think of something to say—a compliment, a comeuppance—the bell rang.

I grabbed my things and chased her and Pat into the hallway.

"Can I sit with you both again tomorrow?" I said.

"You don't have to ask," said Pat. "Of course."

Juneau touched the bruise on my jaw. My entire heartbeat seemed to pulse toward the point where we touched.

"Is that from my elbow?" she said.

"Yeah, but it'll heal."

"It's actually cool," said Juneau. "It makes you look strong."

Without waiting for my response, she walked away. My entire jaw was burning.

chapter 4

Y ou seem distracted," said Anya after school. We were waiting for Ife and Silva in the parking lot. It was so hot that
buses were stalling and the pavement shimmered.

"Just thinking," I said. I remembered that Juneau had my
copy of *Midnight's Children*. I imagined her hating it and felt
agonized.

"About *whom*?" pressed Anya. "Did you meet anyone new
today?" From her tone, I knew she wasn't asking about regular
classmates.

"Nah," I lied. "Anyone for you?" Anya, at least, could be
counted on for vicarious romance. I bet a dozen boys had hit
on her before lunchtime.

"Not really," said Anya, but it sounded like she was lying,
too.

Ife arrived, looking stressed. She was wearing her emergency blazer, the one she kept stashed in her locker should class presidential duties arise.

"Harvey was furious at today's student council meeting," she announced.

"Because of the police incident?" I asked.

"Plus the library vandalism," she said. "It's a bad look. By the way, did I see you walking with Juneau Zale and Patricia Lloyd today?"

"They're in my art studio," I said.

"Two interactions in one day!" Anya was impressed. "You should become friends with them. If they invited us to a party, that would be game-changing."

Ife looked concerned. "You should be careful," she said. "Juneau has a reputation, you know. The administration does not think particularly highly of her."

"That's just because she's *cool*," said Anya. "The administration only appreciates nerds like you and Maya. No offense."

Ife did seem rather offended as Anya continued. "Sam said he knows Juneau's family from church. They're quite upper-crust." She spoke in the lofty tone of someone with insider knowledge, but I was unimpressed. I could already tell Juneau wasn't like the other church families, even if they belonged to the same big-housed elite.

"What did he say about her?" I asked.

"That she's always going out of her way to stir shit up," said Anya. "He called her *insufferable*."

To me, this sounded like a ringing endorsement of Juneau's character, but I remained neutral.

"Well, it doesn't matter," I said. "I'm not even remotely in her social league."

A car honked behind us—Silva was here. "Need a ride?" he called.

As we piled in, Anya's phone rang and she jumped. Ife frowned. "Who's that?"

Anya turned red. "Nobody."

"That makes it suspicious," said Ife. "You could've just said it was your mom."

"I can't lie under pressure, okay?" said Anya, and they started bickering. I never got a sibling, but on drives like these, it didn't feel like I'd missed the experience.

To be fair, we'd practically grown up together. At first it was Silva and me in elementary school, two awkward brown kids shuffled into ELL because of our accents. We met Ife and Anya in middle school, expanding our duo into a quartet. As the three smartest girls of color, our teachers would often group Anya, Ife, and me together, whether or not we asked. Our classmates would, too, their eyes flicking over us without stopping individually. I might've resented this grouping, except I really liked Anya and Ife, who didn't intimidate me with their confidence. I actually admired the way they refused invisibility. In school and in life, Ife and Anya earned respect, reminding me that I deserved the same.

Anya's phone rang again. She grabbed it too late—this time I glimpsed the caller's name.

"*Sam Harvey's* calling you?" I said, and the others gasped. Anya's face fell.

"It's really nothing," she said. "We're just talking."

"Anya, Sam *cheated on you*," I said. "Did you forget that? He and small-tits Sarah who lives in Boca?"

"*I* certainly didn't," said Ife. "If I didn't have, like, college to worry about, I'd kick his ass."

We all looked at Silva, driving determinedly. Ife poked him, and finally he said, "How long have you been talking?"

"Not long," said Anya. "And stop lecturing me, all of you. I know what I'm doing, okay?"

The silence was so pointed in that moment. Silva suddenly turned up the music, a wildly transparent attempt to break the tension that made us all laugh. As the saxophone wailed, Anya smiled. "Thanks, guys, for caring so much. I don't know what I'd do without you all." She spread her arms, making a proclamation.

"We're starting a tradition," Anya announced. "I know that sophomore year's gonna suck, considering we live in Citrus Grove. Still, I want each of you to tell me one thing you liked about today. Ife, go."

"Dear God," Ife said. "Fine. I started this schoolwide service project as class president."

"You're class president?" I interrupted. "I had no idea. You should mention it more."

"Shut up," Ife said, laughing. "Anyway, it's a college clinic for seniors who need help applying. I got a bunch of teachers and parents to volunteer for it."

"That is incredible!" Anya said, hugging Ife. "Well, I'm happy because my English teacher told me I should consider student theater. She said I would thrive onstage."

"She's right," I said.

"Maybe." Anya shrugged. "It was just a nice thing to hear. What about you, Silva?" she said.

"Me?" said Silva. He smiled at me. "Well, thanks to Maya, I auditioned for orchestra. I think it went well. The concert-master said he was astonished he'd never heard me play before."

"Encore!" Anya cried, so Silva pulled over and grabbed his violin. Right there, in a run-down strip mall, to the raucous applause of passersby, he played Bach so sweetly I started to cry.

"What are you crying about?" Anya nudged me. "I guess I never asked you what you were happy about."

I blushed. "Same answer," I said. "All of you. Us."

"You can be so tender sometimes," Anya said.

As Silva performed, I felt so grateful for my friends—Silva's music, Ife's plans to better our universe, Anya's love for traditions, her everyday moments of joy and fanfare. I'd never loved them more than I did at that moment.

chapter 5

The bruise on my jaw faded quickly. I told Amma a partial truth about its origins: that I'd been accidentally elbowed in a crowded hallway. I wasn't in the business of lying to my mother, I just figured that morning's events were a fluke, too random to mention.

In art class, I sat with Patricia and Juneau, occupying a seat at the high priestesses' table that felt laughably unearned. Pat, with her inked-up arms, seemed born for the art studio, and we'd discuss artists we liked: Basquiat, Sher-Gil, O'Keeffe. But Juneau, who sat between us, seemed uninterested in discussion. Not that it limited her work—her charcoal drawings were consistently devastating and imaginative.

Juneau talked mostly to Pat, but when she did talk to me, she'd ask questions in her whirling, straightforward way that left me scrambling to respond. But I'd catch them both watching me. On Friday, I arrived and heard them whispering about me. I could've announced myself, but I waited, afraid to interrupt. Sometimes it was a boon to be invisible.

"I don't know," Juneau was saying. "She would never agree, for starters."

"Maya's not the most obvious choice," Pat said. "But we need her."

Juneau spotted me. "Were your ears burning?" she said.

"Listen, Maya," Pat said. "Juneau and I were talking, and we thought—" She met Juneau's gaze, then modified her statement. "Well, *I* thought you might help us with something."

I glanced at Juneau, but she was impassive. "Like a project?"

"We can't talk here," said Pat. "Want to join us for lunch today? Seniors get to leave campus, so we can drive out of here."

"Oh," I said. I imagined what Anya might say: *What are you waiting for?* Still, I sat frozen. "I'm not a senior," I said. "We'd get in trouble. I know they check IDs for senior lunch. Plus, I've never skipped class before."

"Never?" Juneau perked up. "Not even, like, behind the gym to smoke?"

"My mom works with lung patients," I said. "So, no."

"To be clear." Juneau chuckled. "You've never even been remotely tempted to pack your bags, tell everyone to screw themselves, and drive away?"

"I can't drive," I muttered, embarrassed. "Look. I'm really honored. But sneaking out, or breaking rules, is just not something I'm good at."

"Well, you're in luck, because flaunting authority is something I happen to excel at," said Juneau. "Along with painting, mischief, and disappointing my parents, to name a few."

"I have Chemistry," I said weakly.

"And we don't?" Juneau winked. Something in her seemed to awaken. She no longer seemed standoffish. I knew right then that she, like me, loved a challenge.

When the bell rang, I stood rooted to the spot.

"I can't," I said. "I'm sorry."

Pat sighed. I knew I'd disappointed her, though I didn't yet know how. She left the classroom, but Juneau didn't follow. I could see *Midnight's Children* inside her bag.

"Come on," she said. I hesitated, and she leaned in so close, I could smell her perfume—lemongrass, maybe, or citrus. The book in her bag came alive. I felt it, warm and breathing. "Oh, I—" I tried to shrug my shoulders carelessly like she did, as if throwing off a coat. It didn't matter. Juneau was already out the door. She knew.

I broke into a jog to catch up with her. For the first time in my life, I didn't think twice. I didn't look back.

Juneau was waiting for me in the senior parking lot, minus Pat. "There you are," she said. "I knew you'd come."

I folded my arms and tried my best to appear two years older. Casual, confident. I caught Juneau snickering at me and abandoned the effort.

"No, you're doing it right," she said. "As long as you act like a senior, nobody will question you. See, none of these people are even looking at you."

This was more likely due to my general insignificance than my top-notch acting skills, but Juneau was already marching toward her car.

"Your chariot awaits," she said, pointing to a bright yellow Volkswagen Beetle. It was decidedly vintage but expensively polished, clearly resurrected to make a statement. I'd seen it many times in parking lots around town—after all, how many yellow Beetles could exist in Citrus Grove?—but I'd never realized the car was hers. Now I couldn't think of anything more obvious in the world.

"I like your car."

"I fixed it up myself," she said. "My dad was shit at most things, but he did teach me to hold my own with cars."

She opened the back door of her Beetle, which was an impressive feat, since the interior was jam-packed with half-finished canvases, clothes, and an unthinkable quantity of Styrofoam packing peanuts. There was also a silky bedsheet draped suggestively on the seat. I stared at her, and she smirked.

"I'm not seducing you," she said, and my face burned.

"That's not what I was thinking," I said, getting in the car. "Don't be crass." That was a trick I'd learned from Anya: Make the other person think the embarrassing thing was their idea, and you get off easy.

To my relief, Pat arrived hefting an enormous cardboard box. Together, they squeezed it into the trunk. I tried to peek inside, but Juneau tossed the bedsheet over it. Then she buckled in and jerked the car into reverse, sending me flying back into the seat.

"I'm too young to die," said Patricia, clutching her heart.

Juneau laughed. She swerved through the parking lot, sending seagulls squawking indignantly aside. "Come on," she said. "You've got to admit there's something sexy about dying young."

Our eyes met in the rearview mirror, and I saw her frown. "You okay, rosebud?"

I was breathing hard enough to drown out the seagulls. "Getting flattened in a car crash is literally the least sexy way I can think of to die," I said.

"You won't die," Patricia said, but I wasn't reassured.

"My pulse is too high," I said. "I think I might be entering tachycardia."

"*What?*"

"*Tachycardia*. You know, heart palpitations preceding a heart attack preceding death—"

Juneau slammed the brakes, causing oxygen to physically part company with my lungs. A chorus of horns screamed behind us—Pat flicked a lazy middle finger at them.

"Mayavati Krishnan," said Juneau, shocking me with my full name. She twisted precariously in the seat so I was forced to look her in the face. She was grinning widely, despite the situation.

"In fifty years, when you're enjoying the view from some fancy high-rise corner office, all menopausal and exhausted from a lifetime of changing the world, which are you gonna regret missing more: forty-five minutes of your sophomore Chemistry class, or a lunchtime adventure with me?"

"Well." I stumbled. "When you put it like that..."

It was a lot to process—Juneau's eyes glittering, the adrenaline pulsing through my veins. "I guess let's go, then."

"*Let's go!*" Juneau echoed triumphantly.

We made it another ten feet before Juneau slammed the brakes again. I looked up to see Dr. Harvey blocking the school gates. He rapped on Juneau's window, and my heart dropped.

"Shit. Guys. I don't have a senior ID."

Juneau smiled. "Watch and learn."

"What?"

"Seriously. You're going to want to watch this," said Patricia. "Juneau's a freaking ninja around Dr. Harvey. It's her white girl superpower."

Juneau rolled down her window. "Hello, Juneau," Dr. Harvey said. His eyes darted around the car, lingering on Patricia and me.

"What's up?" Juneau squinted amicably at Dr. Harvey.

"I'm searching cars to make sure nobody's smuggling anything in or out. Just a security precaution, with everything going on. And watch your speed in the parking lot, Juneau. People could get hurt."

The mildness of his tone surprised me. I couldn't tell if we were in trouble or not—Patricia was chewing her nails industriously, but Juneau was completely at ease. Here, then, was her superpower at work. But then I remembered that cardboard box. My stomach squirmed. If I got caught with drugs, or worse...

"I can respect that," said Juneau.

"Once you ladies show me your senior IDs," said Dr. Harvey, "you can head to lunch."

Patricia and Juneau held theirs out. As he checked the IDs, he asked Juneau, "By the way, how is your mother? I barely saw her at church this summer."

Juneau hesitated. "She likes to volunteer in the summers. In other countries, usually islands. She says it keeps her busier than church."

"That's wonderful. We need more women like your mother," said Dr. Harvey. He turned to me. "Where's your ID?"

I froze. "Oh, I don't—"

Dr. Harvey frowned, and I knew he recognized me: the girl who confronted him. That's when Juneau leaned out the window.

"Listen," she said. "I'm going to be honest, sir. Maya's not a senior. She's a sophomore, and she just got her first-ever period. We're trying to find her a tampon so that she doesn't bleed out."

Everyone stared at me, and I felt something brewing inside of me—not fear, but something headier than it, equal parts longing and rage.

"I'm sorry," I lied. "But this is my first time bleeding and I don't know what to do."

Dr. Harvey was at a loss for words. "Juneau, are you seriously asking me to let you drive off campus with an underage student?"

I barely had to pretend; my eyes began to water. I rubbed my eyelids, but it was impossible to stop crying once I'd started. Lying was like free-handing a sketch—and apparently I was good at it.

Juneau sighed. "You're right," she said. "Maya, I can't bring you with me. Dr. Harvey is going to have to take it from here—sir?" She looked back at him. "Can you help her find the right tampon? It needs to be the right thickness to fit her body, and it has to happen soon—"

"For God's sake," said Dr. Harvey. Ironically, it was the furthest from God I had felt in some time. I could see the *choose-your-battles* thoughts waging war on his face, and I knew what he was going to say even before he said it. I knew Juneau did, too, because she was smiling at the sky as if divining meaning from the blue.

"This never happens again," he said, stepping aside.

Juneau needed no further invitation. She stepped on the gas, and we lurched out of CGHS. Pat and Juneau couldn't stop laughing, and eventually I joined in.

"Wow," Pat said. "You really told Dr. Harvey that Maya, a high school sophomore, was on schedule for her first period?"

Juneau was humble. "You have to hand it to men," she said. "They don't know the first thing about women's bodies."

"Can I ask," I said, "where we're going? Also, what's in the box?"

Juneau glanced back. "That would ruin the surprise, wouldn't it?" Then she acted like I hadn't said anything at all.

Juneau drove recklessly through identical suburbs, past small-town churches and citrus trees stretching for miles. Then, without warning, she pulled into the parking lot of a run-down Taco Bell.

"Get out," she said, unbuckling her seat belt. "We're late."

"Hold on," I said. "We drove all this way for chalupas?"

Pat glanced at Juneau. "Shall I do the honors?"

"Go ahead," said Juneau, suddenly serious.

Patricia continued. "Remember how we said we needed your help? We wanted to introduce you to a special group of our people." She hesitated. "We think they may be your people, too."

"What are you talking about?" I said.

Juneau smiled at me. "Maya, I mean this in the best way possible, but you're not a regular person," she said. "You're optimistic. You're willing to stand up for people. You care about justice, so much it sometimes hurts. Please tell me if I'm wrong."

The way she spoke—quiet but commanding, like she'd

never been more certain of anything in her life—it was like she was casting a spell.

"You're not," I whispered.

"We're part of a group of students using acts of nonconformity to change Citrus Grove," Pat said. "We don't identify ourselves publicly, but we get together and do the work. And when we do, people notice."

"Like freeing the library?" said Juneau. "That was us. We think libraries are the last radical space left in this town. Harvey locked it up, so we opened it ourselves."

"We've done other missions, too," explained Pat. "We specialize in pranks, mischief, and chaos—just enough to wake people up. Sophomore year, we outed this rapist on the baseball team. We printed a ton of leaflets and stuck them in the vents, everywhere. That was when we were just getting started." She ticked off her fingers as she spoke. "Once, we nailed lockboxes over the toilet paper in the men's bathroom, just to show the absurdity of making girls pay for tampons. Oh, and last year, we filled the school cop cars with soap and Spam."

"Maybe our finest project." Juneau smiled reminiscently.

"Oh" was all I managed. "I had no idea."

"Yeah, well, we're not in it for fame or anything," said Juneau. "Nobody outside of us knows we exist. And it's not like the school is bragging about our accomplishments, either."

"You're telling me," I said at last, "that you've been running a secret resistance society, or whatever, in Citrus Grove. And you want me to join."

"Well, don't get ahead of yourself," said Juneau. "Pat and I are in charge, but we don't make all the rules. It depends on if the others like you."

"Others?"

"That's why we're here," Juneau explained. "Hurry up. Pat called an emergency recruitment meeting, and everyone else got here fifteen minutes ago."

I didn't get out of the car.

"I still don't understand," I said. "Why me? We barely know each other."

"Truthfully?" said Pat, somewhat apologetic. "We need an artist, and quick. Our next mission's in a week."

"There's a whole studio of artists," I said. "You could've asked anyone else."

"Because this town is a snow globe," said Juneau. "And you have the guts to shake it up." Her voice was so clear I could feel it in my chest. "Do you trust me?"

"Not really," I said, but I followed her into Taco Bell.

The restaurant was sparsely occupied, except for the middle booth, where three kids were eating enough tacos to feed a small country. They turned around when we opened the door, and I waved to be polite, recognizing them as upperclassmen from school. Then one of the guys waved back, and I was startled to see Mateo Chavez.

"Everyone's here," said Juneau.

She slid into the booth next to Mateo, and I sat beside her. Her eyes had a theatrical gleam. "Introductions are in order," she said grandly. "You should get to know the group. We're quite a close-knit circle."

"*Close-knit circle* is a polite way of saying crime ring," said the boy across the table. He was wearing a button-down despite the August heat, and I recognized him from the TV ads—his parents, Fisher & Cho, were prominent attorneys in Orlando.

Juneau rolled her eyes. "Maya, this is Theodore Fisher-Cho. He's a junior. We keep him around mostly for his money. He's a bit of a venture capitalist, if you will."

"Meaning, I bankroll all the crazy shit that we get up to, and my parents can get you out of jail if necessary. Not that it's ever necessary," added Theodore, correctly interpreting my shocked face. He shook my hand. "You can call me Theo. And I prefer *philanthropist*."

"Hello," I offered weakly, but Juneau had already moved on.

"Mateo Chavez," she said. "You both should be well acquainted after Monday morning."

Mateo nodded across the table. "Thanks for standing up for me," he said.

Pat introduced the remaining girl at the table—Tess Osei, the soft-spoken exchange student from Ghana who, according to Juneau, was the logistical brains behind their operations.

Tess said hello, but I sat there staring. None of these people were strangers to me—I'd seen them around school, in supermarket aisles, smoking in parking lots at night. These were kids I knew but had never spoken to. Kids with reputations that other people discussed, like they were TV characters. I tried to follow along, but I felt hopelessly out of place. They smiled when something was interesting; I smiled because they had.

To my right, Tess was sharing with Pat how she'd accidentally called her teacher-crush "Dad" to his face. Instead of fleeing the country, she just laughed.

"He definitely heard me," she said. "And who knows? Maybe he's into that shit."

To my left, Theo and Mateo were arguing. "You need to

handle your shit with Squash," Theo said. "Dr. Harvey's onto us for the library. If you're not careful—"

"It's not about being *careful*," said Mateo. "Harvey's always been after guys like me. We get policed no matter what we do."

"I know, and it's messed up," said Theo. "But you can't draw attention to yourself by fighting."

"I agree with Mateo," said Tess, crossing conversations. "I can't believe we have police at a public school. I knew America was crazy, but to have cops breaking up high school fights? It's like they're trying to punish us."

"Every adult in Citrus Grove is in on it," said Pat, nodding at me. "Remember the way Mr. Taylor talked to me in math class, like I didn't belong there? Racist old ass." She slurped her soda loudly.

Mateo rolled his eyes. "Do you think that shit ends in school?" he said. "I mean, look at the fucking cashier. He's been watching us this whole time, like he's expecting us to rob Taco Bell."

"Well, we probably wouldn't rob it," Tess said ponderously. "Maybe symbolically deface it."

Juneau clapped her hands. "Friends, warriors," she said. "I'm sorry to interrupt, but I hope you're all well fed. It's time to decide about Maya."

Everyone looked at me. My face burned.

"Generally, we start our new recruits with an initiation ceremony," Juneau told me. She took my hand. "Are you squeamish around needles?"

I jerked back my hand. Pat rolled her eyes. "She's kidding," she said. "It's just an interview."

"Oh," I said, though truthfully that didn't sound much better.

"Everyone gets to ask one question," Juneau said. "And you don't get time to think. You just answer."

"First question," said Theo, before I'd realized we'd started. "If you could have any superpower, what would it be?"

"Um, invisibility."

"Really?" said Juneau. "Mine's mind control. In case you were wondering." She smiled. "In that spirit, you can control any person on this planet and make them your personal bitch. Who do you choose?"

"Bill Gates?" I said. "Because then I'd redistribute his money and I could use it to solve basically any world problem I wanted."

"Smart," said Patricia. "What's your greatest strength as a person?"

I bit my lip. "I...can paint?" I said. "And I fight for people I love."

"Have you ever broken the law?" said Mateo. He watched me closely, not joking.

I hesitated, but Mateo snapped his fingers. "I've had wine," I blurted out. Juneau snickered.

"Softball question," Tess said. "What's the biggest crisis facing Citrus Grove?"

"*That's* your softball question?" said Pat.

"So many," I said. "But I think they're all related to one big crisis, and that's power. Only a few people get power in this town, and it's up to them to decide who they use it against, and whose voice actually gets heard."

"All right," Pat said, clapping her hands. "So normally we'd adjourn to deliberate, but since we need to recruit another artist quickly, we're voting right now." She smiled at the table. "All those in favor of admitting Maya, please raise your hand."

For an awful second, nothing happened. I felt tiny, an insect pinned to a corkboard. But then, steadily, Pat raised her hand. Of course: She'd chosen me in the first place. Then the well-dressed boy, Theo, and friendly Tess. I looked at Mateo and Juneau. Juneau was holding out on me—as punishment for my earlier reluctance? I didn't know. All I knew, suddenly, was that I'd never wanted anything more in my life.

Mateo was quiet. He had the clean, sturdy gaze of somebody minted on a coin.

"Pat, I'm not sure," he said at last.

I saw Juneau's face shift when Mateo spoke. Her gaze was tender.

"I think we're rushing this," Mateo said, not looking at me. "Things are riskier than ever. We can't spend our time hand-holding the new girl. Especially an honors student who's never even jaywalked."

His words stung. I felt like a garden of flowers had wilted in my chest.

"That's fair," said Juneau, and my heart sank even lower. "I felt similarly when Pat first suggested her. Maya, any rebuttal?"

"Um," I said, like I was in a play and I'd forgotten my lines.

"I'm not trying to be a dick," said Mateo. "I appreciate your sticking up for me with Harvey. But this isn't just some extra-curricular activity. You don't get AP credit for this. You need to be willing to take risks. Break rules, whatever. And I honestly don't think you're ready for that. Don't take it personally," he added, though it was hard not to.

Deep down, I knew he was right. Under their scrutiny, I paled, insignificant. Juneau, Patricia, Mateo, Theodore, Tess—they sat at Taco Bell like minor gods, assured and self-evident. They smashed locks, lit matches, turned heads. And who was I? A scared sophomore, clearly out of place.

"No, it's okay," I said. "You're right. I haven't taken risks, not like you have." The words spilled out of my mouth, uncareful. "And maybe I don't seem like I can keep up with your team. But I promise there are things I'm good at. Like, I'm an artist. I'm observant, and I can get by unnoticed. And I promise I'll work hard to catch up with you."

I hesitated. "I mean, Pat saw something in me, in my art. Can't that be enough for you?"

"Mateo," said Pat. "I know she's not your top choice, but we need another artist. Maya's the best we've got."

"I'll help her along," said Juneau. "She'll be okay, Mateo. Trust me."

She placed her hand on mine. I felt myself sit up straight, my shoulders jerking into a posture like I'd been knighted. Mateo hesitated. I'm sure he saw it then, what happened whenever Juneau touched me. He must've seen it before anyone. But he nodded.

"Fine," he said. "I trust you."

My heart raced as Juneau raised her soda cup to me, and everyone else followed suit.

"It's unanimous," she said. "Maya, what I am about to offer you is not to be taken lightly."

"God, not that speech again," snorted Pat, but Juneau waved her off, clearly enjoying herself.

"You will shine flashlights into darkness, grapple with

ghosts, and slay dragons," she said. "You might be a painter, but you're a warrior, too."

"What she means," said Pat, interrupting her monologue, "is you're invited to join the Pugilists."

"The *what*?"

"The Pugilists," explained Pat, more gently. "That's what we call ourselves. The secret society of artists and activists forcing Citrus Grove to wake the fuck up."

"Our actions take different forms," Theo explained. "Art, pranks, mischief, or however we're feeling inspired. When we start our next mission, you'll be part of it."

"Some rules," said Tess. "First, you tell nobody that the Pugilists exist. It's called a secret society for a reason, and all of us have serious shit on the line—scholarships, criminal records, futures. You can't even tell your friends."

"Agreed," I said, but Mateo interrupted.

"When Tess says *nobody*," he said gruffly, "that includes extreme circumstances. In other words, if you get questioned by the principal or the police, you need to stay silent." He paused. "You take the fall, if necessary."

I thought about what Mateo had said: *Especially an honors student who's never even jaywalked.* And I remembered what Ife had called me earlier: *the most law-abiding nerd she'd ever met in her life.* She'd only been joking, but she was right. I was never a natural risk-taker. I'd always been so afraid of the known consequences—but what if missing out on unknown consequences was the greatest risk of all?

It really wasn't a choice.

"Agreed," I said again. "Is that all?"

"Our community is built on a foundation of trust," Juneau said. "We just trusted ourselves with you. Now, you'll need to put your trust in us." She passed me a battered notebook. "This is our pact," she explained. "Take a look before you sign."

I opened the notebook to see a list of names. Up top was Juneau's loopy, careless signature, close to Mateo's and Patricia's. Some other names were unfamiliar, including the name on the very first line: *Laila Afzar*.

"Who's Laila?" I asked.

"Laila's our founding leader," explained Mateo. "She recruited our original members two years ago—me, Juneau, and Pat. After she graduated, we kept up her legacy."

I signed my name, but it came out shaky. I knew eventually I'd get to the point where my signature consistently asserted itself, but I wasn't there yet. I'd barely signed anything in my life—just permission slips for school, plus the questionable abstinence pledge girls had to sign in Health Ed. Of my entire class, I feared I was the only one keeping that pact.

I capped the pen, and everyone clapped.

"Welcome," Pat said, "to the Pugilists."

I sat with the Pugilists as the afternoon sun stretched around us. Tess and Theo started singing along to the music so badly that the cashier told us that our two options were to shut up or get tacos elsewhere.

We filed out into the parking lot. Pat left with Tess, so I followed Juneau.

"Back to school?" she asked.

"I can still catch my afternoon classes," I said. I was still hurt by Mateo's *honors student* comment, and I braced myself for judgment. But Juneau smiled. "Your scholarly dedication is admirable."

"Is school not really your scene?" I asked. I tried to imagine Juneau in a classroom boxed in by a desk or holed up doing homework, but I couldn't.

"You could say that," said Juneau. "I mean, I love reading. But the institutionalization of it all? It's soul crushing." She shrugged. "Pat's more like you. She's definitely going to college, and Mateo's expecting a football scholarship, if he doesn't get injured again this season. He got a bad concussion sophomore year."

"You're lucky you're all seniors," I said wistfully. "One more year, and you're free."

"And then *my future* will begin," sang Juneau, making air quotes with her fingers. "Or so I've been told."

I was surprised. "Surely you have plans after graduating."

"Not particularly," Juneau said. "Do you?"

"Me?" I said. "Sort of." I tried to sound casual, like I hadn't daydreamed about it all summer. "I mean, I'd like to go to college for art and business, either in New York or California. Maybe live abroad in India for a bit, launch my first gallery by the time I'm thirty."

"You've really thought this out." She smiled. "Right now, the only plan I have involves getting as far from Citrus Grove as I can. I'll figure out the rest when I get there."

"What about college?" I said, and Juneau rolled her eyes.

"I couldn't get in if I tried," she said. "Not that I tried."

CGHS came into view. Sneaking in turned out to be infinitely easier than sneaking out; Juneau simply drove past the ever-present police cars by the gates. She opened the trunk, and I finally saw what was inside the box—*cans of spray paint.*

"So this is where the adventure ends," Juneau said. For

a moment, I half expected her to pull me back into the car, announce our second destination, the next adventure we'd have together. Something inside me lurched forward. She had more up her sleeve, I knew it.

But she didn't. Instead, she started the car. "See you around," she said.

"Aren't you coming back?" I said. "School's this way!" My voice echoed in the parking lot—*This way! This way!*

She laughed and drove in the other direction.

chapter 6

To my surprise, nobody confronted me about skipping
Chemistry. Nobody noticed I wasn't concentrating in
class. In fact, nobody seemed to care at all, not until Anya and
Ife confronted me after school.

"Where'd you go today?" Ife demanded.

"Chemistry was depressing without you," said Anya.

I tried my best to sound casual. "I left campus," I said. "A
friend took me to lunch."

"Which friend?" said Ife suspiciously. "We're your only friends."

I rolled my eyes. "Fine. It was Juneau. Happy?"

The effect of my words was dramatic.

"I warned you about Juneau," Ife said. "I can't believe she
pressured you into skipping class."

Annoyance clenched my chest. Of course this was how Ife
saw me: helpless as a canoe, easily drifted by stronger winds.

I willed my voice to sound languidly assured, like Juneau's. "I'll just tell my mom to write me a sick note. No big deal."

Ife crossed her arms. "You could get in a lot of trouble. It's only sophomore year."

To my relief, Anya rose to my defense. "Exactly," she said. "It's only sophomore year. That means we have time to screw around before things get serious." She pinched my arm affectionately. "First you stood up for that football player. Now you're skipping class with Juneau Zale, no less. This year's gonna be huge!"

Luckily, Silva arrived to drive me home. I eagerly hopped into the car. I loved Ife and Anya dearly, but I especially cherished moments with Silva. He never judged me, like Ife, or smothered me, like Anya. We had an unspoken code of support. Which is why, in the car, I told him about something else that was weighing on my mind: my father's arrival.

"Do you think you'll meet him?" Silva asked.

"I don't know."

"What does Sujatha Aunty say?"

"We haven't actually discussed it," I admitted. "She's seeing this guy, Ramesh, and I don't want to reopen anything that could hurt her."

"You're being a good daughter," Silva said. I smiled gratefully; he'd said exactly what I needed to hear.

There was a sports car in the driveway when we arrived. Silva whistled. "Fancy visitors?"

I groaned. "I think it's Ramesh. He runs a car dealership, apparently."

Sure enough, inside the doorway I found a pair of men's

leather shoes, right next to my paint-stained flip-flops and Amma's heels. She and Ramesh were snacking on samosas in the kitchen. Spotting me, Amma frowned.

"Maya!" she called. "You're back later than I expected. You should've called. Come eat."

I grabbed a samosa, picking out all the chilies like I was a child. "I'm sorry. I went for a drive with Silva," I said. "I didn't know I needed permission."

Amma's hand closed on mine, a little harder than necessary. "It's all right," she said. She was always cooler in front of her boyfriends. She put on a convincing act like we both weren't drifting apart yet still constantly treading on each other's feet. "How was your day?"

For a wild second, I considered telling her the truth: that I'd lied to the principal, faked my period, and joined a secret cult. Maybe that would wipe the generous smile off her face.

But I didn't.

"Nothing special," I said.

"I was just telling Ramesh about your art class," Amma said. Now I had no choice but to chat with Ramesh, who seemed nice enough but distinctly uninterested in my art or really anything about me. "Study well in school," Ramesh finally declared, and Amma nodded at me. I'd done my job, and now I could go. Before heading to my room, I ate the chilies one by one, so spicy that they bit me back.

I spent the afternoon doing homework. My entire life, school came easily to me, with the exception of English classes. My English teachers liked me—all my teachers did—but I consistently failed their essays. *Stick to your thesis*, they'd write.

Your thoughts are disorganized. My problem was, I meandered to find my truth. Each paragraph surprised me. Maybe one day I'd learn to stick to my guns, but I wasn't there yet.

Out of habit, I opened Instagram. Rajendra's tour schedule hadn't changed. His Orlando exhibit was only two months away.

Staring at my father's account, I kept thinking about Amma and Ramesh, all the failing relationships I watched but couldn't help. I knew what I was feeling was powerlessness. The same way I felt whenever Silva's parents banned his violin, Anya dated shitty guys, or Ife yearned for colleges she couldn't afford. The powerlessness that, upon joining the Pugilists, had burned quickly away, leaving me hungry for more.

My phone rang from an unknown number, interrupting my stalking of Rajendra's Instagram.

"Not interested," I told the caller.

I heard a chuckle, and I froze. "Wait. *Juneau?*"

I'd assumed the call was spam, but instead I heard Juneau's familiar sugarless laugh. I wanted to hang up and die.

"Damn, girl. You are ruthless," Juneau said.

"I thought you were a telemarketer," I said. "I'm so sorry. How'd you get my number?"

"You wrote it inside the book," Juneau said. *"Midnight's Children.* I'm nearly done, by the way, and it's riveting. I assumed you wrote it for me to find," she added after a moment. "I swear I didn't stalk you."

"Oh," I said. "Actually, I wrote it ages ago. So if it got lost I could find it."

"It's funny how that works," said Juneau. "Because this book is very good at finding you. You also included your home address. What if, like, a murderer found it?"

"I somehow doubt a murderer would be interested in reading Rushdie."

"Murderers read all sorts of things. You shouldn't write them off like that."

"Fine," I said. "No murderer would ever bother with me. I'm not very relevant."

"Trust me," said Juneau. "That's exactly how you want it. Living in too many people's minds is exhausting. You're always performing. You never get a break."

I was surprised by her vulnerability.

"Is that how you feel?" I said. "Like you're always performing?"

Juneau laughed. "I did spend the summer after sophomore year touring with Pacific Jukebox. At their Oakland concert, they let me play the triangle."

As an immigrant, I often didn't get references to popular American music. But I knew this band because Silva was obsessed with them.

"*Pacific Jukebox?* They're insanely famous. How did that happen?" Here was Juneau's famous disappearance, explained at last. It didn't occur to me not to believe her. Everything she said shimmered with incontrovertible truth.

"I showed up to their Miami concert and pretended to be the bassist's long-lost daughter," said Juneau. "When they didn't let me backstage, I threatened to call my lawyer. Peak white privilege. I kept saying, *Don't you see the resemblance?* until finally, they saw it."

I pictured Juneau onstage, her hair gleaming, witch-like. The pitch of the triangle. The screaming crowds. I imagined how my friends would react to this story. We'd discuss it for hours, each retelling more fantastical than the one before.

"I have so many questions," I said at last.

"Another time," said Juneau. "I called to check in. What's on your mind right now?"

I decided to tell her the truth, that Rajendra was coming to town for work.

"Whoa. Are you going to meet him?" Juneau asked, just like Silva had.

"I don't know," I said.

"What's the deal with him, exactly?" said Juneau.

"Well," I said. It was strange to explain my father to her, to remember that there were people who occupied entire universes free of Rajendra's shadow. When I shared the story, Juneau scoffed.

"Aren't you furious at him?" Juneau asked. "I would be."

Coming from anybody but Juneau, the question would've been intrusive. But I'd felt so alone in my anger, surrounded by my forgiving, exhausted mother, my kind and gentle friends. In contrast, Juneau understood how I felt. She had rage in her, too.

"I've been mad my whole life," I said. "My mom isn't, though. She makes excuses for him. She thinks there's just a price for loving an artist."

"He's an artist?" Juneau laughed. "That doesn't surprise me. Society gives all sorts of passes to male artists. Like their talent justifies their shitty behavior."

Juneau often did this: abruptly shift the scope of conversations so that a passing remark became indicative of everything wrong with society. But I liked the conclusions she reached. She gave me words to describe my dissatisfactions. She gave my feelings legitimacy.

"How do you know he's coming back?" Juneau asked.

"Instagram," I said. "He's famous online, and he got a fellowship to come here."

Juneau whistled. "And you had me feeling like the stalker."

The space between us crackled with static. "I think you should contact him," Juneau said at last. "Clearly you're in search of some accountability."

"You think so?"

"You deserve answers," Juneau said. "When my dad left us, at least I knew why. I think you should message him right now. I'll stay on the line."

So I put Juneau on speaker. For the first time in my life, I DMed Rajendra.

Good afternoon, I typed. Too formal, I thought, so I backspaced it.

Hello, I wrote instead. This is Mayavati (Maya) Krishnan. Your daughter.

The blank screen stretched before me like an open hand. What could I possibly say?

If you have time during your fellowship in Orlando, I'd really like to meet you. By the way, I'm an artist, too. I post my work here, if you want to look. I scanned over my feed, imagining it through his eyes. Would he find it impressive, or just childish?

I didn't know how to finish the message, so I just typed, Hope to hear from you soon. Before I lost my nerve, I hit Send. "Done!" I said. Juneau cheered. I propped my window open, listening to her talk until she merged with the soft breeze rustling outside.

chapter 7

August ran into September like watercolors. The days left slippery trails behind them. I checked Instagram for my father's reply, but it never came. Though it hurt, Juneau was right. In a way, pressing Send had liberated me.

Juneau didn't call me again, and her school attendance remained sporadic—a layer of inaccessibility that added to her mystery. Meanwhile, whenever I ran into a Pugilist at school, they'd nod. The first few times, I'd turned around, certain they were looking at somebody else. Eventually, I smiled back.

Juneau reappeared on Thursday at lunchtime. I was sitting in the cafeteria with my friends. Squash, whom Anya was officially "talking to" again, sat with his football clan across the room. Occasionally they'd smile at each other; the rest of us exchanged stoic looks.

"We talked for hours yesterday," Anya was saying. "He's

really sorry for how things ended and thinks we can make it work. Plus, homecoming's just around the corner, and we can run together for king and queen. Which I've wanted forever—"

"Who cares?" said Ife. "He's an asshole."

I nodded along, but I wasn't actually listening. I was looking at Juneau, who'd sat down with Pat. I decided against waving. I didn't want to push my luck: I was excited to catch a glimpse of her at all.

Anya poked my arm. "Enough about me and Sam," she said. "How's your love life faring?"

I startled. "Love?"

"You're distracted," Anya said. "That's a good sign."

"I'm not!" I tore my gaze back to earth.

Ife's scoff changed mid-exhalation to laughter. "Don't sweat it," she told me. "Who cares if you and I go to prom single, as long as we kick everyone's asses on the SAT?"

"Ignore Ife," Anya declared. "I'll find you a nice boy. I already have a candidate."

Silva perked up. "Someone likes Maya?"

"What's your opinion on James Quentin?" Anya asked.

"No," groaned Ife. "Not the football player from our Econ class last year?"

"He's Sam's teammate," said Anya. "Do you remember him, Maya?"

I did, vaguely. "Isn't he the one who sat in the back, harassed Ms. Harper for extra credit, and yet ardently opposed 'government handouts'?"

"Bygones," said Anya. "You'll have plenty of time to convert him to socialism, or whatever you're into nowadays."

"What kind of fate would set up Maya Krishnan, Warrior

Artist of Citrus Grove, with some run-of-the-mill Young Republican?" countered Ife, and the two of them started arguing again. Juneau had finally noticed me, her stare unwavering. For a strange moment, I felt the cafeteria fall away, like we were the only ones in the room. I'd never felt more awkward in my life: She was fifty feet away, but we'd already made eye contact, so I couldn't look away without ignoring her. But I also couldn't stare while she walked across the whole cafeteria. And the second quandary: At what distance did I say hello—did I shout an acknowledgment now, or when she was in earshot, or wait until she'd arrived?

"Is that Juneau Zale?" said Anya, craning her neck for a better look.

"Juneau?" echoed Silva, interested.

Ife gasped. "She's coming over here!"

"Hi, Juneau," I said, trying to play it cool. "These are my friends. Anya, Silva, and Ife."

Anya laughed, but her voice was higher than usual.

"I came to check in on you," Juneau said. "More specifically, your pulse. Any risk of tachycardia?"

"Don't condescend to me." The truth was that my heart was, in fact, pounding again. But Juneau didn't need to know that. Her half smile reminded me of Mona Lisa—that is, if Mona Lisa was a suburban teenager with authority issues.

"I need a favor." She pulled me aside to speak privately. "It's for our next mission. Can you meet Theo on the football field after lunch?"

At last, our mission. The reason the Pugilists had plucked me last-minute from obscurity, letting me into their world.

"What is it?" I asked eagerly, but Juneau shrugged and left.

I realized she still didn't trust me; maybe this mysterious errand was yet another test.

"You light up around her," said Anya when I returned. "If I didn't know better, I'd say you had a crush."

"Don't tell James Quentin," I said, and everyone laughed.

"What did she want to talk about?" Ife asked.

"Just art class," I lied. I braced myself for Ife's disapproval, but she, too, looked awestruck.

"Did you know she got a near-perfect SAT?" said Ife. "I found out because I saw her files at the college clinic. Her GPA's shit, but her test score's insane."

"Juneau went to your college clinic?" I couldn't believe how quickly Ife's opinion of Juneau had improved.

Ife nodded. "Her friend brought her, Patricia. To be fair, she looked pissed to be there."

They turned to me for an explanation, but I had none. Juneau told me that she had no chance of getting into college. She didn't mention the SAT, but that meant nothing. Besides my friends, most teenagers didn't give two shits about exams. And yet she'd aced it. If anything, this fact humanized Juneau. In her excellence, she felt just as mundane as the rest of us.

"Maybe she's weirdly good at tests," I said. The subject eventually turned to next month's homecoming dance, which I was grateful for. If there's anything Ife liked more than gossiping about the SAT, it was event planning on a cosmic scale. For the rest of lunch, she regaled us with dance committee drama, and Juneau Zale was forgotten.

69

Theodore Fisher-Cho was waiting for me on the football field. He smelled really good, undoubtedly expensive. Anya could probably identify the cologne.

"Juneau said you needed me?" I said.

"It's easier to show you," Theo said, leading me to the big scoreboard. "We need to measure the scoreboard," he said. "But covertly. Juneau said you'd know what to do."

I stared up at the scoreboard. Atop the blinking numbers, it proudly declared: HOME OF THE CITRUSES. Our mascot wasn't very imaginative. At least it wasn't racist.

"Why?" I asked.

"Juneau said not to tell you until it's time," Theo said. "But there's a big plan for it. You'll see."

"Why?" I said again. "Does she think I'll snitch or something?"

Theo looked apologetic. "Really, it's best not to ask too many questions."

"So I should just blindly follow her?" The question came out sharp.

"You sound like she's a tyrant," said Theo. "She's just brilliant, is all. She has this strange power to make lightning out of thin air. As long as you trust her judgment, things work out."

I must not have looked convinced, because Theo continued, "She and Pat expect a lot from us. They drag the Pugilists out of our comfort zones. But to be part of their world, it's worth it every time."

He pulled out a tape measure. "So how exactly do we measure this thing?"

Questions still burned in me, but I took the tape measure. "Easy," I said. "We use math."

I noted the length of the shadows the scoreboard cast on

the field. It wasn't that tall or hard to measure, but Theo's jaw dropped when I pulled out a protractor to estimate the angle of the sun. He wrote down numbers as I reported them, until finally I seized the notebook, double-checked my calculations, and announced the measurements.

"Juneau said you were smart," Theo said admiringly. "But that was next-level badass."

"It was just geometry," I said, embarrassed. "Though I wish you'd tell me what those numbers are for."

"*That would ruin the surprise,*" said Theo in an uncanny imitation of Juneau's drawl; I laughed. Walking to class, I realized I was still holding the tape measure. The tiny markings reminded me of the art studio's easels with their marked-off inches.

I turned back, but this time I didn't see a scoreboard.

I saw an empty canvas.

I was a little late to Art Studio, and when I saw Pat crying in Juneau's arms, dread pierced me.

"Is everything okay?" I dropped my bag onto the bench.

Juneau winked at me. "Pat, will you break the big news or shall I?"

"I got the email," Pat said. I looked at her phone to see an all-caps **CONGRATULATIONS** from the University of Florida.

"Holy shit," I said. "Pat, did you just get early acceptance to UF?"

"It came in right after lunch," explained Juneau. "She wasn't expecting it. But I wasn't surprised for a second."

"Congratulations, Pat. Oh my god."

To my surprise, Pat scooped me into her hug with Juneau. I felt Juneau, suddenly close against me. Something softened in me, and it was almost terrifying how intense it was. I moved away.

"You're next, Juneau," said Pat. "We're both going to college next year. You promised."

"I already told you." Juneau brushed her aside. "I'm not applying. No matter how many college clinics you drag me to. It's not like I have a chance at them anyway."

"That's not true," I said, unable to stop myself. Juneau and Pat stared at me. I looked down, embarrassed. "My best friend Ife runs the clinic. She mentioned you have a great SAT score."

"You think I'm wasting my talent," Juneau said matter-of-factly, "if I don't fill out the applications."

I faltered. "I just thought college is something to look forward to."

Pat went outside to call her family. I wanted to leave it at that, but I couldn't.

"What about your parents?" The question escaped me.

"What about them?" said Juneau.

"I mean, my mom has always been pretty clear about her expectations for me," I said. "Your parents are okay with whatever you choose?"

"We're crazy rich. My career's not an issue," said Juneau. "As long as I keep up an acceptable facade of a good Christian daughter, I'm fine."

"So what do you want?"

Juneau smiled. "Do you know what Isaac Newton's last words were?"

I shook my head.

"God, I have my work cut out for me." Juneau sighed. "It was like: *I have been only like a boy playing on the seashore and diverting myself in finding a prettier shell than ordinary, whilst the great ocean of truth lay undiscovered before me.*"

The way she said it, there was nothing unusual about memorizing the dying declarations of a seventeenth-century physicist.

She smirked. "I told you I liked pretentious quotes."

"I don't understand," I said.

"It's about refusing to settle," Juneau explained. "Because instead of exploring the spectacular unknown, most people just settle for pretty shells in the sand."

She said this like she'd long figured it out.

"That's really elitist, isn't it?" I said. "You can't say that college is just a pretty shell. For lots of people, that's their best option."

I was surprised by how sharply I spoke. But Juneau wasn't like me. The oceans were hers if she wanted; she didn't have the responsibility to care for her mom, or make her sacrifices worthwhile, or whatever else she considered beneath her. Who was she to talk?

"I see it this way," said Juneau. "If I attend college, I'll pursue a shitty corporate career like my dad, and I'll put my kids through college, after which they'll pursue shitty corporate careers, and so on. And for what? It won't change anyone's life, let alone my own."

"That's why you're in the Pugilists," I said. "You want to be important. You think chasing a normal future would make you irrelevant." I felt strangely worked up, like I'd solved a puzzle.

Juneau opened her mouth, seemingly angry to be read like that, but Pat returned and sat between us. I was grateful for the physical barrier. I felt small, like a girl who'd just been told that "princess" wasn't a real career option. It wasn't fair of Juneau to judge so carelessly, undermine my entire future. Still, she'd gotten under my skin.

"You both seem quiet," Pat said.

"I was going to tell Maya," said Juneau. She smiled at me, like all was forgiven. "The Pugilists have a meeting tonight at Mateo's house. And since you're one of us now, you'd better show up."

"I'll be there," I said. Then the obvious problem struck me. "Actually," I said, "I can't get there. I don't drive."

"Don't worry," Juneau said. "I'll pick you up at six. I'll charm your mother."

Pat rolled her thickly lined eyes. "You do have a way with women," she conceded, and Juneau kissed her cheek.

My friends cornered me after school in Silva's car. They seemed to have gathered for an intervention.

"We're worried about you," Anya said. "You've seemed really secretive lately."

My stomach squirmed. Could she somehow know about the Pugilists? It must have been obvious to her, seeing Juneau and me at lunch today. How my face bloomed with longing, an empty bowl waiting for Juneau to fill it. That was the difference between Anya and me—she got everything she wanted.

"I told the girls about your dad coming back," said Silva quietly. "We want to support you."

"Oh," I said.

I told them about how I'd worked up the courage to send

74

him a DM but gotten no reply. I left out the fact that Juneau had egged me on.

"Poor Maya," said Anya, and her tenderness tugged at me. "No wonder you've been distant." I wanted to cry, or confess, but I did neither. Instead I let her and Ife smother me with hugs.

"That's messed up of him," said Ife. "He left you hanging for thirteen years, and he couldn't even reply to your message? Bullshit."

I knew Ife was angry, and that I should agree with her. Her sense of injustice was as acute as my own. That was something I loved about Ife: her low tolerance for bullshit—which, in Citrus Grove, we sniffed wherever we turned.

"Maybe it's too early," Silva said. "It's only been a few weeks."

"A few weeks is plenty of time to reply," said Ife. "How hard is it to write back, *Hey, thanks for emailing. I'd love to meet up. It's high time I apologized for years of abandonment—*"

"Ife, enough," said Anya.

"No, Ife's right." I rubbed my eyebrow. "Rajendra is the parent. It's *his* job to check up on me." All those moments I'd spent watching him—had he looked for me even once? Suppose he saw me in his audience of fans—would he recognize me from afar?

"So what happens now?" said Silva.

I stared out at the seagulls in the parking lot. Their guffawing cries sounded like laughter. As usual, I wasn't in on the joke.

I didn't know how to explain my feelings, because they didn't make sense. On one hand, I was furious at my father for abandoning me. On the other hand, everything beautiful

I saw from the corner of my eye—sunsets, paintings, wisps of clouds—reminded me of him.

"I want to visit his gallery," I said, and Anya held me close. Right then, it felt like old times. My friends and me, minus the weight of secrets between us. Soon enough, I'd have to deal with Juneau's mystery mission, rising up to meet whatever came next. But for now, I let my friends take care of me.

chapter 8

The doorbell rang at 6:00 p.m. exactly. I'd been stuck watching Indian soaps with Amma and her newest boyfriend, a cardiologist named Vikram. Amma opened the door and there was Juneau standing outside, dressed from head to toe in black. "Nice to meet you," she said sweetly.

"You seem familiar," Amma said. "Have we met?"

"You met a long time ago," I told Amma. "You remember the... *incident*, when I was eight? Juneau was the one who found me."

Amma stared at Juneau, and I was terrified she'd react badly to the reappearance of my runaway accomplice. But Juneau smiled.

"It's so lucky that we found our way back to each other," she said. "Maya's the best student in our class. I knew right away I wanted her in my study group."

The compliment worked like a charm: Amma beamed. "Such hard-working girls," she said. "What class are you studying for tonight?"

"Chemistry," I blurted out, panicked, just as Juneau, unprompted, said the same. She met my eye, looking amused.

"I'd love to send some snacks," Amma said. "I bought very juicy pears at Publix today. It's been so long since Maya brought a new friend home."

"*Amma*," I hissed, mortified, but to make matters worse, Vikram ambled toward us.

"Who's this?" he asked.

"This is Juneau," Amma said. "She's a senior at Citrus Grove."

Vikram eyed her critically. "So you're graduating, then?" he said.

"This May."

"What's the plan after that?" Vikram said, interrogating her.

I turned to Juneau, apologetic, but she crossed her arms. "I don't know," she said. "Travel, I guess. See some places."

"And after that, where are you attending college?" said Amma.

"I don't think it's in the cards for me," said Juneau, but I sensed she was faltering. The Indian music on the TV embarrassed me with its brightness, underscoring the awkward silence.

"What do you mean?" said Amma, ignoring my frantic glares.

"Bye, Amma!" I pushed Juneau through the door. "We'll be studying really late tonight. I'll see you tomorrow."

Juneau chuckled as we drove to Mateo's house. "You've clearly never lied to your mother before."

"Is that a bad thing?"

"It's adorable," Juneau said. "I think your mom's really pretty. You look alike, too."

I ignored the shiver from her compliment.

"I'm sorry about their questions. They're Indian immigrants. They can't imagine why someone wouldn't care about their future."

Juneau's mouth flattened, and I winced. "I didn't mean it like that. I meant, future in the traditional sense. You know, college and all that." I wanted to melt into the seat.

"No, it's okay," said Juneau, though it didn't sound like it.

We parked in front of a Spanish-style duplex. In Florida, you could tell how old a neighborhood was from its trees. Old neighborhoods had big oaks, bowing and grayed with moss. Newer ones had palm trees, transplanted from the coast like toothpicks. This house showed its age gracefully; the massive willow tree in the yard waved a greeting in the breeze.

Tess let us inside. She, too, was dressed in black; I felt florid in my shorts and T-shirt. "Everyone's waiting in the basement," she said.

Mateo's basement was like a secondhand furniture store crammed with all sorts of seating: plaid couches, lawn chairs, a love seat. Even an enormous sculpture of Jesus Christ loomed on the wall.

"Okay everyone," Pat said. "We have a few things to finalize before our mission. Then we should rest up, because we're starting at two a.m."

Theo frowned. "Two a.m. is cutting it close. Are you sure—"

"I'm sure," said Tess. "The security guard's shift ends at two. I've been staking him out all week."

"But the cameras," said Theo. "They'll capture everything."

"Theo, calm down. I worked this all out, remember?" Juneau said. "The guard's out of the picture—Tess confirmed it. The security cameras will be disabled—Mateo's in charge of that. You and Maya scoped and measured the target. And Pat's collected the necessary supplies. Everything is in place." She smiled luxuriously. "Did you really doubt me?"

At last I spoke up. "Excuse me?" I said, resisting the urge to raise my hand. "I still don't know what the mission is."

"You haven't told her, Juneau?" said Pat, looking alarmed.

Juneau sighed. "For tonight's mission, we're getting artistic," she told me. "We're painting a mural on the football scoreboard."

I'd already suspected this was the mission, and that it was massively illegal. Terms exploded through my brain: *vandalism. Destruction of property. Public defacement. Felony.*

"There's only one thing Citrus Grove cares about," explained Pat. "And that's its image. They don't care how they treat their students of color, as long as they *look* like they're not racist."

"So we're going to change that image," said Juneau. "Literally."

"What's the point?" I said at last. "It's so risky and illegal, and for what?"

"You said it yourself, in art studio," said Pat. "You believe art can disrupt narratives."

"When the school gathers on the football field, they'll be forced to confront the truth. Everyone will see how they police their students. It will be right out there in the open," said Mateo. "We're calling them out."

"We'll be safe. This isn't our first mission," said Tess.

"I know, but—"

"Maya." Juneau interrupted me. Her voice was smooth as ever, but this time I heard an edge in it. "We picked you for the Pugilists because we needed an artist. But if you can't handle this mission, I can drive you home right now."

"This is why you waited to tell her," said Pat, annoyed.

My stomach sank, and Mateo sighed. "Are you actually surprised?" he said. No malice. Matter-of-fact.

"It's okay, Maya," Pat said. "No judgment. If you want to turn back, now's the time."

All the Pugilists were watching me now. I could feel it again, deep inside me—the rush of power, the sixth sense I gained exclusively in their presence. I wondered how much of my life I'd spend trying to regain my old, invisible self. I could already feel it slinking away. What version of me would take its place?

"I'm not turning back," I said. "I was just surprised. But I'm here, aren't I? I'm in."

Mateo looked suspicious, but I looked straight, only at Juneau. She smiled, and something inside me loosened and glowed. Nobody could underestimate me now.

"Okay, then," said Pat. "Now that that's sorted out, we need to finalize plans for the mural." She unrolled a giant sheet of paper—I saw her neatly sketched model of Citrus Grove's scoreboard. Everything suddenly became real.

"Tonight's mission is going to be our hardest yet," said Juneau. "We're not just spraying some graffiti or busting up a lock. We're making protest art. So we're going to have to be decisive and precise, working as a team."

Theo was right about Juneau. She really could produce

lightning from thin air. She had a way of commanding the room, making abstract ideas feel so real, they might break down your front door. When she spoke, I believed in our power. With a few strokes of paint, we could rebuild Citrus Grove anew.

"The scoreboard is tall, so we'll use ladders," she was explaining. "And it's a big surface to cover, so we've got tubs of house paint, spray paint, and six pairs of hands." She scanned the room as if double-checking her count. "But first, Maya needs to draw the outlines. She's our artist."

"The outlines?" I said. "Juneau, what exactly will this mural depict?"

"That's your job to design," said Juneau. "But the message needs to be clear. Students are being treated like criminals."

"And Black and brown kids are the targets," said Pat. She smirked. "So, a very pretty picture."

Juneau handed me a pencil. I stared at the blank schematics. Everyone was watching me expectantly, like I was about to pull a rabbit out of a hat—though I supposed that all art, at its core, had that spark of magic. The moment of creation you couldn't explain. You started with nothing, and all of a sudden, you had the world.

I imagined the scoreboard, high above the field. We needed a design that could easily be painted in hours—something repetitive, patterned. Something with colors and rage. Something symbolic.

Some people think with words; I think with pictures. My pencil moved across the page as I thought. I tried something, then erased it, because my next idea was better. I explained it to Pat and Juneau, and we sketched it out together, like we were sitting in Art Studio instead of Mateo's basement.

As the Pugilists passed around the finished sketch, I wondered if my entire life so far had been preparation for this moment. I'd always imagined that my big artistic break would come from a contest or gallery, not an act of vandalism. But this mural—what if it was my calling all along?

Theo was the first to approve. "It's bold. It's a statement." He smiled at me, admiring. "Where have you been all this time?"

As the other Pugilists chimed in with their approval, Pat turned to Juneau. "I kept thinking Maya reminded me of someone," she said. "But now I see it. She's just like Laila."

Juneau flicked her eyes toward me. Her gaze felt so private and direct, it could dissolve the rest of the room. She always had this effect on me. Even in the few photos on her Instagram, it felt like she was only looking at me.

Now that we'd planned the mural, Juneau said we could celebrate, just a little. To raucous applause, Mateo produced a Ziploc bag. I'd never smoked before, but I recognized it from the drug prevention posters at school: weed. Dread clenched my stomach. Just when I thought she'd wrung the most from me—lying to Amma, vandalizing the school—Juneau added illegal drugs to the mix.

"Are you sure now's a good time to smoke?" I said, watching Pat roll a joint. "If we're about to pull off a mission, maybe we should all be sober."

"It's just weed," Mateo said. "It'll wear off in no time."

Just weed? I wanted to protest, but Mateo already thought I was a coward. I wasn't going to add weight to his theory.

"Also, a little blaze from the devil never hurt anybody," said Juneau. "Especially tonight. We need all the divine intervention we can get."

"Keep the devil talk out of my basement," said Mateo, pointing to the Jesus sculpture.

Pat took the first puff. "Holy shit, this is good. Who'd you buy this off, Mateo?"

"Sam Harvey, my dear pharmacist," said Mateo. "He said, and I quote: *This baby will make you feel like champagne on New Year's Eve.* Bless his heart."

Hearing Squash's name, I flinched, but everyone else laughed. Pat rose to make a toast. "To the Harveys!" she cried. "For keeping our community safe and drug-free."

"And to Maya," Theo added. "Our very own artist-in-residence." He smiled at me, a small gesture of kindness that I barely registered amid my panic.

"Let's get this party started," Juneau said. I watched smoke curl from her nostrils like a dragon. Mateo reached for the joint, but she passed it to me.

I hesitated, aware of everyone's eyes on me. "I don't know how to do—*that*." I wanted to die.

Mateo frowned. "You haven't smoked a joint before?"

"No," I said, hoping I didn't look as small as I felt.

"Never?" said Juneau. She leaned toward me, our faces inches apart. I could smell the weed on her breath, musty sweet.

"Never," I echoed, and it was true. I'd drunk with Silva a couple times, mostly wine or beer, but I'd never had enough to get drunk, let alone gotten high, and I had no plans to lose control tonight.

The look on Juneau's face made me think twice. It wasn't pity or disbelief. She was sizing me up, observing me, the way an artist looks at a challenging spread of canvas.

"You don't have to do anything you don't want to," she said.

She was so close I could feel the heat coming off her body. For a wild moment, I thought: *This is who I want to be.* And I did. I thought I could live off her energy indefinitely. Even if

I never touched her, I could stand this close, absorb her vibrations, and that would be enough.

Fuck it, I thought. *To Squash Harvey.*

I sucked in smoke until my breath sweetened like hers, until my body vibrated, and my lungs felt like the eye of a storm. My throat burned, and I coughed smoke into her face. She smiled, like she could taste it. I passed the joint to Theo, who passed it to Tess, who passed it around until it made its way back to me. "Now you're officially a Pugilist," Juneau murmured; I sucked the joint like a juice box.

Minutes or hours later, I found myself lying spread-eagled on the carpet, staring at the enormous effigy of Jesus Christ hanging overhead. His outstretched pose mirrored mine, body chiseled so precisely that every sinew and ridge dripped with sorrow. I reached up to trace his hands with mine, but Mateo appeared out of nowhere to stop me. "Don't touch him," he said. "If something happens, my mom will kill me."

"Oh," I said. "He's beautiful, that's all."

"First time smoking, huh," said Mateo, watching me. "I guess I was your age when I started smoking."

I squinted at him. "Why'd you start?"

"Football concussion, sophomore year," said Mateo. "I still get chronic migraines. Weed takes the edge off it, though. It's the only way I can play. Which means it's the only way I can pay for college."

So that's how he got all tangled up with Squash. *His dear pharmacist.* I suddenly understood that drugs were just another way to leave this place, our pain. The same reason people prayed to God.

"You're not religious, are you?" said Mateo, as if reading my mind.

"My mom is Hindu," I said. "I'm not really anything."

"My family's Catholic," said Mateo. "I went to church all the time when I was little. Last year, I got this." He rolled up his sleeve. His muscles bulged from football season, but I could still make out the cross tattoo.

I smirked. "I could get the Vedic scriptures tattooed on my arm and my mom would still cry."

Mateo snorted. "That's why I haven't let my folks see this one."

"Or the one on your ass," snickered Juneau. I hadn't realized she was listening in. Her fingers, skeletal in the moonlight, slipped into Mateo's mouth. He spat her out immediately.

"We're talking about God, Juneau," he said. "Have some respect. If Jesus saw half the shit you get up to—"

"You sound like my parents," said Juneau. Her voice turned sour, mocking. *"For the love of Christ, Juneau, sit like a lady! Don't talk when you chew! Keep your spirit pure for the Lord—"* Mateo stuck the joint in her mouth like a pacifier, cutting off her tirade.

My thoughts were languid, but I felt sorry for Juneau. I thought of her sweet white parents. Their daughter, a jaded rebel. And Mateo, wearily devoted to the religion Juneau abandoned. I got the sense that something united all of us in this strange lineage of longing. A cool whiff of unsaid words in our lungs.

"Did you know you sound like God?" I said sincerely. My voice sounded distant, like a knock on a neighbor's door.

Mateo and Juneau started laughing—at me, I thought, but I couldn't really tell. I felt for my right arm, fingers dragging across the hairs on my skin. Once I had found my arm, I lost my tongue, and then my toes. I continued searching for myself until Juneau stopped me.

"Honey," she said mildly. "You're way too high."

I found myself sitting on the couch next to her; we sank in like syrup. Everyone was talking too loudly. She started telling me her romantic stories, filled with characters I'd never met, but I listened anyway. She told me about a world like the Bollywood movies Amma loved, except with far more explicit sex. She said falling in love was like diving off a cliff. You fell in love in midair.

"What about you?" she said. "Have you ever been in love?"

She put her head in my lap. I froze with my legs outstretched, flattening my knees until they ached, because whenever I untensed, her hair slipped between my thighs.

"Not the way you have." I stared up at Jesus: I was afraid that if I looked down, Juneau's eyes would be wide open, looking at me. "The thing with brown girls," I explained, "is that we're never sure what love looks like. Half our parents get arranged marriages, and we see our moms suffer, but then when we watch American TV, the only girls who find love look like Barbie. We can't believe anyone would want us, so we settle for guys who treat us like shit. It's pretty fucked."

Juneau simply gazed at me, and I said, "I mean, there are people I love platonically, if that counts."

I found myself talking fast to get everything out, telling Juneau stories until it felt like she'd known me my whole life. I told her about Amma, my father, and the men she tried to replace him with. About Ife, Anya, and Silva. "Silva is the only person in the entire world who can tell when I've had enough," I said. "Like when I'm about to tell Citrus Grove, Amma, Amma's boyfriends, and basically the rest of creation to go screw itself. He tends my anger like a little pet."

"You should date him," said Juneau. "Silva sounds wonderful."

She smiled knowingly, and I realized that nobody had

talked to me like this before, about dating and falling in love and hitting people where it hurts. Anya and I talked about crushes the way little girls do—laughing, scheming, swearing each other to silence—but she acted on them, and I didn't, so after a while I had little to offer. Conversations with Juneau, on the other hand, felt like secret rituals only we could name.

"I don't think I could," I said. "He's my best friend. And I don't know how to approach guys like that."

"You'll get there," said Juneau. "But if you want to give someone your love, you need to own it for yourself, too." She finally got off my lap. "Have you kissed many guys before?"

"That's an assumption." The words flew out with soupy courage.

Juneau chuckled. "Girls, then?"

"Well, no."

"Not many girls? Or guys?"

I was aware of the warmth of her body jammed against mine. I thought: *This is how you know.* When two humans wear each other down, erode until their bodies fit together like clay—that's what love feels like. Sanding somebody's edges and crooks. Settling into their ridges.

"I haven't kissed anybody," I said at last, and maybe it was the weed, but I added: "But when I do, I don't want much. I just want it to be with someone who owns their love, too."

"And you deserve that," she said. "I think your first kiss should be with someone who knows what you need. Someone who knows how to love in reverse."

Juneau's words hung between us. I didn't respond. I could feel her entirely again—it wasn't love, or weed, not even the urge to touch or fuck the way I knew other girls had. I'd never really felt those things before. Instead, I wanted the pull of gravity to be stronger so we'd get swallowed up by the couch. I wanted her to tell me about love, warm and irreverent, like a confession at the end of the world.

Juneau didn't say anything, either. She was looking at me with that clear, even stare that I now recognized as her artist's gaze—sculpting this moment, discarding her inhibitions like snakeskin. This time, I was ready when she said it.

"You don't have to do anything you don't want to," started Juneau, but I interrupted.

"I do," I said, and Juneau laughed as she leaned into me.

Years ago, Anya taught me to kiss by practicing against my reflection in the mirror. Now, despite everything, I thought that was remarkably good training. Juneau's lips were soft like mine, and I couldn't tell which were mine or hers—I just kissed back.

Across the room, Mateo let out a startled shout, and there was a flash of light. I tensed, but Juneau waved him off, laughing— she knew how to play to an audience. There was something too soft and uncooked about her tongue, but the way she grasped my hand and let me feel my beating heart—it felt familiar, organic, like it had happened a million times before.

I came up for air and Juneau asked me how I'd felt.

"Good," I mumbled, and she laughed again. She said now that my first time was a success, I could start having fun with guys. Between us ladies, she said, men were pigs, but I'd soon learn to pick the right ones. She told me that the next time I kissed some-one, it would be glorious, only getting better from here.

As she spoke, I looked around us. Tess, Theo, and Pat were napping by the stairwell. Only Mateo was watching us, laugh-ing so hard I thought he might choke.

"Shit, Juneau," he said. "Give the new girl a break, will you? She's clearly too high to feel a thing."

Juneau's eyes flickered for a second. Then she kissed Mateo, too—so deeply and sweetly I had to turn away. "Don't be jealous. Everyone gets a kiss from me," she said. Then she laughed. "We really are stupendously stoned, aren't we?"

"Squash was half right about you. You *are* such a slut when you're high," said Mateo. I felt a pulse in my stomach, a mix of resentment and awe. This was how Juneau handled people. How she removed their stingers without their noticing. How she loaned them a piece of her to make them feel worthy, when in truth, she didn't belong to anyone at all.

I settled down for a nap, trying my best to ignore Juneau and Mateo. But when I finally looked, they weren't kissing— they were on opposite ends of the couch, Juneau's bare knees hunched up against her chest.

Eventually Mateo fell asleep, and Juneau approached me. On cue, my eyes began to close, so I didn't realize she was whispering to me until she finally said my name.

"What are you thinking about, Maya?"

Stupendously stoned, I thought.

I didn't know how to answer. I tried to pull myself from the web of her words—tried to untangle my fingers—but I succumbed to sleep, swallowed my dry mouth, and mumbled, "You."

chapter 9

My brain must have descended to earth while I slept, because next thing I knew, Patricia was shaking me awake. "It's almost two a.m.," she said. "We need to get moving."

The basement was alive with activity, the Pugilists preparing for our mission. Tess tossed me a black sweatshirt—several sizes too large, reeking of marijuana.

"Is this really necessary?" I wriggled my head through. "I look like a garbage bag. And I smell like one, too."

"Not all heroes wear capes," she said. "Some of us wear hoodies."

"How are you feeling? Back in our dimension again?" asked Juneau. She wore a headlamp over her blonde hair and looked ready to rob a bank.

"Yes," I muttered, embarrassed. "I can't believe I got that high."

"It happens," said Juneau kindly. "You talk when you sleep, you know."

"I do?" My face burned. What had I mumbled inside the eye of the storm? Had I confessed my deepest secrets, admitted my worst fears? Professed a love I didn't understand?

"You muttered math equations," said Patricia, passing me a headlamp. "You nerd."

"We can fit in two cars," Juneau said when we'd all gathered outside. Our headlamps bobbed in the dark like a small solar system, haloing her face. *Chiaroscuro*, I thought, thinking back to Art Studio. Using light and shadow to achieve volume. Stark contrasts to feign fullness.

Mateo and Theo volunteered to drive, so I squeezed into Theo's car with Pat and Tess. I looked around, but Juneau was already in Mateo's car.

I soon learned Theo's chosen driving music was Bach. I couldn't tell if this was ironic or not, a rousing etude to usher in the scariest night of my life. Juneau called us when we neared CGHS. Soft piano provided a background score to her speakerphone commands. "Mateo is parking a block away," she said. "You should park closer since you've got the paints. Make sure your license plate is covered. And that the security guard's gone."

"His car's not in the parking lot," said Tess, peering outside. "We're good."

We parked behind the football stadium. At night, CGHS was a Surrealist painting: Everything looked slightly out of place. Each time I heard a rustle, I jumped, half expecting Dr. Harvey to materialize from behind the trees—but no, it was just us, six teenagers vandalizing the school.

Mateo pulled his beanie low over his face. He sprayed dark

paint up into the corners of nearby buildings. He was covering the cameras.

"Maya, grab a box," Pat commanded, opening the trunk. I seized one at random—it was filled with paints—and followed her across the grass. Theo and Tess unstrapped ladders from the top of his car. We gathered before the massive scoreboard. But this time, I could imagine it as Juneau might: layered with paint, all ours for the taking.

Theo checked his watch. "We have five hours until sunrise," he said. "So where do we start, Maya?"

Three heads swiveled to face me.

"We start," I said, unrolling my sketch, "with the big picture."

I surveyed the scoreboard. The dimensions appeared to me, as obvious and intuitive as the spelling of my own name. I could see the outlines of the faces, all the shapes I could call from the space. An entire mural, invisible to everyone but me.

"I need spray paint," I said, and Tess tossed me one. "Also, someone should start mixing paints." It felt strange to issue orders, even stranger to be obeyed.

I uncapped the spray can carefully. I'd never used spray paint before, and it spurted uncontrollably. It required two hands to hold, like a machine gun. I practiced on the grass until I felt confident. And then I pointed it at the scoreboard.

All the Pugilists stopped to watch as I spray-painted outlines. We didn't have time for realism, so I opted for Cubist flair instead. Watching me, Pat's mouth dropped into a perfect O. My hands shook, thinking I'd displeased her. But when our eyes met, she wasn't upset—she was awed.

"This," she said quietly, "is why you're a Pugilist."

I didn't know what to say. I'd never painted for an audience before. "Thanks," I muttered. I saw that Juneau and Mateo had arrived. Juneau hadn't complimented me, but she was watching me. It was strange: We were surrounded by people, but I was eaten up by her gaze.

"Everyone, grab brushes," I said. I didn't recognize the authority in my voice, but I rolled with it. "Theo, Mateo, Tess—can you start the base coats? Skin tones, please, and let me know if you need help. Pat, Juneau—we'll add details. Features, tints, shadow." I figured it would be better for the more experienced artists to handle that part.

The Pugilists set to work. For the first hour, I barely even painted; I was too busy helping others, salvaging accidental strokes, mixing paints. Occasionally I'd jog across the field, double-checking our dimensions, adjusting our scale from afar. The moon was bright, and we had our headlamps, but it was hard to visualize the entire mural in the dark.

Juneau joined me at the thirty-yard line. "Does it look balanced?" I asked her. "The more I look at it from here, the loopier it gets."

"Well, my eyeballs are fresh," Juneau murmured. She gazed out at the mural, then back at me. "You're a completely different person out here," she said. "I can see it. You're at home."

I rubbed my foot against the dewy field. "I guess painting is the one thing I'm good at."

"It's more than that," she said. "This is what you're meant to do. No rules, no bounds. You know it feels so good." She touched my back, and I felt paralyzed. Was this what happened after you kissed someone? You developed a sixth sense for them; you could find them without looking?

To my relief, Tess jogged up. "We're trying our best," she said, "but it's too dark to paint accurately."

I looked at Juneau, then directly above her. Ringing the field were tall metal floodlights, responsible for the iconic Friday night lights.

"Tess," I said. "Do you think there's any chance we can turn those on?"

We climbed up the bleachers. At the top, perched like an eagle's nest, was the lighting and sound booth. The view up here was prettier than anything I'd seen in Citrus Grove—our surroundings were visible for miles, thanks to Florida's flatness. I could see the theme parks, highway, even my house.

Tess tugged the door fruitlessly. "It's locked," she said, and if I'd ever believed in fate, it was then, because I knew what to do. Silva had taught me to pick locks with everyday tools. In our summer of boredom we'd had to get creative, stealing his older brothers' wine from behind locked doors.

"That," I said, "will not stop us." I showed her my bobby pin. Tess stared in amazement as I inserted it into the lock, jiggled until I felt the tumbler. The door clicked open; the booth was ours.

"Who taught you that?" demanded Tess.

I couldn't resist myself. "I forgot to mention," I said. "They teach it in AP classes."

Inside, I felt for the light switch. I turned on the floodlights, and slowly, the field awoke.

It hit me deep in my chest. I felt like someone had flipped on the lights inside of me, too. I could make out Juneau's hair distinctly, the stadium lights filling it with sheen.

Tess and I ran back down to the lit field. Our shadows

cartwheeled ahead of us on the grass. Juneau grinned wildly at us. "How'd you get the stadium lights on?" she said.

"I may have broken into the lighting booth," I said, holding up my bobby pin.

"Maya Krishnan," Juneau said, impressed. "You're truly full of surprises."

We painted furiously for hours. At first I used a deep brown paint, filling in cheekbones, solidifying expressions. Then I used brightly colored spray paints to add startling highlights, shapes, gleams of eyes. Pat helped me with the facial details. She had an eye for quirky abstraction. To some, our mural might look terrifying, but that night, it looked whimsical, alive.

When my phone rang around four o'clock, I jumped.

"It's my mom," I said. "She must know I'm not home. She's probably freaking out." I thought she'd be at her hospital shift, but I'd somehow miscalculated—

"*Answer it*," Juneau said. "Act natural."

I picked up the phone. "Amma?" I said. I wondered if she could hear the tremor in my voice, if our shared blood afforded her some telepathic powers.

"Kanna, I'm sorry to wake you up," she said. "I think I left the stove on at home. Can you check? I don't want the house to burn down while you sleep."

"*Oh.*" Relief made me almost giggly. "Yeah, sure."

"How was your studying, by the way?" she asked. I could hear the distant hospital intercom, a toddler wailing.

I took a deep breath. "We covered a lot of lessons," I said. "I'll see you tomorrow, okay? Love-you-okay-bye." The last words escaped me in a rush, my nerves failing me.

"I've created a monster," Juneau announced, but lovingly.

As the moon sank lower and the sky got lighter, the mural slowly rose up. It was roughly painted, with dribbled spots and errant sprays, but it looked complete. I'd always struggled with perfectionism in my art, but there wasn't time for that tonight. Already cars were thrumming on the distant highway. Soon enough, people would arrive at school.

"Start packing," Pat ordered the group. "We gotta bounce." She turned to me. "Time for your last strokes, Michelangelo. Make them count."

Had it only been hours ago that I proposed the mural design? What I'd wanted was to paint a collection of student faces. "Students of color, Black and brown, overlapping and swelling together," I'd explained. "Like a garden of flowers, only it's people. To represent our unity, our diversity."

But then—and this was Pat's idea—we'd painted prison bars over the faces, to represent how those students were criminalized. To show CGHS, with all its cops, how it stifled the students it was supposed to protect.

"It'll be beautiful but suffocating at the same time," Pat said. "A whole metaphor."

"We need a tagline, at the bottom," Tess had said. "Something people will remember. Plus, folks here are dense. They'll need it spelled out."

"It should be a demand," Mateo said. "Something to the point."

Pat and I painted the prison bars, working from left and right until we met at the center. At the bottom, I sprayed Mateo's tagline in my strongest handwriting: *STOP POLICING US*.

When we finally stepped back to survey our finished mural, I thought I saw tears in Pat's eyes.

For a moment, everyone paused what they were doing—packing up the paints, folding the ladders—to stare at our mural. In the sugary predawn, it looked grand and beatific, like a stained-glass church window. I felt like if I looked away, the mural would evaporate and I'd wake up in bed, like I'd dreamed the whole thing up. But no, it was here. It was real.

"Well, fuck," said Juneau, for once forgoing a speech. "We did it. We're done."

I couldn't believe that nothing was happening, that no cop cars were screeching toward us. But Juneau led me to Mateo's car. "We'll take you home," she said. "You should rest before the grand reveal."

The ride home felt like the final moments of a dream. I rubbed dried spray paint off my fingers, savoring its proof of tonight. My eyes closed easily. "What happens tomorrow morning?" I asked.

Nobody answered, and I opened my eyes to see Juneau and Mateo lost in a world without me.

In the front seat, Juneau was laughing, and Mateo basked in her gaze. He kept doing that thing boys do where they loop their hand behind a girl's seat protectively. I remembered seeing them kiss on the couch, and a cold fist closed on my windpipe. For a moment, on the field, the sun had been on me, but now Juneau belonged to him.

"Hey, Maya?" said Juneau, finally remembering me. "I wanted to ask you something."

"Yeah?"

"Remember what I said earlier? About wanting to love in reverse?"

I wished she hadn't said that in front of Mateo, but my heart was racing with anticipation.

"So...I worked a little bit of magic. Pulled my strings a bit," said Juneau. "And if you're interested, I found a lover for you." She said this grandly, like a game show host minus the applause. Awaiting my eager response.

"Who?"

"I talked to Theo tonight," she said. "Gave him the green light. He's going to ask you out, and you're going to say yes."

She saw my expression and grinned. "You should've seen him. It was like I'd offered him the last golden ticket."

"You did that for me?" I tried to picture Theodore Fisher-Cho, the lucky golden ticket winner, but all I imagined was Juneau, serving me up like a prize. Looking out for me. Offering me love, in her indirect way.

Mateo watched me impassively through the rearview mirror. Did he notice the way I looked at Juneau? Maybe it confused him, that it wasn't *him* who I watched in that way. He was strong, masculine, accustomed to girls' desire. Like the way Juneau smiled at him, sucked in her breath when his hand touched hers.

"Well, Theo's crush on you was clear as day," Juneau said, oblivious to the silent exchange between Mateo and me.

"Really?" I said. "I didn't notice." I felt sure of her charity, bending the truth to comfort me. But then I remembered Theo's frequent compliments. Pat's gasp when I painted the scoreboard to life. Tess's reaction when I picked the lock. Maybe my Pugilist persona was more crush-worthy than I thought.

"Of course not," said Juneau, laughing. "That's why you're so damn cute."

"Look at you, playing Cupid," said Mateo, with an air of finality; Juneau's gaze had strayed from him for too long. And just like that, I had a prospective lover, and the conversation was over.

I made it home just twenty minutes before Amma did. The stove was off after all; the house was intact. As I limped into bed, exhausted, I almost missed my phone's chime.

I looked, and there it was. Three weeks later, a follow request and DM from Rajendra Krishnan.

Dearest Mayavati, it began. My pulse began to race, and I thought the night was playing tricks on me, but no, the message was real.

Thank you for your message. I'm overjoyed to see that you've followed in my footsteps, blossoming as a painter in your own right. I look forward to seeing your paintings in galleries someday, if they are not there already.

I read greedily, unable to believe my eyes.

Yes, I will be in Orlando next month, staying until winter. My gallery is opening the first Friday of October. Can I meet you for dinner after it's over?

He mentioned a nice restaurant in downtown Orlando. My eyes skipped down to the end.

Keep painting, and I hope to see you soon,

Appa

Appa, he'd signed it. The Tamil word for "father." He wasn't Rajendra Krishnan, the award-winning artist. He signed it as my dad.

It was only when rereading the DM that I realized I didn't know what his voice sounded like.

At first I'd read it in my own inner voice, then I substituted it with some generic booming patriarch voice, like a white dad on TV. I couldn't imagine his voice, so the words pinged impersonally across the screen. Fatherly words, minus the father.

The silence of my own memory agonized me. Who was Rajendra, anyway—a tortured genius, a caring father, or a selfish artist who couldn't support his own family? I knew how Amma felt on this matter. *His true love is his art,* she'd said, as if that excused his abandonment.

Growing up, I thought Rajendra's choice was unforgivable. But after tonight, I finally understood. I'd lied to Amma for the chance to paint the mural, and I'd do it again in a heartbeat. It was a feeling that non-artists would never understand. That rush of power—what would I give to feel it constantly? Whom would I give up?

Maybe it was the aftereffects of the mural, but that night I was trusting. I felt years of anger melt away. My fingers flew to respond.

I'll be there. See you soon.

I logged off and sank into bed. I knew I should be worried about the mural's repercussions, but I wasn't. I felt, for the first time in my life, that I'd figured something out for myself. I was well on my way to becoming a real artist.

chapter 10

Several hours later, I awoke to Silva and Amma watching me with concern.

"What are you doing here?" I jumped out of bed. "How long until school?"

"Technically, school started an hour ago," said Silva.

"I tried waking you up," Amma said. "But you were sleeping like a corpse."

"Apparently nobody can get past the police barricade," said Silva. "So your mom said to just let you sleep."

Now I was fully alert. I jumped out of bed. *Police barricade?*

"The school was vandalized again last night," said Silva. "Just like the library, but a thousand times bigger. Ife's already at school. She said Dr. Harvey's losing his shit."

Adrenaline made my knees buckle—Silva helped me upright.

"Are you okay?" he said, frowning.

"Fine," I said quickly. "I just got up too fast."

"You need tea." Silva helped me to the kitchen, where Amma was brewing chai. She eyed me critically. "Are you sick? Maybe you should stay home."

"*No,*" I said forcefully. "I can't take a sick day. I have Calculus." I turned to Silva. "Who do they think vandalized the school?"

Silva shrugged. "Anya heard the vandals sprayed over the cameras."

"When I was your age," complained Amma, "kids just walked to school, studied hard, and milked their cows. There wasn't any of this vandalism nonsense."

"Times have changed," I said. The chai was blazing a warm trail inside me. As I dressed, I felt panicked, but also excited. So this was how Juneau felt when she held a powerful secret.

"Come on, Silva," I said, slinging on my backpack. "Let's go see what all the trouble's about."

Silva was right—it was nearly impossible to get to school. The traffic was backed up in every direction, clogged arteries thrumming toward the inflamed heart of Citrus Grove. Giving up, Silva swerved into a Publix parking lot, and we walked through the army of police cars surrounding CGHS.

The first thing we saw wasn't the mural. Instead, an enormous crowd of students was gathered on the football field. Reporters swarmed against the police barricade, cameras flashing.

"What is this, the moon landing?" Silva said. We spotted Ife and Anya in the crowd and shoved our way in their direction.

"This is insane," Anya shouted. "Someone vandalized the entire football scoreboard—"

"It's fucking epic," said Ife. "I mean it's a serious crime, whatever. But you should see for yourself."

We made our way to the mural. I'd prepared to feign surprise, but I didn't have to.

In the daylight, the mural sprawled brighter than before. The brown faces were lit by a fierce, uncompromising sun. They screamed with rage, refusing to accept their confines, looking Citrus Grove's racism straight in the eye. The prison bars we'd painted were dark and furrowed. The *STOP POLICING US* looked practically biblical.

Around me, students were posting pictures and muttering. Some students looked angry. Others, like Anya, looked scared, but some were nodding in agreement, their eyes shining. Silva was one of them.

I took it all in, pretending it was the grand opening for my first gallery. This, after all, was the ultimate test for a painter: whether your finished work held its own for an audience. I'd worried, in the dark, that I'd get something wrong—that the lines would look crooked, or the proportions would be off. But we'd pulled it off with a vengeance. Staring at the mural, I felt something churning in my stomach: sleepless, hungry, and full of pride.

Silva whistled softly. "I can't believe the guts of this."

"They nailed it," said Ife breathlessly. "They called the school out."

"This is the shit you were telling Harvey about," said Silva, nudging me. "How the school treats students of color. *Stop policing us.* It's up there for everyone to see."

"Who do you think did it?" said Ife. "It has to be somebody who goes here."

"Whoever did it, they're fucked," said Anya, matter-of-factly. "There's no way the school will let this slide."

"This mural," said Ife ominously, "is a declaration of war."

I tried my best to act normal, but then I remembered I didn't have to pretend—nobody was watching me. I wore my invisibility like armor.

Around us, phone cameras flashed, punctuating snippets of conversations.

"Apparently it's a political statement—"

"*Stop policing us?* What does that even mean?"

"God, this school needs to beef up its security—"

The kids nearest us sounded outraged—not about the issue depicted, but about the mural itself. I realized that to them, this wasn't just a painting. It was a personal threat, holding their normal lives hostage. It meant that the snow globe was shaking.

Behind us, a news reporter had jumped the police barricade and was shouting to the cameras: "Police have been called to the scene at Citrus Grove High School following the appearance of graffiti criticizing their presence at the school—"

Graffiti? I thought, annoyed. *Give us some fucking credit.*

Meanwhile I saw my art teacher, Ms. Meyer, talking to a different reporter. She was gesturing grandly to the mural behind her.

"In the art world, we'd categorize this mural under the umbrella of Cubism," she was saying. "You know, with the fragmented geometry and human degradation. There's a definitive rage in the work. It's certainly a metaphor…perhaps for racism?"

You really think? I wanted to shout. To make things worse, Squash Harvey ambled toward us, having spotted Anya.

"Did you see this shit?" Squash asked like we weren't all standing right in front of the mural.

"We were just talking about it," said Anya. "What do you think, Sam?"

"It's fucked up," Squash said, gesturing to the mural with

the vague disdain I'd reserve for a stain on the wall. "People are so pissed all the time, and for what?"

Anya nodded, and I hated her for it, molding her opinion to match his.

"It's pretty clear to me," I said.

Squash regarded me. "Is it?" he said. His shirt stretched against his chest in a way we were surely supposed to notice.

"It's clear that people are tired of how they're treated," I said. "That's what the mural is all about—policing students of color. If you think they're pissed for nothing, you're either deluded or pretending. And you can pass that along to your grandfather."

Squash smirked. "If these people think that vandalizing the school is an appropriate response, maybe they're the deluded ones."

"Guys, let's not fight," said Anya, but Squash ignored her.

"The problem with people like you," he said, gesturing to my friends, "is that you're angry all the damn time. Always screaming about your victimhood, calling everyone a racist. Maybe if you were civil, there wouldn't be all these problems."

I felt a grenade of rage explode inside me. *People like you?*

"Maya," said Silva quietly. "He's not worth it."

Anya's gaze flickered between Squash and me. I took a breath, even though I felt like wildfire, impossible to tame.

"He's on the warpath," Squash said, pointing to Dr. Harvey. "Whoever did this, they're going to get caught, and it's going to be bad for them. It's your choice whose side you'll be on when that happens."

"I like my choices," I said. Then, before either I threw punches or Squash did, I walked away.

I was halfway to Spanish when someone tapped my

shoulder. I whirled around, ready to rematch against Squash, but it was Theodore Fisher-Cho.

"Can we talk?" he asked.

We walked through the empty hallways; most of the school was still gawking at the mural. Theo asked how I was feeling.

"The victory's a rush, but I hate lying to my friends," I said. "They were all standing there speculating, and I felt like I was going to burst."

"Because you were afraid they'd discover what you did?" said Theo. "Or because you wished they could know it was you?"

"Both?" I said. "This is the most incredible piece of art I've ever made. Like, I left a piece of myself on the football field. My mind, my hands, they're all over it. They're seeing me, but they don't see me."

I bit my lip, afraid of rambling. But Theo smiled at me. I couldn't believe the fullness of his gaze.

"Well, I do," he said. "I see you."

His eyes were brown like mine, and I suddenly wondered why we gave all the hype to greens and blues when brown eyes could swallow you whole. I realized that I was mentally preparing to sketch him, dissecting all the colors and shapes. I flicked my gaze up.

"And...what do you see?" My voice had acquired a flirtatious edge that I didn't recognize. I was copying Juneau's inflections, her questions-as-attacks. It worked: Theo blushed.

"I see a brilliant artist," he said. "Someone who can pour an entire mural out of her mind. For starters." He smiled as he eased into it. "I see you're really smart and caring. And beautiful. Though I'm sure you knew that already."

He was so effortless, I could already imagine Anya's swoon when I retold this story later.

"It's still nice to hear it said aloud," I joked, as though boys praised my beauty every day. I could see from his walk, long-legged and syrupy slow, that he'd done this before. Girls probably launched themselves at him like missiles.

"I could tell you more nice things, if you want," offered Theo. "Tonight, over dinner. Can I take you on a date?"

It felt so surreal. Juneau wanted me to find love, whatever that meant; I couldn't be a good judge of romance, having never seen or experienced it in my lifetime. But maybe now, thanks to her, I would learn.

"That sounds wonderful," I said.

Just like that, I'd done it. As of this morning, I was a girl who'd been kissed, smoked weed, painted a mural, been asked out. The milestones that I'd thought were years away barreled past before I could register them, and as I stood with Theo in the hallway, my life seemed unimaginable.

Since I'd stayed up all night, I almost slept through my date. Luckily, Theo texted me.

See you tonight, he said. A few minutes later: I hope you like nice bread.

I needed to get dressed, but my closet was hopeless—only half my dresses were paint-free, only half still fit, and absolutely none were both. I took inventory of Amma's date-night dresses, but when I tried them on, I looked silly, a girl playing dress-up as a woman. So I called for backup.

Anya picked up my FaceTime immediately. "What's up?"

"I need help. But you have to play it cool."

"Shit. Are you pregnant? Do you need a witch doctor?"

I resisted the urge to hang up, cancel the date, and bury myself in my bedsheets.

"I have a date in an hour," I said. "Right now I'm absolutely naked because I have nothing to wear."

"A date?" She grinned. "Girl, just stay naked. Save yourself some time at the end of the night."

"Anya, focus."

"I'm getting in the car! Tell me who it is."

"No guesses?" It wasn't often that I had something juicy to hold over Anya.

"Is it Jake Quentin? Squash's friend? Last week he told me he likes your art."

"Well, he can have sex with my art, then."

I was grateful it was still normal things Anya expected me to confess to: boys, sex, and crushes, all the secrets she wanted us to share. Certainly not vandalism, parental abandonment, and a strange longing for a girl I barely knew.

So I confessed. "It's Theodore Fisher-Cho."

"Theodore *who*?" Anya's video shook. It looked like she was running every stoplight between my house and hers.

"Fisher-Cho. As in *Fisher and Cho,* the lawyers. He's friends with Juneau. He has an Instagram feed you'd describe as—"

"New money," finished Anya. "Maya, wow!"

I didn't always agree with Anya, but in any crisis, she was always my first call. Moments later, she was in my room. "I brought options, to be safe," she said, handing me a bright red dress. "Does your mom know about Theo?"

"Hell no." I zipped it up. "She'd lock me in my room. Or worse, she'd insist on coming along."

Anya laughed. "You'd think with all her boyfriends, she'd be more relaxed about you dating. Sujatha Aunty's got the middle-aged dick market cornered."

"Please don't ever say those words aloud again." I groaned. "And no, she's still Indian. Protective as hell."

"Makes sense." Anya smirked. "Neither of our parents found out about Squash and me. I can teach you my secret boyfriend tricks if you want." She flopped on my bed, knocking textbooks aside. "Oh, and I called Silva."

"What! Why?"

"Silva's going to chauffeur you tonight," said Anya, ignoring my protests. "Because if Theo picks you up, your mom might see."

"He's never going to let this go, driving me to my own date." I looked in the mirror. "Oh, I like this. I think I look—"

"Anemic," finished Anya. "Red makes you look positively menstrual. Strip."

She tossed me a yellow sundress, and I wriggled inside. This time, I felt it: The fabric hugged me in just the right places. Anya cheered. Silva appeared in my bedroom, stepping gingerly across the dress-strewn floor. "Did you tell her?" he asked Anya, who blanched.

"Tell me what?" I said.

Anya started ironing my hair, perhaps to give her a weapon. "I hooked up with Squash last night," she said. "Don't kill me, okay?"

"You did *what*?" I said, and Anya sighed.

"It was a covert operation," she said. "He had to sneak me in through the window so his family wouldn't find out."

The irony of the situation dazzled me: The same night that I'd snuck out to paint the mural, Anya had snuck into Squash Harvey's bed.

"Anya, I swear to God, if you get back together—"

"We already did," Anya said.

I whirled around. "You're lying," I said. When Anya said nothing, my heart seized. *"You're back together with Squash?"*

"Maya, it's okay," said Silva.

I glared at him. "So you already knew about Anya and Citrus Grove's sexiest white supremacist?"

"Well, it just happened last night," Silva said, fair as ever. "She wasn't trying to hide it from you."

"Is that why you called Silva over, Anya? So you could tag team me?"

Anya shrugged. "I knew you'd be angry."

"Of course I'm angry," I said. "Anya, *he cheated on you.* He called Juneau a slut. He was unthinkably racist about the mural. He—"

Silva shook his head. We had one battle to win tonight, and this was not it. My heart pounded, but I banished Squash from my mind.

"Fine," I said. "Congratulations, Anya."

There was a heavy silence, and finally Silva said, "Where's your date, Maya?"

I checked Theo's text. "The Palmhouse? It must be expensive, because it's downtown."

Anya's jaw dropped. *"The Palmhouse?* Girl, he's rich-rich. Like, two capital *R*s!" I saw Silva's face sour, and I wanted to pinch myself for bringing up money in front of him.

"Rich isn't everything," I said.

"Well, save room for dessert," said Anya. "And when I say *dessert*, I really mean—"

"Got it," I interrupted. "But trust me, it's not happening tonight." I glanced again at Silva, embarrassed, but he'd turned away.

Finally, Anya stepped back. "She's ready for her debut," she announced. "Silva, thoughts?"

Silva's eyes met mine, suddenly formal. I knew him better than anyone, but in moments like these, his maleness felt absolutely alien.

"You look stunning," Silva said at last.

Anya shoved us out of the house, leaving a mess of clothes in our wake. "Go," she said, beaming. "Have fun. Make good choices."

I rolled my eyes, and she pinched me. "Oh! And use protection."

"Anya!"

Silva and I drove out of the neighborhood. There was nothing new about driving around together, except this time I was wearing one of Anya's sexy sundresses, and Silva looked the same as ever in his faded jeans and band tee.

"Can I ask you something, as a man?" I said.

"What's up?"

"I'm not like Anya. Guys don't just *ask me out.*" I didn't want to sound self-pitying, but it was unavoidable. "Do you think it's something about me?"

Silva's eyes met mine in the rearview mirror. "To be fair, I've never known you to like any guys, either."

It was true, but Silva's comment still rankled. "Well, I like Theo," I said. "He's nice and funny. And not an asshole."

"The bar is high, I see," said Silva, but seeing my expression, he softened.

"Maya, it's okay. You're unique," he said at last. "You're really talented and opinionated, and not every guy is strong enough to deal with that. Don't worry about Theo. It's just a date."

"Well, shit. I was planning on marrying him tonight."

"I hope not," said Silva, but he was smiling. "It would be a new low for me to drive you to your wedding."

We laughed, and as Citrus Grove whipped past, we listened to his violin music, so loud it dissolved us.

Silva parked outside the Palmhouse. The entire place was made of glass, sparkling in the setting sun. It struck me as wildly impractical to build a glass restaurant in the hurricane capital of the world. But then I remembered that if you were rich, you could build wildly impractical things like that, just for the look of it. The restaurant was filled with women in cocktail dresses. I felt immediately out of place. Meanwhile, the hostess asked for my reservation.

"Reservation?" I echoed stupidly. I wondered if Silva would take me home if I chickened out of this date.

"What's your name?" The hostess looked annoyed.

"Maya Krishnan." I fidgeted in my dress, wishing it covered more of my legs.

"I don't see anything under that name."

"That's because she's with me."

Theo appeared behind me and smiled. "You look incredible, by the way."

The hostess rolled her eyes. "Come on, kids. Do you have a reservation or not?"

"Yeah, under the name Fisher-Cho. My parents are gold members," said Theo. "We'd like outdoor seating, please."

He said it like it wasn't a big deal, but the hostess's jaw dropped as she checked the name off the list. She looked at Theo, then me, incredulously.

We sat on tall stools outside, my legs swinging foolishly. I could see Lake Eola lighting up, bulb by bulb, preparing for the sunset. Theo saw me staring and smiled.

"The food here is incredible. Have you tried caviar?"

"I don't even know what that is," I said.

Theo laughed. "Clearly we have much to accomplish here," he said. "But luckily, the night is young." He ordered half a dozen different dishes—caviar, calamari, souffle, truffles, and several things I couldn't pronounce.

"Are you sure?" I murmured, watching the waiter's eyebrows rise after the fourth order.

"Of course. We're celebrating," said Theo. "What we did last night—what *you* did last night—was certifiably badass and a little insane."

"More than a little," I said. "But thanks."

"This is the biggest mission we've pulled off, ever," said Theo. "We made the front page of all the local papers."

"I know," I said. "Did you see *Orlando Sentinel* called our mural a *seething meditation on race relations colored by youth rebellion?*"

Theo smiled. "You were right, last night," he said. "The mural doesn't solve anything, not really. But it forces people to open their eyes. They can't act like it's business as usual anymore. And I think that counts for something."

Our food arrived in a parade of servers until there was almost no room on the table.

"Where do we start?" I said, awed. I felt like one of those Renaissance paintings of fat kings at biblical feasts.

Theo opened the nearest lid—caviar, he announced. I must've shown my suspicion toward the viscous black spread, because he laughed. "You go first," he said. "It's life-changing."

I felt self-conscious but strangely flattered by Theo's attention. I had just taken my first bite when the smell hit me, thick and briny, familiar after years of living near the ocean.

"Shit. Theo, is this *fish*?"

"Fish eggs," said Theo, and I spat so vehemently that everyone nearby gasped in disgust.

"I should've mentioned," I said. "I'm so stupid. I can't eat this. I'm vegetarian."

To my surprise, Theo laughed.

"Shit," he said. "Well, I think we'll need to order some more vegetarian dishes, then."

"I'm so sorry. I should've said something—"

Theo had already called the waiter, who looked like he'd rather serve anyone else in the world. This time, I didn't even look at the menu—I asked, point-blank, for cake.

"Bring them all," Theo said.

When the cakes arrived, Theo and I didn't bother cutting them. We ate directly off the dishes. Nearby couples continued to shoot us glances, but Theo didn't seem to care.

Unlike Juneau, who was prone to cryptic questions and long personal anecdotes, Theo was a great conversationalist. His dad was white, but his mom was an immigrant, so we had a lot in common. We shared funny stories about his Korean heritage, my Indianness. We talked about art, and even though

Theo didn't know half the painters I liked, he asked all the right questions and laughed at my jokes. It made it less jarring when he mentioned that his family had inherited a fourth-century Dürer but didn't realize it until they cleaned out their basement.

"I have a rude question," I said. "I would've never guessed you'd be the type to join the Pugilists. You're, you know…" I gestured vaguely to the surrounding finery.

Theo grinned. "You're asking how I ended up as the Pugilists' token rich boy?"

"Kind of," I said.

"It's a fair question," Theo said. "The short answer is, I knew Juneau, and she recruited me. We're both part of this world, and we both have issues with it." He, too, gestured to the restaurant. "I'm grateful for all the privileges I was born with. But I kept thinking, *Things are fucked up.* I wanted to do more with what I have. My parents do, too, except while they prefer pro bono legal work, I chose a slightly different path of resistance."

This world, I thought. Theo's and Juneau's lives, enclosed by sparkling glass.

"I was a hard sell to the other Pugilists at first," he added. "But I can bring the funding. Plus, with all the illegal shit we get up to, it's nice to have a lawyer's son on hand."

I tried not to look at the bill when it arrived, but Theo didn't look at it, either; he simply slid a glossy credit card onto the table, plus a big tip. As we left, I kept looking back at the money perched unassumingly atop the napkins.

Theo drove me home. He parked outside my house, kindly ignoring Amma's angry face in the kitchen window. My stomach dropped—I thought she was at work.

"Thanks for tonight," I said, avoiding eye contact with Amma.

Theo took my hand. "Want to do this again soon?"

My heart was pounding—not from his touch, or even Amma's glares, but from the impossibility of this moment. For the first time in my life, Amma was waiting for me to come home from a date, not the other way around. I wasn't some girl in the background, lost in the blink of an eye. This time, someone was looking at me.

"I think that could be arranged," I said.

"You're not just being nice because your mom is watching, right?" Theo's voice had a gentle tease. "I guess I probably shouldn't kiss you good night, then."

The word *kiss* sent a strange stiffness into my bones.

"She would kill me."

"Next time, then," said Theo, but he was laughing. "Good night, Maya."

Theo waited until I had entered my house before driving away. Unfortunately, this meant I would face Amma alone.

She'd been sitting by the front window dressed for work. Her shift should've started an hour ago. Her boyfriend, for once, was nowhere in sight.

"Where were you?" she said. "I called you three times. I even called your friends."

"You did?" I said, mentally sending prayers for Anya, Ife, and Silva. I saved one for myself.

"They all swore you were with Ife," said Amma. "Since when was Ife a white boy, Maya?" She eyed me. "Your dress is so tight your butt looks picture-framed."

I remembered something Juneau recently told me: *Sometimes it's better to ask forgiveness than permission.* I resigned myself to groveling.

"I'm sorry," I said. "His name is Theo. He's actually half Korean. He asked me to dinner."

"You're only sixteen," Amma started. "Are you being safe? Do you need birth control? Have you—"

"Jesus! No," I said. "It's nothing like that, I swear. It was just my first date—"

"I'm a medical professional, Maya. Do you have any idea what I've seen? Teenage pregnancies, STDs—"

"Amma, *please*. I'm not having sex."

She ignored me. "Even then, to have my daughter coming and going with strange boys in the night? People will think I've raised a wild child."

The anger came sharply and swiftly.

"You're seriously concerned with what people will think?" I said. "Amma, I get straight As and I've never even kissed a boy. How could I possibly be wild?"

"Listen, Maya," she said, and now her voice had an edge. "Maybe you haven't noticed, but *people talk*. It's bad enough that I'm a single mom. The fact that I continue dating—everyone at work knows it, not to mention every Indian in Central Florida."

I remembered what Anya had said today: *Sujatha Aunty's got the middle-aged dick market cornered.* I knew Anya was impressed, not scandalized, but my heart still sank. Then I remembered I was angry.

"I don't need people talking about my daughter's love life," said Amma. "I shudder to think what Rajendra would say when he—"

"Rajendra?"

Amma sighed. "I was waiting for the right moment to discuss this," she said. "Maya, your father's coming to town."

My father. It was a strangely formal title for the man I'd spent years watching in secret, holding his absence close to my heart like a locket. There was no point in lying. "I already knew that," I said.

"I thought so," Amma said. She pursed her mouth. "You've been different lately, Maya. So tense and secretive. If this is your way of reacting to your father—"

"Not everything is about him," I blurted out. "And you don't have to worry about me and Rajendra. We've messaged already."

Amma was taken aback, and it felt good to have the upper hand. "You *messaged* him? And didn't tell me?"

"I didn't realize I had to tell you these things." I crossed my arms.

Amma's face darkened. "You are always so angry, Maya," she said. "It comes from your father. Every day, you become more like him."

"Well, I have questions for him," I said. "About why he left us. And I don't want to hear the bullshit about visas, art, none of that. I want real answers."

This could've been a place for me to tell her Rajendra and I made dinner plans, but I didn't. I realized this was the longest conversation we'd had in a while. Once, our lives had revolved around each other. She was the first responder to every moment in my life. Things changed when I got older; we'd fallen out of orbit, and now I felt us growing apart.

"We were afraid you'd react like this." Amma shook her head. "There's so much you don't understand—"

"I understand perfectly," I said. "He abandoned us, Amma. End of story."

"That's not how I see it," said Amma, more gently. "He still calls to check on you. He still cares."

Questions bubbled over in me, but I picked the biggest one.

"He *calls*? I thought you weren't on speaking terms."

"Kanna, we had a child," said Amma. "You never lose somebody after that. We've stayed in touch."

I felt my anger mounting again. "You still call him? Regularly?"

"Yes, Maya. I do." Amma pressed her palms to her head. "He knows you're angry at him, but I've kept him updated about you, and I want the three of us to meet when he comes. You're his daughter."

All these years I'd spent googling Rajendra in secret, Amma still spoke to him, kept him in her life. The betrayal was staggering.

"To think that you're angry at *me* for hiding Theo," I said. "You've been lying all along."

"Let me explain," she said. To my surprise, she sat on the couch and patted the spot beside her, inviting me to join.

"When I met Rajendra, neither of us knew what we were doing," Amma said. Her eyes were wistful. "He filled my life with grand ideas about life and art until I thought we were invincible."

I thought about all the men she'd dated, trying her best to replace Rajendra, though none of them stuck around. How proud she was when I turned out to be an artist, too.

"I loved him so much, I thought we could overcome anything," said Amma. "When I got my visa, I knew the initial separation would be hard, but I didn't realize how much."

I knew this story well: how Amma had secured her visa sponsorship from the hospital, how Rajendra had tried for years for documents and failed. Amma made it seem like a stroke of bad luck, the roll-of-the-dice nature of immigration. She brushed over how he'd given up on us, too.

"You feel abandoned. And I understand that," she continued. "All I ask is that you give him another chance."

She turned around abruptly, rubbing her eyes. I didn't

know what to say. The last time I'd seen Amma cry was when she and Rajendra divorced, years ago. I had come home from school and saw her on the floor. I didn't even take off my shoes. I stood there, staring. The moment wasn't meant for my eyes.

The truth was, I knew so little about her life. I couldn't remember Rajendra or India. Amma had shouldered that alone, shielding me as best she could. Whenever I needed to find my home, I invariably returned to her. For my entire life, she'd put my needs first—wasn't that exactly what love was?

"I'm sorry," I said, anger subsiding.

"I was sixteen once, too, Maya," Amma said. "I know you have strong opinions. And maybe you won't understand until you've fallen in love yourself. But sometimes love requires accepting the reality of things."

For the first time, I looked at myself as Amma might: a little girl, someone to be cared for, protected.

"Okay," I said.

She put on her lab coat, then gathered me in her arms. I noted, with surprise, that we were finally the same height. Hugging her felt no different than hugging Anya or Ife.

"You have to promise me," Amma said at last. "No more secrets."

It struck me that we'd never had a traditional parent-child relationship. These dynamics predated the Pugilists' influence—maybe they'd started the day we boarded the plane to America. Suddenly the gaps between us felt staggering.

I handed Amma her keys so she could drive to the hospital. "It won't happen again," I promised, though deep down, I knew the secrets were just beginning.

chapter 11

Dr. Harvey's backlash was swift. Following the mural, a dozen cops prowled the hallways between classes. Their squad cars were parked everywhere, sprouted from the cement. Nobody had been caught for the mural, so war was in the air.

"Eighteen days," Silva said as we drove past the mural on Monday morning. It was impressive it had survived this long.

He was right. Eighteen days later, the mural was still clearly visible across the football field—against Dr. Harvey's hopes, the rainstorms had failed to wash it away. Occasionally, passing cars honked at it. When we got closer, Silva, too, honked in support.

"Don't let the Pig Patrol catch you doing that," I said, and he groaned.

"I still can't believe that's a real thing," he said. "Citrus Grove's going off the rails."

Silva wasn't wrong. In response to the mural, Squash Harvey and his friends formed the school's first-ever Student Safety Commission. The Pig Patrol, as we called them, consisted mostly of disaffected jocks and girl-spurned boys who terrorized people they didn't like. They earned an official endorsement from Dr. Harvey—something Ife reported to Silva and me at lunch.

"I spoke out against the Pig Patrol last week," she said. She caught herself. "I mean, the Student Safety Commission."

"Doesn't have the same ring to it," I said.

"Harvey thinks it's *a prudent solution for campus law and order*." Ife imitated his stiff speech.

"This is a school, for God's sake," Silva said. "Not a police state."

We were eating on the football field, despite the sun. We'd stopped sitting in the cafeteria, since the Pig Patrol harassed underclassmen during lunch. More egregiously, Anya was officially dating Squash, and seeing them make out destroyed my appetite.

"You said it yourself, Ife," I said. "The mural was an act of war."

Across the field, Pig Patrol members were covering the mural with heavy white paint, cleaning up for Friday night's football game. They were on their third or fourth layer, but the brown bodies still bared through.

"Please tell me the irony pains you," I said. "They're literally whitewashing that shit."

Ife sighed. "The mural had its moment, but it's probably best they're painting it over," she said. "I'm trying to calm Harvey down, but he distrusts half the student council. Especially me. He thinks I represent whoever did the mural."

"Because you're Black?" Silva shook his head. "That's messed up."

"He's just really shaken," said Ife. "He thinks that we're on opposite sides."

"Aren't you?" I said.

Ife sat up, and when she next spoke, she was using her class president voice. It was the same voice Amma used on the phone calling into work to convince her bosses to take her seriously. Her accent would mysteriously vanish.

"There's no need for *sides*," Ife said. "Obviously I sympathize with whoever painted the mural. But they created more trouble than they might've imagined. Thanks to them, we ended up with extra police."

"So they were right," I said.

Silva leaned forward, attempting to mediate, but Ife ignored him. "You've been skipping class," she said. "You've been mouthing off. Juneau's been rubbing off on you, I can tell. The Harveys think she's behind the mural."

"You're blaming *Juneau*?"

"She's, like, *bewitched* you," said Ife. "You're becoming angry. Reckless. You think I haven't noticed that the mural looks just like your paintings?"

I could feel Ife's gaze burning into me. It was almost refreshing to feel her disappointment, like I was wild, a rebel, far from the quiet nobody I'd been my entire life. Ife must have sensed this, because her next words were gentler.

"You're passionate, but you're smart, Maya," she said. "You create things. You don't burn them down."

I'd expected Ife to shout—she could always be counted on

for a fight—but now I felt myself cave. The old version of me resurfaced, and I said, "I am still those things."

"I could use your help," said Ife. "Bring your new friends to the student council meeting next month. I want student input to convince Harvey to cool off with the cops. You just can't call them 'pigs' to their face."

I imagined how Juneau might respond to this proposition. Probably she'd brush Ife off. *Negotiating with the enemy will never achieve justice*, she'd say, pronouncing the word *justice* with a flourish, like the grand prize in a treasure hunt.

But Ife was right: I wasn't Juneau. So instead, I said, "I'd be happy to help."

"I'm coming early to decorate for the homecoming dance," said Ife.

"Shit. The dance!"

I'd nearly forgotten homecoming, Ife's biggest project all year. She'd spent weeks galvanizing troops of student volunteers, raising thousands of dollars through mysteriously lucrative bake sales.

"Yeah, homecoming," said Ife. "The biggest social event of the semester. The one attended by well-adjusted kids with social lives. Remember?"

"Are you both going?" said Silva, surprising me. Whenever conversations strayed to formal social events, he could normally be counted on to divert it.

"Well, obviously, since I'm directing it," said Ife. "Maya, you should ask Theo to take you. That's the whole point of having a boyfriend."

Despite everything, I blushed. "Shouldn't it be the other way around?"

"You're telling me that you, a die-hard feminist, can't make the first move?" said Ife. Then she yelped. "Avert your eyes," she said. "They're coming."

Squash and Anya were ambling toward the mural holding hands like this was a beach boardwalk instead of an active crime scene. Squash pulled off his shirt and joined the Pig Patrol.

"I have a theory that he gets off to his own naked chest," I said savagely. "I bet he's having a tiny orgasm before our eyes."

"Seriously, why do men insist on baring their nipples like that?" Ife said. She nudged Silva, our in-house expert, but he shrugged.

"Harvey's a different breed," he said. "I don't claim him."

"Look at Anya," I said. "Traitor."

As if hearing me, Anya jogged our way.

"When did you guys start eating out here?" she called. "I looked for you at our usual table."

Silva, pacifist as ever, answered before I could. "It's beautiful outside," he said. "Lunch is only half over. You can sit with us."

Anya bit her lip, an unconscious habit that I was sure drove Squash crazy. "I would," she said, "but I already promised Sam that lunch was his time."

"*His time?*" I repeated. "What is this, a shared custody arrangement?"

"Sam knows you hate him, Maya," Anya said. "Maybe if you were nicer, I wouldn't have to choose between you guys." She flopped down on the grass, resting her head on my thigh.

I stiffened. "I never asked you to choose," I said. "Squash is the one waging war against everyone who challenges his privilege. Not me."

Ife rose up protectively, but Anya brushed her aside gently, like *I got this*. Their teamwork made me so angry I nearly missed Anya's next words.

"Why won't you give him a chance?" said Anya. "Why do you have to make everything so political?" It sounded like she'd rehearsed this statement.

My jaw dropped. "Because it is political, Anya," I said. "Mateo Chavez being dragged down the hallway by the police—you think that's just a freak accident? You think they wouldn't do the same to Silva?"

Silva recoiled. "Maya, it's okay," he said, but it wasn't.

"Don't you see what he's doing, Anya?" I said, pointing across the field, where Squash was busy covering my mural. "He's standing against us."

"Maya, he's good to me," said Anya. I was almost satisfied to see tears glazing her eyes. Then I felt sickened with myself. "You know, we got nominated for homecoming king and queen," she added. "I've wanted that crown forever. I never thought I'd get this close. Why can't you be happy for me?"

I felt numb. The problem with my rage was that it didn't have an *off* switch. Once the lights were turned on, and you saw people exactly as they were, you couldn't return to the darkness.

"Has he introduced you to his parents yet?" I said. "Or is he still keeping you a secret?"

Anya's gaze flickered. "What?"

"Maya," said Ife warningly.

"My parents don't know about Sam, either," Anya said.

"That's because they're Indian. That's not the same, and you know it," I said. "I'm asking why Squash hides you from his family. Everyone knows he's had other girlfriends. He's had a whole harem of white girls that he doesn't hide."

"God, Maya. His family's a bit conservative, okay? I'm pretty sure I'm not what they had in mind for Sam. He's working on them, but that doesn't change how he feels about me."

"Conservative?" I said. "Or flat-out racist?"

Anya was stunned. Her silence was as good as a confession. This time, she didn't stop our friends from stepping in.

"Maya, you promised Anya you'd support her," Silva said. His expression remained mild, but my face flushed, like I was a child being told to play nice.

"If you're looking for validation from a white boy who sneaks you through his window, that's your choice," I said. "Personally, I think it's sad."

"Sadder than following a crazy white girl around, trying to feel important?" said Anya. "Squash said you were brainwashed by Juneau. I'm starting to think he was right."

She was back in fighting form, and we weren't holding back. I was becoming a girl who took shots at her friends, wore her rage on her skin like a tattoo—no wonder they all were staring at me.

"Maybe you should try a coat of whitewash, too," I said. "You know that's exactly why Squash won't let you meet his family, don't you? You don't look the part, not when it's serious."

"Maya, *enough*!" Ife squeezed my arm so tight I feared my fingers would pop like little fireworks. Anya stormed back to Squash, ignoring Silva and Ife shouting that I didn't mean it.

"What's wrong with you?" Ife demanded while Silva stared sadly at Anya's receding figure, like he could comfort her with his gaze.

"I shouldn't have said that," I mumbled. "It just came out."

The truth was, I did suspect what was wrong with me, and it was that I *wasn't* wrong—about any of it. I wasn't wrong about Squash's being racist, and I couldn't comprehend Anya's returning to him. My anger trailed me like a kite.

"You need to apologize to her," said Silva. "That was out of line."

"I know," I said. "I just have a bad feeling about Squash, even if he makes her homecoming queen."

"I hate Squash, too," said Ife. "But that's no way to treat our friend." Silva nodded, looking tense, like he expected me to catch fire. A sticky feeling settled inside me: *guilt.*

"I'm really sorry," I said. "I swear I'm going to fix this."

I sent Anya a text after lunch: Can we talk? And later, I'm so sorry.

She didn't respond, which I knew was her trick for conveying maximal disdain. *Leave a boy on read,* she'd once taught me, *and he'll know you're over his ass.* I tried meeting her eyes in the hallway, but she never looked back.

As gentle as Anya normally was, I knew that her anger, when provoked, was unrelenting. For the next week, I only heard news of her secondhand from Ife and Silva. To make matters worse, she spent even more time with Squash. I watched them together in the parking lot after school. Spotting me, Squash smirked. He called, "Stop checking out my girlfriend!" loud enough to embarrass me, coolly enough to hurt. Anya said nothing, and I was forced to turn away.

And just like that, I learned that wars aren't just fought in football fields or hallways. Sometimes they're fought in people's hearts.

I stopped trying to convince Ife and Silva to support me, and I turned to the Pugilists instead.

Slowly—in conversations with Tess and Mateo, on dates with Theo, over countless midday lunches with Pat and Juneau—I grew aware of, even accustomed to, my sense of rage and injustice. New words appeared to give shape to my thoughts. Words like: *Systemic oppression. White supremacy. Misogyny.*

The world delineated itself neatly, a black-and-white world of winners and losers, good guys and bad guys. The Pugilists versus the Pig Patrol. The people versus the system. Me versus Squash. I didn't know when our showdown would come, but I started looking forward to it. Because when it came, I'd be ready.

chapter 12

As September leaked into October, Anya's absence stung. But all I could think of was Rajendra's impending return. Amma didn't mention him much, still hurting from our fight, but she cut her hair at the salon—an unprecedented luxury. I counted the days until our dinner, stacking them inside me like cards. He'd asked to meet at a restaurant, but I decided I'd go to his gallery opening beforehand, where he was giving a talk and answering questions. Another week passed, and finally he arrived.

Of my remaining friends, I asked Ife to accompany me to Rajendra's gallery. She was reliable and steady, the perfect wing-woman for confronting my neglectful father. I knew she'd hold it down, even if I couldn't.

Amma didn't question me when I told her Ife was picking me up to finish a science project that evening—at least, not like

I expected. If she suspected I was trying to meet Rajendra, she didn't let on.

"Are you sure you girls need to study right now?" she asked. "It's Friday night. Surely you have more exciting plans."

"Maya and I happen to think science is exciting." Ife waved to Amma as we drove away.

"What?" she said, catching my expression. "I wasn't actually lying about that."

"That's why it's so sad," I said.

Ife groaned. "I still don't understand why we can't tell her," she said. "Rajendra is your long-lost dad, after all."

I stared out the window. "She doesn't understand my perspective," I said. "She's forgiven Rajendra, she still loves him, whatever. But I need answers for myself."

"Well, hopefully we get them," said Ife. We parked in front of the Orlando Museum of Art. Arm in arm, we walked inside, following the crowd to my father's gallery.

I knew we were in the right place thanks to the large entrance sign: RAJENDRA KRISHNAN, UNVEILED. My heartbeat quickened. To see my father's name—the name we shared—commanding the attention of an entire gallery was unbelievable.

"Oh my God," whispered Ife. I didn't blame her. I'd seen my father's work online many times, but I still wasn't prepared to see it in person.

The gallery was sleek and modern, evening sunlight slanting through the floor-to-ceiling windows. It was packed with well-dressed art enthusiasts, nearly a hundred people.

Together, we beheld Rajendra Krishnan's famous paintings: religious scenes rendered with oil-slick perfection, portraits of brown people so lucid you might mistake them for photographs, except for the small detail that made you pause—an absurdly curved spine, a trick-mirror smile, an inhuman glint of an eye. The canvases were suspended from the ceiling by blazing golden wires. If you stepped back, the effect was ethereal. The gallery felt alive, flung from the heavens.

"These are beautiful," said Ife. "But I don't understand the paintings. Like, how do you explain this one?" she asked, pointing to a stunningly bloody painting of a lion-headed naked man ripping apart a demon.

Something rose inside me: *pride.* The art spoke to me, naturally and intuitively. I finally understood what it felt like to have your turf, your *home.* My superpower, and my father's, was art: rich and brown-skinned and alive. At last, I felt like I belonged.

I tried dissecting the painting in a way that Ife would appreciate. "Well, the thing about Rajendra's art is that he recolonizes European styles. You can see the Renaissance influence in the muscular bodies, even his chosen medium of oil." I took a breath. "But he applies those principles to Indian religious themes. For example, this painting depicts the myth of Narasimha, the lion-headed god, except he's rendered in the style of a biblical classic. And that's how my dad does it. He raises us to the level of high art."

"Wow. You called him '*Dad,*' " said Ife, ignoring the better parts of my soliloquy.

I bit my lip. "Keep an eye out for Rajendra."

I tried not to nerd out as we explored the gallery. I wondered if people could somehow tell I was his daughter, even though nobody was looking at me. "Oh my God," Ife whispered, tugging my arm. "Look over here."

She pointed out another religious painting—gold haloes,

red-powdered brows, lotuses. It was the biggest piece in the gallery, a focal point for viewers. A plaque identified it as *The Tempest*, his prize-winning self-portrait. In it, my father leaned over the edge of a rock into a roiling ocean, reaching in vain for a face in the depths: a little brown-skinned girl.

"Look at the pain on his face." Ife leaned in close, as if willing the painting to speak back to her. She was right. My father's grief was deep like water, as far as the eye could see.

"Maya, wait." Ife's voice turned hushed. "The girl in the painting...is that you?"

I nodded, stunned. It was thrilling to see myself in portraiture. The painting felt made for me, ignited with special meaning. But then I remembered we were in a public gallery, and *The Tempest* belonged to everyone. The realization made me uncomfortable. Like the painting had walked off with my body.

"I can't believe—" I started, but Juneau Zale appeared out of nowhere, tapping my arm.

"What are you doing here?" I said. I felt like Juneau had intruded on a secret meeting.

"Hello to you, too." Juneau raised her eyebrows. "And if you must know, I'm Patricia's date. She wants us to participate more in the local arts. Supposedly it's the cornerstone of humanity." She rolled her eyes. "I'm Juneau, by the way," she told Ife.

"Ife. We met." Ife was uncharacteristically flustered. "In the cafeteria, remember?"

We were silent for a minute, and I realized Juneau was looking to me to lead the conversation. Maybe because my friend was present, or because we were surrounded by Indian art, but it was like Juneau subtly deferred to me. It felt strange for her to enter my universe when we'd only ever interacted in hers.

"*Maya?*" Pat said, spotting us. "I didn't know you were coming tonight! It's a gorgeous exhibit, isn't it?" She nudged Juneau. "Juneau's ambivalent so far. Though maybe if you convince her, she'll like it." I was flattered to be an influencer of Juneau's opinions.

I introduced Pat and Ife. Ife loved Pat, who always looked effortlessly cool—it wasn't surprising to encounter her here. But Juneau hung back from the crowds. She liked being harder to please.

"What do you think of Rajendra Krishnan's exhibition?" Pat asked. "His art reminds me of yours."

"You think so?" I smiled wide. She had no idea what the compliment meant to me.

"Look at the empathy and emotion in his portraits. The fascination with brown womanhood. And God, the colors," said Pat. "You have so much in common. And not just your last name."

Juneau looked at *The Tempest*, the little girl in the water, then back at me. I saw the doorknob turn in her mind.

"Hold on," she said slowly. "Didn't you tell me that your father was a famous artist?"

I nodded, and her eyes widened. "Shit," Juneau said. "This is him, isn't it?"

Pat's jaw dropped, and even Juneau now seemed interested. "Wow," she said. "So you know about all this art?" Initially I'd felt embarrassed by her arrival, but suddenly I wanted nothing more than to keep her attention. To share everything I loved. To be seen, in my world.

"Yeah, I do," I said. I felt myself standing up straighter. I repeated to them what I'd just told Ife, about my father's reclaiming classical styles. Except now I caught myself point-ing out extra details, offering complicated explanations of the myths. This took a while, because Indian mythology is broad as oceans, involving characters' lengthy backstories spanning multiple lives. Still, by the time I'd finished, Juneau and Pat were impressed.

"This is insane," said Pat. "Where's your dad? Can we meet him?"

I shrugged. "Well, we haven't actually met yet. So these are just my interpretations," I said.

"You haven't met him?" said Pat, looking confused, so I had no choice but to explain my entire parental situation to her. Meanwhile Juneau looked back at *The Tempest*.

"Is that you in the painting?" she asked. "The little girl he's reaching for."

We all gazed at the painting. The longer I looked at it, my sense of unease heightened. I nodded. "I think so."

"You *think* so?" said Juneau. "You mean, he didn't ask you first? Or even tell you?"

I shook my head.

Juneau sighed. "Considering he hasn't spoken to you in years," she said, "doesn't that make it wrong?"

I said nothing, because it felt good to make her work for it. Then Juneau asked directly, "Don't you think it's wrong that he abandoned you as a child, but he's still painting you to win prizes?"

I looked back at the painting, my loss bared for everyone to see. "It's not like that," I said, but I didn't sound convincing. "Well, okay. I guess it doesn't feel entirely right."

"This man exploited your image, and he got an award for

it," said Juneau. "We need to stop acting like artistic genius excuses the fact that men are utter pricks."

I'd often noticed Juneau's vindictive rage toward men who wronged women, from male politicians to catcallers to her own cheating father. I'd normally share her anger, but she didn't know Rajendra. He wasn't hers to judge.

"To be fair, a lot of male artists are exploitative," said Pat, attempting to rescue me. "I doubt that half the artists we've studied got consent from all their subjects. Besides, he's Maya's dad." She glared at Juneau, warning her to play nice.

Blood rose in my face. I wasn't sure whom I was angrier at: my father for painting me, or Juneau for calling him out. Sensing my misery, Ife asked, "Are you okay?"

"I'm fine." The words came out harsher than I intended them. "I'll see you at the Q and A," I told Juneau and Pat, pulling Ife with me.

I found a table with drinks in the back, ignoring Ife's frown as I downed a flute of champagne. "Maya, stop it," she said, grabbing my arm before I could grab another. We sat in the audience, far from the lectern.

"So," Ife said. "You're upset."

"He had the audacity to paint me," I burst out. "No phone calls, not even a lousy email for my entire life. But he still managed to paint me into his great masterpiece." My eyes flicked to Juneau, easily spotted with her white-blonde hair. "I can't believe only Juneau saw through him."

Ife sighed. "Should we just go home?"

"No," I said immediately. "Let's see what he has to say for himself."

The lights dimmed. Rajendra was about to answer the

audience's questions. Juneau and Pat claimed the empty seats next to me, having scored a bottle of champagne. "Want some?" Juneau asked, pouring me a flute—I drank it quickly, ignoring Ife's continuing disapproval. The curator introduced international painter Rajendra Krishnan, whose art evoked themes of third-world liberation, whose magnum opus, *The Tempest*, illustrated radical brown humanity.

The audience hushed as my father approached the podium to answer questions.

I couldn't stop staring at him. In person, our resemblances were even more pronounced—the way he ducked his head when he walked, all his curly hair. Next to me, Ife sucked in her breath.

A white woman raised her hand. "Your work is among the best of its generation," she gushed. My father bowed his head, monk-like. "Could you tell us more about your artistic process?"

Despite myself, I leaned forward as my father tapped the mic.

"Like most painters," Rajendra began, "my process starts with light and colors—physical embodiments that catch my eye and will not leave my mind."

As he spoke, I wondered: *What if everything I thought was mine is actually his?* Certainly our voices sounded nothing alike. He spoke like thunder, his Indian accent a steady rumble, while I spoke fast, my flip-flop American cadence like tides. But the way he spoke of colors, how the taste of manjal made him paint the sun yellow—it was like listening to myself. That's why Pat thought my art looked like his. He'd been reflecting through me all along.

The audience asked questions, one after another, and the

champagne fuzzed my head, so I started to zoom out until Juneau's sharp voice startled me. I looked up to see her holding the mic.

"I'm Juneau," she said. "My question concerns *The Tempest*. I was wondering, who are the figures supposed to represent?"

She gave me a look, like, *If you won't ask him, I will.*

Rajendra cleared his throat. "Thank you for your question, Juneau," he said. He pronounced her name gently: *Joo-no.* "To answer, *The Tempest* is an allegory. You'll see the image of a man—me—perched on the edge of a whirlpool. Inside lies a fearsome girl, tempting him to drown, like the Sirens of the ancient Greeks."

He pointed to the painting. "What draws men to ruination," he said, "is all they regret. When we take the man to stand in for a nation—or humanity, even—the stakes grow higher. The girl comes to represent vice, loss, untold danger—"

"But who *is* she?" Juneau had interrupted Rajendra, causing mutters in the audience.

Rajendra hesitated. "Joo-*no,* art is a nonrepresentative form. It's open for interpretation."

"I understand that," said Juneau. "I just want to know who that girl is."

I wanted to beg her to shut up, but Juneau looked Rajendra in the eye. "Is that your daughter?"

"No," Rajendra said. "I have no children. Thank you for your question."

I stood up, knocking over Juneau's champagne; it spread across the floor like paint. Ife and Pat grasped my hands in solidarity.

Rajendra's eyes met mine across the gallery. His lips parted.

"You also," said Juneau, "have no spine." She smiled, flashing teeth.

The security guards moved toward us; my heart contracted, but my father stopped them with a wave of his hand.

"Mayavati?" Rajendra said. He couldn't seem to close his mouth. Like crying, it was a glimpse of vulnerability, sharp and raw. But unlike crying, he didn't seem afraid—he seemed exposed.

"Mayavati," Rajendra said again. "Please wait. Excuse me," he added to the audience.

We marched out the door, Ife seizing as many champagne bottles as her purse could handle. Juneau turned back to glare at my father. I grabbed her arm, more roughly than I intended. To punish or protect her, I couldn't tell.

"Please, let's go," I said, and for once she let me lead the way. The last thing I saw before the gallery doors closed was my own painted face.

chapter 13

'd never been more humiliated in my life. To his credit, Rajendra messaged me that night.

Maya, I am so sorry for tonight. It was a misunderstanding. Will you give me another chance?

No, I typed quickly, and then I stopped replying.

He messaged again, three times, then four times before giving up. I thought that was the end of it—but then he met with Amma.

Amma confronted me about it the next day. She was in the kitchen, drinking coffee aggressively—she'd either woken early or skipped sleeping to ambush me.

"Maya, sit down," she said. "I know what you did."

For a moment, I thought she'd discovered the Pugilists, and my heart seized. "What?"

"I met with your father today," Amma said. "He said that

you and your friends made a public scene at his gallery opening. What came over you, Maya?" Amma shook her head. "You've lied again. And you've embarrassed your father, after I asked you to give him another chance—"

My face felt inflamed. "Rajendra painted a picture of me," I said. "And then he told the entire audience he didn't have a child, when Juneau asked him specifically—"

Amma's expression darkened: Our story had reached American ears. "*Juneau* was there?"

"Did you miss what he said?" My voice shook. "About his child?"

Amma's voice softened. "Kanna, I know. It was a misunderstanding," she said. "Losing you is your father's greatest regret. Did you really expect him to announce it to the whole gallery?"

My mouth dropped open. "Amma, whose side are you on?"

"Sides?" Amma pressed her head to her temples. I could see the stress catching up with her, causing dark circles beneath her eyes. "There are no sides. This is a family."

"Look around!" I said. "That man isn't here. You don't have to keep making excuses for him—"

"That man," said Amma icily, "is your father, and he is back in my life. I'm no longer asking, I'm telling. You'll put your attitude behind you." She disappeared into her bedroom, leaving retorts unsaid in my mouth.

I couldn't dwell on Rajendra for long, however, because next week was homecoming, and the Pugilists were preparing for war. It was our job to defeat the Pig Patrol, restoring moral order to our universe.

The ball's in our court now, Juneau texted our group chat. They're waiting for us to strike.

But we didn't strike back, not immediately. Even Juneau recognized that we were outnumbered. In direct conflict, the Pig Patrol was sure to kick our collective asses.

We're thinking bigger, Pat added. Mission reveal this week! 😉

To complicate matters, it was also Fight Week. Nobody knew how the tradition started, but the week before we converged on the football field to watch teenage boys collide, CGHS purged itself through violence. If you had a grievance, conflict, debt, or even a minor rivalry, you had one chance to settle it with your fists. Food fights, mobs, and petty theft were all part of the fun.

"This is going to be a shitfest," Silva predicted, weaving between police cars in the parking lot on Monday.

"Fight Week?" I said. "By definition, it's always a shitfest." Already, fights had been declared. Two seniors were supposedly dueling over their homecoming date, and freshmen were fighting for the coveted spot as CGHS's mascot.

Juneau had texted the Pugilists last night: Fight Week is not our fight. Stay out of trouble! Plz!

"Yeah, but this time it's not just dumb teenagers," said Silva. "There's cops with literal guns in the mix. Something's guaranteed to go wrong."

Still, Wednesday arrived in peace. Fight Week was half over, seemingly without bloodshed. I joined Juneau at the computer lab after school because Pat had ordered her to at least *consider* writing some college essays.

We looked at the prompts together. To me, college applications were still a distant prospect, crunched somewhere in my vague mental future space alongside marriage, children, and my own demise. But for Juneau, deadlines were looming. Not that she acted like it—everything in her application portal was blank.

"*Who inspires you?*" I read aloud. "Three hundred words."

"Too corny," said Juneau.

"Fine." I clicked another prompt. "Oh, this looks better. *Describe a hardship you overcame, and what you learned from it.* I'm sure you've had hardships."

"I mean, I'm rich and white," said Juneau. "The freakin' earth was built for me."

Lazily, she pulled a piece of lint off my shirt. She often did this: brushing grass off my legs, once swiping a crumb off my lip. This was what made her such a flirt, I knew, but it also made me feel—secretly—cared for.

"Yeah, but that doesn't mean you don't face bullshit, too," I said. "What about the guys at school? They catcall you, spread rumors, worse. You could write about misogyny."

Juneau's mouth flattened, and I worried I'd offended her.

"Suppose I did write about, say, the summer my nudes got leaked. Or the year every varsity athlete claimed I'd slept with him," she said. "I would get blamed for taking those pictures in the first place. Or for having sex at all." She smiled cheerlessly. "You gotta be smarter than that, Maya."

I felt terrible for mentioning the guys, allowing them to invade our space together. I should have dropped the question entirely, but I didn't.

"You could write about your parents," I said. "What's the deal with them, anyway?"

Juneau shrugged. "They're just really conservative," she said. "You'd hate them if you met them. Like, my mom serves on mission trips, and my dad unironically believes in conversion therapy. They spent my entire life telling me how to act and believe. So you can imagine how they'd feel about some of my . . . proclivities."

"You mean, the fact that you have sex. The drugs and mischief. And the Pugilists, obviously." I spoke as if reciting a list. As I did, I realized that I really didn't know much else about Juneau. My life was simple; it wouldn't fill two pages. Juneau's seemed full and mysterious in contrast.

"I don't understand. How haven't your parents noticed what you're up to?" I asked. "Like, what about all the skipped school?"

"Well, first of all, I phone in pretending to be my mom, so the school excuses my absences. And honestly, my parents have no idea what I'm actually like," said Juneau. "I'm very different at home. I follow all the rules, and they don't ask questions. To my family, I'm a proper, well-bred Catholic young woman. Saving herself for marriage." She pitched her voice ironically, but I didn't laugh.

I couldn't imagine Juneau leading a double life, casting her real self off like a costume. Logically, I'd known that she had to go sleep somewhere, sit at a dinner table, pass some potatoes. Still, how could Juneau so easily switch off everything I liked about her, turn into someone I might hate? How could her parents not see her true power, shining within her like a flashlight?

Before I could speak, the fire alarm erupted. On cue, Juneau's phone rang. We ran into the hallway, filled with rushing students; I grabbed Juneau's arm so I wouldn't get trampled.

"Fight Week!" someone cheered just as Juneau snarled into the phone, "Are you kidding?"

She turned to me. "That was Tess. Mateo's fighting James

Quentin behind the math building." She started running full speed down the hallway.

"Mateo and James? Why?"

Juneau looked angrier than I'd ever seen her before. "I'm only explaining because it's an emergency," she said. "But Mateo has a migraine problem. He got addicted to painkillers, weed, all sorts of things. He depends on Squash's crew to supply him, and he's massively indebted to them. He must've invoked Fight Week to settle it."

A crowd had formed behind the math building. Others were watching from the balconies, cheering and throwing things. Juneau surveyed the damage.

"Find Theo," she told me. "He can help if shit goes down. I'm going to stay with Mateo. He's gonna need a shield."

"*Shield?* From what?"

"The cops," said Juneau. For once, she sounded scared. "They're on high alert, and I'm less likely to trigger them than Mateo. Hurry!"

Frantic, I turned and nearly collided with Silva racing past with his violin.

"Maya!" he said, seizing my arm. "Let's get to my car."

"Have you seen Theo?" I interrupted. "I'm looking for him."

"*Theo?* Why?"

I was too frazzled to explain, so I blurted, "Juneau said so."

"*Juneau said so?*" Silva's jaw dropped. "This looks like a riot. We need to get out of here."

The crowds rammed into us, the combined weight of two dozen students knocking everyone off their feet. Mateo had literally flung James Quentin into the onlookers; as I watched, James rammed Mateo like a rogue asteroid.

"Fuck!"

Silva's violin was knocked from his grip. I didn't even see it break, I just saw Silva's face. He'd never reacted to physical pain before—not even the summer he fell off his bike, requiring stitches. But now, when his violin broke, he looked shattered.

"Shit. Silva—" I grabbed the crushed violin as the fight raged on. Then I spotted Theo in the crowd.

"I'm sorry, Silva, but I have to go." I handed Silva his violin. "I'll follow in a minute."

Silva stared at Theo, who was waving at me. "Go," he said with the kind of cold fury that only a best friend can muster. "Your boyfriend's waiting for you."

I didn't wait to be told twice. I turned and shoved my way toward Theo.

In the gaps between bodies, I caught glimpses of the fight: James's fists wrapped around Mateo's throat, Juneau screaming helplessly at them to *fucking stop.*

"The cops are on their way," I told Theo. "Things could get bad."

No sooner had I said this than Squash Harvey bulldozed into the hallway, followed by the Pig Patrol.

"This is the Student Safety Commission. Everyone, calm down!" he yelled in an impressive approximation of authority. Squash tried separating James and Mateo, but Mateo's leg came out of nowhere and kicked him. Squash and James each grabbed Mateo's arms, looking murderous.

"Two of them and one Mateo," muttered Theo. "This isn't a fair fight."

"What can we do? They're going to beat him up—"

"Not if I can help it," said Theo.

It was a sign that I hadn't known Theo long enough to predict his movements. Because before I could stop him, he dove into the fight.

"Police!" someone shouted just as Theo, his pale limbs a blur, jumped on James.

Four officers burst into the courtyard, uniformed and fully armed. It was almost like a cop movie, except there was no bad guy to catch, just four boys fighting behind the math building.

Spotting them, Juneau's face flashed with panic. Meanwhile Theo pried James off Mateo. Squash whipped around, fists balled. I couldn't tell whether Theo was trying to help Mateo up or punch Squash, but he lashed his arm forward and yelled, "*Touché!*" He swung, missed, and collapsed on the floor with a nasty crunch.

"Theo!" For a wild second, I forgot I was a five-foot girl, and I lunged toward him, narrowly dodging Squash.

Theo's face was pale. "My arm," he said. "I think it's broken—"

"Everyone, stop what you're doing!" The cops broke through the crowd and towered over us. Juneau and I raised our hands in surrender, but the boys continued wrestling. That's when the closest officer reached for his gun.

Suddenly, everything unfolded in slow motion.

Squash and James flung Mateo aside and ducked. Theo pulled me down to the floor.

Meanwhile, Juneau leapt toward the cop with her arms outstretched, knocking the gun from his hand. Her mouth formed what sounded at the time like an indiscriminate scream, but I later realized were words: *You can't shoot us!*

In that moment, she looked less like Juneau and more like

the sculpture in Mateo's basement—a martyr, risking everything for him. A spark of electricity raced up my spine.

The cop shoved Juneau aside, but his gun had clattered to the floor—his partner quickly kicked it out of everyone's reach. As the gun skidded past, I felt Theo's entire body shudder with tension. The sight of the weapon seemed to sharpen the air. I breathed shallowly through my mouth.

"Girl, are you stupid?" the cop shouted, retrieving his gun. "You could've been hurt. You never attack an armed officer—"

Juneau was incandescent with rage. "You were gonna pull your gun on kids," she shouted. "You were gonna pull your fucking gun. What is wrong with *you*?" It shouldn't have surprised me by this point, but I still marveled over the fact that she'd jumped an armed cop and was standing upright.

"Calm down or we'll take you in, too," warned the other cop, and Juneau finally had the good sense to shut up. Mateo was wrested off the ground. James's face, meanwhile, was a patchwork of bruises as the cops helped him to his feet.

"What the hell is going on here?" the cop said. "We're responding to an aggravated assault between two suspects, not six."

Suspects? I realized that half the Pugilists were tangled into this fight, and my heart sank.

"Sir!" said Squash officiously, shaking the cop's hand. As a sign of the universe's cosmic unfairness, he appeared uninjured. "I'm Sam Harvey from the Student Safety Commission. I came to defuse this altercation."

"This wasn't an *altercation*," said Juneau, glaring at Squash. "It was a disagreement that escalated. Everything is fine."

"That's not what I saw," the cop said. "I saw these boys swinging at each other like a game of human Whac-a-Mole. Under the school's new policy, I'm supposed to have them arrested."

"*Arrested?*" said Juneau. "This is high school. People get sent to detention for fighting. Not jail."

"Not anymore," said the cop. "CGHS is now a zero-tolerance campus. From now on, infractors will have to deal with us."

"Excuse me, but who are you arresting?" Squash said. "Like I said, I'm from the Student Safety Commission. I'm here to maintain campus order."

He looked incredibly smug. If the cops weren't right there, I might've slapped him.

"Not you. You didn't hit anyone," said the officer. He pointed at James, Theo, and Mateo. "For those three, however, fighting is illegal."

Squash and Juneau stared at the officer, then at each other. If I wasn't hyper focused on the guns, I might've laughed at the irony: Squash and Juneau were now on the exact same side, united against the cops.

"There's no need for arrests, sir," Squash said. "I'll ask my grandfather to handle it. He's the principal."

The officer stared at us for a long moment. The crowd of students had wisely dispersed; here at CGHS, kids had a sixth sense for trouble.

"I'm reporting them for disturbing the peace. Consider it a warning," he said.

"Thank you," said Squash. James, Theo, and Mateo were each written tickets; Juneau didn't move even an inch from Mateo's side.

The second the cops left, she whirled on Squash. I was shocked to see tears in her eyes.

"Squash, come on," Juneau said. "Can we talk?"

I'd never seen her like this before. I'd seen her laughing, snarling, screaming. But this was different. This time, Juneau was pleading.

"Why?" Squash looked suspicious.

"What are we fighting for?" Juneau said. "We all could've been shot. You need to talk to your grandfather. The cops can't stay on campus."

Squash crossed his arms. "Calm down, Juneau. The officer barely drew his gun. You were stupid as hell to jump on him." He eyed her. "And it's not like they'd shoot *you*."

"Yeah, that's the fucking point," said Theo, glaring at Squash. He was still wincing, clutching his arm. "She's rich and white, for God's sake. But for anyone else, when the police get involved, their lives are in danger."

"It's not the police making this campus unsafe," said Squash. "It's your friends, stirring up trouble. We know you guys were behind the mural. It's only a matter of time until we prove it."

Mateo clenched his fists. "It's only a matter of time before I smash your—"

"Is that a threat?" said Squash. "If so, I would love to call back those officers."

"No, it's not," said Juneau. "Get out of here, Squash. Take your cronies with you."

Despite everything, Squash smirked, making finger guns at us as he disappeared.

"God, if we weren't at school—" started Mateo, but he was cut off by a sharp *thwack*: Juneau had slapped him across the face.

"Stop it!" she said. "The cops almost shot you. You just put all of us at risk. Me, Theo, Maya—"

"I had it under control until you went all female psycho on the cops," said Mateo.

Juneau flinched. "You said it yourself. They're out to get you," she said. "If something happens to you, I swear I'll—"

"You'll what?" said Mateo. With his nose bleeding, he looked ghastly.

"I won't be able to live with myself, okay?" Juneau's voice cracked. I knew she was still reeling from the *female psycho* comment. "Go home, please. Try not to kill anyone on the way."

As Mateo left, she whirled on Theo. "As for *you*—"

"I'm injured," said Theo, raising his good arm in surrender. "Mercy for me, please."

Juneau groaned. "Jesus. Let's get you some medical attention."

We half marched, half carried Theo to the nurse's office. His nose was bruised, but that wasn't my biggest concern. His right arm looked twisted, like the wooden mannequins I used for anatomical drawings.

The nurse took one look at Theo and clucked her tongue.

"Fighting, right?" she said. "I have Band-Aids and ice, but no cure for stupidity. You should take him to the ER."

She disappeared, leaving me to hunt for medical supplies in the cupboards.

"What were you thinking?" demanded Juneau. "You listen to Bach, for God's sake. You have no business in a fistfight."

"I took fencing lessons until I was twelve." Theo sniffed. "Perhaps I overestimated myself."

His nose started bleeding; using a tissue, I tried to stem the flow. I kept my motions clinical, gentle, the way I'd seen Amma treat her patients. Theo's eyelids flickered. "Maya?" he said.

"What?" I said urgently. "Does something hurt?"

"No," he said. He winced. "Well, everything hurts. But I'll deal with that later. I was going to ask: Will you be my homecoming date?"

"You're asking me *now*?"

"Well, this wasn't how I'd planned it," said Theo. "But we're having an intimate moment."

I glanced at Juneau, who nodded wildly, like, *What are you waiting for?* "Fine," I said. "But I'm serious: If you yell '*touché*' in public again, I'll dump you."

Juneau rolled her eyes, ticking off three fingers as she spoke. "Risking my life in a fight between four full-grown boys. Jumping a cop. And now, hanging out with you major-league virgins." She sighed. "This day just keeps getting weirder."

I walked them to Juneau's car. Juneau said quietly, "Don't repeat the stuff about Mateo's drug problem, by the way. He doesn't want people to know. It humiliates him."

"I won't." Although she'd broken Mateo's trust, I felt strangely flattered that she'd done it for me. As she headed for the ER, Juneau shouted back to me: "Are you okay?"

"Both my arms are functional, if that's what you're asking."

"Hold it down for me while I'm gone?" asked Juneau, and by now I didn't have to ask her what she meant.

chapter 14

News of Fight Week spread like a virus, and literally over-night CGHS was infected. There were enough witnesses that no detail was spared in its retelling: how multiple football players were involved, the cops showed up, and Juneau lost her shit. By morning, Dr. Harvey had no choice but to inform parents.

"Sometimes I worry I made the wrong choice, raising you here. Your father certainly seems to feel that way," said Amma, scanning the school email. "This place is so angry and danger-ous, and for what?" Luckily the email didn't identify the fight-ers, so Amma had no idea that my friends were, in fact, the angry and dangerous ones.

"They're mad for good reason," I said, choosing to ignore the mention of Rajendra. "People are tired of being oppressed, Amma. You should understand. You've faced so much racist bullshit at work."

"Don't curse in my house," said Amma. "And all these opinions of yours—on race, oppression, all of that—belong at home. Or, honestly, inside your closed mouth. Outside's not safe. Do you hear me?"

I mumbled something in response. I read the email over her shoulder and was enraged to see that Dr. Harvey had failed to mention the gun sliding across CGHS's sidewalk.

"I'm serious," Amma said. "Promise you'll keep your head down and stay out of trouble."

"I will," I said.

On my phone, the Pugilist group chat was incessant.

Did you see the email? I texted. No mention of the gun.

He's trying to minimize the damage, Pat typed back.

We have to tell people what really happened, Mateo added.

So I typed out an Instagram caption, hitting Share without a second thought: **Yesterday, I saw the police draw a gun on campus. If that doesn't scare the shit out of you, you aren't paying attention. Police have no place at CGHS. They endanger all students, particularly students of color, with their recklessness and violence. Someone could have died yesterday, and if CGHS doesn't make changes, students will make changes for them. We will rise up and demand better. And I hope (for his sake) Dr. Harvey is prepared to answer us.**

My phone lit up with notifications—from the Pugilists, already plotting revenge. From Ife, who warned me to be careful about "incendiary" language. From classmates I'd never really spoken to, either supporting my post or warning me to steer clear of trouble. Even a message from Rajendra: Your mom told me about everything that's going on at school. You should be careful with what you say. I don't want my daughter in trouble. I promptly hit Delete.

When Silva finally FaceTimed me, he was still angry at me for putting myself in danger.

"Is your violin okay?" I said to change the subject.

"No, it's not," said Silva flatly. "It's impossible to repair." It seemed like he wasn't talking only about his instrument.

"I'm so sorry. Maybe I can help—"

"Are you actually sorry?" said Silva. "You talk a big game about keeping students safe, but you were reckless, Maya. And I can't forgive you for that. Even if you don't care."

He hung up before I could defend myself.

Still, miraculously, the Pugilists were spared. In order to cool off controversy before Friday's football game, Mateo, James, and Theo got nothing but detention for fighting. Meanwhile, Theo's X-ray returned clear of fractures. Our near scrape had passed, and we were ready to clap back.

Pat designed our revenge mission, taking place during Saturday's homecoming dance. Unlike Juneau, with her flashy mural, Pat thought cuttingly and logically. During our next meeting, she unveiled her plan. She wanted to wipe out student records—discipline files, transcripts, everything.

"CGHS uses those records to hold kids down," she explained. "That data gets used to track some kids into prisons and some kids into colleges. If we erase the data, we disrupt those processes. And we level the playing field."

If we could hack into an administrator's computer, Pat said, we could get to the digital gradebook. As for the discipline files, she'd discovered that they still weren't digitized, but rather locked away in the police office's filing cabinets. With CGHS distracted by the homecoming dance, we could rob both offices in one fell swoop.

Amid the plotting, I'd nearly forgotten that Ife had invited us to Friday's student council meeting. By this point, I doubted meetings could save us, but I owed Ife one last attempt before the Pugilists waged all-out war.

I asked Pat to accompany me to the meeting. I knew it was risky to speak out together, because that meant we'd be automatic suspects for whatever happened next. But nobody could represent students of color better than Pat.

We met in the library to research police violence on school campuses so we'd have lots of evidence to present.

Ife couldn't stop us from attending the meeting if she tried—which, of course, she did. When Pat and I arrived at school early Friday morning, Ife was waiting, looking worried.

"Maya, I know you're pissed. I saw your Instagram post," Ife said. She'd stepped in front of us, like she thought we might run inside and seize Dr. Harvey by the neck. "Trust me, the student council is going to address what happened Wednesday. Maybe you should sit this one out."

"You invited me to this meeting," I said. "You said I could talk sense into Harvey."

"That was before your controversial Instagram post," said Ife. "The school is on political fire now."

"The cops fucked up," Pat said. "They shouldn't be waving weapons on campus."

Ife ran a hand through her hair. She looked like she hadn't slept in a week.

"I really like you, Pat, so this is hard for me," said Ife. "But as president, I'm ruling that this meeting is closed to you both. Sorry."

"Nice try," I said, "but I read the CGHS Constitution. According to the bylaws, all meetings are open to public participation."

For a moment we stared at each other. Ife, empty-handed, arms crossed over her chest, and Pat and me, clutching anti-policing leaflets we'd printed at the library, as well as the entire student constitution, to be safe.

Eventually, Ife's eyes filled with reluctant respect. "You read the bylaws?"

"All eighty pages. There's some hidden gems. Did you know it's decreed that female students can't wear skirts above the knee, or else teachers are legally permitted to spank us?"

"It really says that?" Ife reconsidered. "Actually, I'm not surprised at all. Nobody's updated it in decades."

"Are you saying you *haven't* read the whole constitution, Ife?"

"Fine. You did your homework." Ife rolled her eyes. "You win—this time. Come on."

Ife led us inside, and for a moment, I felt our old connection return: Ife and me conquering books in the library, verbally abusing Anya's exes, facing down my father. Just like nothing had changed.

The meeting was held inside the auditorium; the council members sat onstage, and Ife and Dr. Harvey presided at the podium. In the audience, I saw a handful of parents, teachers, and most of the Pig Patrol, including Squash. Pat and I sat down as Ife opened the meeting.

"First, we'll review our final plans for the homecoming festivities—tonight's football game and tomorrow's dance," she announced, after greeting the crowd. "And then students can make comments about Wednesday's event. Which, to be clear, is their right," she finished as Dr. Harvey glared at her. She shot me a look, like, *I'm doing my best.*

I practiced our arguments in my head as Ife talked about budgets and fundraisers in her steady, presidential voice. It was boring, but still: Ife was in her element, leading a group, and she kicked ass at it.

Dr. Harvey's booming voice alerted me again. "I am concerned," he said, "that you have not discussed homecoming police presence, Ms. Asefa."

Ife looked ruffled. "Respectfully, sir, I don't foresee a need for excessive event security," she said. "I worry it could escalate things—"

Another administrator sighed heavily. "Matters at this school are already out of hand," he said. "The mural brought us a lot of bad press. I can't imagine that will be the last from those criminals. I've half a mind that we shouldn't be hosting homecoming at all."

Pat and I smirked, but there was fire in Ife's eyes: Homecoming was her hill to die on.

"I know people are shaken," she said. "But, speaking on behalf of the students, it seems like a bad idea to clamp down too hard during homecoming. It's supposed to be a time for togetherness—"

"You don't speak for all students," someone interrupted. Horribly, predictably, I saw Squash stand up. Anger lanced through me.

"The Student Safety Commission feels differently," Squash continued, indicating his goons seated around him. "We have to make a show of strength. We need to let students know what sort of behavior isn't tolerated on our campus."

To her credit, Ife spoke calmly instead of cursing him out, which is what I would've done. "I am firmly against bringing police to these events," she said. "We have adult chaperones, and that is enough."

Some of the other council members nodded their agreement, but the administrators weren't having it.

"I'm sorry, Ife, but police presence is nonnegotiable," Dr. Harvey said. "They will be protecting students. That's final."

Pat waved her hand, but Dr. Harvey shook his head. "Now's not the time for open comment," he said pointedly when she persisted.

"Squash just commented quite openly," I said, which earned me a stare-down, too. "Patricia should be heard."

Pat cleared her throat, and when nobody stopped her, she opened her binder to the research we'd prepared.

"With its heavy police presence, CGHS is contributing to a phenomenon known as the school-to-prison pipeline," she read aloud. "Police, and policing, on campus will disproportionately hurt Black students like me."

I watched in awe as Pat laid out her case. "CGHS," she said, "is on track to become a majority-minority high school within the coming decade. That means it's time to start taking the needs of students of color into better consideration. Instead of police, we need guidance counselors, college advisers, peer educators—"

As she spoke, I surveyed the audience. The administrators

looked stony-faced; I wondered if this was their way of concealing shame. Ife was nodding along quietly. But Squash and his friends were muttering among themselves. Their utter disregard for Pat incensed me; I couldn't help myself. "Shut up," I hissed at them, which raised eyebrows all around.

"Instead of amping up police presence at homecoming, I'm encouraging CGHS to consider de-escalating," Pat continued. The longer she talked, the more I could tell that people were getting uncomfortable. She seemed to radiate with truth. I realized that some people needed megaphones, billboards, podiums to get their point across. Pat didn't need all of that. She captivated us with just her words.

"In conclusion," Pat said at last, "stop policing us."

It was a cheeky move, quoting the tagline from our mural. Around us, people muttered. Dr. Harvey leaned forward.

"Ms. Lloyd," he began, disregarding everything else she'd said. "You wouldn't happen to have anything to do with the vandalism, would you?"

Pat's mouth opened, but I jumped up protectively. "Are you accusing her?"

Squash smirked. "Defensive, aren't you," he said.

"How dare you," I said. I could feel myself getting heated in a way that I never had before—a throw-it-down, start-a-fight kind of heat. "Patricia just did this entire meeting a favor by educating you about students you never think about otherwise. And you're, what, calling her a vandal?"

"Maya, sit down," said Dr. Harvey sternly. "Attending these meetings is a privilege, not a right. If you don't behave with respect—"

"Yeah, let's talk about that *privilege*," I snapped back. My voice gained steam. "You don't care about us, do you? If you did, students wouldn't be getting arrested by police. They wouldn't be beating each other up and nearly getting shot for it—"

Instead of responding to me, Dr. Harvey turned to Ife. His gaze was hard. "Ms. Asefa, these are your friends?"

"I—yes," said Ife, shooting me a glare. "Maya, Pat, you need to go now. Please."

I didn't know whose stare burned worse—Squash's, Dr. Harvey's, or Ife's. I didn't stick around to decide, though. Instead, I stormed out of the council meeting.

chapter 15

I was so angry, I considered going home after that meeting. But I'd already skipped too many classes, thanks to the Pugilists, and I figured the day couldn't possibly get worse. I was wrong.

Inside the cafeteria, Juneau ran up to me. "I wanted to tell you personally, before everyone finds out." She took a breath. "Mateo and I finally talked through our feelings for each other, and we decided to start dating. Officially."

I felt like my chest had deflated. I suddenly had a wild, inappropriate vision, a mix of imagination and premonition: Juneau naked, having sex with Mateo. My face burned. I'd never pictured her like that, and I felt disgusted with myself.

"Wow," I said. "Congratulations." An absurd response, since it wasn't like she'd gotten a promotion or had a baby. But Juneau beamed.

"Thanks," she said. "I guess having a gun waved at you makes you finally go for what you want, right?" She bought a salad and sat down, leaving room for me. But I didn't sit.

I knew I shouldn't be surprised by this development. After all, Juneau jumped a fully armed cop to save Mateo's life. They had years of history together. Still, it gnawed at me.

"Do you actually love him?" I asked. "Like, *love-in-reverse* love him?" I spoke our shared phrase aloud, holding it out like an offering. Juneau considered, salad fork midway to her mouth.

"Who knows?" she said, biting the kale with a crunch. "I know my *hormones* are pleased to see him. Isn't that enough?"

"Sure." I shrugged. "I guess I expected grand romance for you. Not just hormonal gratification."

Juneau chuckled at that. "You hold me on such a pedestal," she said, coming up for air between laughs. "You're adorable."

"I'm leaving," I said. "I have homework to finish." I left her laughing alone at the lunch table.

I often felt that Juneau possessed the ability to charge the air around her. Like the gases I studied in Chemistry, she expanded to fill the containers she was in. Perhaps we got along because I permitted Juneau to do just that: fill me up, push me to my limits. So many of my firsts belonged to her—first smoke, first kiss, first crime, first boyfriend—that I imagined her accumulating them like pennies in a piggy bank.

Juneau scored another "first" that night: my first football game. Organized sports were never my scene—I hadn't even learned the rules of football, a game that Amma considered a cranial health hazard.

Mateo is playing, she texted me. *As his brand-new girl-friend, I'm legally obligated to support him. And as my sweet friend, you're legally obligated to support me.*

No thanks, I typed. Juneau's laughter at lunch still rang in my ears.

Juneau persisted. *Homecoming is the quintessential American high school experience. Plus, Theo's coming. What do you say, peach?*

Normally I'd make excuses: My homework is due. I'm on my period. I have cramps. But it was homecoming, and Juneau was right. *At some point, Maya, you need to let yourself live. It's possible to save the world and be a stupid high school kid.* So I went.

At school, the bleachers were packed. Everyone was wearing our ghastly school color, citrus orange.

"Maya!" Tess spotted me and waved. She, Theo, Pat, and Juneau were sitting together. In a satirical display of school spirit, Juneau had temporarily dyed her hair bright orange, though the blonde showed through.

"Since when were you a loyal fan of Citrus Grove football?" I had to shout over the band.

"Don't be so bourgeoisie," yelled Juneau. "Where else would I get to publicly avow my genetic lust for violence?" She drank covertly from her tumbler of beer. "White people invented football for the same reason we pick fights, launch nukes, or colonize land. Because we're aimless, hungry, and bored."

"Interesting take," said Pat. She pried the beer from Juneau's hand and passed it to me. "When you start soliloquizing about colonization, that's when I know you've had enough." I finished Juneau's beer in two gulps, even though it tasted like pee.

I sat next to Theo, who was sporting a temporary arm sling. He draped his uninjured arm around my waist. I suddenly wished Juneau would notice.

"How are you feeling?" I asked Theo.

"Now that you're here? Exquisite," he said. "Any bets on who wins?"

"I have to admit," I said, "I don't understand football."

"Me neither, to my white dad's cosmic disappointment." Theo laughed. "Let's just clap when everybody else does."

The whistle blew: The game was now afoot. The second Mateo charged out onto the field, we all cheered, and Juneau pretended to swoon.

The rival team, I learned, was from East Orange High— apparently Florida's stockpile of school names had run dry. Their team was dressed in a similar shade of violent tangerine, so the plays were nearly impossible to follow. Eventually, I gave up on watching. Instead, my eyes landed on Juneau, who was pelting popcorn at the field.

"Faster, boys!" she yelled. "For America's most homoerotic sport, you'd think this would be more entertaining!"

"Juneau, shut up," Tess begged. "You're going to get us kicked out."

Citrus Grove scored its first touchdown—or at least, I assumed we did, because the crowd rose to its feet and roared. It was a level of ecstasy I'd expected from drugs or lovemaking. Our school mascot, an inflatable orange, cartwheeled across the football field.

"*We got the juice!*" the cheerleaders screamed.

"Squeeze us like a titty," Juneau followed, under her breath.

I noticed Ife standing down on the track. Our eyes met, and I realized she'd been watching me. I waved, but she looked away too fast to seem natural.

My heart ached. Just last week, she'd driven me to the museum, held my hand in the gallery. How quickly we'd become strangers, torn apart by this war.

During halftime, Pat gave us assignments for tomorrow's revenge mission. You'd think it was too bold, discussing our crime at a wildly crowded football game, but it turned out to be the perfect place. Everyone was yelling, plus we were out in the open, defying any suspicions.

"We'll strike during the dance," Pat said. "The buildings will be unlocked, and everyone will be distracted. Also, we'll be spotted dancing, which will give us an alibi."

Pat was methodical, plotting every movement like a military general. We'd divide into two teams, she said. The first team, consisting of Theo, Tess, and me, would hit the principal's office. While Tess hacked Dr. Harvey's computer, wiping out student grades, Theo and I would keep lookout. The others would strike the police office, stealing the disciplinary records.

"The tricky part," said Pat, "is that we won't strike at the same time. That way, one team is free to keep an eye on the Pig Patrol."

Nobody checked to see if I felt comfortable with the risks, and that's how I knew I was finally one of them. I wasn't the new girl anymore, nearly chickening out in Mateo's basement. Now I broke locks without blinking, smoked weed without coughing. Like I'd known how to do it all along.

The game raged on, but the audience was losing juice. The

crowd thinned out significantly after halftime. "I'm bored." Theo nudged me. "Would Juneau hate us if we ditched and got milkshakes?"

I glanced at Juneau. I'd come at her invitation, but she'd hardly spoken to me all evening. After all, this was Mateo's game, and I was the least of her priorities.

"Nah, let's just go," I said.

Halfway to Theo's car, we ran into Ife. She'd appeared in the parking lot, probably teleported. She was wearing the fluorescent CGHS varsity jacket, which made her look like a menacing traffic cone.

"Where are you going?" she asked.

I noticed the tenseness of her posture, one hand gripping her phone. Theo nudged me, and I said, "We're getting milkshakes. This is Theo, by the way."

Ife acknowledged my miraculous new boyfriend with a quick nod of her head, and I understood this wasn't a friendly conversation. She was onto me. The mural, the Pugilists, all of it. She'd followed me so she could catch me in the act.

"Is your car parked here?" she said with a practiced authority, but she couldn't fool me. Her voice curved anxiously upward, like her words might break free and escape.

"It's a parking lot, Ife," I said.

Ife flushed. "Can I walk you to your car?"

Our eyes met.

"Sure," I said. "Theo, lead the way."

As we walked, Ife kept a careful eye on Theo and me. She walked as close to me as she could without making it a three-legged race until finally I said, "Ife, can we talk?"

I pulled Ife behind the car.

"You've been watching me all night," I told her. "You think I'm going to do something."

Ife said nothing, but her face gave her away.

"Don't bullshit me," she said at last. "I know you better than anyone. You're planning something tonight. You, Juneau, Pat, Mateo, and Theo, too, I'd bet. The mural was just the beginning."

"You can't prove that was us."

Like me, Ife was small, but she always looked so tall when she was right about things. At that moment, she towered over me, the whole parking lot, even.

"Come on," she said. "You think I can't recognize my best friend's art? The mural was brilliant, Maya. Only you could have done it."

She thought it was brilliant. I held on to this like rope.

"Why are you so obsessed with the mural?" I said. "It didn't hurt anybody."

Ife's face was pained. "You should know, I'm covering for you," she said. "Not just because I love you, but because I think you're right—about all of it. But I can't let you risk everything just to make another statement."

"I think some risks are worth taking," I said. "But maybe we'll never agree on that."

Ife sighed. "Harvey's expecting more crimes at the game tonight," she said. "He asked me to keep an eye on you." I raised my eyebrow, and she added, "No matter what, I'll protect you, you know that. But you're making it really hard."

So this was why she'd followed me to the car. Just like I'd attended the student council meeting to make peace, Ife was reaching out, hoping to stop me from blowing things up. How did we end up on opposite sides?

"Please promise you won't do anything crazy tonight," said Ife. "Promise, and I'll let you go."

I felt like my heart was splitting in two, but I nodded. There was still time for Ife to join our side, I thought. After tomorrow's revenge mission, the whole school would see we were right. Maybe I was naive, but I truly believed this.

"Nothing's gonna happen tonight," I told her. Not a lie, and still a lie.

Ife watched until I'd gotten into Theo's car. She didn't move until we'd driven away.

After the game, she texted me again.

I'm sorry I doubted you, she wrote. Game went well. We won, if you can believe it. And then, Theo's such a cutie. Score!

I imagined the final euphoric roar of the crowd. Squash, the captain, basking beside a whitewashed mural. Juneau kissing her victorious boyfriend. Maybe he'd sling her across his quarterback shoulders, lift her up like a trophy. I wasn't there, but I pictured it all in placid slow motion.

That night, I dreamed about Juneau. She was kissing Mateo, and I don't remember if more happened. All I could recall was this: When Mateo looked into the mirror, he had my face.

chapter 16

By morning, I realized I'd forgotten to buy a homecoming dress.

Amma drove me to the mall three hours before the dance. "I'm surprised you're here with me," she said. In neighboring dressing rooms, we tried on clothes, something we hadn't done in years. "Isn't Anya the one you bring for fashion advice?"

"Anya's busy. She needs the whole day to get ready for the dance." I was lying. Anya hadn't spoken to me in weeks.

"Well, I'm glad you asked me," said Amma. "I've barely seen you since school started. You're always with your new friends. And that boy—Theo?" she asked, though she knew his name perfectly well.

I started feeling guilty, but Amma's voice softened. "I was too harsh on you about dating," she said. "After discussing with your father, I've decided it's all right with me."

I couldn't believe my ears. "You guys approve of Theo?"

"Don't get ahead of yourself. I'm saying *I get it*," said Amma. "Rajendra reminded me that dating boys is normal for American girls like you. I won't stop you." She reconsidered. "Unless you get pregnant. In which case, I'd ship you to a Himalayan monastery."

She knocked playfully on the wall between us. She couldn't see the question burning on my face.

"What if it wasn't normal for me?" I said. "What if...I didn't want boys at all?"

Amma fell quiet, and I feared I'd gone too far.

"What do you mean, Maya?"

She sounded genuinely confused. Even I barely knew where this was coming from. Only that I'd kissed Juneau, and now I couldn't shake her. She followed me like a stone in my shoe.

"Do you know women who aren't attracted to men?" I said. "Who...want other girls instead?"

I got as close as I could before swerving around the confession. Amma had never given me "the talk" before, the one involving birds and bees, the firsthand knowledge that Juneau preached like gospel. Here was my attempt to test the waters. She would think it meant nothing at all.

"You're talking about lesbians," Amma said at last. "But you have a boyfriend."

Suddenly I wished the wall was transparent so I could see her face. I needed to see that she was matter-of-fact, motherly. A new fear crept in, slouching and insistent. Did Amma suspect what I was? Was she disappointed?

"I know I'm not. I'm just wondering if you knew any," I said.

"Oh, Maya," said Amma. Was that relief? "They're a minority. I've never had a lesbian friend in America, and certainly not in India. Maybe a few patients, but no more."

"Why not?" I said. I sounded too quick, breathless.

Amma considered.

"I suppose because their lives are difficult," she said. "They can't help who they are, but their lifestyles are challenging. It brings a lot of suffering to their families. To be truthful, I pity them."

I stared at the wall between us. A crawl space opened inside of me, something worming its way deep. Of course she felt pity. She was a nurse, attuned to all sorts of suffering and brokenness. Some people were so doomed, she felt preemptive sorrow for them.

"Come out, kanna," said Amma, knocking on the door to show me her dress. Except we'd accidentally picked the same one: black silk, perfect for poisoning an ex-lover. At first she looked like my reflection in the mirror. But the distinctions bloomed immediately—how the silk hugged her body but pressed flat on mine. How hope shone in her face but secrets lurked in mine. She was so trusting; I felt guilty. She really knew nothing at all.

"Now I feel silly!" Amma covered her face with her hands. "I'm too old to dress like a teenager."

"Stop it." I managed a smile. "You look beautiful."

She ended up buying both dresses. Even though they were on sale, she used her coupon book and bullied the cashier until they were nearly free.

"I love you, baby," she said, carrying our bags. "I know we've had our disagreements lately. You're just growing so fast, and I'm trying to keep up."

"Who knows," I said. "Maybe I won't become a complete failure."

"*Chee!*" Immediately, Amma pressed her knuckles to my temples, then her own, moving fast to reverse my jinx.

I thought about how much of love is a conscious act. How hard we work to smooth the disappointments of others into a velvet sheen that we could love. This was what Amma must have felt when she continued playing nice with Rajendra. Was this why she couldn't give him up?

The good news was, I knew how to lie. I started envisioning the possibilities: marrying a man I didn't love, because I loved Amma more. Living with a so-called best friend or roommate, spinning an endless lie. Juneau was right—faking it wasn't that difficult. You just had to pretend it was the easiest thing in the world.

To my relief, Theo arrived in his own car, not a limo. As he slipped a corsage onto my wrist, his hands lingered on mine. Anya would know what to do: If our places were switched, I knew she'd lean into the moment. Was this how the crushes my friends described felt?

Luckily Amma arrived, insisting on taking pictures in the backyard. At first Theo and I stood rigidly apart, like a painted Gothic couple. After a few camera clicks, Theo slung his arm around me. Amma didn't react to his boldness, and I finally remembered to breathe.

Theo parked outside the gym, two rows from where Squash's Porsche was parked. It was an eyesore: shiny and red as a fire hydrant. What was it with rich people and vintage cars? It was tradition for the homecoming king, coronated at the dance, to drive the queen for a victory lap in his car. According to Anya, there was a second, secret part of the tradition: sex in the back seat. "It's not homecoming if you don't come," she'd joked.

Seeing it, Theo shook his head. "The victory lap tradition is odious," he said. "And so is that car."

We walked into the dance, and Ife had outdone herself: The gym was completely transformed. Somehow she'd gotten our impoverished public school to spring for strobe lights. The dance radiated around a center stage, where the DJ blasted hip-hop with the curse words bleeped out, though everyone screamed all the lyrics anyway. Adult chaperones skulked in the corners, plus Dr. Harvey and a handful of sullen cops.

"Shall we dance?" asked Theo, leading me to the floor.

It felt like I'd dived into a volcano. The temperature rose several degrees, wet heat coiling from tightly packed bodies. I spotted Anya and Squash dancing together, and even from afar I could tell she was drunk. She was surrounded by Squash's Pig Patrol lackeys—identical football jocks paired with girls in strappy dresses—but her eyes were only on Squash. They were grinding so aggressively they didn't need the Porsche's back seat. They looked maybe three seconds away from having sex right there in public.

Mateo and Juneau pushed their way toward us. Mateo slouched behind her, but Juneau was clearly at home on the dance floor, turning heads as she walked. Of course she did: She looked like the sun.

"Mateo's liked her forever. I'm glad they're finally dating," Theo said.

"Me too," I lied. I'd braced myself for this moment, but

seeing them together still sent a dull quake through my chest. Squash and Anya might be frontrunners for homecoming king and queen, but Juneau and Mateo looked like real royalty.

"There you are," Mateo said. His quarterback frame strained through the clothes, like someone had stuffed him, scarecrow-style, into a suit. But I didn't look at him for long, because my eyes were drawn, inevitably, to Juneau.

I'd never seen so much of her before—she wore a white dress that changed colors in the lights, showing off her best features: her curved legs, her delicate neck, which was bare except for a tiny pendant. Her hair was loose, unbothered. I thought, *This is how you do it.* This is how you accomplish womanhood.

"Maya!" Juneau hugged me like we were long-lost lovers, so close I could feel that she wasn't wearing a bra. "You look irresistible," she said.

I pictured myself through her gaze. It occurred to me that my skin might be glowing beneath the sweat. Maybe my hair shone like black silk. If Juneau declared it, such miracles became possible.

"You too," I managed. I forced myself to smile at Mateo. "Congrats on yesterday's game."

"Let's hope the good luck runs into tonight," Mateo said.

Juneau pouted. "I thought I was your good luck charm."

"Are you kidding? You're an agent of chaos." Mateo kissed her. "Let's find the others."

Mateo took Juneau's hand, Juneau took mine, and I was already holding Theo's, so we made a strange procession over to Pat and Tess. "Thank God," Tess said, spotting us. "If another man tries to gyrate against me I'll vomit."

"We're all here," said Juneau. "Pat, let's review positions?"

Pat got to business. "Theo, Tess, and Maya," she said. "You'll visit Harvey's office during the couples dance, right after they crown the homecoming royalty. Juneau and Mateo, we'll handle the cops' office after they're back. Everyone, keep an eye out."

My skin burned from pre-mission nerves. "What do we do until then?" I said.

Juneau laughed. "Now we dance," she said. She wrapped her arms around Mateo and they shimmied closely. They weren't as awful to watch as Squash and Anya, but only barely. I tried to dance like girls I'd seen on TV—throwing it back, twisting my hips—until I realized Theo and I were the only couple not entwined with each other; our pelvises were unfused. How did these motions come so easily to other couples? What would it take for me to kiss Theo, press my body against his?

As if reading my mind, Theo twirled me—actually twirled me—so the dance sped into a blur. I caught sight of Juneau mid-twirl. This time she was kissing Mateo, his hands sliding up her dress.

Something boiled inside of me. It wasn't envy, not exactly; I had no right to feel possessive over Juneau. What I felt cut deeper than that. All this time, I'd viewed Juneau as a myth descended into our midst—but here was Mateo, groping her like any horny teenage boy. Juneau wasn't unattainable: She was simply out of my reach.

"Where'd that come from?" I asked Theo, breathless.

He smirked. "I dabbled in ballroom dancing in middle school."

I snorted. "I'm sure ballrooms are much classier than this," I said, indicating the varying levels of foreplay unfolding around us. I tried to direct my contempt toward Mateo like a knife.

"Not really," Theo said. "All dances are about intimacy. Done correctly, even waltzes are erotic."

It took me a moment to realize he was joking. Talking with him always felt this way: unserious, fun. If only things could stay this easy. Theo would never pressure me, but surely he'd noticed that we weren't grinding or kissing. Suddenly I wished those things had never been invented.

"I can teach you to waltz," said Theo. "If you want."

He spun me around again, but then I tripped on a boy's foot. The boy swore loudly, and I found myself face-to-face with Silva, who looked pissed to see me. Still, I played nice, introducing Silva and Theo. "I didn't know you were coming to the dance," I told him. "You look good."

It wasn't the first time I'd felt that Silva was attractive—I saw how other girls reacted to him, and I wasn't blind, either— but it still felt vaguely unsettling, like spotting your teacher in the grocery store or catching your mom in a lie.

"Thanks," said Silva stiffly. Mentally I prayed for an escape route—to God, maybe, or whoever handled such mercies. Fortunately Ife appeared, wrapping me in a hug. "Maya!" she said. "You look like a model."

"This dance is great," I told her.

"Thank you," said Ife, slightly breathless. "So far, no problems. Thank God, because Dr. Harvey's on edge." She rolled her eyes. "But you're here, so I feel better already."

I ignored the stab of guilt. Beside me, Theo fidgeted.

Silva touched Ife's shoulder comfortingly. Seeing them together, my heart lurched. I knew I'd made my choice—I was here for the mission, with Theo and Juneau—but right then, all I wanted was my friends. "Can we get a picture together?"

I asked. "There's a photobooth in the lobby. I know it's cheesy, but I want to save this memory forever."

We said goodbye to Theo and crossed the gym. As we waited in line for the photobooth, Ife unleashed her usual scathing commentary about who screwed up the decor, who tried to stuff the homecoming ballots, and whom she'd separated as they made out under the bleachers. But then she paused.

"I'm sorry," she said. "But we can't do this without Anya. It feels wrong."

I frowned, but Silva said, "Agreed. The drama's lasted long enough."

I didn't want to cave so easily. In my view, the battle lines were already drawn. Anya had chosen Squash, and thus had not chosen me. But Silva and Ife were right. Anya's absence tunneled through me like a train. "If you want," I said.

Silva texted Anya to come. Unfortunately, she came hand in hand with Squash.

Just as I'd known immediately that she was drunk, I now saw that Anya was really happy. Next to Squash, she looked elegant and important, like a first lady. "Look who learned to dress herself," she teased.

"I did okay without you." My words felt measured, cautious. Squash hulked behind, looking bored. Suddenly, jealousy clenched inside me. I wanted Squash to notice me, all the ways I outnumbered him in our war for Anya's heart. I took her hand.

"I wish I could paint you," I said truthfully.

Anya's eyes lit up. "This has been on my vision board since middle school, remember?" she said, which of course I did. "I dreamed of winning homecoming queen. Ife, you counted the ballots, right?"

"I'm not going to tell you if you won," said Ife, appalled. "That's leaking results. I could lose my position."

"Yeah, but Sam isn't gonna tell Dr. Harvey," said Anya, beaming. "Are you, Sam?"

Squash looked startled—or was he annoyed? The longer I stared at him, the more my insides boiled. He knew he was in enemy territory, but he wasn't acting hostile. He was indifferent.

"Yeah, whatever," he said. "Just take the picture, okay? I'll get drinks."

We crammed ourselves awkwardly into the photobooth. "Props!" Anya declared, looping us all inside a feather boa. She smiled at me, and for a split second our closeness returned. In that second, I might've told her anything. That I was halfway through a Pugilist mission. That I couldn't kiss Theo. That I loved her more than Squash ever could.

"Ife, please give me a hint," Anya begged as the photos printed. "If I won, I need to gather myself now."

"My lips are sealed," said Ife, but she couldn't resist a wink, and Anya gasped.

"These are actually really cute," Silva admitted, distributing the pictures. He was right. Our faces looked sweaty, our sobriety questionable, but we all looked radiant. Anya and I could be sisters.

Squash was waiting outside the booth. He tried to pull Anya away, but she didn't follow. "Sam, wait," she said. "I want a picture with you, too."

Squash simply stared at her. She was so pretty, so hopeful. I knew her expression intimately, because I'd seen it many times on Amma's face, in the final stages with various boyfriends.

The ride-or-die face, the hold-it-down face. Carrying the relationship on your shoulders, even if it crushed you.

"Don't be tacky," said Squash. "Come on, let's go smoke. The guys are waiting outside."

I couldn't believe it: Squash was refusing Anya in front of her friends. And maybe Anya couldn't believe it, either, because she said, "Okay, but can you introduce me to your granddad first? I would *die* if Dr. Harvey met me after I got high."

"Later, babe. I promise he'll bore you either way." Squash's voice was low.

To her credit, Anya stood her ground. "Sam, we're about to become homecoming royalty. Don't you want me to meet your family?"

She reached for his arm, but he moved his shoulder, just by a fraction, so she missed him. I'd learned to notice these gestures, to systemize her faults like a man might. Our eyes met.

Squash was ashamed, I realized. Of *her*.

Just then, the music faded. Ife shot up like a rocket. "Duty calls," she said, making her way onstage to the mic, joining Dr. Harvey, the administrators, and the other student council kids. The homecoming crowns now sparkled onstage.

"It's happening!" said Anya, momentarily forgetting Squash's rudeness. "Fix me, please?" she asked me. Without question, I started smoothing her hair and dress. That's when I realized: I didn't care about fighting. I just wanted her to be happy.

The crowd hushed as Ife called the homecoming nominees onstage: boys first, then girls. It was mostly varsity athletes—Mateo was nominated, along with Squash and half the football team. Most of the girls had been nominated as part of a couple, like Anya. I briefly wondered if CGHS would ever nominate a lesbian couple. Then Juneau's name was called, and I lost my train of thought.

"Juneau Zale?" Ife called again, and then the whistles started. The freshmen boys behind me grew excited, and I caught a snatch of their conversation. *"That's Citrus Grove's most bangable chick,"* one whispered, like he'd learned this from a book. *"She's got the highest body count of anyone at this school."*

"Shut up, pigs," I told them, and they cowered.

There was no way that Juneau hadn't heard anything. But she continued walking onstage. It seemed to me like a spotlight was shining on her, or maybe that's just how I always viewed her. Anya, too, stood out to me. She was the only brown girl in a sea of white, gazing across the stage at Squash. Was I imagining that Squash was avoiding looking back?

"And now, your homecoming king," Ife announced. She opened an envelope, and the Pig Patrol started cheering preemptively. "Sam Harvey," she called, surprising nobody, and Squash loped forward to be crowned.

Ife had to tap the mic several times to restore quiet. "Next, the homecoming queen," she said. There was a hush of anticipation. Anya stood a little taller.

That's when Dr. Harvey plucked the mic out of Ife's hands. "This year's homecoming queen is Emma Sowers," he announced. "Thank you all very much." The mic screeched as he switched it off.

A pretty blonde girl stepped forward amid equally wild cheers. There were a few scattered murmurs—it was strange, after all, for a non-coupled pair to win—but that was it. Emma accepted her crown effortlessly, like she was made for it. The

DJ started the music, and Squash and Emma led the couple's dance.

Dimly, I recalled that the couple's dance was my cue to start the mission, but instead Silva and I rushed toward Anya. She stood frozen, the only girl onstage without a dance partner. Strobe lights caught her hair, tinting it blue and pink. Even in her shock she was beautiful.

Finally, she spoke up. "I think there's been a mistake," Anya told Dr. Harvey. "Sam and I are a couple. We should've—"

Dr. Harvey glanced back, and the way he looked at her, she wasn't even a disruption—it was like she was nobody at all.

"Stand back," he said quietly. "It's already been decided."

A bright flash: Squash and Emma were posing for pictures. Anya's body tightened. I could feel her desire to sob as if it were inside my own body.

"Sam," she said, prodding his arm. "What's going on?"

He shook his head at her. It was a minuscule gesture, but Anya's face crumpled. Dr. Harvey gave his grandson a curt nod.

He's fucking dead, I thought.

Ife ran toward us. "This is wrong," she said. "Anya and Squash got the same number of votes. Couples on the ballot were voted in jointly."

"Get back onstage and issue a correction," I said. "That crown belongs to Anya."

"I can't publicly contradict Harvey." Ife looked desperate. "But I'm going to sort this out." She disappeared into the crowd. Meanwhile, Anya rushed out of the gym, crying. Squash finally had the decency to follow her.

"There you are," said Theo, appearing with Tess. "That was heartwarming, wasn't it? No surprises with King Harvey, though." He offered me a cup of personally spiked punch for good luck: I downed it in three gulps. "Shall we go?"

Without thinking, I pushed Theo aside. "I can't," I said. I knew I was ruining Pat's carefully timed mission, but I didn't care. "I'm going to murder Squash."

I slipped past Theo's outstretched hand, seized Silva's instead. Anger was coursing through me, hot and sticky as syrup. As I ran after Anya and Squash, I felt sickly powerful. Like if I willed it, the roof would collapse on our heads.

I knew the moment I reached the parking lot that I was asking for a fight.

Anya was sitting on the hood of Squash's Porsche, and Squash appeared to be comforting her. The Pig Patrol was gathered with coolers of beer, celebrating Squash's victory.

"Maya, wait." Silva caught up, panting. "What are you doing?"

I was already removing my earrings for safekeeping. "I'm going to tell Squash what he's severely in need of hearing," I said. "That he's a piece of shit for rigging an election because his racist family won't accept Anya."

"Wait!" Silva said. "I don't think you should—"

I whirled on him. "You don't think I should intervene?" I said. "I guess only one of us grew a pair here."

Silva looked like I'd slapped him. "You're out of control," he said. His voice had a new edge to it. "How could yelling at Squash possibly help Anya?"

"At least she'll know I give a shit," I said. "I actually *try*. I don't sit around in my room writing music for nobody to hear while everything collapses around me."

I knew I was being cruel, but I couldn't bear to look at Silva. Instead I crossed the parking lot, trying my best to channel my inner Pugilist.

"Hey, Anya," I called, recklessly loud. The fruit punch was starting to hit. "Want to get out of here?"

Her wet eyes flashed like danger signs, but I couldn't leave.

"Come back inside and dance with me," I called, louder this time. Squash smiled lazily at me, like the Cheshire cat with white privilege. "Hey, Maya," he said, his eyes lingering as he looked me up and down.

I grinned with all my teeth. I had his full attention. "I know you and your granddaddy rigged the homecoming election," I announced. "It's pathetic, really."

Around me, Squash's cronies muttered. Squash stood up straight. Men were predictable like that. If a woman insulted them before their friends, they burst like balloons. He flexed a thick, heavy hand on the Porsche—a hand capable of punching a wall, a window, a person.

"Fuck off, Maya," he said. "I know you have it out for me. But this time, you're stretching."

I ignored him. "If e counted the votes," I told Anya. "That crown should've been yours." I glared at Squash. "We both know Anya won homecoming queen, and you took it away from her. I just want you to admit why."

"You and Juneau are the same. So desperate to find a villain. Acting like everyone who's not a white guy is automatically a victim. Like the *Pig Patrol* is some kind of racist cult." Squash smiled widely. "Yes, I know that's what you call us. And I know exactly what you are."

I took a deep breath.

"Tell her why she's not homecoming queen," I said.

Anya looked like she'd rather be anywhere else in the world. Staring down at the pavement, she said, "Why did you ignore me onstage?"

Squash looked startled. "Babe, I'm sorry. Please," he said. Those words should've been kind, but his tone made them dismissive. "That shit doesn't matter anyway. Homecoming's just a stupid ritual."

"It mattered to me," said Anya. She still wasn't looking at either of us, but her voice gained strength. "Sam, why can't your family see us together?"

She was so radiant, I felt like we were watching her in a play. One filled with broken hearts and shitty men and lovely, disaffected leading women. Except the pain on her face was real, whereas Squash still had a homecoming king smile plastered on his face.

"Come on, Anya. You know what my family's like," he said. I could tell he was choosing his words carefully. "They're just old-fashioned."

I had to hand it to Squash. He'd somehow admitted his family was racist without actually using the word. Behind me, Silva scoffed.

"They want you to drive Emma on the victory lap. Not me," Anya said.

"I'll take you out after," said Squash. "Look, it's just a tradition for my family. I know we're just messing around, but for them this shit's serious."

Anya flinched. I wondered, then, if this was what love was: a wound that opened in you even if you didn't want it.

"Just messing around?" she said, her voice rising. "Sam, we said we loved each other."

Everyone was listening now. Not just Silva and me, but the entire Pig Patrol and random passersby. I pictured this moment through Squash's eyes: He, the football captain, was being publicly embarrassed by the small brown girl he couldn't seem to quit. Her love was hurting him, too. I saw his face turn ugly, and fear fluttered in my chest.

"I do love you," he said. Again, his words were kind, but with a layer of forced calm brushed over them. Like if she continued to embarrass him, there'd be hell to pay. "My family decided who'd win long ago. They wanted a girl like Emma. It's nothing personal."

"They think I'm not good enough for you," said Anya. "I'm not white enough."

"You know I don't see color," said Squash, attempting to salvage the situation. "I hate what happened, too."

Until then, I didn't think a rich white boy could hate anything about his life. But Anya nodded slowly, and my heart sank. She was going to forgive him. I could scream at Squash, but I couldn't make Anya respect herself.

Then Anya stepped away. "That's fucked up, Sam," she said. Her words were calm, matter-of-fact. "If you loved me, you'd stand up for me. I'm tired of being your secret."

People around whispered, and I saw Squash redden. He moved toward her, and something leapt up inside me. I thought, *That's it.* Anya had gone too far, and now the cruel version of Squash had awakened, the version who'd tackled Mateo on the first day of school. I stepped toward Anya, protective.

Squash noticed me, and his eyes hardened. Then he said, loud enough to carry: "This isn't coming from you, babe." He pointed to me, aiming the blow. "It's coming from this jealous dyke."

The slur hit like thunderclap. Around me, people gasped.

"Excuse me?" I said stupidly. I heard a rushing in my ears. The word *dyke, dyke, dyke,* like the beat of a drum.

Squash smirked at me. "I thought it was obvious. You know, with your pathetic crush on that cunt Juneau Zale…"

His words hung in the air. I clenched my jaw, but I could feel it all pounding at the back of my head, begging to be released: Rage against Squash. Rage against Silva. Rage against Mateo. Rage against my father. Rage against every vilely ignorant man who'd catcalled Juneau, disrespected girls, stopped jealous dykes from speaking their minds.

And I let it all out in one furious run-on breath:

"Even-if-I-was-a-dyke-there-is-absolutely-no-shame-in-being-one-so-your-point-is-both-ridiculous-and-laughably-ignorant-in-fact-the-actual-shame-is-being-so-pathetic-that-you-get-off-on-policing-and-threatening-people-and-abusing-whatever-power-you-can-get-and-calling-women-gay-in-a-painfully-transparent-attempt-to-cope-with-your-own-fragile-masculinity-in-fact-if-you-haven't-seen-a-therapist-for-that-you-probably-should-you-sad-little-boy-you-will-be-lucky-if-anyone-remembers-your-name-in-a-year."

Then, with all the venom I could muster, I snarled, "In summary, go to hell."

Spots danced before my eyes. I dragged Anya into the gym, panting, as shouts erupted behind me. The only thing that could've made the moment more cathartic was if the parking lot had blown up in my wake.

chapter 17

Back inside, my stomach squeezed. I ran to the toilet and threw up my insides, fruit punch, rage, and all.

Afterward I felt better. As I stared at myself in the mirror, for once I liked what I saw. My hair was a lion's mane, wild and strong. I looked like the kind of woman I'd draw from a dream. I suddenly wished I were a man so I could go head-to-head with Squash. I could kiss Juneau in front of the world. I could punch the next person who called me a dyke. I wouldn't need to paint well or talk smart—I could scare people just by raising my voice.

I found Juneau, Pat, and Mateo on the dance floor; Theo and Tess were gone. They looked surprised to see me.

"Maya, where'd you go?" Pat demanded. "Your team left without you. They said you ditched the mission—"

"Something happened," I said. I told them about my

confrontation with Squash. When I mentioned the word *dyke*, all of their jaws dropped.

"He called you that, in front of everyone?" Juneau whispered. "Just out of the blue?"

"Well, not exactly. He..." I weighed the words on my tongue, but I knew the story would spread regardless, and it was better for me to say it. "He called you a cunt. He accused me of having a crush on you." I delivered these words with an incredulous tilt, hoping to neutralize the blow.

"Why would he say that?" asked Mateo, his voice flat.

I couldn't answer. Juneau looked at me for the briefest instant, and she read my mind. She came to my aid.

"Does it matter?" she said. "Squash came for one of us, and that shit can't slide."

When nobody contradicted her, she took a deep breath.

"We're changing the mission," she announced. "Pat and Mateo, go ahead with our plan. I'm doing something extra. Something off the books."

"*What?*" said Pat.

"I've thought about doing it forever, and if not now, when?" said Juneau. "I'm going to steal Squash Harvey's Porsche."

We stared at her like she'd spoken German. Mateo said, succinctly, "What the fuck?"

"It's easier than other things we've done before," said Juneau. "My dad taught me about cars, remember? I know what I'm doing."

"I don't care how easy it is," said Mateo. "Juneau, this is grand theft auto. Use your brain!"

Juneau's eyes hardened. "I won't *steal-steal* it. I'll just relocate it. He'll find it eventually," she said.

When Mateo shook his head, Juneau turned to Pat. "Back me up here," she demanded. "Tell my boyfriend I'm right." Sometimes it maddened me, but now I loved how perfectly bitchy she was. I wanted to learn her ways.

"Hell no," said Pat. "I think stealing Squash's car crosses a line."

"No, Squash crossed the line when he insulted Maya," said Juneau. "If I get caught, I'll take the fall."

"Screw that," said Mateo. "You're not stealing his car, Juneau. Not even you could get away with that. End of discussion."

He looked angry, and I didn't blame him. I knew Juneau was being reckless, drunk on her own confidence. And yet, when Juneau spoke, I could see it like a movie. Squash and Emma would lead the crowd out for their victory lap and find the Porsche missing. Squash would rage until he deflated. He'd be afraid. Just for a minute, the axes would tilt in our favor.

I wanted him to feel small. I wanted him to hurt.

Juneau crossed her arms. "I wasn't asking for your permission, Mateo." She turned to me. "Will you help?"

It wasn't even a question. "Yeah, I will."

Mateo made an awful sound, half-laughing, half-choking. He stared at us both like we all were meeting for the first time.

"I can't believe you, Juneau," he said. "All this because of one thing Squash said? Does that mean it's true?"

"Drop it," said Juneau firmly. "I'm tired of the way girls get treated here. Didn't you hear what guys were saying when I went onstage?"

Pat nodded, and Mateo glared at Juneau, but it was suddenly like he didn't see her at all. He was looking at all the men who wanted her, all the men who ever would. He realized he was outnumbered.

"I'm sorry about that," he said. "But—"

"You wouldn't understand, because you're a *man*," said Juneau. She somehow made the last word sound like its own slur. "Those boys are your teammates and friends. When they call me that shit, *I* feel it, not you, and I'm telling you that they need to pay."

The way she talked, jumping between ever-accelerating arguments, made little sense. Her logic uncoiled around the edges. But I listened to her like one might a preacher. Everything I wanted, she spoke into existence.

"Fine." Mateo turned to me. "If you won't listen to me, maybe you'll listen to *her*. Maya, tell Juneau she needs to calm down."

"No," I said. "I think Juneau's right."

Mateo's eyes narrowed, and Juneau clasped my hand. One gesture, and something fractured between Mateo and me. I saw jealousy light his eyes.

Despite everything, I thought, *What a shame.* Because honestly, I liked Mateo. He was the sort of man I'd want to be if I could. He played football with men like Squash, but his beliefs set him apart, made him protect others, resist injustice. The kind of man who, despite his strength, was unafraid to be soft with the people he loved. We both loved Juneau. There was no need to fight at all.

"You're a coward if you won't stand up to her," he told me, but I knew he would concede. I got the strange sense that I could read Mateo's mind. When two people share something so personal, like loving the same girl, you end up with a bond. Mateo and I stood on the same train tracks, unable to step aside from what we knew was coming.

"I can't support this," he said. "Sorry."

Juneau shrugged. "That's fine. I'll take Maya." She must've said this to punish him, but I sidled up to her, predictable and loyal.

Mateo shook his head. "Whatever. Choose her. I'm sticking to the mission." He disappeared into the crowd. Pat hung back for a moment.

"I don't condone this for a second," she said. "But Juneau, be careful. Look out for Maya, okay?"

Juneau rolled her eyes and led me out of the gym, moving too fast to ask questions. She grabbed a toolbox from her car, and we crossed the empty parking lot toward Squash's Porsche.

The Porsche was so glossy we could see ourselves in the reflection. I couldn't fathom how a teenager could drive a car worth more than some families made in a year.

"How can I help?"

"I've got it," said Juneau. "You just keep a lookout. I can probably start the engine with the screwdriver."

I stood by nervously as she climbed through the open top. I kept an eye on the gym doors, but it was a pointless gesture; I wasn't sure what I'd do even if somebody did come out. Instead, my eyes wandered back to Juneau. It almost felt like we were in art class, where I loved watching her work. Even years later, this would be how I remembered her most fondly: with her face snarled in concentration, hair spilling over her eyes. I'd say something irreverent, and she'd respond and reveal that she was just as unhinged, too.

For several minutes, Juneau worked the screwdriver into the keyhole. Then, without warning, the engine turned and roared to life.

"It worked!" she said. "It fucking worked. I didn't think—"

"Oh my God. Juneau, you're a genius."

She threw the car in reverse, but the Porsche screeched. Juneau slammed on the brakes.

"What's wrong?"

Juneau groaned. "The steering wheel's locked," she said. "I could start the engine without the key, but that's not enough." She flung her head back, punched the wheel. *Fuck, fuck!*

Her reaction scared me. "It's okay," I said. "We can just go back. We've done enough."

In a way, I was relieved. It was true that the Pugilists were already causing damage. Stealing the Porsche would only be the cherry atop an unquestionably malicious night. But Juneau frowned. "Don't go soft on me now, Maya."

The steering wheel could've been an excuse, and I could've returned to the dance. Part of me wanted that. But another part wanted to fulfill the sick propulsion building in my chest.

"Fine," I said. "Take a few more minutes."

Juneau ducked back into the car. Then, without explanation, she got out and crawled under the Porsche. All I could see was her lower body, which started to shake.

"Juneau?" In a panic I dropped to the ground, where Juneau was laughing hard.

She emerged holding a key. "Dumbass had a spare taped to the bottom."

We stared at each other and I started laughing, too. "How'd you know it was there?"

Juneau grinned. "I didn't. But my dad always told me that under the car is the first place that thieves look for spares. So I thought, what the hell?" She didn't wait for my response. "Get in!"

Her excitement was infectious. I hopped into the passenger seat. The fact that we'd waltzed in with the key made it feel less than massively illegal. Running my hands along the leather seats, I finally understood why Anya was so enamored by Squash's wealth.

Then Juneau slid into the driver's seat, still laughing, so beautiful that I knew I'd take her over the Porsche every time I had the choice.

"Now what?" I said.

"Now, baby," said Juneau, imitating Squash's drawl, "I'm taking you for a ride."

She whirled out of the parking lot. We sailed past the school, merged onto the highway. I kept looking back, expecting cop cars to screech after us, but nobody did.

"Fuck, this is majestic," said Juneau. She stepped on the gas, and the Porsche responded energetically, gracefully. The speed dial soared upward and a scream rose in me, loud and full of joy. I bit it down.

A second later, I decided I didn't care.

Juneau laughed as I yelled. She put the headlights on full blast as we coasted down the road. The lights refracted across the road signs, glinted in her eyes.

"*Music!*" she demanded, so I turned on the radio, landing randomly on a country station, bland and vaguely Waspy. Somehow the twanging guitar made everything a million times funnier, or maybe the adrenaline had unhinged us, because we were laughing like we were drunk.

At Juneau's request, I looked through Squash's glove compartment, stealing spoils for ourselves: a rosary for Juneau, a pen for me. It was weird to touch someone else's things—without context, Squash's most personal items turned into junk. A box of condoms spilled out. I was embarrassed, but Juneau shrieked, "*What size? What size?*"

I squinted at the label. "Magnum, extra-wide," I said, and Juneau looked disappointed. "Aw, shit," she said. "I was sure this car was compensating for something." But even this disappointment was soon forgotten in her next rush of speed.

She abruptly swerved off the highway onto a dark road.

"Wanna take the wheel?"

I laughed. "I don't drive, remember?"

"But you know how, right?"

"I took Driver's Ed, if that's what you're asking. But I don't—"

"Come on," said Juneau. "Are you seriously passing up the chance to drive a stolen car?"

I took a deep breath. There was a chance Juneau would drop it if I refused, but I didn't want to disappoint her. That would be worse than disappointing myself, because Juneau always believed in me. If she hadn't taken a chance on me, flipping every light switch in my mind, how long would I have stayed in the dark?

So we switched seats. It was surreal to see the world from the driver's seat, the road wide and passive before me. Juneau touched my hand, sending shivers through my skin, and my confidence returned. I stepped on the gas, and we lurched into the night.

The light turned red almost immediately, but I didn't brake in time. Juneau sucked in her breath as I shot through the intersection—as cars honked, Juneau ordered, "*Don't stop don't stop just go!*"

I felt something rising in my chest, bright and certain as the sun. It should've worried me, how I only felt like myself when resisting things. How I only felt alive when escaping things. But I was with Juneau, and her presence pushed me forward.

As I ran the red light, she squeezed my hand, like I was seeing her through a birth. "Jesus Christ, I hope you never get a license!" she gasped. An unholy laugh rose in my belly, and then she started laughing, too.

Once I got the hang of driving, things became fun. Juneau cheered as I hit higher speeds. Lifting her arms like a world leader giving a speech. Our eyes met, and I felt invincible. In that moment, the whole world was our crash pad.

We parked the Porsche in the junkyard amid torched-out, rusty cars. I took a shaky breath, unable to believe what we'd done. Then I saw Juneau watching me and quickly assumed an expression of courage.

"Why are you looking at me like that?" I said.

"Because I'm proud of you," she said. She leaned toward me and my heart skipped a beat. She whispered in my ear, "I fucking love you, you know that?"

It was the first time she'd said those words to me. And maybe because I'd heard those words many times already— from Amma, Anya, Ife, Silva—I didn't react at first. I always told my friends I loved them. It was possible Juneau was also being friendly—or worse, saying she loved me the way you'd say you loved iced coffee or cute puppies. But when I looked at her, she didn't seem to be joking.

Deep down, I thought, *If every choice I'd ever made led me to this moment, stealing a Porsche and driving off with Juneau, I'd be okay with that. I'd gladly accept the risks.*

I should've laughed it off, played it cool. But I hugged her back and said, "I love you, too." No qualifiers, no joking tone. Earnestly, like a child.

I felt her head turn and she kissed my forehead. Swift and light, a bird swooping. She must've meant it as a friendship kiss, a *holy-shit-we-stole-a-Porsche* kiss. Except my heart swelled, and I lifted my face so our lips brushed—not a full makeout, but not a chance encounter, either. She didn't lurch back, not immediately. Her mouth lingered, and I leaned in for a deeper kiss.

The second she tensed, I knew it was a mistake.

"Oops," she said, laughing. And just like that, the bubble popped. "I wasn't trying to kiss you like that," she said. She was apologizing like it was her silly mistake, even though I was the one who kissed her *like that*, and we both knew it.

"Maybe we'll not mention that to our boyfriends," she said. Then she laughed. "If Squash Harvey could see us now..."

"He'd probably get off to it," I said.

"Speaking of boyfriends," she said. I didn't realize she'd ended our moment until it was over. "We should probably call Theo for a pickup. We're stranded."

It was strange to remember that there was an entire world outside this car, beyond Juneau and me. If it was up to me right then, we'd drive away, but so much was waiting for us. There were the Pugilists, the dance, and men, so many men. The one I was dating, the one dating Juneau, the one who stole Anya away.

We called Theo, and it was almost funny how matter-of-factly we explained our situation, but he arrived twenty minutes later.

"Does this make me an accomplice to grand theft auto?" he asked, driving us back. Juneau had dived into the back seat and closed the door, so I sat up front. It was probably because as Theo's girlfriend, I had front seat rights. I knew I shouldn't read too much into our seating arrangements, but what if Juneau was trying to distance herself from me? I felt guilty for kissing her. The boys hooting at her tonight—what made me any different from them?

I realized Theo was waiting for a response. "Probably?" I said. "I'm sorry for ditching you earlier."

"That's okay. Pat filled me in," said Theo. He started telling us about Dr. Harvey's office—how Tess had logged into his computer, wiped all the student records. They'd nearly been caught by a janitor, he said. But they'd made it.

It was a good story, but I was suddenly exhausted, so I let Juneau ask all the questions. Out the window, I saw the same roads I'd driven with Juneau, now in reverse, like our fairy tale was over.

When we snuck back into the gym, the dance was still raging. I tried not to look resentful as Juneau raced back to Mateo. She gave him Squash's rosary as a gift, which hurt a little: I thought she would keep it as a souvenir of our night. Meanwhile, Theo pulled out a flask. "I brought us a post-mission treat."

It was Gatorade mixed with vodka, sharp and fruity. We swigged in a corner and then went back to dancing, the bass grinding satisfyingly against my bones. The Gatorade kicked in, stronger than I expected. I finally understood why people got drunk: the rush of energy, loose-bodied fun. How had I missed out on this for sixteen years?

But my fun didn't last long. Halfway through the sultriest random Macarena of my life, the gym lights turned on. It made everything instantaneously ugly—sagging streamers, trash everywhere, suspicious puddles on the floor. The DJ cut the music, and everyone groaned.

Dr. Harvey came on the intercom. "Attention Citrus Grove," he boomed. "We've had another campus incident. The police are on their way, and the dance is canceled. Everyone, go home."

The effect of his words was dramatic—everyone started protesting. "Let me be clear," he said. "I know that the perpetrators are at large on this campus, possibly at this dance. I want them to know that justice will be swift, and it will be—"

What else it would be, we never heard, because everyone was booing. Then Squash raced across the gym and pulled the fire alarm.

Chaos ensued—the alarm blared, lights flashed, and sprinklers started pouring overhead. But it worked: Everyone rushed out of the gym. Theo and I staggered into the parking lot. "I need to sit down," he said, so we collapsed onto the curb and watched the drama unfold—people yelling, piling into cars, a girl reversing into a bush. Theo rushed to her aid, but I barely paid attention. I was looking for Squash.

I spotted him loping through the parking lot, accompanied by his friends. They were talking animatedly, probably about the break-ins. He was still wearing his stupid crown. He didn't know what was coming for him.

By now he'd reached his parking spot, facing the empty asphalt. He turned around a few times, like he'd forgotten where he'd parked it. Then he started giving orders. I watched his friends fan up and down the rows of rapidly depleting cars. They returned, shaking their heads: no Porsche in sight.

As a small army of cop cars descended upon CGHS, Squash shouted, "Who the fuck stole my car?"

The glee I felt was so deep I thought I might explode,

revealing myself as the thief. But everyone was watching Squash Harvey as he threw an honest-to-God tantrum in the CGHS parking lot.

"Oh my *God*," Theo whispered. "I think you broke him, Maya. He's short-circuiting."

I spotted Juneau in her car with Mateo, watching the drama unfold. Seeing them together sent a stab through my gut. The victory had been ours, but at the end of the day, she was Mateo's girl.

Right then, I had two realizations. One, I couldn't keep watching Juneau like this from afar, pining for her in moments when she clearly wasn't thinking of me. Two, I knew exactly how to crush those feelings. I turned to Theo.

"Follow me," I said. "I want to be alone."

I took Theo's hand, leading him to the football field. We sat together atop the empty bleachers, and it should've been gross with all the trash from last night's game, but I could see every star in the sky.

"Were there these many stars the night of the mural?" I said, tucking my body into his. I willed him to lean closer—I knew he would. Until then, I kept talking. "I guess if there were, I didn't notice. I wish I could name them. I think—"

I turned around mid-speech and found my face an inch from Theo's. His eyes were dark. Nobody had ever looked at me like that before, except maybe Juneau, right before she kissed me—and thanks to her, I was ready. I knew what to do.

"You're so perfect," he said, leaning in. "Do you mind if I—"

Without waiting for him to finish, I kissed him.

Or maybe he kissed me, I wasn't sure of the chronology: just that I was alone with Theodore Fisher-Cho, and his mouth was soft on mine. As we kissed I had a sticky, gooey feeling of watching myself. Just like how I'd mentally viewed Juneau fucking someone else, the way I'd replayed our kiss all night.

Theo's breathing got heavier the longer we kissed. I let his hands slide up my body, feel me in places I'd never been felt before. Because he seemed to like it, I got bold: I climbed on his lap and straddled him. Except Theo was gentler than Juneau, and maybe that was why I didn't feel the stirring inside me, the warmth, the inevitability of it all—no matter how hard I focused, my thoughts returned to Juneau's mouth, the way she smiled when she kissed, like it was an inside joke known only to us.

I pulled away from Theo, my heart pounding. He wasn't smiling. I realized I'd gone completely stiff.

"Are you okay?" he said. "You look like you've seen a ghost."

I might've told him he was right—except my ghosts weren't cold and dead, but alive, in love, a warm breath on your ear catching you in a lie. *I am in love with Juneau Zale*, I thought. Then: *I am fucked.*

"I'm fine," I said. "Just...tired. It's been a crazy night." I wanted him to know I was telling the truth—about that, at least.

"Do you want me to drive you home?" Theo asked.

"No," I said, too fast. I could feel the air fracturing between us, and I pulled down my dress. "I mean: No, thank you." My heart was beating, but I didn't feel warm.

"Did I do something wrong?" said Theo.

"What?" I said. "No. It's not you. I just—I don't want this."

"What do you mean?"

"I don't want to be your girlfriend," I said, and the words plunked ear-splittingly between us like a spilled bag of marbles.

"Oh," Theo said.

"I value our friendship," I said. "I just don't have the words for this."

He didn't say anything, so to fill the space I said, "I'm sorry for being like this."

At last, Theo stood up. "You have your phone, right?" he said. "Text me when you get home safe."

I watched him climb down the bleachers, lanky legs moving faster than usual, refusing to look back. I tried not to think about the kiss with Theo, and the kiss before that—what I knew I wanted but could not have. And then, because I had no friends left to drive me, I walked all the way home in my heels.

chapter 18

Classes were canceled on Monday after the dance. News of three crimes had set Citrus Grove ablaze. And yet, the days after homecoming were the quietest I'd had all semester. I'd broken up with Theo, the Pugilists were lying low, and my friends were angry at me, so I didn't have anyone to see. Instead, I stayed home with Amma and followed the copious media coverage.

"Can you imagine who would do this?" Amma said, watching the TV. "I'm worried to send you back to school tomorrow."

"I'll survive," I said absently, scrolling through reactions on Instagram. It was thrilling, seeing evidence of our mission onscreen, even if we could never take credit.

"How are your friends handling all this?" Amma asked. "I haven't seen them around."

It was a good question, but I couldn't answer. Ife and Anya

wouldn't return my texts. After five calls, Silva picked up only once.

"I'm not ready to talk to you," he said tersely. "I need space."

"Have you heard from Anya and Ife?" I said. "Are they avoiding me, too?"

"Yes, and I don't blame them," said Silva. He hung up, leaving unsaid apologies in my mouth.

I was dreading returning to school on Tuesday, but Juneau called me early that morning.

"What's going on?" I sat upright in bed. "It's five a.m."

"I'm almost at your house," Juneau said. "Wear long sleeves. I'm taking you on an adventure."

"What about school?"

Juneau sighed. "I'd rather skip today. I need a break from seeing Mateo," she said. "Now get up. Google Maps says nine minutes until I arrive."

I didn't need more convincing. Nine minutes later—just long enough for me to leave Amma a note claiming I'd gone to school early—Juneau rolled into my driveway. "What's all this?" she asked when I climbed inside. I was holding a bag of the first food I'd found in the kitchen: clementines.

"It's early," I said, embarrassed. "I thought you might not have eaten."

"God, you're a gem," she said. "Can you peel them? We need to get moving."

Juneau revved toward the highway. She opened her mouth, not taking her hands off the wheel, so I fed her an orange wedge. I tried not to stare at her lips when she chewed.

"So I heard you dumped Theo," she said. "What happened? I was rooting for you two."

"He's a sweetheart. I just…didn't see it working out."

"I'm sorry, babe. Breakups are no fun." She opened her mouth for another orange. This early in the morning, I4 lolled wide and empty like a tongue.

"Why do white people always apologize for things that aren't their fault?"

"To be fair, most things are." Juneau smiled. "If it makes things better, Mateo and I are going through a rocky patch, too. He's being a jealous bitch because I took you in the Porsche."

That did, in fact, make me feel a million times better, though I'd never admit it.

To my surprise, Juneau parked in front of the Orlando Museum of Art.

"Wait. Why are we here?" I had a flash of panic, remembering the fiasco with my father.

"Don't worry," she said. "I have a treat for you. My friend just told me there's a new shipment of eighteenth-century international art. Even the curators haven't seen it yet."

"Then how are we going to see it?"

"Because my friend," said Juneau, "is the security guard."

My heart pounded. "So we're sneaking into the museum?"

"Honey, no. How gauche," Juneau said. "We're letting ourselves in with the key."

We walked up to the museum doors. Like I expected, they were locked—the OMA wouldn't open for a few hours—but Juneau knocked with confidence, like she was running for office.

A young man in a museum uniform opened the door: Juneau's friend. He handed her the key, plus gloves for us to wear.

"You have an hour," he said. "And if you damage anything, I hope you have a couple million dollars lying around. This shit's the real deal."

"I wouldn't expect anything less," said Juneau, unlocking the door.

The warehouse was cool and sterile, filled with art in its rawest form, unguarded by frames or glass. Now I understood why we'd worn long sleeves and gloves. Even the slightest contact with human skin could damage the works.

We riffled through drawers of paintings. Several canvases were unpinned, spread wide like maps, so we could lean in close to every paint stroke. Juneau didn't say much to me, but that somehow felt even more intimate.

"Whoa," said Juneau, pulling out a modest book-size canvas.

"What is it?"

Juneau showed me an oil painting of a small yellow sun sinking low over blue-shuttered windows. She pointed out the artist's signature: *Vincent*. The handwriting unearthed a memory in my mind—art history books, posters, famous pictures online.

"Wait—*Vincent*?" I said. "As in, Vincent van Gogh?"

Juneau cradled the painting reverently. "I think so," she said. "This is one of his lesser-valued miniatures—*Sunset in Vienna*."

"*Sunset in Vienna*," I repeated. I'd never seen Juneau this excited. Suddenly I wished I had more opinions about Vincent van Gogh, an artist I'd only read about in books. I wished I'd done nothing but ponder his art for all of my sixteen years.

We sat down on a funky wooden bench. Or it might've

been a modern art installation, I couldn't tell. Juneau pulled out her notebook and tore me a sheet. "It's time for my favorite museum activity," she said. "Writing love letters to artists. Today, Vincent van Gogh."

"He's dead, you know."

"Then that should take the pressure off things." Juneau smiled.

I watched her write. Poised on the museum bench, she looked like a sculpture herself. Before I could stop myself, I tucked her hair behind her ear.

"Less flirting, more writing," Juneau said.

I blushed, feeling the painted eyes of a dozen portraits judging me as I tore my gaze away from Juneau. I wasn't actually impressed by *Sunset in Vienna*. I couldn't understand why this tiny painting had captivated Juneau.

Before I realized it, I'd covered my paper in words.

"Done?" she said. She rubbed her hands like a mad scientist. "We're going to share now."

"Do I have to?"

"Of course. Unless... Did you write a dirty letter?"

"Shut up," I said, lowering my eyes to the paper. "Dear Mr. Van Gogh," I read. "My name is Maya Krishnan. We have a lot in common. We both hope that people can see us through our art in ways they can't if they pass us in the street."

I kept going, too embarrassed to look up.

"*Sunset in Vienna* is beautiful. But if I'm honest, I can't find anyone in your painting. I only see myself, the onlooker, longing to get swept up in something majestic. Your sunset is a blank, unpopulated void."

I took a deep breath. "I think that's kind of cool, though. It reminds us that it's unfair for us to romanticize others, like our feelings for them are the only ones that matter. We think we know a person, or a painting, but we really just know our own desires, reflected back at us."

Juneau clapped when I finished. "You reminded me of the male gaze," Juneau said. "How guys put all their expectations and fantasies onto women. Trying to own all the pretty things."

"All these naked paintings of women," I said, gesturing to the boxes. "You'd think we exist for people to look at. They stare at us like they can see themselves in reflection." I looked back at Van Gogh's sunset. "I want to build a museum just for women."

"And you will, one day," said Juneau. "You're going to be so famous, Maya. Girls are going to sit in art museums and write love letters to you."

Sometimes I'd feel annoyed at Juneau's grandiosity, but every now and then she'd say something like this, and everything inside me would melt. But before I could thank her, Juneau opened her own notebook.

"Dear Vincent," she began. "I've always thought art could change the world," Juneau read. "How incredible is that, to play God with a paintbrush, bringing beauty into existence? A lot of this universe comes predesigned, but art lets us alter it."

She turned the page. "I think a lot about how you painted better worlds for yourself, with all the yellow suns. I think it's incredibly inspiring."

I thought she was finished, but Juneau continued. "Somewhere I heard you used to eat yellow paint. You thought it'd make you happy, since yellow is such a joyful color. You didn't know that it was slowly killing you inside. So maybe something else to remember is that we've all got our yellow paint." She closed the book.

"You know, that's not true," I said.

Juneau frowned. "What's not true?"

"He didn't actually eat yellow paint," I clarified. "That's a really popular myth in art history, but it's been debunked. I read about it."

"No way," said Juneau, unconvinced. We started walking, but I couldn't stop thinking about yellow paint. Her historical basis was shaky, but Juneau was right. There was nothing crazy about eating yellow paint. It was no different from Anya's dating Squash, for example, or Amma's forgiving Rajendra. It didn't matter if they hurt you, because you felt seen.

"Look at this one." Juneau unwrapped another painting, soft-hued and angelic. Upon closer glance, it depicted an orgy of naked women. I covered my face, scandalized, and Juneau laughed.

"They don't care if you look."

I uncovered my eyes a little, and Juneau snickered, thrusting the painting in my face. "Perv."

We looked a little longer at the women. I got the sense that Juneau was thinking of something. Thirty seconds later, she proved me right.

"Can I ask you a very personal question?" she asked.

I nodded.

"I know Squash started the rumor, and he's a dick, and it doesn't matter anyway," she started. "But are you—"

"Gay?" I finished.

"Feel free to smack me for asking," she said.

"No, it's okay," I said, because it was, sort of, at least coming from her. "Well—"

I felt my mastery of the English language melting off my tongue, like when you say a word over and over and it loses its meaning entirely. "I mean, I've been doing some internal number crunching, and maybe I'm not a rigid hundred and eighty degrees of straightness. If that makes me gay, then—"

I shut my mouth before I rambled. I felt Juneau's hand on mine.

"It's okay, Maya," Juneau said quietly. "I understand. I fell in love with a girl before."

"What?"

"I was in love with Laila, actually," Juneau said. "You remember her, right?"

How could I forget Laila? During my first Pugilist meeting Pat had said I reminded her of Laila, like it was a compliment. Of course, I'd never actually seen her—just her handwriting in the Pugilists' notebook and the mysterious legacy that followed.

"It was real love," Juneau continued. "The kind of love that made me think that humans are worthy of the art we make."

I realized I wasn't actually surprised by her confession. I remembered how Juneau scoffed at religion. Her willful abandon, her reckless magnetism, the way she'd kissed me in the car. And though, in many ways, she was like every other white girl, striding through Citrus Grove like it was built for her, she carried that special sensitivity, that rare ability, through side glances and shared vulnerability, for gay women to find their way to each other.

"Did Laila love you back?" I asked.

Juneau frowned, and I thought I'd upset her. But the

moment passed as soon as it came. "It doesn't matter," she said. "Either way, it passed."

"Oh," I said. "That's too bad."

"No, it's okay," said Juneau. "I've moved on. Lovers throw themselves at me, with my stunning good looks and rapier wit." She winked, but I couldn't laugh. Not now.

"Juneau," I said finally. "You're a living legend at Citrus Grove. You can afford to be gay, or however you identify. You could make it something to be proud of."

She raised her eyebrows. "You mean, if I came out?"

"If you fell in love with a girl again," I pressed. "You could open up about it. You could normalize it."

Juneau shrugged. I understood immediately that I was one of the few people Juneau had ever confided in.

"Maybe," she said. "But I'm not really a fan of labels."

"Labels?"

"In art, labels are important," said Juneau. "You know— Impressionist, Cubist, the like. But on humans, they're the greatest burden of all."

She smiled, but the look she gave me was fragile. How could I tell her what I truly wanted: to know her heart, to be the only thing inside it?

I said nothing, and Juneau squeezed my shoulder. "Come on," she said. "Let's get high."

"Where?" I asked. "We can't go to my house. My mom's still there."

"My place, then," said Juneau. "We'll make a girls' day of it."

Bypassing my house, we drove toward the rich neighborhoods, multistoried and landscaped with fountains. We parked in front of Juneau's. I'd seen her white picket fence as a child, but I'd forgotten about her expansive front porch, the bird bath.

"Welcome to my humble abode." Juneau bowed as she opened the door.

Except it was hardly humble. I stared up at the massive spiral staircase, the shiny countertops. Even the sunlight felt expensive. As I felt the plush carpet between my toes, my heart sank. The awful truth: Juneau was even richer than I expected. Somehow this felt like a betrayal, a cord cut between our lives.

The biggest thing in her living room was a life-sized family portrait. At first I thought it was a photograph, but then I realized it was an actual, honest-to-God oil painting. There were pictures of her family on mission trips surrounded by dark-skinned children. A tiny Juneau, gap-toothed and laughing, hugged a man who shared her green eyes.

"This is your family?" I asked.

Juneau glanced up. "Yeah, and that guy's my dad. I'm surprised my mom hasn't sliced him out with scissors."

"Who are all the boys?" I pointed to the family portrait.

"My three brothers," said Juneau. "They're at school. Otherwise they'd be giving us hell right now."

"Three brothers?" I said. Then I noticed dirty soccer cleats slung across an armchair. A photograph of her brothers dressed as the three wise kings for a nativity play. How hadn't I known Juneau had three brothers?

"I'm the oldest," said Juneau. "They're in middle school. They're sweet, for now. Kinda sucks that they're gonna turn into men."

"What's being the oldest like?" I imagined occupying

a world with multiple versions of myself in it. Citrus Grove scarcely felt large enough for Juneau, let alone four Zale kids.

"It can be frustrating," said Juneau. "My mom treats my brothers differently than me. At their age, I was attending manners classes, getting shipped to youth groups at church. She lets them play soccer, basketball, whatever."

"Just because you're a girl?" I said. "That's messed up."

"My parents," said Juneau, "would hate me if they knew the truth about me. I don't know what they'd do. Probably disown me."

I looked around the massive house. It really was a lot to lose. "If they thought you were gay?" I said.

I wasn't watching her directly, but I felt her stiffen. "I wouldn't stick around to find out," she said; I couldn't tell if she was joking. It was strange to remember Juneau hadn't willed herself into existence—she, too, had parents overseeing her life, higher powers to consider. I couldn't imagine her obeying anyone other than herself.

"Want to watch TV?" she said. "My brain needs a break."

"Sure," I said, and Juneau belly flopped onto the couch.

"You're really something, you know that?" she said, browsing channels. "I'm positive you'd have any girl flipping sides within, like, a week."

"That's kind of you," I said. The TV flickered, dizzyingly fast. I caught snippets of a soccer game, a telenovela, a dance-off. At last, Juneau settled on the home improvement channel, a strangely escapist house-hunting show where a couple moved into a customized cave and practiced feng shui.

Suddenly it felt like Juneau and I were in a cave of our own. Like we, too, were escaping our real lives. It felt like I'd known

Juneau forever: the way she yelled at the TV, refused to laugh at the punch lines—everything felt familiar. I wondered whether Mateo had ever seen her this way. They'd spent years creating mischief together, but I couldn't picture his staying home with Juneau, watching trashy TV, letting her let down her guard.

"Can we smoke?" Juneau asked. She saw my expression and laughed. "I'll make sure you don't get too high this time."

"Okay," I said. Juneau lit me a bowl, not bothering to open a window—I looked up and saw that the smoke alarm was dangling from the ceiling by a wire.

"What if there's an actual fire?" I said, pointing. "We do live in the lightning capital of the world."

"You worry too much," said Juneau. "Luckily this will help. Deep breath now."

This time, I didn't cough. I leaned back and closed my eyes, let Juneau smoke me out, breath by breath, the way Amma fed me applesauce on sick days as a child. Eventually I felt cotton-candy soft.

"Juneau?"

"Maya?"

I'd been waiting to catch Juneau off-guard since the museum. I thought if I asked her my question when she wasn't expecting it, she might answer me—and not with a riddle or mystery, as she usually did. What I'd learned was that being obedient was the best way to do it. As soon as she thought she had the upper hand, she'd tell me everything she knew.

"Why did you say that, in the museum, about labels?" I asked.

"What?" Juneau asked, though I knew she remembered.

"I asked you why you wouldn't come out. And you said labels were the greatest burden of all."

Juneau curled her body against mine. Her warmth filled my chest like a balloon. "I think you know why."

I could imagine the reasons: her parents, Mateo, men, religion, society. But I wanted to hear her say it.

"No, I don't. Why are you so scared?" I hadn't meant to say it so baldly, but the words slid out before I could stop them.

"Aren't you?" said Juneau.

I said nothing, and she sighed.

"How many gay women have you met before today?" Juneau asked. She said it like we'd had this conversation a million times before.

She already knew the answer—we lived in suburban Florida, after all—but I said it anyway.

"None," I said. "But someone has to be the first."

"Don't you see? We already are," said Juneau. "Women are always forcing the world to give us our first chance. I mean, how many of the pieces in that museum were by women? Let alone women of color?" She sighed. "To give society another reason to say no—it's too fucking much to bear."

I didn't want to sympathize with her, but I did. Because although I conquered canvases and calculus with self-assurance, I'd never faced the fear that some doors were permanently barred to me even if I strived. Amma had warned me this world wasn't built for me, that I'd have to be twice as good as everyone else—except as a gay brown woman, it wouldn't be *twice* as good. It would be four times, ten times, a thousand.

"I'm sorry," Juneau said. "That was literally the worst thing I could've said."

"No, I understand," I said, because I did. And I felt like I understood Juneau, too, more deeply than before. She wasn't a fearless activist. She wasn't a Renaissance masterpiece, or an unimaginable mystery. On the couch, stripped down to her softest, I saw her at last: a questionably straight, unquestionably vulnerable girl.

"Are you going to tell people you're gay?" Juneau asked.

"Probably not." I felt like an empty bottle drifting out to sea.

"I want you to know," said Juneau at last, "your secret is safe with me. I just need you to promise me the same, okay? Nobody can know about Laila. Not even the Pugilists. I love Mateo, but he wouldn't understand."

I sucked the bowl too hard, like if I tried I could suck us back in time, to a moment as children where one of us might have acted differently—trading sandwiches at lunch, bumping heads on a trampoline—a choice that would land us together today. What might have changed things for Juneau and me? At what moment was it too late?

"I promise," I said. It didn't matter, our secrets. Even if I believed these choices were ours to make, Citrus Grove had already been devised.

On TV, the home improvement couple strung lanterns across their cave. The wife curled up in their new hammock bed. Her husband tried to coax her out, but she was too cozy to move. She said she could stay there for the rest of her life. In my mind, I imagined the cave woman getting her own movie. I pictured Juneau in the starring role.

When the credits rolled, Juneau turned to me. "Tell me a story," she said.

"A story?"

"About us," Juneau said, like we'd discussed this at length. I wondered, not for the first time, whether she could read my mind. "Give us superpowers or something. Fill it with plot twists."

Superpowers, I thought. Weeks before, I'd told Juneau that the superpower I craved most was invisibility. I hadn't known it back then, but I was wrong. Anybody could be invisible. The real miracle was to be known, to be loved as you were.

"Close your eyes," I said. Because I was high and could get away with it, I touched her hair and pretended that was all I wanted. I tried to recall the plot of a movie, a made-up world, a life I no longer belonged to. I touched her hair until I felt her relax. She trusted me.

"What should I imagine?" Juneau said. "Tell me what to see."

I made a mental note to intercept the telephone call that would come to my home this evening, reporting my absence from school. This day would leave no records; it would belong just to Juneau and me.

"Nothing," I told her. "In this story, everything is quiet. Everything is safe."

chapter 19

Another day, another message from my father.

Hello, Maya. Your mother told me about unrest at your school dance. Are you doing all right? I've been meeting Sujatha, but perhaps we all can meet soon.

I pressed Delete without a second look. I still wasn't ready to deal with Rajendra. While playing hooky with Juneau felt like vacation, on Wednesday, my real life resumed with a vengeance. CGHS was a war zone, and I was rumored to be a dyke. To top it off, my best friends still weren't speaking to me. But I figured I could win Silva back if I played my cards right.

I dumped Theo, I texted him. He FaceTimed immediately.

"I will permit you a bit of gloating, just this once," I said.

"I wasn't going to gloat," said Silva, but he became noticeably friendlier. "How do you feel?"

What a difficult question, I thought. By this point the

feelings were blurring together—fury at Squash. Longing for Juneau. Guilt from dumping Theo. Loneliness without my friends. Resentment toward my parents.

"I'll tell you when you drive me to school," I said.

We kept talking in his car. I felt a bit like Juneau, recounting the relationship like a veteran telling tales from war.

"You broke up with Theo *mid*-hookup?" said Silva. "That must've been dramatic."

"Having the cops sweeping campus? That actually helped move things along."

We pulled into school, and as we navigated the parking lot, Silva slammed the brakes: Anya was waiting in his parking spot. When we got out of the car, she grabbed my arm.

"I know what you did," Anya said without saying hello. "And you should know—it had consequences for Ife."

"What happened?" Silva said.

"Dr. Harvey kicked her off student council this morning," said Anya. "Homecoming night was her responsibility, and this was the consequence."

My heart dropped, but Silva looked confused. "That makes no sense," he said. "He can't punish her for someone else's crimes."

"Well, it happened on her watch," said Anya. "And it couldn't have helped that she protected Maya all this time." She turned to me. "You know how important student council was to her. How could you take that away?"

I was stunned by Anya's rage. I'd never faced this sharp, unsugared version of her.

"Go to Dr. Harvey and tell him where Sam's car is," said Anya. "You have to make this right."

"*What?*"

"Don't lie. I know you stole the Porsche," said Anya softly.

Her gaze burned holes through my skin. This was the difference between girls like Anya and boys like Squash. Yelling, threats, I could take. But Anya's quiet fury was agonizing. I almost wished she'd raise her voice.

"Maya," said Silva gently.

"No, don't *Maya* her," said Anya. "She needs to understand the seriousness. Sam said he's definitely pressing charges."

At the mention of Squash, my fury returned.

"You're still talking to him?" I shook my head, disbelieving. "After what happened at the dance?"

"Sam is not the one who stole a car," said Anya slowly, like I was a child. "He doesn't deserve what you've done—"

"How can you still love him?" I burst.

"The same way I still love you!" Anya was shouting at last; several passersby stopped to stare. "But you're making it so hard for me—"

"Being Sam's girlfriend will not protect you," I said, and Anya flinched. "You're not one of them. You're just as brown as me. We all saw how he treated you at homecoming." I took a deep breath. "The second you stop putting up with him, he'll treat you exactly like you are."

I wanted to shake Anya, but deep down I understood her feelings. I understood so much it hurt. Girls like us were invisible until someone like Squash, or even Juneau, decided to give us attention, anointing us with meaning. Anya's compulsion toward Squash was as hopeless and natural as a moth to a light bulb.

"Good speech," Ife said behind me.

I whirled around. If I'd found Anya's anger terrifying, I was wholly unprepared to face Ife's.

"Ife, I'm so sorry. Dr. Harvey shouldn't have—"

"I thought you were better than this," Ife said. "I hoped the mural was the end. You promised me, at the football game, that nothing else was going to happen."

"Ife—"

"You used to be different," Ife said. "But Juneau got into your head."

Now it was my turn to get angry. "Okay. Why does everyone have such a problem with Juneau?" To my embarrassment, my voice had ascended an octave.

Ife shook her head. "It's because you're acting like Juneau's little bitch," she said. "And you've forgotten who you are."

"This is exactly who I am," I said.

"Squash was right about you." Ife smirked. "Your crush on Juneau is too big for you to see past."

She shouldn't have gone there. She shouldn't have said that, but she did anyway. Rage transformed me into a live wire.

"You're not actually angry at me. You're scared," I said. "You know how bad things are, but you're not brave enough to fight back. You just play pretend, going to all your student council meetings, because you don't have the guts to do anything that counts." I took a deep breath. "Soon you'll realize you picked the wrong side."

I walked away, unable to shake the fear that I'd made an irreversible mistake. I'd cut myself off, set myself adrift. Without my friends, I was a kite with nobody holding the string.

I'd known, when I signed the contract in Taco Bell, that joining Juneau's world meant accepting the consequences of rebellion.

Already I'd lost Anya and Ife. As the hours passed, I imagined Dr. Harvey's rage simmering as well. I was almost relieved, in AP Calculus, when the bomb finally dropped.

The classroom phone rang, and Mr. Taylor stepped away from an eye-watering array of integrals on the whiteboard. The rest of the class, frantically copying the notes, seized the chance to catch up.

I rubbed my eyes. For the first time in my life, math had stopped yielding a steady stream of As for me. This month, I'd gotten a record-breaking C, even a D. Skipping classes, replacing homework with artistic revolution—my shifting priorities were catching up to me.

"Maya and Pat?" Mr. Taylor called. "Dr. Harvey wants to see you in his office."

In any other classroom, this announcement would have solicited snickers. But in AP Calculus, nobody reacted. Pat froze in her seat.

"Did he say why?" she said, but Mr. Taylor shrugged. "He just said to bring your things. Apparently this could take a while."

My stomach dropped. I tried to communicate telepathically with Pat: *What could he possibly know?* And, *Are we fucked?*

As we walked to his office, I tried my best to calm myself. I felt like a lump of clay was stuck in my throat: I wanted to cry, but I couldn't. I imagined a worst-case scenario—expulsion, police, and, worst of all, Amma's disappointment.

Juneau and Mateo arrived from the opposite hallway. Juneau's eyes glittered with apprehension.

"Did you get summoned, too?" she said.

"Yeah. What's happening?"

"But nobody else?" continued Juneau. "Not Theo or Tess?"

"No," I said. "Just Pat and me."

"That's good. They haven't figured out everything," Juneau said. "They don't know about the Pugilists. I bet they're just targeting the troublemakers." On this dramatic note, she knocked on Harvey's door.

"Wait. What's our plan?" I whispered.

I realized I'd misread Juneau's expression. She wasn't apprehensive. She was delighted. To her, this summons posed a challenge, a chance to up the ante.

"Juneau, I'm scared. I—"

Dr. Harvey opened the door.

Up close, his resemblance to Squash was more pronounced—except for the web of wrinkles around his eyes. His office wasn't empty. A stern-looking man and a police officer stood inside. "Sit down," the stern man said, so we did. Dr. Harvey sat at his desk, steepling his fingers. Dangerously calm.

"Juneau Zale, Patricia Lloyd, and Mateo Chavez," he said. "And May—" He stumbled over my name, then looked down at his papers in case they included a pronunciation guide.

"Mayavati Krishnan." I said my name loudly and slowly, to embarrass him. It succeeded. He flushed, and Juneau smirked.

"Well," he said at last. "Do you have any idea why I've called you here?"

"Nope," said Juneau. "But I'm guessing it's important, since you've seen it fit to interrupt our education for it."

"Please, Juneau," said Dr. Harvey. "You can claim to care about your education, but your GPA tells a different story." He pointed to the two other men. "Let me introduce the county superintendent and the chief of police," he said. "They're here to help me get to the bottom of things." The men nodded grimly. I imagined them perched like unsmiling vultures coming for their prey.

"Wonderful," said Juneau. "We have enough people for a cozy game of charades."

I wanted to beg her to stop provoking them, but my mouth didn't work. Mateo and Pat looked equally distressed.

The superintendent crossed his arms. "Is this a joke to you?" he said.

"Well, it's not funny," said Juneau. "Maybe you should stop with the interrogation techniques and tell us why we're here."

"As we all know, CGHS has been targeted by a malicious gang," said Dr. Harvey. "A car was stolen, on top of all the destruction inside school offices. We have reason to suspect your involvement."

The vultures leaned forward, watching our reactions, and my insides earthquaked. Juneau finally sat upright.

"Well, that was dramatic." Her voice was casual, but her eyes were alert. "What gives you that idea?"

"The car theft victim issued statements against you." The cop spoke gruffly. "We're investigating them very seriously."

"I can see that." Juneau looked unimpressed. "So you have rumors and gossip. What else?"

Dr. Harvey cleared his throat. "It's also not escaped us that you all seem to have a public vendetta against this particular student, and the school in general." He nodded at me. "Ms. Krishnan, you were seen harassing Sam shortly before his car was stolen. You and Ms. Lloyd also made a pointed outburst at the student council meeting."

I felt my heart grinding inside my chest, but I also felt Juneau's presence beside me, cool and unbothered, and I held it together.

"The point of those meetings is for students to express their opinions," I said. "That's all we did. But maybe we inspired somebody."

Juneau laughed, and I felt a brief flash of victory. But the moment didn't last long, because the fact remained that Dr. Harvey held all the power.

"I was surprised to hear of your involvement, Ms. Krishnan," said Dr. Harvey. "I looked up your record. It's spotless. You have one of the highest GPAs at CGHS. There's an impressive future awaiting you."

I said nothing, and he sighed. "It's a shame that you're associating with bad influences," he said. "If you help me put a stop to this madness, there's no reason to jeopardize your future."

Still I stayed silent. Mateo was drumming his fingers frantically against the chair. I couldn't bear to meet his eyes.

"Which leads me to this special offer," said Dr. Harvey. "Right now, based on reasonable suspicion alone, I have grounds to notify your families. Mr. Chavez, I will also be placing a call to your future university coach. I understand you're expecting to attend FSU on a football scholarship?" He smiled. "And Ms. Lloyd, you've gotten into UF?"

The precision of his malice shocked me. Pat flinched. Juneau snarled, "Seriously?" and Mateo leaned forward, his voice low. "You can't do that," he said.

"Of course I can," said Dr. Harvey. "This is serious business. I will be making those calls promptly—that is, unless someone comes forward about the stolen car."

The room got quiet. I felt the floor disappear beneath me, everything falling away.

"Ms. Krishnan," he continued. "Perhaps you have something to share?"

All six of them—Dr. Harvey, the vultures, Pat, Mateo, and Juneau—were staring at me now. Juneau's expression was unreadable. For the first time, she seemed to falter.

"Well?" said the police chief. "Are you speaking up, or should we start making calls?"

I could feel Pat's and Mateo's stares burning my face. The situation was cosmically unfair. Neither of them had stolen the car—Juneau and I had, against their wishes. I remembered what Mateo had said on homecoming night: *You're a coward if you won't stand up to her.* Had he been right?

"I think—" I started.

"Enough," Juneau said, interrupting me.

We all stared at her. She rubbed her temples like she had a headache. "I'm sorry, but aside from unsubstantiated rumors and a bias against student activists, do you have any evidence?"

Dr. Harvey hesitated, and Juneau pounced. "Do you have camera footage?"

I already knew the answer—we all did. "No," said the superintendent. "But—"

"Do you have witnesses who saw us committing the crimes?" said Juneau. "Do you have evidence that we did anything but dance that night?" She looked like someone had lit a match behind her eyes.

The vultures were silent, and Juneau stood up; without hesitation, I copied her.

"So what I'm gathering," Juneau said, "is that you can't prove anything. You're scared out of your wits and lashing out against students who make you uncomfortable. Do you want my family to file a discrimination complaint? Because I can make things difficult for you, too."

I couldn't believe her courage, but it seemed to cascade over us, protecting us like a shield. Dr. Harvey stood up, looming over us. For the first time, he looked truly angry at Juneau.

"Ms. Zale, if you don't watch your tone—"

"If you have proof, expel us all right now," said Juneau. Her voice gained momentum. "I dare you. Arrest us right here. You already have an armed cop for the job."

She didn't even wait for Dr. Harvey's response. I felt the thrill of victory emanating from her: the rush, the electricity. Juneau as the sun, object, and shadow. I marveled again at how she'd flipped the entire situation on its head, shouting at Dr. Harvey like he'd fucked up, not the other way around.

"That's what I thought," Juneau said. "Tell your Pig Patrol to stop harassing our friends. Kick the cops off campus while you're at it." She nodded at her friends, breaking us from our shock. "We're leaving."

Dr. Harvey blocked the door. "Not so fast," he said. "Juneau and Maya, stay. There's another reason I called you both here."

"Yeah?" said Juneau.

"Truancy," said Dr. Harvey, producing two slips of yellow paper: referrals. "Both of you were reported absent yesterday. Quite the coincidence, isn't it? Skipping school is a serious offense."

Juneau read the papers. "You're giving us detention?" she said. "Are you joking?"

"Every afternoon this month," said Dr. Harvey. He couldn't keep the smugness from his tone. "And I'll be informing your families of the truancy."

"That's ridiculous," said Juneau. "You're just looking for an excuse to punish us."

"You didn't make it particularly hard," said Dr. Harvey. "It's time for you to understand that your actions have consequences." In that moment, he sounded exactly like Anya.

"Fine." Juneau pocketed the slips. "Catch us in detention, then." Despite the dire situation, I couldn't look away from her. Her voice burned with a rage so deep, I thought even her silence could scald.

"You all are dismissed," Dr. Harvey said coldly. "You have until the end of the week to come forward. If not, I won't be lenient."

Juneau waved to the vultures as we left—there was nothing dead here.

The second we'd escaped the office, Mateo pulled us into an empty classroom. I'd never seen him this angry before, and my insides twisted with guilt.

"I told you two," he said. "I fucking told you not to steal Squash's car. That's why Harvey's on our asses: You made it personal. Now my scholarship's on the line—"

"UF wouldn't rescind me for this," Pat said tremulously. "Would they?"

Juneau had been fuming silently about the detentions, but now she returned to herself. "I know you're scared, but you can't show it," she said. "Harvey clearly doesn't have evidence. He's trying to tear us apart. If we stick together and hold our ground, nobody goes down."

She looked at her boyfriend, but Mateo looked enraged. I couldn't blame him.

"I guess there's no way you'll just take the fall for the car, will you?" said Mateo flatly, and even Pat nodded her agreement. "Save all of our asses?"

Juneau's expression darkened. "Don't be ridiculous," she said. "I can't admit to one crime without potentially exposing everything we've ever done. I won't be able to protect you."

Mateo said nothing, but Juneau was right. Whether we'd agreed to it or not, our fates were intertwined. Sensing this, Juneau offered us her hands. "Let's make a pact right now," she said. "No matter what happens, nobody cracks. We just ride this out."

Pat scowled. "Do you know how much you're asking of us?"

"Hell no," said Mateo. "If Harvey doesn't back down, I lose my scholarship. I can't just *ride it out.*"

"Mateo, I love you," Juneau said. "I won't let anything happen to you." And it didn't matter whether she was manipulating him or not, or if she even had a plan or not, because I knew that she truly did love him. With her right hand, she grasped mine. Her left hand hung softly by Mateo's. He hesitated.

"Come on." Juneau leaned in and kissed him. It worked like a charm; Mateo relented.

"Fine," he said. "For you, okay?"

He took my hand stiffly, then Pat's, and we shook on our pact. Right there, it was decided: Nobody would break.

Mateo and Pat headed back to class, leaving me with Juneau. She looked pensive.

"I know they're upset, but they'll get over it," she said. "What I'm gathering is, we really scared Harvey. He's stretching. He can't actually touch us."

She saw my expression and stopped. "Maya, are you all right?"

I hadn't said a word since we left the office. My eyes stung with held-in tears.

"That was so messed up," I burst out. "Harvey had our futures in his hands. And you just laughed through the whole situation—" I shook my head. "Harvey was right about you. You don't care."

"Harvey got to you, too." Juneau looked annoyed. "He's trying to play us off each other, make us scared. And it worked."

"I wasn't scared of Harvey." I tried to turn my gaze to steel, like Juneau's. "I was scared of you."

Juneau was taken aback. It occurred to me that I'd hurt her feelings, that her feelings could be hurt in the first place.

"Look," I said. "You aren't the same as the rest of us. I've seen your life. The others don't have the options you do—to get arrested, not attend college, any of that. Our families can't file complaints against the school. Regardless of what happens, you'll be okay. We won't. It scares me how you seem to forget that."

For once, Juneau had the decency to act ashamed. "I'm sorry," she said. "I didn't mean to scare you."

She took my hand, brought me in close. It was almost romantic. Why did she keep doing this? She knew how I tensed when she touched me. She could handle me just like she handled Mateo. I heard her voice, soft in my ear: "You should know. Even if something does happen, I'll protect you."

"I know. It's okay." I pulled away from Juneau. I didn't want her to touch me with the same hands that touched Mateo, that put his future at risk.

"You're not actually scared of me, right?"

"I didn't mean that." What else could I say?

She smiled. "Good. Because I meant what I said on home-coming night. I love you, okay?"

"I know." I took a deep breath.

That afternoon, instead of going home, I shuffled toward the school basement. I looked determinedly at the floor, bracing myself to be stopped and questioned—*Where are you going? Don't you know that way is detention?* But nobody said anything.

I didn't know anybody there. Everyone looked restless and bored. In the corner, Juneau was reading a book.

The detention monitor, one of the librarians who often checked out my books, reached for my slip. At the sight of my face, she did a double-take.

"What are you doing in detention?" she said.

"Truancy," I muttered, indicating the line marked OFFENSE.

The librarian's eyes widened. "I guess you can't judge a book by its cover," she said. She and I spent the entire detention pondering my descent into potential delinquency.

At home after detention, I showered so long, I started to feel bad for the environment. But I granted myself this allowance because I needed to scrub the day away for good.

As I dressed, my phone rang. To my surprise, it was Mateo. We'd never called each other before. I didn't even think he had my number saved.

"Listen, Maya. I have a question for you," Mateo said. He didn't sound sober.

"Yeah?"

I assumed he was going to yell at me for my cowardice in Harvey's office, and I prepared myself to accept his wrath. I wasn't prepared for what he actually said.

"Are you and Juneau hooking up?" Mateo asked.

I nearly dropped the phone.

"Why would you ask that?"

"Because I see the way you look at her," said Mateo. "You do whatever she says. Even unhinged shit, like stealing Sam's car. The day you two skipped school. Harvey was right, it wasn't a coincidence. You're in love with her."

My stomach burned. "God, Mateo. No. She loves you."

"You kissed her, that night. Everyone saw it."

For a second I thought he was referring to what happened in the Porsche. Then I realized he was talking about the kiss in his basement—a moment so laughable it embarrassed me. "I was high out of my mind," I said. "And to be fair, she kissed you next."

"You two stole the car, even when I told you not to," Mateo continued. "That was a betrayal. I can't just let it slide."

He paused for a second, seemingly losing his train of thought, and I seized my chance.

"I know about your drug addiction." I announced it before I could stop myself. "I know you're in debt to the Pig Patrol. You're high right now, aren't you? No wonder Juneau's so worried about you."

A brand-new cruelty had overtaken me. I remembered what Juneau had said when revealing Mateo's secret: *It humiliates him.*

"She told you about that?" Mateo sounded stunned.

"I—"

"Of course she did," said Mateo. "You can't trust these white girls, Maya. I swear they're so careless with us. She'll want me on the football field, or in public, but I'm not worth her actual respect. Of course she told you my personal shit."

His words took me aback. The way he warned me about white girls, it was almost like he was looking out for me. He might be a football player, Juneau's boyfriend, but he was a brown man, and that made him vulnerable. "Has she told you what happened with Laila?" Mateo said.

"What does Laila have to do with anything?"

Yesterday Juneau told me Laila was her crush, nothing more. But hearing Mateo's question, doubt crept into my chest. Had something actually happened between them?

Mateo chuckled. "I don't even know where to begin with Laila. Ask Juneau. I dare you to."

"I will," I said, trying to sound cold.

Mateo continued like he hadn't heard. "I've known Juneau for a long time. And I should warn you, she uses and discards people. Especially people like us. You saw what she did in Harvey's office today, how she handled us both."

There it was again: that supposed solidarity between us, even though I didn't know what he wanted from me.

When I didn't respond, he continued, "She uses sex to get favors or secrets. She gets something from everyone. But I can't imagine what she wants from you."

"Why are you telling me this?" I said at last.

"Because if you're sleeping with Juneau, you deserve to know all of her," Mateo said. "Juneau isn't just this weed-smoking white girl. She has a dark side, too. Eventually you'll end up on it."

By now his voice definitely sounded slurred. I hung up because I knew he was too stoned to care. Still, I'd learned a lot from him, perhaps more than Juneau would have wanted.

chapter 20

After Dr. Harvey's call, Amma was beside herself with rage. "You promised me no more secrets," she said at dinner. Even before he called, she'd been tenser than usual. It had been going on for weeks, ever since Rajendra reached Orlando, his presence like an invisible third member in our home. "And now you're getting detention for truancy?"

"I'm really sorry," I said, but Amma slammed a crumpled paper on the table—my failing math test, fished out of the trash. My heart sank. The truth was leaking everywhere, damning and messy. How much longer could I conceal the ways my life was falling apart?

"Your grades are slipping," Amma said. "Why did you skip school with Juneau in the first place? You used to excel at school."

"Are you going through my garbage now?" I demanded. "What happened to trust?"

"Maya, *enough*." The last word came out desperate, like she was trying to reclaim the version of me she knew. "How can I trust you? All these horrible crimes going on at your school, with vandalism and stolen cars—you know, the principal is concerned about you. He seemed to think you were involved somehow. He asked me what I thought."

Fear surged in me. Dr. Harvey knew he could get to me through my mother. Already he'd gotten between the Pugilists. "What did you tell him?" I said.

"I said you wouldn't do such a thing," said Amma. "Of course I said that! But you're terrifying me, Maya. I never dreamed I'd be getting phone calls about you. I really don't know what to do."

I felt the resentment piled up between us, sharp and uncrossable as a wall. I'd felt it building for years. I couldn't pinpoint the exact moment everything had changed—maybe one day Amma came home too late, or I'd said something too harsh, or she'd fallen in love with the wrong man. Either way, we'd grown apart.

"Clearly something isn't working here," Amma said at last. "So I'm implementing some changes. First, I'm officially forbidding you from seeing Juneau. From now on, you'll keep your distance."

"Are you serious?" I stared at her, but Amma didn't relent. "Amma, you can't stop me from seeing Juneau. She's my friend."

"She's a bad influence," Amma said firmly. "She made you skip school, and your principal thinks she's leading you on a dangerous path."

"He doesn't know anything about Juneau," I said vehemently. "And neither do you."

Amma ignored me. "Also," she said. "I've invited your father over for dinner next week. He'll be here next Friday, and I expect you to be on your best behavior."

"You didn't even ask me if I wanted him to come," I said.

She buried her face in her hands. Had she always been this weary? "Honestly, Maya?" Amma said. "I can't do this alone. I don't know how to talk to you anymore. I think having Rajendra back might help work things out for both of us."

I stared at the table. I suddenly couldn't eat, because my stomach felt heavy with grief. I hated the idea that my mother was too tired to handle me alone.

"Well," I said. My voice came out rusty. "I'll make things easy for you, then. I'm going to bed." And then, because I was grounded and had nowhere else to go, I fell asleep with rage churning in my head.

When I saw Juneau in the art studio the next morning, she was standoffish. She worked brusquely at her paintings, like she was trying not to be as good as she could be. Maybe I was the only one who noticed, though, because her painting was still excellent. She couldn't help it.

"What's wrong?" I whispered.

She said nothing, and nerves unspooled in my stomach. There was a real art to scaring people with your silence.

"Juneau, did I do something?"

"Not you," said Juneau. "Mateo. He broke up with me."

A span of reactions shuffled through me—shock, an awful glimmer of satisfaction—before the biggest problem hit me. My heart started to pound.

"Fuck. Because of the car? Is he planning on going to Harvey?"

"That's not why," said Juneau, and then she burst in an angry whisper, like she'd been holding it all in. "He accused me of cheating on him with you. He knew about me and Laila. It's all ridiculous, but—"

A deep hole opened in the center of my stomach.

"You told me that you and Laila never did anything," I muttered back. I'd nearly memorized our conversation in the museum.

"I lied," Juneau admitted. "Laila's old history anyway. I just wanna know how Mateo found out."

"Found out what?" I said. "That you're gay?"

Juneau gripped her paintbrush. "I told you I don't believe in labels." She had returned again: the scary-quiet Juneau.

"Who else knows, then?" I asked, but the final bell rang, cutting off Juneau's response. Patricia rushed in, nearly late. In one fluid motion, Juneau rose to her feet.

"Just you and Pat," she answered coldly.

After Amma's endless breakups, I'd developed a sixth sense for conflict. Or maybe I'd finally become a seismologist of Juneau's mood, could sense the tremors before they came. I planted myself in front of her.

"Don't fight here," I said, grabbing her arm. "Juneau, come on..."

"Outside, then." Juneau glared at Patricia. After class she brought us outside the studio. "What did you say to him?" she demanded of Pat. "Pat, I swear—"

"I heard Mateo dumped you." Patricia looked bored. I wondered how it felt to be Juneau's best friend, her equal. To manage her rage instead of bowing to it.

"He knew about me and Laila," Juneau said, pronouncing the name like an accusation. "You're the only person who knew about her. He accused me of being, you know—"

"Gay," I finished, and Juneau flinched. "Mateo said that he couldn't trust me, and he wanted to know all these things about my past. He has theories about me and Maya—"

"You and *Maya*?" said Pat, to my embarrassment.

"We're not a thing," Juneau and I said at the exact same time. My embarrassment multiplied.

"Hold up." Pat raised her hands. "You think *I* outed you to Mateo?"

"Who else?" said Juneau. She jabbed a paint-stained finger at Pat. "Is it because of the car, or—"

"Of course I didn't!" Patricia said.

"Then how'd he find out?" Juneau said.

Pat sighed. "Honestly? We all knew, Juneau," she said. "It was so obvious, even back then, what was happening between you and Laila. You couldn't hide it. You didn't have to. Mateo shouldn't have accused you of cheating just because of your sexuality. But why are you so afraid for people to know that you're—"

"Gay?" I supplied for the third time, and Juneau actually snarled; she looked completely unmoored. *She has a dark side*, Mateo had said, and he'd been right. I saw it at last, and I couldn't unsee it.

"Because it's nobody's business," Juneau snapped. "All of you people, always trying to pin me down like a goddamn butterfly—" She flapped her arms like wings.

"Okay, enough," interrupted Pat. "You're not the victim here, Juneau. You fucked him over first when you stole the

239

Porsche. We didn't agree to it ahead of time, and now all of us are in danger."

I had to hand it to Pat. In the face of Juneau's fury, she held her ground. As a novice in that regard, I admired the work of a master.

Juneau scoffed. "You're taking Mateo's side?"

"Yes, I am. You've been reckless," said Pat. "And if anyone calls you out—even your friends—you act out. I'm tired of it."

I thought about Juneau, how she demanded our allegiance, gathering our secrets while showing nobody her own. That was how she liked herself: holding all the cards. Guiding our lives. The moment the facade cracked, she panicked.

Juneau laughed, but for once the sound didn't fill me with warmth. "Patricia—"

"No, I'm talking," said Pat. "You suck up all the oxygen in the room. You put all of us at risk. You keep secrets. And you expect us to follow whatever you say. No questions asked, right?"

I realized suddenly that Pat was right. Juneau had gotten me high, claimed my first kiss, coaxed me into coming out, and collected my secrets, but I barely knew hers. How many times would she bulldoze me—how many times would I let her?

For a moment Juneau didn't say anything. I couldn't fathom what she was thinking. I looked away, afraid to anger her with my attention.

When she finally spoke, her voice was quiet.

"I thought you all wanted a mystery," she said. "You all want me to be your leader, or your love interest, or both. And I've been delivering. What more do you want from me?"

She was monologuing now. I'd never seen Juneau get

defensive. And yet, her words gave me a deep, sticky guilt. Wasn't that precisely what Mateo and I wanted from her?

"I've been putting myself on the line for you all. I've been holding it down, giving you all a community, a sense of purpose," said Juneau. "I thought we all believed in the same things. That's why I brought the Pugilists together—"

"No, Laila did that. And then we did it together," snapped Pat. "You're not her. You're too lost in your white savior complex to realize you're treating us like shit."

She'd touched a nerve. "Is that really what you think?" Juneau said.

Yes, I thought.

And perhaps Juneau, as usual, could read my thoughts, because she turned to me. "Maya," she said. "Be honest. Do you agree with Pat?"

"Don't drag Maya into this," said Pat, sparing me. Her voice was calm, but each word hit like a punch. "We're not your pet projects, Juneau. Mateo isn't your drug-addicted damsel in distress. I'm not just your Black sidekick. And Maya isn't just your—"

I didn't want her to finish that sentence. "Stop, please," I said. "Let's not fight. We have bigger problems right now."

They both stared at me, and I pressed on.

"Juneau, you're being an asshole," I said, which was the strongest word I could muster. "And Pat, Juneau's just been dumped, which is why she's lashing out. Can you please forgive each other?"

Pat looked like she'd rather do anything else in the world. I couldn't escape her disappointment. She'd wanted me to stand up for myself, starting the moment Juneau suggested we steal a car. And more than anything, I wanted to. I wanted to shake Juneau, to shout: *Why are you so self-centered?* And, *Why can't you say the word* gay?

"You're right. I fucked up," Juneau said at last. She looked so tired, I could see the individual creases under her eyes, as if drawn with a ballpoint pen. "Pat, I don't know what came over me. You both are the most important people in my life. I'm really sorry."

One day, maybe, I'd learn not to permit people to tell me those words: *I'm sorry.* Or at least I'd pay attention when they did. But that day, I felt like something had opened between Juneau and me. Her facade had cracked, and I might never see her the same way again.

After school, Pat pulled me aside. "We need to debrief," she said.

"I have detention," I reminded her.

"It'll be quick," she promised, so I followed her to her car.

"I don't know what happened this morning," I said. "But I'm really sorry. For stealing the car, for all of it." I wasn't sure if I was apologizing for myself or Juneau.

Pat sighed. She had a soldered air about her, like someone doomed to roll a boulder for all eternity.

"It's not just about the car," said Pat. "This moment is two years overdue. Juneau still hasn't come to terms with Laila, and she's been taking it out on her friends."

"Laila?" I couldn't keep the resentment out of my voice. "I keep hearing about her. Everything except what actually happened."

Pat rubbed her eyebrow stud. "That's Juneau's story to share," she said. "But I'll tell you the ending: Laila disappeared right after graduation. She didn't tell anyone, didn't say good-bye. One minute she was scheming with us, and the next she was gone. She totally abandoned us. All the Pugilists were shocked, but it really fucked with Juneau."

It took me a moment to process.

"You're saying that Juneau Zale got her heart broken by a girl," I said. "And that's why she's . . . I don't know. Controlling? Careless? Manipulative?"

"It's definitely not an excuse," said Pat. "Or the full picture. I'm sure you also know, by now, about her family. They're horrible. She's extremely privileged, but also repressed at home. I think she escapes by rebelling with the Pugilists. She pours her frustrations into the missions, but she gets reckless."

I remembered Juneau's house: the wide staircase, the mission trip pictures. At first I'd resented her for it—how she could raise hell with the Pugilists one night, return home comfortably the next. But now I felt sympathy. Being rich didn't mean your home life was perfect.

"Everything is a facade," I said, quoting her art portfolio.

"We both care for Juneau," Pat said at last. "But she can be toxic to the people who care for her. Your love can't fix her, Maya."

"I don't love her," I said a little sharply.

Pat's eyes were sympathetic. "I don't want to make assumptions," she said. "And I can't speak for the other Pugilists. But I want you to know, whatever your sexuality is, you're safe with me."

I held Pat's gaze. Had it really only been months ago that

Pat, Juneau, and I met in the art studio, flipping through each other's sketchbooks? We'd run our fingers across the drawings, complimenting them grandly. *This will be a masterpiece,* I'd announced. *I can already see it in a gallery.*

"Thanks, Pat," I said. "But you don't have to worry about me." I climbed out of her car, Juneau's name still burning on my tongue.

chapter 21

Juneau offered to drive me home after detention. "We'll take the long way," she announced, swerving onto an unpaved road I'd never traveled in my life.

"What are you thinking about?" Juneau poked my arm.

I looked at the road ahead, how it seemed to veer and disappear beneath the car. *You*, I thought. *It's always you.*

"Is Mateo still pissed at you?" I asked. I'd picked up another trait of Juneau's: answering questions with questions. A transformation so subtle I'd barely realized.

"He's still angry about the car theft," Juneau admitted. "And that's his right. But I told him that my sexuality's not his concern. Long story short, he's leaving the Pugilists."

She seemed calmer, but I was still nervous. "He's not going to turn us in, right?"

"We have our pact, and he's an original Pugilist," said Juneau. "We'll always protect one another."

"So you're finished with him?" I asked. "That's it?"

"Mateo's the first man I loved." Juneau shrugged. "I doubt we'll ever be finished."

We drove for miles but I didn't count them, passing house after house. I felt sorry for everyone stuck within those boring walls.

"Everything's unrecognizable," I said at last.

Juneau looked over, and I sketched the details of her face. For years I'd seen her from afar, and only in glimpses. Now she was familiar from every angle.

"The Pugilists are falling apart," I explained. "I lost all my friends. Rajendra's coming home. There's nobody left on my side—"

"You have me," said Juneau.

"I barely know you," I said.

"What do you want to know, then?"

"Laila," I said. "What happened with her?"

"Laila. Of course." Juneau sighed. "Where do I even begin?"

Her voice softened. For a moment I'd had the power, but now we slipped back into our roles: Juneau talking, me listening. Juneau in the driver's seat, me in the passenger's. The natural order of our universe.

"Laila was a once-in-a-lifetime person," said Juneau. "She took us under her wing: me, Mateo, and Pat. She had the idea for this secret group, the Pugilists, and we followed without question. She was this gutsy brown lesbian in the middle of Citrus freakin' Grove. Can you imagine?"

Our school library had archives of yearbooks, and earlier

I'd looked up Laila Afzar. She'd graduated the summer before my freshman year, so our paths never crossed. But I understood why I reminded people of her. We both were dark-eyed brown girls, stronger than we looked.

"She sounds wonderful," I said. Then I hesitated. "Wait. You're using the past tense. Is she—"

"She's not dead," said Juneau quickly. "Sorry. Some people just live better in past tense, you know?"

That statement was deranged, but coming from Juneau it made perfect sense.

"At first it wasn't a relationship," Juneau continued. "I was surprised she even liked me. Back then, you wouldn't have pinned me as a Pugilist. I fucked awful guys like Squash. I was a rich white girl with too much rage for her own good. But Laila knew that rage, too. She helped me shape it."

"That's why you loved her?"

"Laila had this righteous desire to transform Citrus Grove," Juneau said. "She brought us all into her vision. I'd never felt that way about the world before—or another girl. But we went for it."

"It was the kind of love that made you believe that *humans are worthy of the art we make*," I said, and Juneau smiled. It fazed neither of us that I'd memorized her words.

"It was," she agreed. "But we knew our parents wouldn't allow it. Not to mention, you know, our greater society. Fucking Citrus Grove. This absolute wasteland."

She didn't need to say more. I understood. It felt terrifying to occupy a space nobody had before, acutely visible and invisible at once. In our school of four thousand students, there were no openly gay girls. When did we collectively agree to this silence?

"But you tried anyway," I said. "She was your girlfriend."

"Not publicly," said Juneau. "My parents would've been furious, and Laila thought her family might kick her out. So we kept it a secret. And it was good until she moved away."

"Pat told me that part," I admitted. "How Laila abandoned the Pugilists."

"It was maybe the worst heartbreak I've ever felt," said Juneau.

The dashboard beeped—we were almost out of gas. I looked at the empty road, knowing there wouldn't be another gas station for miles. But Juneau kept driving.

"I have another question," I said. "If you've had real love with a girl, then why bother with all the shitty guys? They use you, hurt you. All they want is sex."

I wished I'd phrased the question better. I sounded naive— or worse, resentful. My virginity had never been more obvious.

"Guys aren't the only ones who want sex. I can use them, too," Juneau said. "Besides, nobody really wants to love me. They just want to hate me, discuss me, or fuck me. I'm well aware."

I realized we never had these conversations face-to-face. She was usually behind the wheel, and I was next to her. Or I was high as hell, and she'd gotten me there, my body melting into hers. Either way, she never looked me in the eye.

"Not everyone," I said. "There are people who care about you, Juneau. You can let us in."

I wanted to reassure her but didn't know how. "When you came out to me at the museum, it meant everything to me," I said. "You made me feel less alone. I never loved you more than I did that afternoon." I didn't mean to say *love*, but it slipped out.

"You're special, Maya." Juneau sighed. "No wonder Mateo thought I was sleeping with you."

"Is that so crazy for him to think?" My heart wouldn't stop pounding.

Juneau smiled. "Maybe not," she said. "It's not like the possibility never crossed my mind. Or yours, I believe." In the rearview mirror our eyes finally met, and something splintered in my chest. "Am I wrong?"

I became acutely aware of all the things between us: my thigh touched my seat, which touched the cup holder against her seat, where her legs rested, long and tanned. I was grateful for the physical barriers—not because I disliked it when we touched. Because I wanted it too much, without permission.

"No," I said. It came out breathless. "Why didn't you go for it?" I couldn't believe my own daring. "There were so many moments…"

Juneau shrugged. "Good question," she said. "I knew we were attracted to each other, that much was obvious. I guess I didn't want to complicate things."

"Complicate things?" I shook my head. "Juneau, since when were you afraid of complications?"

"Fine." Juneau laughed. "Honestly? You're so *good*, Maya, and I'm just not. I thought I'd never get so lucky."

My breath caught in my throat. I wasn't sure I'd heard her right, but then she smiled at me. She was Juneau Zale, after all: an enigma and a challenge to the end. She looked unreadable and vulnerable all at once. She'd shown me her cards and simultaneously disarmed me.

"That's only because you never pushed your luck," I said. I felt it strongly: the blind leap, sink-or-swim courage my mother instilled in me. "It's okay if it's too soon after Mateo, or if you don't want me like that," I said. "But I've liked you since the moment I met you."

I gathered the spikes and aches within me. "I don't know what any of this is supposed to feel like, or how to express it," I said. "But if you feel the same way, then I'm not looking back."

Before my courage or the engine gave out, I took her hand. She didn't pull back.

"Are you sure?" Juneau said, and now she sounded a little breathless, too. "Maya, do you want to—"

"Yes," I said, and she squeezed her fingers around mine. A spark rippled through me, and Juneau stepped on the gas.

We swerved toward the first exit we saw, ending up in a field filled with tiny yellow flowers. Juneau parked and pulled me into the back seat filled with packing peanuts, and then she kissed me with everything I'd come to associate with her art: fierceness, color, fire.

"You are making me crazy," she whispered between kisses so deep I couldn't tell who was breathing for whom. "You've been making me crazy for weeks, did you know that?"

Her grasp was firm but painterly, her touch sending sugar rushes through my body. I thought: *This is what it's like to be sculpted.* To be hewn from rock and molded into something beautiful, something from the mind of Juneau Zale.

Juneau started to remove her shirt, and I tensed. Juneau stopped. "Is everything okay?"

"Better than okay," I whispered. "But I don't know how to... I haven't..." I wilted.

Juneau's eyes softened. "Really?" she said. "Not even with Theo?"

I blushed. "No," I said. "I'm sorry," I added, though I didn't know why.

"No apologies," Juneau said. "We'll take it slow. We don't have to do anything unless you're ready for it."

"Are you sure? Juneau, if you wanted—"

Juneau silenced me with a kiss. "We have a long road ahead of us, Maya," she whispered. "And I intend to enjoy the journey." She touched my hair, and I let myself dissolve into her.

In the middle of nowhere, in the back seat of her car, was nothing like I'd imagined things would start. But it was exactly how she'd said it would feel: like falling through midair.

Afterward, we sat on top of her car. It was hot as a stovetop, but I didn't mind.

"It goes without saying," said Juneau, "that we're not telling anybody about this."

I'd been waiting for her to mention this. "I know," I said.

"I just want everything to be clear from the start," Juneau said. "This won't be a relationship. We're not going on dates or kissing in public, none of that. I want this to be easy and safe."

When I said nothing, she pulled me closer, so I felt the knock of our hips. "Maya," she said. It was almost unfair, the effect she had on me. Every time she said my name, I felt like a tongue was sliding down my neck. "You understand why, don't you?"

I remembered the first time we met as children, how she entered my life like a thunderbolt. Even then I was in love with her. I'd spent a lifetime following her adventures until one day she invited me along—an act of kindness that was never anything but dazzling to me. She chose me, trusted me, and now, at last, was kissing me. How greedy would I be to ask for more?

I nodded, and Juneau smiled. "Okay, good. Because I don't want to fuck this up."

It's okay, I thought. In moments like these, removed from Citrus Grove, I could have her alone, and that could be enough. Here in the flowers, we could feel like the last inhabitants of an empty planet. Like there was nothing left between the sun and us.

chapter 22

For the next week, I was a woman reborn. It felt like all my life until now had been backstory, a series of events meant only to guide me to Juneau. There was a time when I'd look for her whenever I entered a room. Now I didn't need to search. Across crowded hallways our eyes always met, she'd give me a look, and that was all it took. I'd stop everything and follow her—behind the gym, to her car, once even to the lightbox above the theater. Wherever we could be alone. I still wasn't talking to Anya, Silva, or Ife, and in that black hole, Juneau sucked me in. She didn't have many friends left, either, and maybe that's why I let her swallow me.

At home, however, Amma was domesticating aggressively, preparing for Rajendra's visit. She made me scrub every inch of the house, even replant the flowers on our doorstep.

"Amma, it's just dinner. I doubt Rajendra will care if our peonies are thriving."

She glared at me. "We need to make a good impression. On that note, you shouldn't mention that you're in detention all month, either."

"You win," I said, resigning myself to the flowers.

On Friday, Amma summoned me to the kitchen, where she'd balanced four hot pans on the stove; steam billowed through the vent. "Will you finish this sambar, please? It still needs seasoning."

I opened the pantry to confront her spice collection, all stored in repurposed salsa jars. I couldn't remember the last time Amma cooked—no wonder she looked frantic.

"How much should I add?" I said.

"Use your judgment. Don't ask stupid questions."

I carefully sprinkled in the proper spices, and Amma clucked her tongue. "Have your taste buds gone American?" she said. She stuck her entire fist into the jar—no measuring spoons in our kitchen.

"I thought dinner was going to be simple," I said. "It smells like a whole Indian restaurant in here." Already I counted three subzis, sizzling vadas, and a dozen cloud-soft idlis.

"I got a little carried away," Amma admitted. "But Rajendra mustn't think his daughter goes hungry in America."

I spent the day helping Amma cook and clean until the doorbell rang. Amma answered it and Rajendra's voice filled the house.

"You look beautiful as ever," I heard him say in his rhythmic rumble.

And then Amma called, "Maya, your father's here!" so I had no choice but to greet him.

Rajendra Krishnan strode into the living room, a painting come to life. He stopped a pace behind Amma, his face adopting the same austere expression as in *The Tempest*. Amma might've interpreted this as shyness, but he and I knew what he really felt: shame.

Amma was uncharacteristically upbeat as she introduced us. "Rajendra, she's been very excited to meet you."

"Mayavati," he said gravely.

"I go by Maya," I said. "Welcome to our home."

Rajendra turned to Amma, who'd been watching nervously. "Can I have a moment alone with her, Suj?" he asked.

Suj? I thought, annoyed by his familiarity.

Amma smiled. "Take all the time you need. I'll go finish up dinner," she said, even though we'd wrapped up hours ago. It was a small lie, but I resented her efforts to make him comfortable.

At first Rajendra didn't speak. He looked up at the walls, covered in my paintings. "These are yours?" he said. Then he answered his own question. "Of course they are. They're magnificent."

"Thank you."

The sound of my voice seemed to awaken him, because Rajendra turned pleadingly to me. "I understand that you're very angry at me, Maya. But is there any way you could give me another chance?"

"N—I could," I said, changing my answer midway. Maybe I'm weak, because I have a hard time being cruel to people's faces. "I've been reading your messages. I know you're sorry. I just needed time."

Rajendra's expression broke into relief. "I'm glad to hear

that. Because you deserve an explanation." He took a deep breath. "Mayavati—*Maya*, that is. I'm so sorry for what I said in the museum. Your friend's question caught me unaware, and I panicked. I was so deeply ashamed."

"Ashamed of me?" I said.

Rajendra flinched. "Of course not," he said. "Maya, I'm so proud of you. Every time your mother called me or sent me your artwork, I felt like a piece of my heart was flowering. I could never be ashamed of you."

I now understood why Amma had called him charming. When Rajendra praised me, something inside me softened. But I wasn't gullible. I stood firm.

"Then why were you ashamed?"

"Chellam, I was ashamed of myself," said Rajendra. "Look at you both. Your mother is the greatest beauty I've ever seen. And you're the greatest beauty I've ever created. How could I let you both go?" He touched his heart. "Please, Maya."

Looking at Rajendra, I experienced a strange sensation: power. I realized that I'd never had a man approach me like this, offer his regrets and wait for my judgment. Rajendra looked truly apologetic, scrunching himself into this unfamiliar living room, hoping for my kindness.

I wasn't required to forgive him—Juneau, for one, would never. But Rajendra was staying for dinner, and Amma would kill me if I didn't behave, or at least pretend to.

"It's whatever," I said. "We can try to start over."

I led him to the kitchen, where Amma had arranged the food. We'd awkwardly unfolded an extra chair—our tiny table usually only sat two. At first nobody said much: We were too busy putting food on our plates, our arms crisscrossing gracelessly.

Soon Rajendra started complimenting Amma's cooking, which was exactly what she'd been hoping for. She watched expectantly as he took a bite of each dish. I wished she would wipe the hostess smile off her face.

"I've been eating bland American food for so many days, I've gotten too thin for my clothes," he announced. "Thanks for cooking, Suj."

I still couldn't believe he was calling her that, *Suj*. I should've expected that my mother had nicknames I didn't know about. She had an entire life of her own, with people who knew her by names other than Amma or Sujatha Aunty or Nurse Krishnan.

Amma blushed deep. "It took no time at all," she said: another tiny lie.

I stared as Amma and Rajendra lost themselves in stories of the past. The way they talked, you wouldn't guess they'd split up a decade ago—it was more like I'd intruded on their date. I noticed how they anticipated each other's needs, remembered details, finished each other's sentences.

At last Rajendra turned his attention to me.

"So, Mayavati," he said. "What got you so interested in art?"

I'd answered many versions of this question before, asked by men who were actually interested in Amma but had to pretend to care about me. It struck me as an extremely thoughtless question, akin to *What got you so interested in breathing?* But coming from Rajendra, the question bothered me less. Maybe it was because he was an artist, too.

"I guess it's always been a part of me," I said, inadvertently sitting upright, as though I were in an interview. "Painting is how I process my life here in Citrus Grove."

"I've always thought she got it from you," said Amma, and Rajendra looked pleased. He kept asking me questions about my art, not in the perfunctory tone of a bored adult, but earnestly, as if I was a serious artist. He asked me all about my opinions on art, my portrait subjects, my inspirations.

"Have you been officially trained?" he asked.

"Not really," I said, suddenly self-conscious. "I'm self-taught. I tried attending a class once, but it felt too exclusive, so I quit. And now I'm in my school's advanced studio. Though sometimes it still feels like I don't belong."

Rajendra leaned forward at this comment. "Why do you say that?"

"I don't know," I admitted. Rarely had adults taken such an interest in my opinions, so I felt unprepared to defend my statements. "It feels like a lot of posturing, living up to somebody else's ideal of what a great artist looks like. I just want to paint my own world. I wasn't really asking for white people to give my work meaning."

The last sentence slipped out a little too sharp, and I realized I'd spoken as if I were with the Pugilists. I bit my lip, waiting for my parents' response. I saw Amma frown—she hated when I spoke out of place. But Rajendra nodded solemnly.

"I understand completely," he said. "The whiteness of the art world—it's stifling. You should see how some of these Western critics review my art. They'll call it *exotic* or *otherworldly*. Singling out everything that makes it different instead of what makes it unique."

"Wow," I said. "That's so...diminishing."

Rajendra smiled at me. "I'm impressed to see that you've chosen to focus on your own world in your art. Painting your culture, what feels natural to you. It's so easy to succumb to the pressure, to become someone you're not."

"I try my best," I said, unsure how else to respond. And yet I felt strangely seen. I wondered if Rajendra and I were bonding. He asked me more questions about my favorite artists, and I told him about the Amrita Sher-Gil poster in my bedroom, my love for Jamini Roy. At the mention of the Indian artists, his eyes lit up.

"Oh, you must come to paint in India," he said. "The painters you'd meet, the art stretching back centuries..." He launched into a passionate reverie about his travels across the subcontinent, the ashrams where he'd painted in moments of dizzying inspiration. Amma smiled, and who could blame her? When he spoke of art, she remembered all the reasons she loved him. But all I could hear were the reasons he'd left us. I felt myself growing resentful again, like I was on the losing end of a competition.

Eventually Amma brought out dessert: kulfi. As the dinner wound down, I started to get the sense that Rajendra was brimming with something. I watched him poke at his dessert. Then he set down his spoon.

"I was waiting for the right moment to say this," Rajendra said. "There's something I must share."

Amma looked up eagerly. This seemed to bolster Rajendra: He smiled. "So my lecture series was quite successful at the Orlando Museum of Art," he said. "They weren't expecting such interest in Indian art."

"That's wonderful news," Amma said.

"That's not all," Rajendra said. "They've made me an offer. They'd like me to stay on as their artist-in-residence for the rest of the year."

Amma simply stared at him. When neither of us said anything, Rajendra delivered the punch line: "They're ready to sponsor my visa."

His words seemed to puncture the air. I was the first to recover.

"You're joking," I said.

But before I could continue, Amma said softly, "After all these years?"

"I know it's unexpected," said Rajendra. "But yes, assuming a visa extension, we could work to reunite our family. If, of course, that's what you want."

My heartbeat pulsed in my ears. As a child, I'd dreamed of this moment: the precise instant when my father would appear at our kitchen table, promising to stay. But now I was older, less naive.

"Raj," said Amma, still looking tender. "What are you saying? This is everything we dreamed of. Of course I want that—"

"Well, I don't," I said, shocking everyone. "It's too late."

Both my parents stared at me. I flushed but held my ground. The evening had started with promise, but now years of rage returned to me. Empty Father's Days, sparsely attended parent-teacher conferences. Amma's explaining my abandonment over burned tacos. The smack of humiliation in the museum. It was all too much to handle.

"Maya," said Amma warningly. To Rajendra, she added, "She's going through a difficult phase right now. She doesn't mean that."

The betrayal stung. "Excuse me," I said. "But you can't let him just waltz back into our lives. Amma, you said it yourself: He made his choice when he stayed in India."

Rajendra's face darkened. "Is this how you let her speak to you?" he asked Amma in Tamil. He assumed I wouldn't understand. He was wrong.

Amma looked startled by the question. I stood up.

"You haven't been here, so maybe you wouldn't understand," I said. "But we have a life on our own. We don't need you."

I turned to Amma, but she wouldn't look at me. She was staring at the food she'd spent hours preparing. My heart sank, knowing I'd lost her.

"You know what? He's all yours," I told Amma. And then, before either of my parents could do it, I sent myself to my room.

chapter 23

When I went to the kitchen the next morning, Rajendra was setting up an easel. The kitchen table was covered in paints, plus a half-eaten bowl of cereal. On the canvas, he'd sketched a Renaissance-style portrait of me and Amma, our hair intertwined. He'd barely started painting, but it already looked majestic.

"What are you doing here?" I said.

Rajendra turned, surprised. "I'm eating breakfast," he said. "Here they say it's the most important meal of the day."

"No, *that*." I glared at his makeshift art studio.

"Your mother," he said, "has graciously invited me to stay here and work for a while."

"You *slept* here last night?"

We didn't have a spare bed, which meant he'd slept with

Amma. It was bad enough to know your parents were sleeping together, even worse when they'd divorced.

"Sujatha didn't want me sleeping at the rental anymore. Not when I had family around," Rajendra said; I silently cursed Indian hospitality. "Anyway, I rose early. I was feeling inspired. I thought I would paint you a portrait to show my gratitude."

Only the knowledge that his paintings sold for thousands of dollars kept me from retorting. I ate cereal, aware of his intense gaze. I couldn't tell if he was watching me as a caring father or as an artist observing his subject. It was hard to keep those separate.

"I'm sorry about last night," he said eventually. "I understand you have no reason to like me. But I hope, with time, you'll grow to trust me." He had one of those earnest, trustworthy voices, like the narrator of a movie.

I looked at his canvas. He'd aged me up, so Amma and I looked like sisters. I'd never seen a real painter at work before. I couldn't help myself: I wanted to watch him paint.

Just then, Amma returned from work. She nearly tripped over Rajendra's shoes, piled unexpectedly by the doorway. Seeing us sitting together, I saw her puff up with hope.

"Were you two having breakfast?" she said.

Now that she was here, Rajendra was no longer my responsibility. I clattered my dishes into the sink. "Yeah, but I'm late for school. See you later," I called, even though it was Saturday.

Right before the door closed, I saw Amma hug Rajendra, and I heard a snatch of their conversation: "You ate together?" Amma said. "Am I dreaming?"

"Yes, we did," Rajendra said. I prayed to God they weren't

going to have sex. "Things are changing in the Krishnan household. Just you wait and see."

———

It normally wasn't my business whom my mother was falling for, but picking my father seemed to cross the line. Our house grew crowded with his enormous presence—his art supplies, his booming voice, his pounding footsteps. Pre-Rajendra, Amma and I never ate dinner together, because she had to leave early for work. Now we ate together as a family, at 4:30 p.m., like old white people.

At dinner, Rajendra was full of questions about my art, classes, friends. I was used to Amma's boyfriends trying to get to know me. The only difference was that I shared half of Rajendra's DNA. So the questions carried a heavy veneer of parental concern, like he was playacting the role of my father.

"What was the name of that girl with you at the museum?" he asked. "The blonde one."

"You mean Juneau?"

"Right," said Rajendra. "She seemed to be quite protective of you."

Amma's expression soured. I calculated how to steer the conversation away from Juneau, whom Amma still considered a terrible influence.

"I've seen her driving you home all week," continued Rajendra, failing to read the room. "When I'm painting in the kitchen, I see you through the window."

I wished he hadn't said that. My heart pounded. I'd been forbidden from hanging out with Juneau. Amma glared at me.

"I thought Silva was driving you home," she said.

"Sometimes Silva has orchestra practice," I lied quickly. "Juneau's just helping me out."

Amma shook her head. "I swear to God—"

"I didn't mean to cause a confrontation," said Rajendra, looking alarmed. "I just wanted to make conversation."

"Yeah, well." I eyed Amma, daring her to criticize me. "We don't always get what we want."

"Maya!" said Amma, momentarily forgetting Juneau. "Apologize to your father at once!"

The dinner ended like most—in tense silence. Amma and I were angry, and Rajendra watched us both carefully, like we were a puzzle he hadn't quite solved.

Amma could scold me all she wanted, but she couldn't actually stop me from seeing Juneau. In a sad way, hiding from Amma was easy because we were also hiding from the rest of the world. Juneau had made it clear we could never hold hands in the hallway, kiss in public, go on dates to the movies. Those love stories didn't exist for girls like us.

Maybe I'm naive, but I'd always thought that when I loved someone, it would be so visible, like a ray of sun connecting us. But in reality, nobody noticed or cared. Walking through school, I'd sometimes get the urge to shake the nearest person, like: *Do you know that I get to kiss Juneau Zale?*

Still, when we were together, I forgot that I was Juneau's secret. She loved me, and that was a million times more important than public validation. I finally understood why Anya agreed to date Squash in secret. That feeling of belonging to another person—it was worth all the costs.

On Friday, instead of going to lunch, Juneau said she wanted to take me somewhere.

"Come on," she whispered to me in the hallway. The sound of her voice against my ear was enough to raise goose bumps on my arms. "I'm taking you to my happy place."

We snuck into the woods behind campus, ignoring the KEEP OUT signs.

Like the rest of Florida's wilderness, the woods were damp and slippery. With each footfall, tiny lizards scurried out from under twigs. "*This* is your happy place?" I asked Juneau. She walked a few feet ahead, graciously holding aside palm fronds so they wouldn't snap back into my face. "It's full of mosquitoes."

"Just wait," she said. "We're almost there. I swear it's incredible."

She pushed aside a bush, and as usual, she was right. In the middle of the trees, occupying a sun-filled clearing, stood the remains of a metal jungle gym. The sun hit the dome from above, turning the metal translucent. We climbed inside. In these woods—quiet except for the low drone of insects—I felt like the last survivor of an apocalypse. Time slithered slowly, a parallel universe where nobody else existed.

This was the perfect place, I realized, to disappear.

"Welcome to the Smoking Hole," Juneau said, lighting me a joint. "It's my favorite spot in Citrus Grove."

"Why didn't you take me here before?"

"Because I didn't want to spend all my surprises too soon," Juneau said. "And because I reserve these happy places for only the most special people."

I wondered, briefly, how many other people had inhabited the Smoking Hole with Juneau. As if reading my mind, she blew smoke in my face. "I'm talking about you, peach."

"Oh." I wondered if I could blame my reddened face on the sun. "I'm honored."

I opened my mouth to exhale smoke, but Juneau kissed me, trapping its musky scent between us. "That was the next surprise," she said.

"Very sneaky." She'd caught me off-guard, but now I leaned toward her, and with the extra courage supplied by the weed managed to slip my hand under her shirt. She seemed amused, holding the lit joint away from our bodies. I'd never initiated touching her before. I reached out hesitantly, gently, afraid I might upset her.

"I'm not made of china, Maya," Juneau murmured. "I won't break if you touch first."

My face burned. "I know that. I just don't have a lot of practice with this."

Juneau laughed aloud at that. "This isn't one of your AP classes. You're allowed to make mistakes."

"Am I making a mistake?" Now I was definitely embarrassed. I felt this way often around her, conscious of my inexperience.

Sensing my discomfort, Juneau relented. "No, you're doing great," she said. "Welcome to Intimacy 101. I will be your instructor. I'm guessing you're a visual learner." To my relief, she took the lead, and I leaned into her.

We whispered in each other's ears about all the countries we wanted to visit, all the places Juneau could kiss me. "There is so much waiting for us," Juneau promised.

"I hope so," I said. "I've only ever lived in two places in my life. Here and India."

"And you've never once thought about packing up and leaving?"

"I think that's more your style."

"If you could run away," Juneau said, "where would you go?"

"Why would I be running away?" I'd never seriously

considered it—except, I guess, for all the times I had. Plus, hadn't I spent the entire summer planning my grand escape to college, adulthood, freedom? Maybe I had an escape artist in me, too.

Juneau rolled her eyes. "Use your imagination. I don't know. A natural disaster, maybe."

"Oh." I considered. "Somewhere warm, obviously. Tropical. Why?"

She ignored me. "So your soulmate is on that tropical island. But everyone else is stuck on the mainland. All your friends and family. Would you come back for them?"

"That doesn't make sense. Why—?"

"I'm forbidding that word. It no longer exists. No more questions."

"This alternate universe feels dictatorial."

"I'm serious," Juneau said. "Would you come back?"

I didn't know how to answer. How typical of Juneau, to see life as a zero-sum game, so that even her thought experiments involved dramatic choices and sacrifice. Moments like these reminded me that we were not the same.

"So I'd have to choose between my soulmate and family?" I said. It occurred to me that my mother had made some version of this choice when she immigrated to America without Rajendra.

I wasn't opposed to the made-up island. I liked my private moments with Juneau, these small vacations from the real world. Things were easy right now, even if they couldn't stay that way forever. Already I was thinking of the next step: actual sex. I knew it was coming, and I wanted to be ready. But for now, I lay in the Smoking Hole with Juneau, letting everything sink in: her touch, swizzled-soft every time.

We returned to class a little high, and I ended up acing a Calculus test, which made me wonder if marijuana had unlocked some latent mathematic ability. I'd never been high at school before, but it was delightful, how relatable my classmates suddenly appeared to me. All these kids were fighting their parents, doing drugs, and hooking up—and I was finally part of the club.

After school, I walked home alone. I didn't ask Juneau for a ride, because Rajendra might see and tell Amma. Besides, it was almost Thanksgiving, and the cool air gave me the chance to clear my head before I started my research.

Inside my bedroom, I googled something I never had before: *lesbian sex.*

Just typing these words sent a little shiver up my spine. I'd previously tried reading about it in books, because I preferred lyric description over straight-up porn. I'd flipped straight to the sex scenes, hoping for clear descriptions, but they weren't good without context. So now I surrendered to Google.

I had to hand it to the lesbians of the Internet: I didn't think there were many of us, but they were vocally pornographic. Websites advertised informational articles, such as "10 Ways To Know She's Really Into You!" and "I Slept With a Straight Woman! Now What?" and "Ever Wondered About Sex Toys?"

If anyone caught me reading these, I'd be humiliated. Luckily I'd thought ahead, opening a separate browser with my science homework. At a moment's notice, I could become a conscientious student of chemistry. In truth, I was learning a new science altogether, one that involved tops and bottoms and two to three fingers and writing the alphabet with your tongue.

I almost wished I hadn't googled it in the first place, because with every question answered, a million new ones arose.

At some point it all became too much. I cleared my search history and stared at my reflection in the laptop's black screen. I expected to see some proof of sex on my face, lingering residue from what I'd just read. But my face looked soft and blameless as ever. Some girls managed to suggest sex just with their bodies—how had I missed out?

More than anything, I wished I could talk to Anya. She'd make me feel confident about sex, even excited. I had to admit it: I missed my friends. Without them, my life felt like the island Juneau described. I was overcome by loneliness.

chapter 24

Rajendra's portrait still wasn't finished. Each afternoon, a new detail emerged: a golden-hued hand, a sharp, dark eye. He'd painted Amma quickly, but it seemed like he couldn't pin me down. Over the week, he'd altered me constantly: widening my eyes, softening my cheeks, only to toughen me up again.

"I've been struggling with your face," he confessed on Monday.

"Really?" I said. "My face looks just like yours."

Rajendra was pensive. "Maybe you can figure out what I'm missing." To my surprise, he offered me his paintbrush. "Go ahead, give it a try."

"Are you sure?" I said. Rajendra Krishnan's paintings were world-famous; what if I made a mistake?

"Of course. Show me what you've got," said Rajendra. He offered me his stool but stood close behind, preparing to intervene in case of disaster. I wondered if this was how normal teenagers felt when they learned to drive from their fathers.

I initially stuck with the colors he'd already mixed, but then I added some hues of my own. Each time I paused to dip my brush, I sensed him surveying my work. Sometimes he'd make a small noise of affirmation.

I started to relax. I couldn't believe I was painting with my father. It actually did feel like Rajendra and I were getting along better lately. Our conversations grew less stunted. At dinners, I'd comb my days for interesting anecdotes, rack my brain for artists to mention—anything to provoke his interest.

But then Rajendra said it out of nowhere: "I'm proposing marriage to your mother this weekend."

My hand jerked, sending a sloppy streak through my eye.

"No, you're not," I said flatly.

"Your mother is struggling." Rajendra grabbed a paintbrush and started repairing my mistake. "She needs me, Maya. I'm hoping, for her sake, that you'll be supportive."

I didn't know what to say. I should've seen this coming, but it still hit like a punch.

"She doesn't need you," I said at last. "She has me."

We were both still looking at the portrait, and the gentleness of the art felt ironic. It was tough to be a painter when what you really wanted to wield was a sledgehammer.

"Is that true, Maya?" said Rajendra. "Does she know the truth about Juneau?"

"What are you talking about?" My voice shook.

"I saw you kissing Juneau in the car," Rajendra said quietly. "I was taking a walk around the neighborhood, and I saw you waiting at a stop sign. It was in broad daylight. Anybody could've seen."

My stomach squeezed. Juneau and I were careful in public, but sometimes we let our guard down in the car, when we thought we were alone.

"Did you tell Amma?" I said.

"No, I haven't," said Rajendra. "I wouldn't dream of burdening her further. You worry her sick, Maya."

"You don't know anything about me," I said. Guilt tangled inside me. I tried to focus on the painting, but my hand-eye coordination wasn't working properly.

"Trouble in school, your slipping grades, cutting class with Juneau," said Rajendra, rattling it off like he'd memorized the list. "She thinks you're acting out because of me. But that's not the case, is it? Something else is going on."

His voice remained neutral, like we were still discussing painting techniques. But I could hear the accusation underneath.

"What I'm doing with Juneau is nobody's concern," I said.

Rajendra surveyed the painting. My painted self smiled back at us, innocent and devious at once.

"Your mother's been very hard on herself," he said. "At first I tried to reassure her. I told her I was equally rebellious at your age. But now I think I understand the problem."

I wasn't sure whom I was angrier at—Amma, for confiding in Rajendra, or Rajendra for confronting me. Another part was angry at myself. How could I have been so naive to think Juneau and I could slip by unnoticed?

I spoke slowly so I wouldn't say anything I regretted. "I

think," I said, "that you don't like Juneau. She called you out at the museum, and she was right."

"Are you a homosexual?" Rajendra asked. And just like that, he won. He knew what I was, and he could tell Amma or the whole world if he wanted. And if the truth got out, how could I protect Juneau?

"Of course not," I said. I hated how automatically the lie slipped out. I rushed on: "I know what you saw, but I promise it won't happen again. There's no need to tell Amma."

The words stung in my mouth. To deny who I was, to deny my love for Juneau, felt about as natural as denying the existence of gravity or the pull of tides. But what choice did I have? I remembered Amma's warning about lesbians. She'd be devastated if she discovered the truth about me. If I could have one wish, it would be this: No matter what happened with me or Rajendra, Amma would be spared.

"Good," said Rajendra. "Because if she found out, it would break her heart."

My rage spiked. "I think that's your specialty, actually."

I'd meant to wound him, and the blow landed. "Listen, Mayavati," Rajendra said. It was the first time I'd seen him angry, like a man. "I've tried to do this nicely. But you're tearing this family apart, and someone needs to intervene."

I didn't know we'd started fighting until things had gone too far. Suddenly the man who'd eaten dinner with me, who'd knelt on the floor and asked for my forgiveness, was gone.

"*I'm* the one tearing us apart?" I said. "I—"

Just then, Amma appeared in the doorway, carrying groceries.

"The painting's coming along nicely," she said, oblivious to the tension. Rajendra kissed her, which angered me. I wanted him to know all the ways she'd prospered on her own, all the reasons that our life was better without him.

It was four thirty, time for our early dinner. Rajendra and I set the table, trying our best to avoid each other in the tiny kitchen. My heart was pounding. I felt Rajendra's knowledge hanging over me like a hammer.

"The Thanksgiving holiday starts this weekend," Rajendra said. "I thought we could take a family vacation. I've booked a hotel in Miami by the beach."

A family vacation was the last thing I wanted: to be stuck with my parents, far away from Juneau. But Amma smiled. "That's a lovely idea," she said. "What do you think, Maya?"

I didn't want to let her down, but it seemed I was already becoming a cosmic family disappointment. "I'd love to come, but I can't," I said. "I've been falling behind in school." This, at least, was not a lie. "I think I should stay home and study."

"Oh," said Amma, crestfallen. "In that case, let's cancel the hotel. We can all stay home with you."

Rajendra watched me unblinkingly. I could hear his words echoing in my head, reminding me of all the pain I'd caused Amma. A good daughter would make her mother happy while she still could.

"No, it's okay," I said. "You should go without me."

Amma hesitated. "Won't you be lonely at home?"

"I'll be fine." I looked at Rajendra, swallowed hard. Was it my turn, now, to sacrifice for Amma's happiness? "Besides, it might be nice for you two to get alone time."

"You've raised a very thoughtful daughter," said Rajendra.

Amma gave a small smile. "I guess it would be like old

times," she told Rajendra. To me she said, "I'll call you every day, okay? And you'd better pick up."

"I will," I promised. I tried looking on the bright side. With Rajendra on vacation, the coast would be clear for Juneau and me. I just wished my mother wasn't the price.

⁓

Amma and Rajendra spent the next morning packing for their trip. They looked happy, so natural together. Before heading to school, I asked Amma to make me a sandwich for lunch—something I hadn't done since I turned nine. Her eyes brightened.

"I thought you'd never ask," Amma said, busying herself with the jelly. I ignored Rajendra, watching us. I didn't really want a sandwich: I just wanted to feel Amma doing it for me. In these small gestures, she still was mine.

I walked to school armed with a PB&J. I headed straight for the senior parking lot, where Juneau was waiting for me in her car. In the mornings we liked people-watching, inventing stories about our classmates' lives. I'd become especially fascinated by girls in relationships. Watching them kiss their boyfriends, I'd guess how far they were from breaking up or having sex. Since this was high school, I figured most girls were in their first relationships. It was jarring to think that those lanky, careless boys might permanently alter the way they saw love for the rest of their lives.

Suddenly Juneau stiffened. "Look who's back," she said quietly.

I followed her gaze to the parking lot gates. A line of student cars chugged through. Then, like a bad nightmare, Squash Harvey pulled up in his Porsche.

It seemed to happen in slow motion. We stared as he swerved triumphantly into his parking spot, revving the engine so obnoxiously that if Juneau and I hadn't independently verified his penis size, I'd feel certain of his deficiency. A crowd gathered, observing the miraculous reappearance of his car.

"Who told him where his car was?" My voice shook.

Juneau shrugged. "We left it in the junkyard," she said. "Anyone could've seen it. He doesn't know how it got there."

"I know," I said, but my mind was spinning. What if we'd left behind traces: loose hairs, an earring? I tried to summon the confidence I'd felt the night of homecoming, but now all I felt was fear. "Do you think Mateo said something?"

"Enough about Mateo," Juneau said sternly. "You're spiraling."

Outside, Squash was clearly enjoying everyone's attention. He slammed his horn suddenly, causing people to jump.

"Okay, what a pissant," Juneau said, unbuckling her seat belt. To my horror, she marched out of the car toward Squash, leaving me no choice but to follow.

Spotting us, Squash stepped out of the car.

"Glad to see you're reunited with your Porsche," said Juneau before he could speak. "I mean, how else would you symbolize that you're destined to peak in high school?"

To my surprise, Squash didn't scowl at the insult. It was worse: He grinned. "You have no idea," he told Juneau. "You have no idea how fucked you are."

He got up in her face, way too close. Juneau stood to her full height, but next to Squash, she looked small.

"I know you stole the car," Squash said. "And as of today, I can finally prove it."

My heart pounded, but Juneau laughed, haughty as ever. "Nice try," she said. "But your grandfather already confronted us."

Squash wore the gleeful expression of a kid who tears insects apart limb by limb. Drawing it out, just for fun.

"Didn't you hear what I said?" he asked. "This time I have proof. You slipped up, baby." The last word came out as an awful drawl.

My heart dropped. I'd thought Juneau was invincible. I'd seen the ways she flaunted authority, wearing her skin as a shield—her laughter as a weapon, cool and capable of revenge. She could get away with almost everything, outmaneuver almost anyone. Anyone except for Squash.

Squash must've known it, too, because he was still grinning as he walked away. "Don't say I didn't warn you," he said, and my week of hell officially commenced.

chapter 25

Fuck," I said. I didn't seem to be capable of saying anything else. My breathing was shallow.

Juneau bit her lip. "He's probably bluffing."

"He's not." I felt this with chilling certainty. The parking lot seemed to tilt around me. I imagined all the versions of myself that had ever existed here: the quiet girl who followed Juneau to Taco Bell. The angry girl who shouted at Squash. The reckless girl who stole a car, certain she'd get away with it. At what point had I lost myself?

Juneau sighed. "Then we'll have to figure something out."

She kissed me on the cheek. It was a small gesture, but the fact that she'd done it in public, just to comfort me, filled me with warmth. "It's time to woman up," Juneau said. On that somber note, we went to class.

It was an award-worthy feat, in my opinion, that I managed

to feign normalcy, taking my Spanish quiz like there wasn't a chance I'd get arrested for grand theft auto. What else could I do? Juneau was right: There was probably no evidence, and therefore nothing to do but woman up and maintain my invisibility, my innocence.

At lunch, Juneau and I sat at the window table reserved for seniors so popular that nobody else ever sat there. Ife, seated nearby, was still ignoring me, and Silva was with her, which made him off-limits. Spotting me, he looked away.

Juneau noticed. "Your friends will come around," she told me. "They always do."

"To be fair, you don't have many friends left," I said. "I think I'm your only one."

We startled at the sound of footsteps approaching our table. Anya was standing behind us. For once, Squash was nowhere to be seen.

"We need to talk," Anya said. She glared at Juneau. "I'm Anya, by the way."

"I know," said Juneau. "Squash's girlfriend, right?" She said it like an insult, and it worked: Anya winced.

"Will you two join me in the ladies' room?" she asked. I immediately recognized our old code: Anya wanted to share a secret.

Despite everything, my heart swelled. "I guess," I said, instead of what I was really thinking, which was *Yes, yes, yes!*

Inside the restroom, Anya waited until all the stalls were empty before speaking.

"Mateo talked to Squash," she said, uncharacteristically direct. "He gave him evidence against you, and it's only a matter of time before Squash uses it."

My heart sank. I knew Squash hadn't been bluffing, just as I'd known, deep in my bones, that Mateo would be the first to crack.

"What kind of evidence?" I asked.

Anya shrugged. "I don't know exactly," she said. "But they made a deal after school yesterday. Mateo gave him a bunch of shit. Including a necklace."

"A necklace?" I turned to Juneau, bewildered, only to see that she'd gone pale. "Juneau, what's wrong?"

"Remember when I told you to search Squash's glove compartment?" she said—Anya's jaw dropped at the blatant confession.

"Yeah. I stole, like, a pen. And you took—"

"Squash's rosary," said Juneau, and my heart dropped. I had a fleeting memory of the rosary in Juneau's palm, bright like pearl. My jealousy when she'd given it to Mateo. "If Mateo returned it to Squash, he'll know we got it from his car. It links us to the crime."

"Well, that was idiotic," said Anya. "That's all the proof Sam needed."

I wasn't sure what was more shattering: the fact that Juneau was so careless, Mateo ratted us out, or that Anya, of all people, was warning us. My worlds collided with terrifying violence.

Meanwhile, Juneau looked like she'd been slapped. "I just don't understand," she said. "Mateo wouldn't do this. We made a pact."

I wanted to shake her, but Anya cut across. "If it makes you feel better, he's the one who sent me," she said. "Mateo says he's sorry, Maya. He said Juneau will be fine, but you won't. That's why he asked me to warn you."

I still couldn't stomach Mateo's betrayal. All this time, he'd acted like I was the Pugilists' weakest link, yet he'd been the one to cave. And still, in his fucked-up way, he was looking out for me.

"So what do we do?" My voice shook.

Juneau crossed her arms. "Well, there's really only one option, isn't there?" she said. "We steal the rosary back. Without it, Squash has no evidence again." She turned to Anya. "Do you know where he's keeping it?"

Anya blinked. I couldn't believe how swiftly we'd fallen apart. Had it been only months ago that Anya hugged me on the first day of school, convinced our lives would change for the better?

"It's in his locker," Anya said at last.

For a long moment, I looked at Anya. It hurt beyond words to see a stranger looking back. I wished we could break through the resentment and find our old intimacy beneath, like poking a crusted-over tube of paint.

"Screw it." Anya sighed. "You need to go right now, okay? I'll keep him busy at lunch." On a scrap of paper, she jotted down numbers in her neat, curved handwriting: Sam Harvey's locker combination.

The enormity of her gesture struck me. "Anya, what are you doing?"

She glared. "I'm taking care of you."

Juneau looked at me frantically, like, *What are you waiting for?* But I turned back to Anya. "Are you sure?" I said. "If Squash finds out…"

"What choice do I have?" Anya's eyes filled with tears. "If you get caught for stealing the car, your entire future is ruined. I can't let that happen."

"Maya," said Juneau warningly. "Lunch period's almost over. We need to go."

"Go," said Anya. She wouldn't look at me. "Please."

I didn't have the words to thank Anya. I wanted to remind her of how, at age ten, we'd devised a theory about time travel: that if you hopscotched backward fast enough, you could go back in time. Neither of us believed that anymore. It was impossible, we knew, to fix the past. But maybe our future still had a chance. For our sake, I had to believe this.

Juneau and I waited outside the boys' locker room watching the athletes file through.

"I can't go in," Juneau said. "It has to be you."

"*What?* Why me?"

"Because they know me, okay?" Juneau scowled. "You, on the other hand..."

My face burned. "I get it. I'm unmemorable."

Juneau was exasperated. "No, you're a motherfuckin' ninja, okay?" She nudged me toward the doors.

Luckily the locker room was nearly empty. But it was still bizarre to see teenage boys in their natural habitat. I realized that I'd never actually seen a penis before, not until a fully naked basketball player exited the showers and I had to dive behind the lockers. *I'm a motherfucking ninja*, I reminded myself.

Once the naked boy left, I used Anya's note to find Squash's locker. It opened easily.

The inside looked normal, stacked with clothes. Then I slipped my hand inside his sweaty sneakers, which took guts, and found Ziplocs full of drugs. Mostly weed, but also some pills I didn't recognize. Classic Squash, selling drugs at school with impunity. Fuck it, I thought—if I was burglarizing a drug dealer's locker, I might as well treat myself. I stashed some weed in my bra.

Eventually I found what I was looking for. Although I'd only seen the rosary once, it winked familiarly at me, like an old friend. I didn't push my luck. I slipped that, too, down my bra, fleeing the locker room as if Squash himself was chasing me.

When the cops showed up in AP Government, I knew even before hearing my name that they'd come for me. The entire class gaped as I followed them outside, the floors creaking like they knew the danger I was in.

The principal's office was filled with people. Cops and administrators sat around a conference table as if pitching the next billion-dollar company. Sitting on opposite sides of the table, studiously ignoring each other, were Juneau and Mateo. It reminded me of a Last Supper painting: the dark expressions of the participants, the doomed finality of it all.

Mateo was hunched over the table looking utterly tormented. I pretended not to see him, sitting with Juneau instead. She didn't really acknowledge me, either, because we were being watched. But she straightened slightly, softening the air between us. The fact that she was sitting up bravely, trying to make me feel better, made me want to cry. Our worst-case scenario had arrived, and we'd face it together.

"Thanks for joining us, Maya," said Dr. Harvey smugly. I gave him the nastiest look I could muster. "Just a few more minutes now. We're waiting for Sam."

We all waited tensely, but nobody else arrived. Dr. Harvey's eyes jumped to the clock. Sensing weakness, Juneau leaned forward.

"What fresh set of accusations are we facing today?" she said. "We've been here before, remember?"

Dr. Harvey was unfazed. "Mr. Chavez has finally decided to do the right thing and hand over evidence," he said; Mateo turned red. "The game's finally over, Ms. Zale."

Juneau opened her mouth to retort, but the doors opened with a bang, shaking the table. Squash burst in, looking murderous.

"What did you do?" he said. "What the hell did you—"

"You're late," said Juneau.

Squash stalked toward us. "How'd you get into my locker?" he said. "The rosary is gone. I know you stole it—"

"Stole what?" said Juneau, smiling widely. She'd gambled, and now she'd won.

"What's going on?" said Dr. Harvey, looking at his grandson with mounting concern.

Squash looked at everyone, and I saw disappointment crush him. It was almost worth the trouble of being summoned by the cops, just to watch his reaction. He struggled to explain himself. "Chavez gave me the rosary that Juneau stole from my car. It was in my locker. It was—"

He stopped, because Juneau was laughing.

"Right," she said. "Let me guess. This rosary was your only proof that we got inside your car. And now you've lost it? That's convenient." She turned to Dr. Harvey. "Is that the best you've got?"

Dr. Harvey was finally flustered. "Be quiet, Juneau," he

said. "Sam, I called this meeting because you said Mr. Chavez returned your rosary. Now you're saying it's gone?"

Squash balled his fists. "I'm telling you, it was in my locker, and now it's not. I don't know how they got in there, but—"

I couldn't help myself. "Are you sure someone broke into your locker?" I said. "I mean, was anything else missing?"

Squash's gaze hardened. We both knew what I was referring to, and we both knew that Squash couldn't press the point, not without revealing that his locker was full of drugs.

"I've gotta say," Juneau said dismissively, "things have a habit of disappearing around you, don't they?"

Squash turned red. "Screw the rosary," he said. "Chavez, just tell everyone what you told me—that they stole the car and you tried to stop them. Tell them right now."

"Hold up," said Juneau. "This isn't fair. You can't take his word against ours—"

"I'll decide what's fair." Dr. Harvey turned to Mateo. "It's okay," he said. "You can speak freely. Did these girls tell you they intended to steal Sam's car?"

For an awful moment, all eyes turned to Mateo. I had absolutely no idea what he was going to say. He was a wild card now, and even Juneau knew it. I saw them look at each other, communicating silently, and I felt a pang of old jealousy. Did she still have him wrapped around her finger? Did I want her to?

Then Mateo shrugged. "I don't know," he said, stunning us all. "It was chaotic at the dance. I can't really remember what was said. Sorry."

Dr. Harvey looked incredulous. "Are you changing your story, son?"

Mateo stared at the ceiling, as if personally bargaining with God for an out. "No," he said. "I'm not saying they *didn't* steal the car. I'm just saying I'm personally not sure what happened."

Squash slammed his hand on the table. "What are you doing?" he said. "We had a deal, Chavez. You told me the truth."

Mateo's expression was blank, but Juneau gave me an airless smile. We'd reached a standstill, and the tension in the room was palpable.

"I'm giving you one last chance, Mr. Chavez," Dr. Harvey said. "You don't owe these girls anything. You can tell the truth, and you'll be protected."

Mateo actually laughed at that. "Who's gonna protect me? Your cops? The same cops who've been harassing me since I entered this school?" He crossed his arms. "I told you, I have nothing to say. Can I go?"

Squash looked about ready to explode. "Man, what are you on?" he said. "Tell them she gave you my rosary!"

"What rosary?" said Juneau innocently.

She'd set him off. Squash lunged at her, forgetting that we were surrounded by cops—or maybe he figured they'd take his side anyway. My adrenaline spiked, and I stood up, even though I was no match for Squash. But it didn't matter, because Mateo got there first. With athlete-fast reflexes, he blocked Squash's path to Juneau.

"Take a breath, Harvey," he said quietly, facing down his teammate. Squash blinked, like he'd finally remembered where he was. He turned to his grandfather.

"Why are you just standing there?" he said. "Those bitches clearly stole my shit, and they're lying about it!" When nobody responded, he whirled on us. "When I find out how you got into my locker, there will be hell to pay," he promised. "I'm not letting this go—"

Dr. Harvey covered his face with his hands. When he spoke, his voice was tight with anger.

"Sam, get ahold of yourself," he said. He looked at Juneau, Mateo, and me. "The rest of you: Get out of my sight."

We didn't wait to be told twice. We darted out of the office. As we left, I overheard Dr. Harvey shouting at his grandson: "You just made a mockery of yourself!"

I felt a powerful rush of relief. I couldn't believe we'd gotten off for the second time. But Juneau didn't share my glee. She seized Mateo's arm.

"What the *actual hell*?" she said. Even though I wasn't the target of her rage, I felt a secondhand thrill of fear. "What happened to our pact? I never guessed you were a backstabber."

Mateo looked equally furious. "I didn't have a choice," he said. "Harvey threatened my scholarship. And I didn't break the pact, not directly. I went to Squash instead."

Juneau's rage was meteoric. "How noble of you," she said. "You almost screwed us anyway. If we hadn't gotten tipped off by Maya's friend—"

"Yeah, you're welcome for that. I sent her," said Mateo. He was back in fighting form, not letting Juneau steamroll him. "Even after everything you put me through."

Juneau shook her head. "To think I jumped on a cop for you," she said. "Maya, we're leaving." She looped my arm possessively in hers. Seeing this, Mateo scoffed.

"You move fast," he said coldly.

"What?" said Juneau.

"You and Maya," said Mateo, gesturing obscenely between us. I twisted my arm free of Juneau's, but it was too late: Mateo looked vindicated. "You two are together, aren't you?" He answered his own question—Juneau's face was as good as a confession. "Of course you are. After you lied to my face that you'd never cheat..."

"I didn't cheat!" Juneau insisted. "Mateo, you need to calm down."

That was the wrong thing to say. Mateo did not calm down. Instead, he stared at me and Juneau, looking utterly repulsed. He told me in a soft and measured voice, "Squash was right about you on homecoming night, wasn't he?"

My voice shook. "Screw you," I said.

I kept replaying our phone conversation, when Mateo first accused me of sleeping with Juneau. He'd known what I wanted from the beginning; he must have. Looking at me was like looking in a mirror, his desire for Juneau reflected back to him. For Mateo, that was probably the worst part: not Juneau's leaving him, but whom she left him for. She'd picked a *girl*, and worse, she'd picked the quiet nobody, the girl who never should've posed a threat.

Mateo smirked at Juneau. "I guess it doesn't matter now," he said. "You hurt me, I hurt you. From now on, we're even. I don't owe you shit."

He stormed away, and even Juneau couldn't think of a retort to yell back. She stood there gutted like a fish.

Now that we were free, my adrenaline crashed, and I realized how hungry I was—I hadn't eaten my lunch, having been too busy burglarizing to eat.

Juneau watched me scarf down my mom's sandwich.

I couldn't fathom what she was thinking. Finally she sighed heavily and proclaimed, "All men are terrorists." We raised our water bottles, tapped them together, and drank.

We'd escaped by the skin of our teeth, but it didn't feel like a victory. After detention, we went back to the Smoking Hole. Juneau wouldn't stop venting about Mateo.

"Not to sound like a raging feminist, but it's toxic masculinity, I'm telling you," she was saying. "That's why Mateo allied with Squash. Like, forget the Pugilist code. Men's loyalty to each other is even stronger. He could never handle my sexuality, my power, you know? He wanted to put me in my place."

Anya texted me. It was jolting to see her name on my phone after all these weeks of silent treatment. Squash is livid, she'd written, so I'm guessing you got out OK?

Yeah, we're okay. I owe you my firstborn child probably.

Yes, babe, you do. Because pretty soon he's gonna figure out I helped you break in...

Juneau's monologue continued. "But I still can't believe he betrayed us," she said. "He owes Squash, whatever. But—"

"Maybe he thought it was fair," I interrupted. I was being belligerent, but I didn't care. Juneau's misplaced confidence had landed us in this predicament, and for once, I wanted her answer for it.

"You're taking his side?" Juneau glared at me.

"No. I'm not." I rubbed my temples. "I just think your relationships are rarely equal, Juneau. And you endangered Mateo first, when you stole Squash's car—"

"You mean, when *we* stole Squash's car," said Juneau pointedly.

"Yeah, yeah, I know." I tried to backtrack. "I just...He's not the villain of this story, Juneau. Squash is. We can't lose sight of that."

Juneau relented. "Yeah. I thought Squash was gonna cry in the office." Her eyes lit up at the memory.

"That reminds me. I got you a little gift." I put Juneau's hand up my shirt, against my bra. She gasped, finding the weed baggie I'd stashed earlier.

"Are these Squash's joints?" She laughed incredulously. "You stole them?"

"Yeah. Are you proud of me?" I meant it as a peace offering, and it worked: Juneau leaned in for a kiss, Mateo entirely forgotten.

"Of course I am," she said. "And I wish everyone could know how proud I am of you."

My heart ached. Remembering Mateo's reaction, I asked, "You're not worried that someone knows about us, are you?"

"I'm always worried," said Juneau quietly. She fished in her bag for her lighter, lit Squash's joint. "Which is why it's so lucky we have weed."

She took a deep drag, then handed it to me. "For you, m'lady."

Something hard and cold settled in my stomach. "We can't have all our discussions high, Juneau," I said. I put out the joint, causing her to frown. "I'm trying to be serious here."

"About what?" Juneau lay down.

"I want to know what comes next for us," I said. "We can't constantly be afraid for the next shoe to drop. You heard

Squash: He's never gonna leave us alone. And Mateo knows we're together. We need a plan."

"I don't know what to tell you." Juneau shrugged. "There is no plan, Maya. There's no way to not be afraid. We just have to learn to live with it."

The resignation in her voice flattened me. But she was right. Since neither of us could come out, we'd always fear discovery. And as long as we attended CGHS, the Harveys would keep trying to punish us. There was no end in sight. No wonder Juneau needed weed to talk with me. When fear is packed so deeply into your bones, sometimes it takes divine intervention to break free.

"Fuck this homophobic-ass town," I said. My voice gained fervor with each grievance. "Fuck Mateo. Fuck Squash. Fuck Dr. Harvey. Fuck my dad."

It felt cathartic to utter these curses, but Juneau frowned. "What happened with your dad?"

Amid today's drama, I'd forgotten to fill her in about Rajendra—how he'd caught us kissing, his impending marriage proposal.

"Why are our parents so determined to keep us from being happy?" Juneau said at last.

"If I ever have my own kid," I said, "I'll love them no matter what. I think that's what you sign up for when you become a parent."

Juneau pulled me closer. Her arms were warm, and for a second I felt like she was my mother. I know that's not the most romantic thing to say, but it was the purest expression of love I'd ever known.

"That's how it should be," she agreed. "But other things often get in the way."

"What got between you and your parents?"

Juneau considered. "Religion," she said. "But also I think maybe it's a power thing. That's certainly the case with guys like Mateo and Squash. They just can't imagine a world where women don't owe them love. Because that means they can't control us."

Her words sank in. "Wow," I said. "I think you're right."

"What about your mom?" Juneau asked. "I thought she'd be accepting."

"Sometimes Indian culture can be homophobic, too," I said. "Maybe that's where my mom got it. Or maybe…" I hesitated. "Maybe she knows how hard life was for her, and she wants things to be easier for me. It's hard to believe that my mom's heart is full of hate. I'd prefer to think it's just misguided love."

"I know she loves you so much." Juneau's eyes were sympathetic, but her breath was soft against my ear, so even factual statements felt seductive.

The sun was finally starting to set, but the day felt so long. Maybe this was the secret to time, to relativity—that not all moments were the same length. When I kissed Juneau, time seemed to disappear, but right now, things felt so stagnant. More than anything I wished we could fast-forward our lives, skip ahead to when we escaped Citrus Grove. I imagined the moment the clouds would part and sunshine would pour out. It felt so real, yet impossibly far.

"That's enough wallowing," Juneau said. "Now, if we're done talking about parental trauma, I can think of better things to do." She rolled over, pulling me against her.

At home, Amma kissed me goodbye. She and Rajendra were vacationing early, driving out tonight. Amma had exchanged her usual scrubs for a sundress, and she looked beautiful. I couldn't believe that she might get engaged to Rajendra. "I have frozen meals in the fridge, okay?" said Amma. "If anything goes wrong, one call, and we'll come straight home." Then she frowned. "Why is there grass in your hair?"

I realized I was covered in grass from the Smoking Hole. I dodged her attempts to groom me by hand. Like a good daughter, I waved until their car headlights had shrunk into pinpricks. She'd been gone for only minutes when loneliness filled me up.

So I gave myself a treat. Instead of homework, I watched TV until I fell asleep. It was the first good sleep I'd gotten that week—and also the last one for a while. Because overnight, all hell broke loose.

chapter 26

Silva called early the next morning, startling me awake. I was sprawled on the couch, the TV still airing reruns of the same shitty game show that had put me to sleep.

"Have you checked Instagram since, like, midnight?" he said.

"No." I hesitated. "Silva, is everything okay?"

"Check. Right now." Silva's voice was heavy. "It's Squash, that bastard. He and Anya had a fight and broke up, and...he violated her."

I raced to Instagram and saw that the app was blowing up. A post was circulating from an anonymous account. Seeing it, my heart dropped.

There will be hell to pay, Squash had promised, and he'd meant it. The photos were of Anya—but they were the kind of pictures that very few people had the right to see. The sequence of events played awfully in my mind. Anya had betrayed Squash, so Squash had pulled off the cruelest vengeance he could muster: leaking Anya's nudes.

Despite the photos' explicitness, her face wasn't covered, which meant she'd taken them trustingly, willingly. The post had only been up for a few hours, but cruel comments were pouring in.

"Where is Anya right now?" I said, sounding much calmer than I felt. "Is she okay?"

"Of course she's not okay," said Silva. "She called me as soon as she saw the post. Ife and I are at her house right now. We reported the post to Instagram, and they'll probably take it down, but screenshots are going around."

I ignored the stab of grief in my stomach. I wasn't Anya's first call.

"Her house?" I said. "Okay. I'll be there."

Silva hesitated. "Maya, should you really?"

He wanted me to stay away from Anya after I'd directly caused her suffering. But we were at war with Squash, and that made our internal conflicts shrink by comparison.

"Of course I'm coming," I said. "See you in twenty."

I dressed haphazardly, unable to view my own naked body in the mirror without picturing Anya's. Even I, a virgin, knew how disastrous a nude leak was. It didn't matter if the girl had a boyfriend—one leak and she'd be branded a slut forever. Before leaving the house, I forced myself to print screenshots from Instagram, covering the explicit parts with Sharpie, in case she needed evidence of what Squash had done. Then I raced to Anya's house. School buses passed me in the other direction, but I couldn't imagine attending class right now. How dramatically your priorities realigned themselves when a girl's life had been ruined.

Silva let me inside. Ife sat on the couch, and the TV was playing, even though nobody was watching. Anya lay forlornly in her lap. Ife glared at Silva, like, *You let her come?* I paid her no attention. Instead, I knelt by Anya.

"Hey," I said, because I didn't know what else to say. To my embarrassment, tears rose to my eyes. I wiped them away because I wasn't the victim—far from it. "I'm going to fix this, Anya."

"*You?*" said Ife. "What could you possibly do?"

I felt like my heart was splitting. What exactly *was* I capable of? All the times I'd felt powerful with the Pugilists—painting the mural, stealing Squash's Porsche—felt useless now. I realized, awfully, I'd never actually had the power to do anything at all. Except to stand up, speak my dissent, even if I burned everything down.

"I'll figure it out," I said. "But, Anya, I need to know everything. Like, how'd he get those pictures? Was it consensual?"

Remembering the tone Amma used with distressed patients, I prodded Anya gently for information. It was a strange role reversal since Anya was always the one who'd cared for me: braiding my hair, holding my secrets, preparing me for my first date. Everything I knew about womanhood I'd learned from her. How had things gotten this bad?

"I sent them when we were dating," she said. "It was so stupid, I know. I really thought they'd make him happy—"

"Did they make *you* happy?" I asked.

Anya looked surprised by the question. I knew immediately that nobody had asked her that before, and I felt appreciative of

Juneau, who constantly asked what felt good to me. "I mean, I guess, yeah. I felt beautiful. I—"

"Then it wasn't stupid," said Ife fiercely. But Anya sobbed.

"Everything is ruined," she said. "All the guys have seen those pictures. To the whole school I'm some kind of slut."

"Nobody could blame you for this," Silva said. "Not when those pictures were clearly leaked."

She sank under the covers. "Don't be stupid, Silva," she said. Her words resurfaced a memory in my mind: Juneau, working on her college essays. She'd mentioned the summer her nudes were leaked.

"I think I know who can help," I said.

To my relief, Juneau picked up my call. "Are you with Anya?" she said. "I noticed that none of your friends are at school today. You should probably keep her away for a while. Squash is—" She took a breath. "He's bragging, Maya."

Fury unfurled in my chest. "He leaked her nudes, and nothing's happened to him?"

"Don't tell me you're surprised."

"Didn't this happen to you, too?" I asked her, desperate for guidance.

"Unfortunately, I am familiar with revenge porn."

"*Revenge porn?* That's what it's called?" The name sounded fitting. At the same time, it was depressing that this occurred often enough to warrant an official name.

"Yeah, when a guy leaks his ex's nudes to get back at her. It's basically legal in Florida, plus there are no school rules about sexual harassment." Juneau paused. "This is our fault, isn't it?"

I suppressed my mounting guilt. "We need to talk to Dr. Harvey. If anyone can rein in Squash, it's him."

Juneau didn't sound optimistic, but she offered to pick me up. "We'll talk to him together," she said.

Hanging up, I turned to my friends. "Juneau's taking me to school," I said. "We're gonna fix this, I swear."

Anya was unresponsive, so I turned to Ife. I sensed something passing between us: not quite forgiveness, but a mutual stalemate. Today, Anya's needs came first. "Ife, Silva, you'll stay with her?" I asked.

They nodded, and I waited for Juneau outside. I couldn't breathe normally. I felt uncontrollable, like something sleeping deep inside of me had opened one eye. I was tired of being a girl, resigned to whatever men threw at us. What they expected us to do was pretend we'd agreed to it all. To smile and laugh along, even when the joke was on us.

"Maya, wait," Silva called. "I'm coming with you."

I didn't know what to say. How quickly we'd all become strangers to each other, like awkward neighbors encountering one another in the street.

"You don't have to. This is my mess to clean," I said.

Silva shook his head. "No, it's not," he said. "It's my job, too. I know what other men are like, especially the Harveys. They won't listen unless another guy backs you up."

We gave each other a long look. I saw our reflections in Anya's polished front door, our brown faces melting into the wooden brown surface. The door opened, and Ife and Anya stepped outside.

"Maya," Ife said, stiffly. "There's only one person to blame for this, even if you provoked him."

A honk on the street: Juneau was here. I didn't even have to turn to know it was her. I felt the air between us.

"Go," said Anya, squeezing my hand. As the door clicked shut I felt like something else was closing—an old era, a simpler life, the girls we used to be. We had finally outgrown ourselves: the girls who drank spiked lemonade, braided each other's hair, and told each other's fortunes like we could control anything in the world.

In Juneau's car, I wondered if Silva would notice something between us, but Juneau drove fast, and Silva's fingers drummed against the window, playing an urgent rhythm only he could hear. There was no time to register my worlds colliding—Silva, my best friend, plus Juneau, my first love, their significance only vaguely known to each other—but it was decidedly weird.

"So what's the plan?" I asked Juneau.

"I don't know." Juneau sighed. "When this happened to me, I never confronted the guy or tried legal consequences. I was just a freshman, and I was afraid of further debasing myself." She shrugged. "I think our best shot is if Dr. Harvey intervenes. He can make a school policy to ban spreading the photos."

"So our plan is to appeal to Harvey's better nature?" Silva shook his head. "In that case, we're screwed."

We'd all been thinking it, but now Silva said it aloud. Juneau pulled into school. It was the middle of a class period, so the campus was deserted. We ran to Dr. Harvey's office. He was in a meeting. Not that it mattered: Juneau shoved open the door.

"What's going on here?" Dr. Harvey said. "Juneau, I don't have time for this."

"*Make time*," said Juneau. By now, her boldness had ceased to startle me, but I saw Silva's jaw drop. "Are you aware that your grandson has been posting explicit images online?"

I'd expected Dr. Harvey to flinch, but if he was shocked,

he covered it well. He ushered us into an inner room and closed the door. "I was not," he said. "And I'm similarly unaware of why you are telling me about this."

"Because the photos," said Juneau, "are of a CGHS student."

Now Dr. Harvey did look uneasy. "What are you talking about?"

I hesitated. I'd wanted to keep Anya's name out of it, but given the situation, it seemed unavoidable. "The victim is Anya Patel," I said, handing him my censored screenshots. We stared at our feet, unwilling to watch Dr. Harvey look at the photos. "She's Sam's ex-girlfriend."

Dr. Harvey glanced at the door, ensuring it was tightly closed. "These photos are being circulated around the school?"

"They appeared on Instagram last night," said Silva.

Dr. Harvey sighed heavily. "They were posted to Sam's account?"

"Well, not exactly," I admitted. "They're from an anonymous account."

Saying this aloud felt akin to clattering a weapon onto the table. Dr. Harvey seized it, his eyes bright. "So it wasn't Sam," he said. "It could've been anyone."

"But Sam's the only one she sent the pictures to," I said.

Dr. Harvey stood up. "I am disgusted," he said. "Both by these photos, and by the groundless accusations you're making. If Ms. Patel is the sort of young woman who takes these sorts of photos, God knows whom she's been sending them to. For all we know, she posted them herself for attention."

I felt my breath catch in my throat. "No, she sent them to *Sam*," I insisted. "They were dating. They were only meant for him."

Dr. Harvey's expression was steely. "Listen," he said. "That girl made her choice when she took those pictures. I pity her, I do. But it's about time you girls accept the consequences for your actions. I would be well within my rights to expel Ms. Patel for spreading this sort of filth—"

"*You girls?*" Juneau echoed icily as the bell rang. A slow roar built up through the walls; students were changing classes.

Silva leaned forward valiantly. "Sir, she's being violated," he said. "You could put a stop to this. Talk to Sam, create a school-wide penalty for anybody who shares the pictures—"

"I'm sorry, son, but you should leave," Dr. Harvey interrupted. I saw Silva deflate, and even though he wasn't my real target, I hated him for always giving in so easily. "There's nothing I can do to reverse Ms. Patel's poor decision-making."

"Her only poor decision," I burst out, "was dating your piece of shit grandson."

I hadn't meant to curse, but the words tore out of me with a vengeance. Dr. Harvey slammed his hands on the desk. In that gesture, he reminded me so forcefully of his grandson.

"Get out!" he said. "Or I'll expel her, I'll expel you all—"

Desperation sawed through me. I wanted to stay and yell at Dr. Harvey, but Silva pulled me into the hallway, which was flooded with people. I saw Silva's head turning around. He locked eyes with his target: Squash Harvey.

I opened my mouth fruitlessly as Silva yelled Squash's name.

Squash looked genuinely confused: He didn't know Silva. But spotting Juneau and me, his face hardened. He walked toward us, but Silva shoved his chest—hard.

"Watch where you're going," Silva said. "You fucking creep."

Nearby students tensed, sensing the start of a fight.

"What's your problem?" Squash said.

"Anya," said Silva. "We know what you did."

Squash laughed. "Who the fuck are you?"

By way of answer, Silva punched him in the face.

I lunged forward, but Juneau pulled me back to safety; instead I watched helplessly as Silva punched Squash repeatedly. He was a skinny violinist fighting the football captain, but somehow he had enough rage to give Squash Harvey a nosebleed. I'd expected him to be wild, but Silva's hits were steady. And I knew right then this wasn't a random act of violence. It had been building up forever. All these years I'd criticized him for sitting on the sidelines, letting the world pass him by—he'd finally risen up with a vengeance.

"Silva, stop!" I begged, but it was too late. The cops burst into the hallway, followed by Dr. Harvey. Silva got in one last, sickening blow before they converged on him, four cops versus one kid. They slammed him against the floor, my gentle best friend, his limbs splayed like a shot-down bird.

I lurched toward one of the cops handcuffing Silva. "Please," I said, or something useless like that.

The cop pushed me aside easily, and I learned right then that I did, indeed, belong to the weaker sex. I watched them read Silva his rights and drag him away.

"Where are you taking him?" I heard Juneau demand.

The cop regarded her coolly. "Down to the station to book him," he said. "Then he's going into lockup."

"Assault is a zero-tolerance crime," added Dr. Harvey, helping Squash to his feet. "It's time that CGHS learns respect for the law."

"You're trying to make an example of him," said Juneau. "He's just a sophomore."

"He's gonna pay," snarled Squash. "And so are you." Blood streaming from his face, he shouted a bunch of terrible insults at us both, including a few that I mentally stored for future use. He and his grandfather rounded the corner, leaving splatters of blood behind them. And then Juneau and I stood in the empty hallway as my world fell apart.

chapter 27

I was nearly incoherent when I called Theo, but he knew what to do.

"Maya, deep breaths," he said. "My parents can help. They deal with assault cases all the time, plus Silva's a juvenile. He'll be free by midafternoon."

"He can't hire a lawyer," I choked out. "His parents don't have money. Theo—"

"Maya, it's okay. You have a rich ex now, okay? I'll meet you at the station."

Juneau drove me to the Citrus Grove police station. The receptionist frowned when I presented my learner's license as ID. As promised, Theo was already there. This time, he was flanked by his equally well-dressed parents, the famous Fisher & Cho. "You did the right thing by calling us," Mrs. Cho said. "Anything we should know before we go in?"

"The guy he punched is powerful," said Juneau. "Sam Harvey. His dad's a local real estate mogul, and his grandfather's the CGHS principal."

"Sounds like a highly punchable candidate," said Mr. Fisher. I could see Theo's humor in his smile.

Mrs. Cho clasped my hand. "We'll handle it from here," she said. "And we'll discuss the revenge pornography later."

"Thank you so much," I managed, and they went inside. Juneau left to pick up her brothers from school, leaving me alone with Theo. For several moments, we sat in awkward silence.

"You saved the day," I said at last. "I don't know how I'll ever repay you."

"It's my pleasure to help any friend of yours." Theo was modest. "Especially someone who retraumatized Squash's nose."

"I didn't think you'd pick up." I looked away. "And I wouldn't blame you. I'm sorry about how I ended things. It wasn't very appropriate of me."

Theo laughed, but not meanly. His eyes crinkled in their familiar friendly way. "Maya, it's okay. I'm glad you're still comfortable calling me. Though, to be honest, it's weird to bail out your new boyfriend." His mouth flattened. "Silva's the reason you dumped me, right?"

Now it was my turn to laugh. "Silva's not my boyfriend," I said. "God, Theo. You have no idea."

Theo looked a little hurt, and maybe that's what propelled me to say it. I cast my words like sand into the wind. "Theo, I'm gay."

It was the first time I'd said those words aloud, in a sentence, together. Coming out to Juneau had been different—hushed, confessional, my heart split by longing. And maybe it was the absurdity of the situation, the solitude of the police station, but I no longer wanted to hide.

"I didn't realize it until we started dating," I explained. Then I winced. "Not to say that you turned me gay. Quite the opposite. It actually confused me, because I really liked you."

Slowly, Theo smiled. "Wow." His hands wrung awkwardly. "Sorry, I'm still processing. Is it appropriate for me to congratulate you?"

I laughed. "Yes. But I'm not publicly out. So, if you don't mind—"

"Your secret is safe with me," said Theo, and my heart lurched. How I wished the secrets could end and Juneau and I could be free. But after what Squash did to Anya, I was no longer naive about these things.

Mr. Fisher and Mrs. Cho came back outside, clutching their briefcases. Following behind—slightly bruised, but miraculously free—was Silva. Relief swelled in me, and I threw myself at him. He wasn't expecting it, but he still managed to catch me, his arms familiar and warm.

"I'm so sorry," I said. I was afraid to look at his face, because then I'd see pity, and that was the last thing I deserved. "I can't believe you got arrested. It's all my fault." I was crying uncontrollably.

"No, it's not. Squash had it coming," said Silva, which only made me cry harder.

"Let the man breathe," said Theo, sparing Silva. He handed me a pressed handkerchief, causing me to laugh through my tears. Only Theodore Fisher-Cho would bail my best friend from jail and bring clean linens, just in case.

In the car, Silva looked older than I'd seen him before: a dark bruise accentuated his jaw.

"You look different," I said awkwardly. "I guess prison really does change a man." To my relief, Silva laughed at the joke.

"So, let me get this clear," said Theo. "You broke Squash's nose? Right in broad daylight?"

Silva nodded, and Theo whistled. "Congratulations to you, sir. You've done humanity a favor."

Despite the situation, Silva grinned. "It was about time," he said. "You were right, Maya, when you said we needed to stand up for ourselves. I just wish it hadn't taken me so long."

At Silva's house, I insisted on walking him inside. I still couldn't stop crying. Outside his house I remembered us as children new to Citrus Grove. When someone's part of your life for so long, you assume that they'll be there forever. You don't think that you'll hurt them.

"I don't deserve you," I told Silva. He shook his head, but I was thinking of Juneau.

You deserve love in reverse, Juneau once told me. Juneau, who wouldn't hold my hand in public. Juneau, who pushed me to dangerous extremes. Juneau, who I sometimes thought showed me kindness only so she could see the gratitude on my face. What exactly did I deserve?

At home, Rajendra's half-finished painting opened like a window into another world. I couldn't escape my sense of guilt. In the past month alone, my actions had resulted in Ife's losing her job, Anya's nudes getting leaked, Pat's and Mateo's futures threatened, and Silva's going to jail.

It occurred to me that I was just as bad as Juneau.

I mean, the parallels were impossible to ignore. We both endangered our friends, weaponized our love, hit people where it hurt. My friends might blame Juneau for ruining me, but only I knew that Juneau had merely awoken something that always existed. I deserved Juneau, and she deserved me.

Once I realized this, there was no point resisting my desires. I couldn't spend another night alone. So I called Juneau.

"Is everything okay?" she asked.

"Can I come to your house?" I said.

"Like, for dinner?"

"I already ate," I said. "I want to sleep over."

She was quiet, and I sensed the possibilities churning in her mind. "I'll pick you up," she said.

Juneau drove me to her house, but this time we weren't alone. Juneau's mom and brothers were in the dining room looking like they'd been plucked out of a Norman Rockwell painting.

"Maya!" Mrs. Zale wrapped me in an embrace. "It's lovely to meet you. You're welcome to stay here, since your parents are out of town."

"Thank you," I said with a brief glance at Juneau. After everything she'd told me about her mother, I'd expected Mrs. Zale to be the suburban devil. A raging racist, at the very least. But she looked mostly like an older version of Juneau, sweet-toned and friendly. Maybe that's what made her so dangerous.

"Please, sit down and eat with us," Mrs. Zale said. "Juneau mentioned you're vegetarian. I took the liberty of starting a salad."

"She already ate," said Juneau.

"She can speak for herself," said Mrs. Zale. "Maya, would you like salad?"

"That sounds wonderful," I said.

Juneau rolled her eyes, but Mrs. Zale brought out a magazine-worthy salad. She made us all bow our heads for prayer—Juneau hissed, *Mom, she's not even Christian!* But I didn't mind. I closed my eyes and said "amen" a beat too late. It was nice to feel someone pray for you, even without your permission.

Mrs. Zale asked me a dozen questions as I ate: what neighborhood I lived in, what my parents did for work. Then she wanted to know where I was from. *Really* from, she clarified.

"Mom," protested Juneau, but I'd been anticipating this question. I'd been answering some version of it constantly since I was three.

"I was born in India," I said. "But I've lived in Citrus Grove practically my whole life."

"Ah," Mrs. Zale said, like she'd solved a puzzle. "No wonder. Your English sounds perfect."

"That's enough," said Juneau. "We're going to my room." I barely had time to thank Mrs. Zale for dinner before Juneau whisked me away.

"Don't stay up too late, girls," Mrs. Zale called. She gave me a piercing look, but I returned it with what I hoped was a trustworthy smile.

"Thanks for letting me stay," I said.

"I'm so sorry," said Juneau when we were out of earshot. "My mom's awful. I told her not to say anything."

"She was sweet," I said. "But yeah, a bit regressive."

"Come to my room. I'll make it up to you," Juneau said. Her tone made me blush. She was so good at this, I thought. Just being alone with her made my knees weak.

I entered Juneau's room for the first time. I hung my sleepover bag on her chair and put my sketchbook on her desk, which was covered with photos—mostly of friends and family—but in the back, I spotted a familiar girl with black hair. She was smiling, the kind of smile a girl only wears when she really, really likes you.

I knew who she was without needing to read the handwritten caption at the bottom of the photo. *Laila Afzar: art connoisseur, mischief-maker, best friend, etc.*

"Wanna watch something?" Juneau asked me. "You can pick. You've had the shittier day."

I ended up choosing a classic—*Thelma & Louise*, which felt fitting. I tried to watch the movie, but it was hard to focus on anything but Juneau. I'd told her I wanted to sleep over. We both knew what that meant.

When the movie ended, I ran my fingers through her hair. I knew I wanted her, but it was more than that—I thought when you liked someone the way I liked Juneau, you didn't need to have sex. You could just sit next to her. You could listen to her heartbeat until you couldn't tell where yours ended and hers began. It takes more than sex for your heart to forget that it's beating. To mistake someone's pulse for your own.

"What are you thinking about?" Juneau smiled at me.

Instead of answering, I kissed her.

She glided her fingers down the side of my waist, down to my thigh. She stopped there, her hands safely on top of my jeans, but I sat up.

"Could you—" I said, feeling a sting of embarrassment. I couldn't find the words to tell her what I wanted. It felt like my old childhood nightmare where I studied for a test, only to show up and face the questions in Latin. And certainly, this seemed to require a different language altogether. When had I ever voiced these desires, told someone exactly how to touch me? What should desire even feel like?

I took a deep breath and tried again. "Could you...keep going?"

Her hand suddenly clamped down on my thigh. I was intimidated, and she laughed. "You mean...keep going like this?" She kissed me back, softer this time, but I didn't want softer. My heart was racing.

"No," I said. "Or, I mean, maybe. I don't know how you'd do it." I winced. "I mean...I don't want to stop at kissing. I want more."

She softened in place, her mouth still somewhere behind my ear. "Are you sure?" she said.

"Yeah," I said, my voice coming out rusty. "All of it. Any of it. Whatever you want."

"What do *you* want?" Juneau said. Maybe I imagined it, but her voice went low, too. "Maya—"

"Just...you know." I felt so shy because there was something different in her eyes. "I don't know the mechanics for any of it. You're the first person I've tried to do this with..."

She started laughing, and I worried I'd spoiled the moment.

"*Mechanics?*" Juneau said, and I blushed deep. "God, Maya. We can have sex right now. I just wanted to know how you'd want it."

I didn't know what to say. The word *sex* felt like a snake released from a tank. Its weight moved between us.

"Or, how about this," Juneau said. "I'll try some things, and you tell me how they feel, okay?"

Grateful, I nodded. I'd spent the week watching things online, studying for this moment. But when it came to Juneau, I always felt unprepared.

"You'll have to keep it quiet though," Juneau said. "The walls are pretty soundproof, but my family's downstairs."

I'd never wanted something more badly in my life. With a boldness I didn't know I had, I kissed her, and she eased on top of me like the world's easiest geometry.

The kiss continued past where Juneau normally stopped: my neck, my collarbone at the lowest. Then, slowly enough so I could tell her to stop, but with the single-mindedness of ripping off a Band-Aid, Juneau took off my shirt. I lay there in my bra—a boring cotton bra, now I wished I owned something prettier—not that it mattered, because she took that off, too. She unclipped it with a one-handed flourish, like a magician pulling a rabbit from a hat.

"That was smooth," I said, and Juneau laughed.

"It's a good thing I have practice," she said. Then she pulled off her clothes, and I saw her for the first time.

Fuck, I thought. I felt stoned. I'd imagined her so often it almost felt like memory: the curve of her hips, the swell of her chest, her soft thighs—except now she was right in front of me. I almost forgot my own nakedness. I just stared at Juneau, miraculously up close. I almost expected to see paint strokes, but no, her skin was real and smooth. She was better than art. I didn't think I would paint the same way again.

"You're so beautiful," she said, stealing the words from my mouth. I tore my eyes away from her and looked down at myself. A burning quite separate from desire sparked through me: *shame.*

Juneau sensed it. "Are you still okay?"

I'd never worried about my body before, but suddenly I felt terribly conscious. It wasn't like nobody had seen me naked before—I'd changed in front of my friends. But not like this. Our bodies were the same, but they couldn't be more different. She was sensual, effortless, and I was so awkward. It was a good thing I was lying down, because I didn't even know how to carry myself.

"Yes, of course," I whispered. "I'm just—I don't know what to do. I don't know how to touch you." I tried to sit up. "But I want you to show me."

"We'll get there, I promise you," said Juneau. "But first, just lean back. Relax for me." She was bossy as ever, but her hands were gentle. "Let me take care of you."

She kissed me again, got back on top of me. My chest brushed hers. It was like she was a magnet: my body lifted off the bed, suddenly floating. I let Juneau run her fingers along me, and I let myself melt into her. She kept asking me how I was feeling, and I wanted to say, *like a brand-new coat of varnish*, but then she'd laugh, and it's not like I could say much anyway, because strange sounds kept escaping me.

"Are you ready?" she said at last. I felt like my heart might explode in my chest—if not my heart, then another part of me—and I nodded. One singular thought: *Juneau Zale is going to have sex with me.* Me, the girl who looked at others, saw herself only in reflection. The girl who watched Juneau for years from afar, never dreaming to ask for more.

When my jeans went overboard, I lost track of linear sequence. I felt her fingers and mouth. Her skin, so pale compared to mine. Our hair, lots of it, untied—my scrunchie

314

somehow slipped loose from my head, reappeared on her wrist. She surfaced, and the pendant of her necklace clacked into my teeth. I tried to pay attention to exactly how she did it, each touch and shock, but theorizing became impossible. Instead, I absorbed her heat, let her form me like clay in her palm.

I was afraid to touch Juneau, but in the dark, it was easier than I thought. Her body was like mine, everything merging naturally. She guided me with her hand, and I followed. Was I doing it right? I looked up but couldn't see past the slope of her chest, where it softened into rib cage. The sound of her, like rage mixed with surprise. I didn't care if Mateo had heard those sounds before. I was with Juneau, and that was enough.

Afterward we talked ourselves to sleep. I made her laugh, like I chatted up naked girls in bed every night. When I wondered aloud whether I'd feel different as a nonvirgin, Juneau smiled.

"Of course you will," she said. "You'll never be the same. Soon you'll have sex with a million other girls, but no matter how much time passes, you're always gonna compare them to me." She paused, cocky as ever. "Girl, I *deflowered* you."

I didn't want to make a big deal of virginity, since the whole concept was invented by men. But I was afraid she was right: I might always think about her.

"Do you think about Laila?" I said. "She was your first girl, right?"

"Shh. Don't turn my words against me." Juneau pulled me in close. "Right now, I'm thinking about you."

That was the right thing to say. I felt warm and safe. I should've known then that this moment couldn't last. Still, as we drifted off to sleep, the sex kept replaying in my mind, and when my phone rang the next morning, I thought I had imagined it.

chapter 28

I was half-asleep when Rajendra called, so I ignored my phone. He called again, and the phone rang louder.

"Maya, please," Juneau mumbled. "It's too early for this."

Still, I picked up.

"Hello?" I whispered.

There was silence, and I thought it was an accidental call. But then Rajendra's voice crackled through the speakers.

"Maya?" he said. "Where are you?"

"I'm at home. *Sleeping.*"

"Don't lie," Rajendra said. "Are you with her right now?"

Texts were flooding in, my phone flashing like a siren. It was too much to process. "Who?"

"I'm talking about Juneau. We saw the picture on Instagram. They're spreading," said Rajendra. "You need to come home now."

Amma's voice echoed distantly. "Maya?" she said. "What have you done?"

I had never heard her like this before. I'd heard her happy, tired, furious, but this time, she sounded terrified.

I jumped up and scrambled for my jeans but found Juneau's instead. "Picture?" I couldn't hide my panic. "Where are you?"

All I could hear was her crying. Rajendra's voice resumed. "We're almost home. Your mother insisted we drive back immediately."

"Rajendra, wait!" I clutched the phone, but he'd already hung up.

How did they know about Juneau? I remembered what Squash had said: *He's gonna pay. And so are you.* I knew in my gut that he'd outed us. Here was his revenge.

I still couldn't find my jeans. I threw open the curtains, flooding the room with light.

Juneau stirred again. "What are you doing?" she said. "Come back to bed."

She smiled at me, one sleepy hand outstretched. Something inside me seemed to swell and burst. For a wild, aching moment, I imagined going back to bed. I could curl beneath the covers and refuse to leave. In that moment, it still felt possible.

"What time is it?" Juneau asked.

I looked at her. How could I tell her that the clock was counting down?

My phone lit up with texts from Silva: **ARE YOU UP?** Another from Ife, then Anya: **You need to see this.** She'd sent an Instagram post. When I saw it, my heart dropped.

The post was from Squash's burner account, the same one that exposed Anya: a grainy picture of Juneau kissing me, our bodies intertwined. Thanks to the large Jesus sculpture, I recognized our very first kiss, lifetimes ago. I hadn't realized there was a picture until I remembered the flash of light. Based on the angle, I knew exactly who'd taken it.

As if on cue, Mateo texted me: I'm sorry, but I warned you.

Rage exploded in me, unexpected in its violence. Mateo had given Squash the picture, the exact ammunition he needed to put me in my place for good.

"Maya, what's wrong?" Juneau said.

I took a deep breath. "I don't want you to overreact," I said. "But something happened."

Anya texted again: The post has dozens of comments. We need to take it down.

Ife's response came immediately: Maya, hang in there.

"Squash posted something new." I took a deep breath. "About us."

I handed her my phone. The photo wasn't as explicit as Anya's, but the comments were worse. He'd tagged us in it, and many of our followers, which is how lots of people, including Anya, Silva, and my dad saw it. Guys from our school were asking for threesomes, calling us sluts, dykes, worse. Some of the commenters didn't even go to our school, or they were using fake accounts.

In spite of everything, all I could think was: *Squash won.* He'd dealt the final blow. Here I'd been thinking that Juneau held all the cards, when in reality Squash ran the game.

Juneau leaned back and closed her eyes. Her silence scared me more than anything so far.

"Juneau, what do we do?"

I waited for what I was sure to follow: Juneau would rise to her feet, a manic gleam in her eyes, convince me of our next vengeful act. Instead, she started to cry.

"Oh no. Juneau." I started stammering. "You'll be okay." I reached for her hand, and she gripped it viciously. I recognized her symptoms, because Amma had described them once: a panic attack.

No sooner had I realized this than Juneau started hyperventilating. It was terrifying, like watching her die.

"Shit. Juneau. Hold on." I held her in my lap. I started counting down. My voice, gentle and soothing, sounded calmer than I felt. "Breathe with me," I said, and she gasped, and I said it again. "Breathe through the numbers. Come on."

I had a sinking feeling in my stomach—the way I felt, swimming in lakes in the summer, when I'd try to put my feet down, only to feel cold water below, deeper than I'd thought. "Juneau, please. Say something."

"I can't," Juneau mumbled. "I'm fucked. When my mom finds out, I'm fucked."

"What do you mean?" Perhaps panic was contagious, because my throat was closing up, too. "Juneau, you've done worse. Your mom seems nice. Everything will be okay—"

"No, it won't. You don't understand," said Juneau. "She already gave me one pass."

Mascara was running freely down her face like ink. I didn't know she wore mascara.

"Are you talking about Laila?" I said. A strange combination of emotions rose in me like bile—confusion, jealousy, panic.

"I never told you how that story ended," Juneau said. "Laila and I got outed, too. My mom found out. It almost destroyed everything."

For a moment Juneau wasn't there. She was still looking at me, but her eyes were far away, looking at another girl who loved her, another girl who might have held her, wiped her tears as I did now.

"You got *outed*? By who?"

"Her parents," said Juneau. "We tried to keep it a secret, but inevitably we slipped up. They caught us kissing. Laila was a senior, so after graduation, they moved out of Citrus Grove. I never saw her again. They told my mom, and she lost her shit. It was so bad I ran away that summer."

I thought about Juneau, all the things I'd thought were true: her thirst for adventure, her knack for mystery. The summer of her rumored disappearance, when she'd played the triangle for Pacific Jukebox—she'd told me what she ran toward, but not what she'd run away from. Now I knew.

"Did you try to get her back?" I said.

"I was too scared," said Juneau. "Laila kept trying to get back in contact. Once the worst was over, she thought we could be together for real. But I had too much to lose. Like, my parents' financial support. And this house. I wasn't ready to give that up." Her voice was dry, unfeeling. "Luckily, Laila had been exiled from town, which meant the situation was contained. I cut Laila off, promised my mom I'd do better, and I came back home. I never told the Pugilists what happened. I just continued her work."

I felt numb. "I thought Laila abandoned you," I said. "But that's not true. You abandoned her."

My heart was aching, but it had nothing on Juneau's pained face. "I'm sorry," I whispered. "I shouldn't have said that." I tried again. "With Laila, you were really young and scared. But that doesn't mean that things are ruined for us, too."

"Aren't they?" said Juneau. "Everyone at school knows. The picture is out. It's only a matter of time before my mom finds it."

I thought of Amma, and my stomach hurt. What would she say when I returned home?

"We'll figure out how to delete the picture," I said. "But first, I need to talk to my parents." I tossed Juneau her clothes. "Can you drive me home?"

"You seriously want to go home now?"

"Things will be worse if I don't," I said. "I owe my mother this much."

As a portrait artist, I'd had a theory that people looked most like themselves when sleeping—their faces relaxed, all pretensions stripped away. But I'd been wrong. Right now, driving me home, Juneau looked more vulnerable than ever before. It wasn't sleep that stripped you down: It was fear.

The drive between our houses usually took fifteen minutes, but Juneau floored it, and we were there in eight. We ran up the driveway, and Rajendra opened the door.

"Maya, get inside," he said. "Juneau, go home."

Juneau teetered on the doorstep. "I don't want to leave you," she said.

"No, you need to go," said Rajendra. "You've done enough. This is family business."

Juneau's protests were cut off by the sound of thundering footsteps. All three of us jumped to see Amma standing in the foyer. I'd never seen her this furious before, not even when I'd run away as a child.

"You were with her?" she said, pointing to Juneau.

"I can explain," I said, desperate to defuse her rage. "She wanted me to get home safe."

"No, she's a pervert," said Amma. "And she took advantage of you."

"Amma, please," I said.

Amma shook her head. "She has ten seconds to leave." She started to count down.

"Ten," she said.

"Amma!" I said, but she kept counting.

"Nine. Eight. Seven, six, five..."

The seconds fell like sharp stones. Juneau was frozen.

"Four," said Amma. "Three. Two—"

"Can you stop?" I yelled; Juneau flinched, and Rajendra's jaw dropped. We might have been a reality TV show, I thought wildly, as my mother leaned toward Juneau.

"Get out of my house," she told Juneau. "Get out before I make you."

She wrapped her hand around the doorknob as if demonstrating what she'd do to Juneau's neck. Even I couldn't tell if she was bluffing.

"Amma, she's my friend," I insisted, but Rajendra interrupted.

"That girl is not your friend," he said. "Your mother tried to warn you—"

Juneau didn't keep silent. She never could.

"At least she wants me around," she told Rajendra. Her tone was as unbearably cocky as it was in the museum. "Which is more than you can say. And I take care of her. I make her feel good. I do it better than you ever could—"

"Juneau, *please!*" My heart skipped a beat as Rajendra lashed forward in rage.

Amma jumped to grab Rajendra so he couldn't throttle Juneau, then slammed the door on her. Outside I heard the squeal of Juneau's tires. I felt a stab of panic. I knew she was terrified and hurting. I didn't know where she'd go next.

"Maya, you're so young," Amma started. "I know you think you can act however you want. That some girl matters more than your family. That your relationship is healthy or normal. But it's not."

I wanted to tell her that she was wrong: that loving Juneau felt like the most natural thing in the world. That I couldn't imagine a love like her and Rajendra's, withering across oceans, when I could love a girl I'd follow to the ends of the earth. But I didn't have the words for any of that. Instead, I stood my ground.

"Excuse me," I said. "But somebody has publicly violated me. Shouldn't that be your bigger concern right now?"

"You can't imagine how I felt when I saw what you'd become," said Amma. She had tears in her eyes. "Why did you have to pick that girl? How did you end up—" She couldn't finish her sentence.

"I didn't just *end up* gay," I said. For the first time in my life, I cringed at the label. It sounded like an admission of guilt.

Now I knew how Juneau felt.

"Then why do you choose this?" Rajendra said. "Is this your way of resisting us? Of punishing your mother and me?"

I felt a flare of annoyance. "Of course not," I said. "This might come as a surprise, but my life doesn't revolve around you."

"Maya, enough!" Amma moaned. "Kanna, you're so young. You don't have to ruin your life like this. You could have anything you want. Any life, any man—"

"Except I don't want one," I snapped. "Amma, you're better than this. There's no way you actually believe that being gay is wrong."

"This is my fault," Amma said, all rage burned out of her. "It's because I never had a steady man in the house. If I'd kept one, then maybe you wouldn't have become—"

"This is not your fault," I insisted, but Rajendra interrupted.

"It's time to stop being selfish, Maya," he said. "The choices you're making, they'll destroy our family."

"You mean, like you did?" I knew I was shouting, but I didn't care.

My father stood up to his full height, and though I knew he wouldn't hurt me, my heart still raced. His shadow seemed to fill the room, washing Amma out entirely.

"I've held my tongue long enough," he said. "Sujatha, clearly something is broken in this home. I've begged you for years, but now it's time to act upon it. We need to move her back home."

"*What?*" I said.

"You heard me," said Rajendra. "Your mother and I have been discussing it for weeks. It's time to move our family back to India."

His words echoed through the room.

"Are you serious?" I said. I turned to Amma. "Amma, come on. You wouldn't do this."

To my horror, Amma nodded. "I think Rajendra's right," she said. "I can't do this alone."

The betrayal was awful and plummeting. My mother wanted to take me away.

"You've gotten out of control in Citrus Grove," continued Rajendra. "It's time you learned some respect. I'll make sure of it myself—"

"Good luck with that," I snarled. I stalked across the room toward his unfinished portrait of Amma and me, the paints still slick and wet. "Maya, *no*," Amma begged, but it was too late.

I didn't know if the violence came from fear, or maybe I'd just been waiting for the opportunity to strike. Because in one swift motion, I ripped the portrait off the easel, paints pinging to the floor. I seized the edges, tore it clean in half. In maybe thirty seconds, I ruined a month of Rajendra's work.

The way my father screamed, you'd think I'd murdered his family. In a way, I guess, I had. I stood in the living room, grinning wildly, my hands dripping with paint. *Like father, like daughter*, I thought. We both were artists, fucked up to the core.

Rajendra didn't touch me, but he scared me enough that I lurched backward, tripping over the easel. He was shouting at me, blurring English and Tamil so I didn't fully understand him. Amma shoved him away.

"*Rajendra, no!*" Amma shouted. She stood in front of me, protective.

My father glared at us both. Then, to my mingled surprise and horror, he backed out of the room.

"I've had enough," he said. "This is it. Sujatha, I'm sorry, but I can't stand for this. I—"

"Raj, what are you saying?" said Amma as Rajendra continued his slow retreat toward the door.

"I can't handle this anymore," Rajendra said with a finality that punctured us all. "Unless you're coming back with me, I'm leaving."

And then Amma was raising her voice, trying her best to stop what was coming. "Don't you dare," she was yelling. "If you take one more step toward the door—"

There was no way we hadn't woken up the entire neighborhood. For a wild second, I imagined how we'd look to onlookers, three brown people breaking things and shouting with our full chests. It was a miracle nobody had called the police.

Rajendra slammed the door behind him. I scrambled to my feet, also hoping to escape, but Amma caught my arm. "Not you, too!" she said. "Maya, *sit down*."

"Amma, I'm sorry. Please let me go." With Rajendra out of the house, my anger broke down, replaced by pure grief. I clutched at my mother, smearing paint on her blouse. Helpless as a child. With surprising strength, she pulled me to my feet.

"I can't look at you right now," she said, and that's what did it. I collapsed, limp, let Amma pull me into my room.

"You're not going to move me," I said. I hated how I sounded, begging like this. Amma stopped in the doorway, her face flat and cold.

"What choice do I have?" she said. She shut the door with a rattle I felt in my bones.

My heart pounded as I paced my bedroom. If I stayed here, my parents would take me to India. They'd ship me thousands of miles away from everything I knew, everyone I loved.

A small mercy: My phone was still in my pocket. I called Juneau.

"They want to move me back to India," I said. "I don't know when I'll see you again."

"You're joking." Her voice crackled with static.

"I'm not. At least, they're definitely not," I said. "Where are you?"

There was a pause. "I'm at the store. I'm buying road supplies," Juneau answered. "Screw this place. I'm heading out of here."

My heart dropped. "You're *leaving*?"

"There's nothing left for me here," Juneau said. "I need a break from Citrus Grove. At least until things blow over." She paused. "Do you want to come with me?"

Through the window, I saw Amma and Rajendra yelling in the driveway. The sound of their arguments reminded me so forcefully of childhood, it was like I'd been transported. I remembered feeling small and helpless as my parents fought.

Even then, I'd only had one choice: I'd packed my bags and left. The world sprawled before me; the meaning of life lay only paces away. I was just a child, but now I marveled at my premonition. Somehow I'd run, and I'd found Juneau. I still didn't believe in miracles, but something had drawn us together. I didn't doubt it then, and I didn't doubt it now.

"Where would we even go?" I said. I thought that by asking questions I could delay the inevitable. We both knew I was coming.

"It doesn't matter," Juneau said. "Anywhere we want. The whole goddamn world is ours. I'm gonna empty my debit card, bring it in cash. Just pack a bag."

"Yeah, but—"

"You can't give up on us now," Juneau said quietly. "You said it yourself, this doesn't have to end the same as Laila. We just need to get out for now."

The sound of Laila's name worked like a charm. "Okay," I said, and I didn't have to see her to know she was smiling.

After hanging up, I felt a newfound clarity. It was like my instincts took over, just like when I was so immersed in a painting my hands would pull strokes from thin air. I started packing my bag. I realized I'd left my sketchbook in Juneau's bedroom. But that was a small loss, all things considered. Once I'd packed, I called Silva. To my relief, he picked up.

"Are you okay?" he said urgently. "Where are you?"

The sound of his voice filled me with relief. "Silva, I fucked up," I said. "Can you come get me?"

I knew I sounded like I'd gone crazy, but I didn't care. My words blurred together as I finally told him the truth: that I was in love with Juneau, that Rajendra was planning to take me to India, and Amma would let him.

There was a pause on the phone. I realized that Silva was choking up.

"I'm so sorry, Maya," he said. "I feel like such an idiot. I was so hard on you."

Then we were both crying. "Silva, I need to get out of here," I said. "I need to get to Juneau. I need—"

"I know," he said. "I'll be there soon."

Running away from home was easier than I'd expected.

When Silva arrived, parking down the street so my parents wouldn't see him, I climbed out my window and got into his car. It felt almost normal, like we were heading off to school. The only difference was that I wasn't coming back.

For the first few moments of the drive, we didn't say much.

He'd just been violently arrested. I'd just been publicly outed. What else was left to say? But then Silva looked at me. "Do you have everything you need?"

Looking at Silva, I thought longingly of our summer together, his violin music, the easy times I hadn't known to cherish.

"I'll be with Juneau," I said. "She has money and shit. It'll be okay." I wasn't sure if I was reassuring him or myself.

We pulled into the gas station where Juneau had promised to meet me. I was half afraid she'd leave without me, but her yellow Beetle was there, and she was waving at me, so hot and bright. I thought, *I finally did it.* I flew too close to the sun.

I looked at Silva. I wanted to thank him, but I couldn't find the words. I tried anyway. "I know I've caused so much trouble," I said. "And you and Anya and Ife probably never want to see me again—"

"Maya, please," said Silva quietly. "I'm here right now, aren't I?" He squeezed my hand. "I promise the others will come around. You've been so brave, Maya, and…" He trailed off, and I realized that he, too, was searching for words. There was a terrible air of finality to all of this. That's what pushed me to say it.

"I love you, Silva," I told him. "I know you've loved me so perfectly and I can never pay it back, but I want you to know it. I really love you. I do."

I was getting tearful again. "Well, shit," Silva said, but he was teary, too. "Don't get all soft on me now."

When I reached Juneau she kissed me, right in front of Silva, with all the tenderness in the world. We waved as he drove away.

"Are you ready?" Juneau asked.

She was looking expectantly at me, but I didn't see her. Instead, I saw Amma crying in the kitchen, wishing Rajendra and I would repent for our cruelty. I saw Ife's disappointed stare. I saw Anya, terrified and exposed. I saw Silva, pinned down by the cops. And I saw Citrus Grove, cold and impenetrable. There was nothing left, no way forward, except into the sun with Juneau.

"Yeah," I said, climbing into the passenger seat. We didn't say anything else; we didn't need to. Even the sky could see that our love ran deep, and it held fast.

chapter 29

Citrus Grove is miles behind, but all I can think of is Juneau. Her in the driver's seat, me in the passenger's: the natural order of our universe.

We keep passing the usual exits, driving northwest until we've crossed state lines, until any hope of normalcy is in the rearview mirror. All these years I've lived in Citrus Grove, and I've never driven out this far. And suddenly I'm leaving, with no plans to come back.

I've never been on a road trip before, and I try to savor the experience—we play music, honk too loud, make up stories about the other drivers. We have a full tank of gas, plus four thousand dollars in cash, emptied from Juneau's spending account. At Juneau's instruction, I've turned off my phone so my parents or the police can't track me. "Trust me, sweetheart," she murmurs, putting my phone into the glove compartment.

I can tell she's still shaken by today's events, but her eyes blaze with the inevitability of it all.

Where we are driving *to*, that's our big mystery. I've escaped my parents, but I haven't planned far past that. Once Juneau filled my head with talk of visiting tropical islands, exploring museums overseas. The sudden possibilities make me giddy.

Four hours away from Citrus Grove, we stop at a diner. It's the first time we've been on a real public date, requesting a booth for two. It's a cute old-timey diner where the waitresses deliver food on roller skates. This only heightens my sense of incongruity, like Juneau and I exist in a bubble separate from reality and time. Juneau pours sugar packets onto my tongue and then kisses me, so sweet it burns, and if anyone is watching, we no longer care.

A plate of pancakes materializes before me, and I devour them. When I finish one plate, Juneau orders another.

"What do you want?" she says several pancakes later. I know she's not talking about the menu.

"I want to go west," I say, marveling over the ability to speak my future into existence. "My mom might change her mind about India, or maybe not. Either way, I can't go home, and I've never explored beyond Florida before."

Juneau smiles. "I was thinking that, too," she says. "And I know where we can stay, just for a little bit. I have an old friend in New Orleans who will let us use her house."

And just like that, Juneau's done it again. She's pulled another trick from her sleeve.

"Really? Are you sure?" My heart is beating. "Who's your friend?"

Her smile reminds me of when we first met, how omniscient she seemed. She doesn't feel that way to me anymore.

"Are you sure you want to spoil the surprise?" She laughs. "Don't worry. My friend's really nice. I'm sure you'll get along."

Juneau pays for the meal in cash, tipping with bills big enough to raise suspicion, but we don't stick around. We climb into the car, and then we're off to New Orleans.

I'm excited, but I can't quite shake my sense of mounting unease. I don't know exactly where we're going. So much could go wrong. But we keep driving because there is nothing else to do. Besides, without a plan I wouldn't function. I need small steps, brushstrokes, slow and steady. One more breath, one more mile. New Orleans keeps my panic at bay.

New Orleans is ten hours west of Orlando on a good day. If I was a good driver, we could've alternated driving shifts, and we might've made it in one stretch. But I'm too nervous to drive, so everything falls on Juneau. She doesn't show it, but I can tell she's getting tired, especially as the afternoon wears into evening. Our conversation dies out, and my ass aches in the seat; I've had to pee for fifty miles. I wish I could check my phone. I want to stretch my legs.

It's in the twilight hour that things start to fall apart.

I catch Juneau's eyes fluttering as we cross the border to Alabama. We're starting to drift in the lane. At first I don't realize the danger is Juneau—I assume it's the high speeds, curving road. But then the car veers sharply, and I turn to see that Juneau's eyes are closed. They're closed!

"JUNEAU-FUCKING-LOOK!" I gasp as we barrel toward a ditch. She startles and swerves the car, slamming the brakes with a screech that makes me want to curl up and cry.

"Holy *shit*," she says, leaning forward, knuckles white on the wheel.

"You fell asleep," I say, unable to contain the accusation in my voice. "We could've died."

Juneau bites her lip; I feel a tinge of her displeasure. It's pitch-dark except for our headlights, twin beams cutting the air. "I got distracted for a moment," she says. "Sorry I scared you."

"I think we should stop for the night," I say. "You're tired."

"I'm fine," Juneau insists, but she can't stifle a yawn. The darkness outside feels oppressive.

"No, you're not," I say. "You can't drive for another four hours. That's how far we are from New Orleans. You need sleep."

Aside from the near crash, a new fear is piercing me—we're two queer women alone in the middle of nowhere. We have a shitload of cash in the trunk. If we get stranded, who knows what might befall us? I close my eyes like I can wish myself back into bed.

"What the hell, Juneau," I hear myself say. "What are we even doing here?"

"We need to make it to New Orleans." Juneau is speaking to me like I'm a child. "I told you, my friend's going to take care of us. I'm going to keep driving, and we're going to make it. Trust me."

"Trust me, me, me," I say. I sound incoherent, but I don't care. "Juneau, this is a terrible idea. We shouldn't be doing this. We need to stop and think—"

She starts driving, ignoring me. I feel frozen with dread.

"Juneau, we need to stop the car. We can't keep driving like this," I say. The inner alarms that I've ignored for so long, the self-preserving instinct that should've roared to life long before—the moment we stole Squash's car, the moment I met Juneau, even—are now blaring with a vengeance.

Juneau laughs, startling me. And for a second I don't feel like Maya Krishnan, Juneau's crime-committing lover, but Maya Krishnan, the quiet sophomore from art class. The girl who kept her head down, watching Juneau from afar, hopeful for her love—except now that I've gotten it, it's too searing to take.

"You're just scared," she says. "When we get there, we can unpack all this shit, but right now I need you to woman up a bit—"

The car gains speed. Ignoring Juneau's previous instructions, I reach into the glove compartment and turn on my phone.

The screen lights up with messages. Amma's text is bright on top: Maya, I'm worried out of my mind. I've called the police. Please respond.

Guilt seeps through me, rollicking and all-consuming. Still, I don't call my mother. Instead I call Silva, desperate to hear his voice. But I don't get the chance. Because when she hears the phone, Juneau startles. "What are you doing?" she demands.

"Calling Silva," I say. "My mom called the police, and—"

Before I can react, Juneau grabs my phone from me.

"Give it back!" I lunge for my still-ringing phone, and in a panic Juneau flings it out the window.

For a moment I'm too stunned to respond. Then my rage returns to me, familiar as an old friend.

"*Juneau!*" I shout. I forget that she's driving and I reach toward her—she flinches, and this split second of vulnerability sends another spasm of rage through me. *I* am the vulnerable one. She is Juneau, in control until the very end, and I don't know who I am anymore.

"Stop the car, Juneau!" I yell. "My phone—why did you just—"

"I'm sorry!" she gasps, but she stops. "I told you, we can't use our phones. The police can track our locations. I'm eighteen, legally an adult, which means I technically kidnapped you—"

"I don't care! Juneau, you can't just—" I keep saying her name.

"I'm sorry," Juneau says again, this time tearfully. And, because our relationship has started to feel like a zero-sum game, when she starts crying, I stop, because one of us needs to hold it together. "I got scared, okay? I thought you were going to call the police or leave me alone—"

I know better than to suggest we retrieve my phone; there's no way it survived a fall at sixty miles an hour. But rage still pounds through my body.

"Fuck this, Juneau," I say. "We need to stop now. I'm not asking. I'm not going farther tonight." She wipes her eyes, but because she feels guilty, she obeys my instructions to park at a motel.

The clerk glares suspiciously when we request a room for two. Of course he does: We're two weary-looking teenage girls paying in all cash.

"Where are your parents?" he asks.

Juneau looks exhausted. "My dad's a lawyer, okay?" she says. "He gave me this money to stay the night. Do you want me to call him?"

The clerk doesn't say anything after that. He just takes us to our room, which turns out to contain a single bed, because of course all the doubles are occupied. I'm angry at Juneau, so I move a pillow onto the rickety sofa, but she rolls her eyes. "Don't be ridiculous," she says. "Just sleep here with me."

I consider being stubborn, but I don't have a phone or money of my own; Juneau is all I have. In bed she presses her face into my arm and mumbles about how sorry she is. Over and over, until it feels like we aren't two separate girls anymore, and I relent.

"This is just the first day," I tell her. "Tomorrow will be better."

Tomorrow we will reach New Orleans. Or we won't. But right now I'm tired, so tired. Juneau falls asleep first, one arm slung possessively over me like she's afraid I'll go rogue overnight. Instead, I lie awake and think about my life. When I was little, I wanted to be an artist like my dad, then a nurse like my mom, then a pet groomer—I don't know where I got that one. But now all I want is to be happy. And safe, if that's not too much to ask.

In the morning we return to Juneau's car. Last night was our worst-ever fight, but in the morning it feels blameless and empty as an eggshell. We consult the maps, and then we're off to New Orleans.

As we cross the border into Louisiana, Juneau seems to awaken. "New Orleans is amazing I've heard," she says. "The food, the music, and oh! The art..." She tells me about all the places we could go, all the buildings we could see, and her excitement softens me. This is why I love Juneau, after all: her boundless possibility. I resolve to be more supportive of her. Then my sleeplessness catches up to me, and I nap until Juneau pokes me.

"Wake up," she says, and then she can't contain herself. "Maya, we're here!"

I open my eyes, groggy. We've parked in front of a tiny house on a residential street. It's late afternoon, the sunlight making everything luminous.

"Where are we? Your friend's house?" My mouth tastes horrible and my hair is mussed.

"Well, sort of," says Juneau. "Maya, there's something I need to tell you." She takes a deep breath and hands me something from her pocket. I look down to see a well-worn postcard of New Orleans.

When I turn it over I see the message, *The house, four walls, and garden—I have it all, minus you.* I skip down to the signature: *Laila Afzar.*

"Holy shit. *Laila?*" I say. "Is this her address? Is *she* your friend?" I reread the message a few times: *I have it all, minus you.* I feel a whine in my gut, pitchy and insistent, growing slowly into a howl.

"Yeah," says Juneau. She smiles widely, like we're at a birthday party and she's just given me the most wonderful gift. "Laila lives in New Orleans now. This is her house. We can crash with her, at least until we've figured shit out."

Laila. I can't believe it. For so long Laila has felt like a mythical creature to me: utterly tangential, functionally make-believe. But now, in a strange twist of destiny, she's become the object of pursuit, the final step of our quest. Amma, Silva, Anya, Ife, Theo, Mateo, Rajendra—all the people who once filled my life—now feel like fictional characters, remnants of an old dream. Nothing feels real.

"Juneau, how could you—" I start. I mean to ask her how

she could bring me to the house of the girl who took her virginity, when two nights before she took mine? How exactly does she expect me to feel? But instead I ask a more practical question.

"What about her homophobic family?" I say. "Don't they hate you?"

Juneau laughs aloud at that. "Laila's not a kid anymore," she says. "She doesn't live with her parents. She's a grown-up person with her own house. We're safe."

Something cracks open in my chest. I try to picture adulthood, freedom, but I know so little about the world or what it takes to live in it. Does Juneau really believe that Laila Afzar, with her grown-up house, can promise us safety?

"But I thought you haven't spoken to Laila in years," I say. "She wanted to get back together, but you were too scared to respond."

"Yeah, and?" Juneau doesn't seem pleased with this line of questioning.

"Have you talked to her since then? Or at least asked if we could stay?" I ask.

"No, I haven't," Juneau admits. "But I know she lives at this address."

I can't seem to keep my mouth closed. I try again. "How can you be sure this is it?"

Juneau looks bored. "Because I looked the house up once," she says. "When Laila first sent me the postcard I found it on Google Maps. We used to talk about it, you know? The house we'd live in once we were safely out of Citrus Grove. I wanted a city apartment, but she wanted a proper house. Four walls, a garden, no shoes worn indoors."

You planned for a house? I stare at the Juneau I know: the girl who told me we could never have a relationship, who barely thinks through the present, let alone plans for her future. How did Laila inspire, or perhaps invent, the other Juneau? I knew Laila was special, but now I feel a sting of resentment. What we have—whatever that is—can never compare.

"Juneau, I don't care. We can't stay here. I don't want to." The howl in my ears has built into a scream. "Are you still in love with her or something?"

Juneau sighs. "Jealousy isn't cute on you, peach," she says, and I stiffen. I can't tell if she's teasing, but her words feel razor sharp.

"Maya, come on," Juneau pleads. "Please let me at least knock on the door. See if she's there. Can't you imagine how I feel?"

"I—" I have a startling, intrusive image of myself in two years. What if Amma and Rajendra made good on their promise, sent me to India? If I managed to return, would I be able to control myself from knocking on Juneau's door? Besides, we're all the way in New Orleans, and there doesn't seem to be another choice.

"Fine," I say, though my heart feels like it's sinking. I follow her up the driveway.

How do you present yourself to your current not-quite-girlfriend's long-lost first love? I awkwardly finger-comb my hair as we wait. For several tense moments nothing happens, but then a young brown woman opens the door. It's Laila, in the flesh. She's even more beautiful than in her pictures. Despite myself, I feel my heartbeat quicken.

"Laila," says Juneau, holding up the postcard. "Is...is now a good time?" She's using a soft voice I've never heard before, and I realize that Juneau, uncharacteristically, is nervous. My heart aches as she hugs Laila. But Laila stands stiffly in the doorway, mouth open.

"Juneau," she says at last. "What the hell are you doing here?"

chapter 30

Laila makes us leave our shoes outside, a small gesture of normalcy that feels almost absurd. Her house is clean and colorful, swiped out of an IKEA catalogue—I half expect to find Swedish meatballs cooking on the stove.

"Laila, wow," says Juneau. She stares at the living room like a child in a candy store. "This is just...wow."

I find it strange that Juneau, with her big house, is so impressed by Laila's tiny place. But then I remember this is the first time she's seeing Laila all grown up, with her own house and rules. Laila's moved up in the world, and Juneau can't see her the same way.

"Yeah, well. Don't make yourself too comfortable," says Laila.

This wounds Juneau; I see her face fall almost comically. "Laila," Juneau tries again. "Can we talk?"

Laila sighs. "Sit down," she says. "I have to finish in the kitchen. Maybe that will give you a few moments to get your story together."

I stare at Laila as she disappears. She's small like me, but her hips are full, her clothes sensible, and gait confident in a way that marks her as a woman, not a girl. I calculate in my head—she's twenty or twenty-one, given her graduation year. She definitely has a job, I'm guessing, judging by the multiple-monitor setup in the living room.

When Laila returns, I suspect she wasn't actually in the kitchen, because her hair, previously in an unglamorous bun, has been brushed, and she's no longer wearing sweatpants.

"So," says Laila, nodding at me. "Who's this kid?"

Kid? I think, indignant. Juneau scoots beside me on the couch. "This is Maya," she says, giving Laila no indication of the fact that she and I are sleeping together. "We need help, Laila. Things are bad."

Laila's mouth flattens. "I'm sure they are," she says. "They must've been really bad if you couldn't stay in touch for two years." Despite her critical words, Laila has the flat affectation of a disappointed adult, like she doesn't actually care.

Under Laila's unyielding stare, Juneau has the decency to falter. "I'm sorry," she says. "I got your postcards and your texts. But shit was bad at home. My mom was really pissed. I just—" She trails off, out of excuses. "Are you okay?" she says at last. "What happened with you?"

Laila relents slightly, but her tone remains guarded. "Yeah, I'm okay," she says. "Let's see. I got my associate's degree, I got my graphic design job. My girlfriend, Rosie, rents this house with me, but she's at work. Life is fine."

It's fascinating to me, the details people prioritize when giving others the rundown of their lives. Undoubtedly years of trauma and recovery are packed into Laila's matter-of-fact summary of the past two years, but she doesn't divulge them.

"You have a girlfriend?" says Juneau. Is that jealousy I hear? "What about your parents?"

Laila shrugs. "I'm an adult, June," she says, startling me. All these months I've known Juneau Zale, and I never knew she went by *June.* "Once I got my own job and moved out, they couldn't really say shit to me. Our relationship improved with time. It's not like high school anymore. I guess you'll get there soon enough," she adds, looking at Juneau. "You're almost graduating."

Juneau looks down. "That's kind of the problem," she says. "I messed up."

I see something flick on in Laila's eyes. She goes into protective mode. "Tell me everything," she says.

Laila sits down, and Juneau starts speaking. She tells Laila about the Pugilists, the war we found ourselves embroiled in. She tells her about Squash, Mateo, the leaked nudes, the public outing. Laila's eyes rake over me, the girl who loves Juneau, following her to the ends of the earth—or at least to New Orleans. She doesn't seem impressed by Juneau's escapades. Instead, with each damning detail, her mouth gets flatter.

"So you fucked up," she says when Juneau finishes. "You finally went too far, and now you're running away. Does that sum it up?" she says.

Juneau stumbles. "Yeah, but—"

Laila cuts her off. "You were so close. We talked about it, remember? How close you were to getting out of Citrus Grove?"

She shakes her head. "Now you've dragged this kid down with you."

There's that word again. *Kid.* It's not just because I'm a sophomore. Laila's assuming that I'm powerless against Juneau. While it stings, she's right. All this time I've been following Juneau's wishes, and it's taken a perfect stranger exactly five minutes to notice.

I stand up. "Juneau, we should go," I say. "This was a terrible idea." I'm not sure if I'm referring to our visit to Laila's house, our decision to run away, or something more essential than that: our friendship, our love.

Juneau looks despairing. "Maya, wait," she says. To Laila, she says, "Laila, I know I screwed up. I *am* screwed up. But I need help. I just need somewhere to stay for a bit, just until Maya and I can sort things out—"

Laila snorts. "June, I'm sorry, but I'm not running a halfway house for short-sighted teenage girls. Harboring a runaway minor is illegal, and so is running away with one, you know that?" She leans back in her chair. "Those days are behind me. You two need to leave."

I don't even have to look at Juneau to know that she is completely and utterly crushed. But I manage to speak to Laila.

"Look. I know you don't know me," I say. "You have no reason to care about me. But I just got outed, my family's turned their backs on me, and I have nowhere to go."

Laila glances at me with surprise. Maybe she didn't think I could speak. To be fair, I've provided no evidence to the contrary. Why is it only when Juneau shuts down that I finally wake up?

"You of all people should know what that feels like," I add.

I could be crossing a boundary by invoking Laila's past, but luckily it works; Laila's face falls, and I know she's going to cave. When did I get this manipulative? Perhaps I learned it from Juneau—or perhaps it's been part of me all along.

"Fine," Laila says. "But only for one night."

Juneau splutters. "*What?*" she says. "Where are we supposed to go after that?"

"Laila, thank you," I say, interrupting Juneau. Laila gives both of us a piercing look, her gaze especially tough on Juneau.

"June, I've got about an hour, if you'd like to speak outside. After that, I'm going to meet Rosie," Laila says. "We'll be back around dinnertime. You two can find whatever you need around the house. And later tonight, you and *I*"—I assume she's talking to Juneau, but instead she's pointing at me, and I startle—"are having a little chat."

With that, Laila disappears, taking Juneau with her.

Through the window, I watch them walk down the street. It's like they develop new personalities around each other: Laila, who was previously reserved—possibly because we crashed her house—now talks animatedly, whereas Juneau listens closely, hands jammed in her pockets. I have no idea what they're discussing. So I wait.

After what feels like ages, Laila gets into her car and Juneau returns to the house, looking defeated.

"Hey," I tell her, instead of what I mean to say, which is: *What were you and Laila talking about?* And, *What comes next for us?*

But Juneau is too upset for words. I've never seen her like this before. First she disappears to take a long shower. Then she inspects all of Laila's things—her books, her drawers, the pictures of her new life pasted proudly on the fridge—before stepping out to smoke. When she returns, the weed must've worked, because she seems peaceful. But I'm not. I'm humming with rage at Juneau for shutting me out.

Still, because I'm me, I try to play nice.

"Maybe we should talk while making dinner. We could fix something up before Laila gets home," I suggest. It's late afternoon, fading quickly into evening. "You know, as a thank-you for letting us stay."

"You're such a good person," says Juneau. "Doesn't it get tiring sometimes?"

"Less tiring than being so stubborn," I say. Juneau's eyes fly open, but before she can speak, I say, "I told you we shouldn't just waltz into Laila's house like this, and I was right. She has a new life, Juneau, a good one, without you. Who are we to invade it?"

Juneau is angry as she raids Laila's kitchen for supplies: a box of pasta, tomatoes, and garlic. She says nothing, so I push harder.

"This is the problem with you, Juneau. You never think anything through. You never think about other people. How did you really think Laila would feel? Or me, for that matter?"

Juneau chops tomatoes with the intensity I have normally attributed to her artistic practice. I boil water for pasta. The scene is hilariously domestic. I imagine us five years from now, in a serious relationship, fighting in our shared kitchen. The same arguments, same problems. It never gets better, just turns around.

"Juneau," I say. "What did you fucking think would happen?"

There's a terrible pause, and then Juneau sets down her knife.

"I think," she says at last, "that maybe running away together wasn't a good idea. Maybe…" She swallows. "Laila and I talked it through, and you shouldn't have come."

Her words sink in. This wasn't what I was expecting her to say.

"No, that's not it," I protest automatically. "I wanted to be with you."

"Bringing you was the wrong idea," says Juneau, tears in her eyes. "We can't actually survive out here together. I can't take care of you, Maya. Not like you deserve. You're right. I keep fucking up, and I'm so goddamn difficult, and—"

I touch her hand. "Okay, so you want to go back to Citrus Grove?" I said. "We'll work something out. Hopefully things have simmered down—"

"No, *you'll* go back," says Juneau. "That is, if you decide to. Obviously I can't force you. But even if you go, I'm not coming back. I'm done."

It's those last two words, uttered with terrible finality, that make me start crying, too.

"What are you saying?" I say. "Of course you can come back. It's only one more semester to graduation, you can get through it with me."

What I mean to say is, *I can't get through it without you.* But instead I beg, "Come on, Juneau. It'll be okay."

"No, it won't," says Juneau flatly. "Do you see Laila's life? I want this. I'm ready for it. I'm eighteen years old—I can move anywhere and find work. Laila can help me get set up, and then I'm on my own."

My heart feels like it's grinding itself to pulp. "Where will you go?" I ask.

Juneau shrugs. "I'm thinking California," she says. "I'll figure it out from there."

California, I think. On the other side of the country, which might as well be another planet. A land of sunshine, not unlike Florida. Except while our hometown crushed Juneau's soul, I've seen enough movies to know that California will welcome her with open arms.

The abandonment hurts so much it's like layers of my own skin have been ripped away. The pasta is boiling, and I'm still crying, unintentionally salting the water with my tears. All I can think is, *Not you too.*

"You'll be okay, Maya," says Juneau. "Your future's so bright, and you've got two more years of school. Your friends will have your back. And whatever's going on with your family—Laila thinks she can help you with that. I'm still looking out for you. I promise."

I know she's right. But I still can't believe I'm being broken up with by Juneau Zale in her ex-girlfriend's kitchen.

When I've composed myself, Juneau leans over and hugs me. It feels rare, like love in reverse. Juneau is rarely a hugger; she's all kisses and flirtatious winks. Hugging seems too intimate for her. It seems to break the spell or ruin the magic. Because up close, Juneau isn't sexy or confident or indomitable. In my arms she's small and shivering. Skin and bones.

"Maya," she says. "I'm so sorry to disappoint you."

Perhaps I'm a little shaky, too, as I stare at her face. She is pale, drawn, nothing like the Renaissance portrait I first imagined her to be. Her hair is plastered to her cheeks, her face blotched with tears.

Beautiful.

"I don't know what to say—"

"Then don't," she says. She's so close I can smell her citrus perfume, and maybe I'm just imagining it, but fresh paint and grass, too. I close my eyes and kiss her face, the one I've always longed to draw.

We stand there sobbing and cooking pasta. At some point Laila comes home, now accompanied by Rosie, and we eat dinner. Laila's in a far better mood now that she's had a chance to process everything. She and Rosie drink glasses of wine, which they pointedly refuse to share with us.

"Maya and I talked it out, and we need another favor," says Juneau. Seeing Laila's expression, she says quickly, "We're leaving tomorrow, don't worry about that. But we need some help getting there."

After exchanging glances with Rosie, Laila nods. Juneau tells her our plan. She can pay her in cash but needs Laila to buy her plane ticket with her credit card. Moments later on Laila's laptop, a one-way trip to San Francisco appears for Juneau. I swallow my pasta and try not to cry.

"There's also the matter of the Pugilists," Juneau tells me. "The Harveys are still on our asses, but I think I know how to fix it. Once you're home safely, Maya, I want you to go to Dr. Harvey and put the blame on me. For stealing the car, for all of it," she says loudly, as I start to protest. "I don't want you, Mateo, Pat, or anyone else to be punished. I'll be gone anyway," she adds. "And then—and I know Pat agrees—you and Theo should take over the Pugilists. You can continue our work next year, however you choose. I know Theo's been angling for us to go aboveground anyway. If you guys did public, legal advocacy, you could be just as much of a pain in the ass, but you couldn't be punished for it. It could be a nice change."

Beside her, Laila smiles. It's the first time I've seen her smile, and it transforms her face. Despite how young she is, she's still unreal to me. She founded the Pugilists. She set into effect this cascading chain of motions that brought Juneau and me together, and while she never intended it, I'm still grateful to her.

"I'll do my best," I say, both to Juneau and Laila, and I mean it.

After dinner, Laila asks me to join her outside for our chat. I follow her with a sense of trepidation, sensing Juneau's eyes on me. I am Juneau's current girlfriend, if you can even call me that, talking to her ex. What could Laila possibly want to say?

"I think," Laila tells me on the porch, "it's time for you to call your mother. Don't you agree?"

She interprets my expression correctly as one of terror. "We'll talk it through first," she says. "And then you can use my phone, because Juneau told me what she did with yours." She winces. "It wasn't so long ago, when I was in your position," Laila says. "I was really terrified when my parents found out about my relationship with Juneau. I was always afraid they wouldn't understand my sexuality, and I was right. They didn't."

I stare at her, wondering whether she is actually trying to make me feel better, and if so, how she will accomplish it.

"My parents reacted...strongly," she continues. "They couldn't recognize the daughter they thought they knew, and they wanted to get things back under control. Our entire family moved out after graduation. Juneau says you're in a similar situation, right?"

I nod.

"At the time, I was so angry at them, Maya, and I'm sure you are, too," Laila says. "I thought I was in love, so why were they keeping me from Juneau with their horrible beliefs? They thought something was wrong with me, and I thought something was wrong with them. Is that how you feel?"

That is, in fact, a very accurate explanation of how I feel. I didn't expect Laila to understand me so perfectly.

Laila looks at me bracingly. "Listen," she says. "I'm going to tell you what I wish I knew when I was in your situation. You can do with it what you will. If you decide not to go home, that's up to you. Juneau could take you to California if you really wanted."

I briefly imagine Juneau and me in California. Smoking weed under palm trees, dancing on the Golden Gate Bridge. Even in fantasy I know it's ridiculous. I look at Laila. "How did it get better?" I say.

Laila leans back in her chair. "Back when I was outed," she says, "I was too angry at my parents to discuss it with them rationally. And who knows?" she adds with a smirk. "Maybe if I'd run away like you, it might've forced that discussion. Or at least I would've gotten some space to process and decide what I wanted. I definitely would've gotten my ass beat."

"Ass-beating isn't off the table for me, either," I say darkly, and she laughs.

"Look. It took me a long time, and plenty of soul searching, to figure some of this out," Laila says. "But ultimately, here's what I realized. My parents weren't freaking out because they hated me. They were reacting out of love. Even if it was suffocating and frankly traumatic." She paused. "Their love was the problem, which meant it could be the solution, too."

I nod slowly as she continues. "Our parents have two sets of beliefs," Laila explains. "First, that we are the most important people in their lives. We're the reason they immigrated, the daughters they've been working themselves raw to protect. The second belief is that those daughters should only date men, or not date at all. It's when those beliefs conflict that things get tricky for them. Since those two beliefs are impossible to reconcile, they're going to have to let one of them go. And I'm betting your mom's not willing to lose her place in your life. Which means, eventually…"

"She's going to change her mind about my sexuality," I finish. "You're saying my mom will come around because she loves me so much, she has no choice?"

"I'm not saying it'll be painless." Laila shrugs. "It's taken me two years with my parents. I had to move out, get a job, go to therapy, learn to stand on my own before I could stand up to them. But things will improve. I promise they will."

I stare at her. With the exception of Juneau, I've never spoken to an older girl about love before, and certainly not a girl who looks like me, who understands the painful tussle of love with my mother, the gaps that tug us apart at the seams.

"Are you afraid that your mother will hurt you?" Laila says quietly. "Like physically beat you, kick you out, anything like that?"

"She would never," I say immediately, and Laila nods.

"That's the wonderful part of being the daughters of

immigrants," she says. "We're our parents' whole hearts. It can be a painful burden, but most of the time it's a gift, because they'll never let us go." She sighs. "Sometimes we don't give our parents enough credit. They crossed oceans and climbed so many hills to give us better lives. I promise it's not your queerness that will be the hill they die on. You just have to give them time."

She smiles a bit at this, and I do, too. I take a deep breath. "Can I borrow your phone?" I ask.

Amma picks up on the second ring. Her voice swells with emotion. "Maya, thank God," she says. "I thought you wouldn't call. I thought—"

She chokes up, unable to finish the sentence. And then she is so upset with me. As she unburdens her soul aloud—it's a miracle how much human grief a phone line can carry, because if you somehow could put it on a physical line, that shit would be crushing—it takes all my willpower not to cry, too.

Soon I realize that Rajendra isn't present. With his loud voice and intrusiveness, I would know by now if he was.

"He's gone," Amma says when I ask.

"Gone?" I echo blankly.

"He's not coming back," Amma says faintly. "He left after you did. He said things in this family were too far gone, and he didn't want to have anything to do with us."

My fists tighten around the phone. Instinctively I'm relieved, but I know how much pain he's causing Amma. "I'm so sorry," I say. "You're all alone at home. He shouldn't have left."

Amma interrupts. "I don't care about him, kanna. I care

about you," she says. "Where are you, Maya? Whose phone are you calling from?"

I tell her I'm at a friend's house in New Orleans. "I left with Juneau, but I changed my mind. I'm coming home," I say. And then, before I can stop myself, I add, "I don't care about her, either, Amma. I care about you."

It's this simple admission that opens the floodgates in me. I launch forward before Amma can interrupt. "But before I come home, I want to discuss some things," I say. "First, I want you to promise that we're not moving, not until we've talked about it. I love our life in Citrus Grove, just the two of us, and I'm not ready for anything else."

Amma takes a deep breath. I try to picture her now; our tiny house suddenly enormous, her lonely voice echoing against the walls. "I think with your father gone, India is off the table anyway," she says. "I do want to take you back to see your motherland. But it will happen one day as a blessing, and not as a punishment. Does that sound fair?"

"Yes," I say, which is all I can manage without sobbing.

Amma has no such reservations—she's crying openly. "I know we've had our differences," she says. "But I never wanted you to run away from me. You are everything to me, don't you know that?"

I think of what Laila just said: *We're our parents' whole hearts.* I wonder, one day, if I will have a child, and thus allow another human to have such a particular chokehold on me. It is a terrifying thought.

"I know," I say. "Which brings me to my second thing. I don't want to lie to you, Amma. Not about where I'm going or what I'm doing, and definitely not about who I am." I trail off.

"You're referring to your sexuality," Amma says.

"Yeah, but it's not just that," I say. "I'm an artist, Amma. I'm going to be loud, sexual, openly political. You might not agree with how I choose to express myself. I can't always be the safe daughter you want me to be."

For a moment Amma doesn't say anything. I'm afraid I've gone too far. But then she sniffles and says, "You're really your father's daughter, aren't you?"

Grief goes through me like a lance. I cling to the phone like it's my mother herself. "And yours," I say. "Mostly yours."

After I hang up, the sleeplessness of the last few nights catches up to me. Laila doesn't have a spare room, so Juneau and I sleep together on the floor of her living room. Either due to our recent breakup or out of respect to Laila, Juneau makes a point not to let our bodies touch. I don't know if either of us actually expects to sleep. But as we both stare at the ceiling, I ask, "What's the first thing you'll do when you get to California?"

I can't see her, but I picture her smile in the dark. "Probably call you," she says. Then she catches herself. "That is, once you get another phone. But I'll reach back out as soon as I can. I'll be thinking about you the whole time. I promise."

Even then I know she's lying. The moment she's free, I suspect she'll never think of me again. That's the difference between Juneau Zale and me. She is the main character of my story, but I was just a subplot in hers. My story will end without her.

Or will it? I think of everything that life has in store for me. Juneau might have California, that bright and sunny paradise. But I have my mother waiting back home, my mother who gave me everything, crossing oceans with her complicated love. I have Ife, Anya, Silva, who know me better than anyone, whose love comes free of sharpness or pain. I have the Pugilists and a better school to build. And I have my art, my ability to bring worlds into existence. Two more years, and Laila's right: I'll be a grown woman, I'll be okay. It's the okayness of the situation that holds me like a blanket as I finally fall asleep.

chapter 31

The next morning we drive Juneau's car to the airport so Juneau can catch her flight to San Francisco. Juneau's leaving the car with Laila for safekeeping. Instead of sitting with me, she climbs up front with Laila. Like she's weaning me off before the final departure.

"I'll reach out as soon as it's safe," Juneau promises. She kisses me fast, before I can savor it. It doesn't feel like a goodbye kiss—with her lips, she's promising more and more. "Be brave," she says. And then she's gone.

From the airport drop-off line I blow Juneau a kiss. Cars honk behind us, forcing Laila to keep driving. The clouds don't part when we do. I look back at Juneau once; the rest is memory.

"Are you okay, kid?" says Laila as we merge onto the highway one woman down. I still hate that she calls me that, but I force a nod.

"I know this is the right decision. But I'll miss her," I say. That's all I can manage without crying, which I refuse to do in front of Juneau's ex.

"Oh, I know," says Laila. "Trust me, I know."

The car ride feels blurry, like a drug trip. I watch the glow of streetlights dance on Laila's face. Passing drivers might think we're sisters as we drive to the bus station.

"Good luck, Maya," says Laila. I look absolutely pitiful with my duffel of clothes and Juneau's rumpled hoodie, like a child sent home early from a sleepover.

"Thanks for everything," I say, and I mean it. I sit in the back of the bus wishing I had my sketchbook as the landscape rumbles past. Curling around my grief like an animal. After everything, all I can think is this: I don't know what I was expecting to happen in New Orleans. A cathartic, third-act coda to bring our lives full circle? A grand, undiscovered truth at the end of our quest? I don't know. But now I'm going home, minus the girl I love painfully, from whom I've rescued myself.

I spend the bus ride imagining alternative endings to our road trip—one where Juneau tells me she loves me, one where Citrus Grove disappears, one where we crash into the farmland, Thelma-and-Louise-style. Finally I settle on the perfect finale: the one where everyone on earth finds what they're looking for. Someone to love, a place to call home, something as simple as a yellow sun. Where they find their needs inside themselves, as if they were there all along.

My mother, steady and unfailing. She's waiting at the bus station for me, just like when I was a kid. For the first decade of my life, hers was the first face I'd see after school. When I disembark, she hugs me fiercely, unwilling to let go.

"I'm sorry," I keep saying.

"I know you are," she responds. "But I'm still scared. I'll be scared for a very long time."

We keep talking in the car. "Can I tell you the truth?" she says after a while. "I know I've always said that I was thinking of you when I immigrated here. That I wanted to give you the best opportunities, all of that. But the truth was, I didn't think about you at all."

She pauses. I have no idea where she's going with this. But it's rare when Amma tells me about her own life, so I shut up and listen.

"I walked into it with my eyes closed tight. I was too busy trying to keep a job, to survive. When your present is so unstable, how can you dream of the future?" she said. "I didn't know how to raise you or how single parenthood might affect you or how to help you make friends. I didn't even teach you your own native language. Kanna, you learned so much on your own. Now you know so much that I don't. You'll live a life that I could never. And where will that leave me?"

Her eyes focus on the road. We're almost at our house. *Find your home*, I remember dimly. Why didn't I know it was here all along?

"You're right," I say at last. "You didn't get a chance to dream of the future, but I do. I get to think about art and changing the world, all of those things." I wipe my eyes. "And you know why that is? It's because I never had to worry about the survival part. Because you handled it for me."

Then, before I completely lose it, I say, "The only difference between you and me? It's that I had you."

At home my mom makes me shower and eat. I was only gone for three days, but the house smells new and distinct: a mix of cleaner, spices, incense. Anya always said the Krishnan household had a certain scent, but I didn't believe her, because I was accustomed to it. Now the smell marks me as an outsider. I'm back, but a small part of me remains in New Orleans. That part will never return.

And neither, it seems, will my father. Even though Rajendra has gone—absconded with his easels, leaving nothing but dried paint on the floor—it takes Amma weeks to forgive me. By driving him away, I've dealt her a terrible wound. I don't know if she'll ever regain her trust in me. But for now, she's willing to give me a chance. She allows me to return to school on the condition that she drives me herself. She tells me we need to see a therapist, and I agree.

We start taking long walks in the evenings. Amma has adjusted her work schedule so we're in the house at the same time. At first I think she switched it just to keep an eye on me, but then I notice that she's happier the longer we spend together. On those walks, she tells me her stories. About her life in India, before she was Rajendra's wife or my mother. Back when she was just a girl.

"I want you to know that I understand you," she says. "Or I did, at some point in my life. And I promise I'll get back there. It might just take time. And by the way," she adds, "your friends want to see you. They've been calling me every day."

And so, after dinner, Anya, Ife, and Silva show up to my house. We spread out towels on the yard to talk. I apologize, for what feels like the millionth time, for all the pain I've caused them.

"I know it's not nearly enough," I finish quietly, looking to my friends for their responses.

Silva, who specializes in being the bigger person, nods encouragingly. He knows I need an easy landing. Beside him, Ife is quiet—she doesn't know what to say, and I can't blame her. One day I hope she'll trust me again, and what's more, she'll help when it's time to rebuild the Pugilists. But then Anya leans forward and hugs me, and something inside me sighs with relief.

That's when Anya tells me that thanks to me, she's finally been protected. Theo, at my request, reached out to Anya, and it turns out that she has a powerful legal case against Squash. Theo's parents informed Dr. Harvey that since Anya is a minor, any student who shared the pictures is guilty of distributing child pornography. Which means that half the Pig Patrol are potentially sex offenders.

"If I agree to it," Anya says, "they're pretty sure they can file a successful case against Dr. Harvey for creating a schoolwide culture of sexual harassment. All I'd have to do is testify."

My jaw drops. "Are you going to do it?"

Anya shrugs. "I never wanted the spotlight," she says. "Fighting the system, that's more your style. But..." She pauses. "It means we have the power now." Unconsciously she flexes her fingers, as if she's physically gained a new strength.

"Whatever you choose," I tell her, "I'll stand behind you. I promise." For the first time since homecoming, I see Anya smile.

I had planned on making a clean break from Juneau. Without my phone, I can't call or text her. But one afternoon, in a moment of weakness, I log into my email account and write to her. For a full week I await her response. But she doesn't reply—she's moved on. It's time I do the same.

Following Juneau's orders, once I'm settled into school, I march into Dr. Harvey's office and turn her in for our crimes. The mural, the break-ins, the car theft, all of it. Dr. Harvey is not as gleeful as I imagined, because he has bigger problems: He might get sued by Anya Patel.

The threat of a lawsuit is wearing heavily on Dr. Harvey when I visit his office.

"You realize," he tells me, his wrinkles more pronounced than ever, "that by admitting mere knowledge of Ms. Zale's crimes, you are implicating yourself, becoming open to disciplinary action?"

I shrug. I know I've made the right choice by coming forward, because it means I can protect the other Pugilists. I'm not afraid of what comes next.

"Do with me what you will," I say. "I'm just telling you the truth. I can't stop Anya from suing you—and she might—but I can promise you that with Juneau gone, the crimes will stop. In exchange, I hope my friends will stop being harassed by the cops and the Pig Patrol."

He sighs. "I'll have no choice but to report you to the police," he says. "Unless, of course, we can meet to settle things... extra-judicially."

A wonderful phenomenon: mutually assured destruction. I meet with Dr. Harvey again after school, and by this point I have Fisher & Cho on speed dial. I call Theo's parents, and they join me for the meeting. They threaten the Harveys, reminding them they can't prosecute me for Juneau's crimes unless they're ready to get publicly blasted for sexual discrimination. For a brief, glorious instant, I am more powerful than a man. My fate is staked on Sam Harvey's bright future—and I cannot believe how much that makes me worth. My stellar grades are trotted out, including my shiny math trophies. I summon tears and repentance at a moment's notice. My final sentence is laughable: academic probation and community service. God bless Fisher & Cho.

The downside of turning Juneau in, though, is that I've effectively sealed her fate; now she can never return to Citrus Grove.

I can't yet face the fact that I'll never see her again, so I focus on a smaller problem: My sketchbook is still in her bedroom. I deserve it back, not the least as compensation for everything she's put me through.

During school, I skip my lunch period and walk to Juneau's house. I know better than to try the door—Mrs. Zale is likely to have a jacked-up camera system. I would, if I owned that house. Instead, I wedge her bedroom window open like I've been breaking into homes my whole life.

My sketchbook is exactly where I left it; I slip it into my bag. But looking around Juneau's room, I can't shake the feeling that I'm back in a museum. Like I'm looking at artwork frozen in time, trying to imagine the majestic civilizations past, and through her objects I see her. All her memories, the varied ways that people touched her life.

It occurs to me that in life, unlike in art, we cannot make other people into who we want them to be. Humans are not canvases to be molded and altered. It is imperative to keep the two separate. Otherwise we could all end up like Vincent van

Gogh, mistaking sculpting for painting and accidentally carving off our own ears.

With time, I could learn. I could stand up for myself but still accept others as they are—my mother was right about that. It is a hopeful thought.

Something I tell my new therapist: When someone you love leaves, they don't leave you all at once.

"You've had a history of abandonment," the therapist tells me kindly. "I can imagine it makes your breakup with Juneau even harder."

"Maybe not," I tell her. "I have plenty of practice."

I want to explain how with someone like Juneau, you break up with her in bits over time. First her scent fades from your clothes. The texts stop coming, and you forget the sound of her voice. Eventually you make a list of everything that's missing until you stop checking the list, and it disappears into a desk drawer with overfilled sketchbooks—and just like that, you're free.

But I don't. Instead we talk about my coping strategies. Facing the holes Juneau left behind, waiting for me like ghosts whenever I turn a corner.

"You're a creative," my therapist reminds me. "You are capable of filling these holes yourself."

At her urging, I keep on painting. In the art studio, at home, in my bedroom until late at night. I work diligently on my art portfolio: *Femininity in Color*.

The next painting is the largest work I've ever done: a six-foot life-size portrait of a woman overgrown by sunflowers. Her expression is tranquil as I hang it in the art studio.

"Maya Krishnan."

Behind me, Patricia is gazing at the painting. Post–college acceptance, Pat's attendance has suffered. She now skips class almost as frequently as Juneau, so I rarely see her. She looks more depressed than ever, or perhaps it's just the eyeliner. I remember that when I lost my first love, she lost her best friend.

"Patricia Lloyd," I say, mirroring her.

She sighs. "We haven't really talked since...you know," she says. "How are you holding up?"

"I'm doing okay," I said. "I haven't been speaking to Juneau. But I'm living with my mom again, Dr. Harvey's not actively trying to prosecute us, and my friends don't hate me. Small victories."

"Look how far we've come," says Pat.

I study Pat, remembering her and Juneau's epic falling-out. Somehow I thought she'd look different afterward—you can't face a supernova head-on and walk out unscathed. But Pat is calm and regal as ever, her piercings glittering like stars. She is a constellation unto herself.

We're quiet for a moment, and I say, "Juneau thinks I apologize too much. But I still feel like I should apologize for how things ended."

"That's bullshit," Pat says. "Apologizing too much, I mean. Like, I get that women need to stand up for ourselves, whatever. But it's never a weakness to say when you're wrong. In my opinion, at least."

"Well, I *was* wrong," I say. "I stood by Juneau and kept putting you in danger, and I shouldn't have. I was processing a lot back then—I still am—but you were right. I needed to stand up to her. And I didn't."

"Well, you're here now," says Pat. "And she isn't. So you must be doing something right."

We turn back to the painting, and Pat smiles. "That's one hell of a painting," she says. "It's so...you."

It's strange. I met Pat first, but I never really got to know her, not without Juneau's presence between us, coloring every interaction we had.

"It's missing a little something, though," she adds. "May I?"

I raise my hands in surrender and step back. Pat approaches the still-wet painting with a palette in hand. It never occurred to me that there could be so many shades of black, but Pat wields them all with expertise. For the better part of an hour, she paints and repaints.

"What do you think?" she says, stepping back.

My gasp is initially one of panic, but midway it changes into delight.

Because with her well-placed strokes, Pat has transformed the entire painting. She's turned the sunflowers from too-perfect, cloying yellow bunches into the kind of flowers that you'd see growing on the dark side of the moon. They cast shadows on the woman, dark and hauntingly beautiful.

Chiaroscuro, I think numbly.

"It's perfect," I say. "God, Pat—"

She grins, and it feels like a gift. Despite the piercings and eyeliner—or perhaps, because of it—her smile is unexpected and radiant, like the moon flowers she's just landscaped my painting with.

It's a Florida winter, so Citrus Grove continues to bloom. The swamp seems to glisten, orange trees budding with a ferocity unmatched by art. I do my homework with the windows open, feeling the sun on my skin.

It's not easy, being the talk of the school. I take my lunches alone, though my friends walk with me sometimes, just to update me on their lives. We head down to the football field after school. Ife has gotten a full-ride scholarship to a leadership program at Stanford. And Anya, formerly Sam Harvey's dirty secret, now shines onstage—she's leading the spring play. They're healing, they reassure me. They're okay.

"And you?" I ask Silva. "What's new with you?"

"I uploaded my music online," Silva admits. "Which I guess you missed, since you don't use modern communications or hang out anymore." He pulls out his phone to play it for me.

He's right. My phone is still on a road in Alabama, and I've been grounded until marriage probably. Once Juneau kept my phone constantly buzzing, had me in ever-accelerating motion, but we don't talk anymore. And I'm not heartbroken like you might expect. A lifetime without Juneau sprawls before me, and I'm plenty content on my own. Our paths crossed once, and who am I to be greedy for more?

I'm okay, I keep telling myself. For the rest of the semester, then the school year. *I'm okay.*

And then, in the blaze of summer, her postcard arrives.

At first I don't realize it's from her, slipped between magazines and bills. But then I see her name, and my heart quickens.

I read it too fast, and then I read it again, savoring new details each time—the swoop of her ink. My name on the back.

Her perfume sprayed all over. One postcard, that's all it takes. The picture paints itself in my mind.

In it, I can see her so clearly. I could spend a lifetime studying her, and I'd never scratch the surface. I half expect us to start floating. I wait for a miracle, and I know I won't be disappointed.

She steps out of the car, and I see her eyes, her artist's vision. She can tell the time from the warmth in the air, can guess the paints that mix into the color of the sky. There's a shy way she looks at me, both terrified and hopeful. She wants me to speak, I realize. For once, she's waiting for me.

"Juneau?" I say, like the first word of a song.

"Come on," she says, and my heart cracks in two. "Promise you won't look back?"

She takes the first moon-man jump into the sky, but I stand on my two feet. I hold myself down while the sky lifts her up, like curtains poised to rise.

ACKNOWLEDGMENTS

When I first dreamed up *All the Yellow Suns* in 2018, I identified strongly with Maya; years later, I feel more like her big sister. To me, this shows how much I've grown up while writing this book. I drafted most of it during a gap year in 2020. It was my plague year, my pizza crust year, my "year that asked questions," to paraphrase fellow Floridian novelist Zora Neale Hurston. I was experiencing my own queer coming-of-age pretty much in real time alongside Maya, learning so much about love and art. That year, I discovered how friendships, mentorship, and found families can change your life. In that spirit, I would like to thank the following people:

Neha Kamdar, the first person to formally teach me creative writing and the first person to read this book. For ten weeks in my freshman winter at Stanford, you taught me magic. My learning curve was so steep. Thank you for pushing me hard.

My dearest Miranda, for making my life feel rich, profound, and more romantic than fiction. When you helped me edit chapters over FaceTime during winter break, it was the sweetest gesture of love I'd ever known.

All my friends who read this book in its earliest stages, including Alana; Ana; my fierce sister, Deepika; my writing workshop cousins; and my beta readers. Allison, my mentor and literary fairy godmother; my agent, Steph Kip Rostan; my editor, Sam Gentry; and the wonderful team at Little, Brown Books for Young Readers: Thank you for believing in this baby author.

Thank you to my Stanford professors and the communities I found in HerLead, Women's March Youth, and the Bryan Cameron Education Foundation for investing in me as a young writer. A special shout-out goes to YoungArts, and especially to Joan Morgan, for giving me the first affirmation for this book in 2019.

I'd also like to thank everyone who loved me at age sixteen, when I had too much rage for my own good. This includes my high school friends and family friends, whom I introduce as my aunties or cousins because that's just easier. Thank you to my fellow burnt-out former teen activists, whose bravery inspired this book. Thank you also to my queer friends of color, for bringing all the fire. To all the girls I've loved before. To every queer creator of media who helped me imagine who I could become. To all the luminary women of color who inspire me to write.

Last but not least, thank you to my Amma and Appa. Things haven't been easy, but I hope you're proud of what I made.